Hillcity Press

Edited by Monica Wanat

Cover art by Damián V.

Cover design by Mibl Art

Map by Maarten de Wekker

ISBN 978-1-7379425-0-4 (hc)

ISBN 978-1-7379425-2-8 (eBook)

BLADE OF ASH

• SCEPTER AND CROWN BOOK ONE •

C. F. E. BLACK

HILLCITY PRESS

For Dad, for all your wisdom.

To read a free Scepter and Crown short story, follow the link below and sign up to be a reader VIP. My VIP readers get early access to cover reveals, first dibs on ARCs, and other exclusive content like deleted scenes.

https://vip.cfeblack.com/join

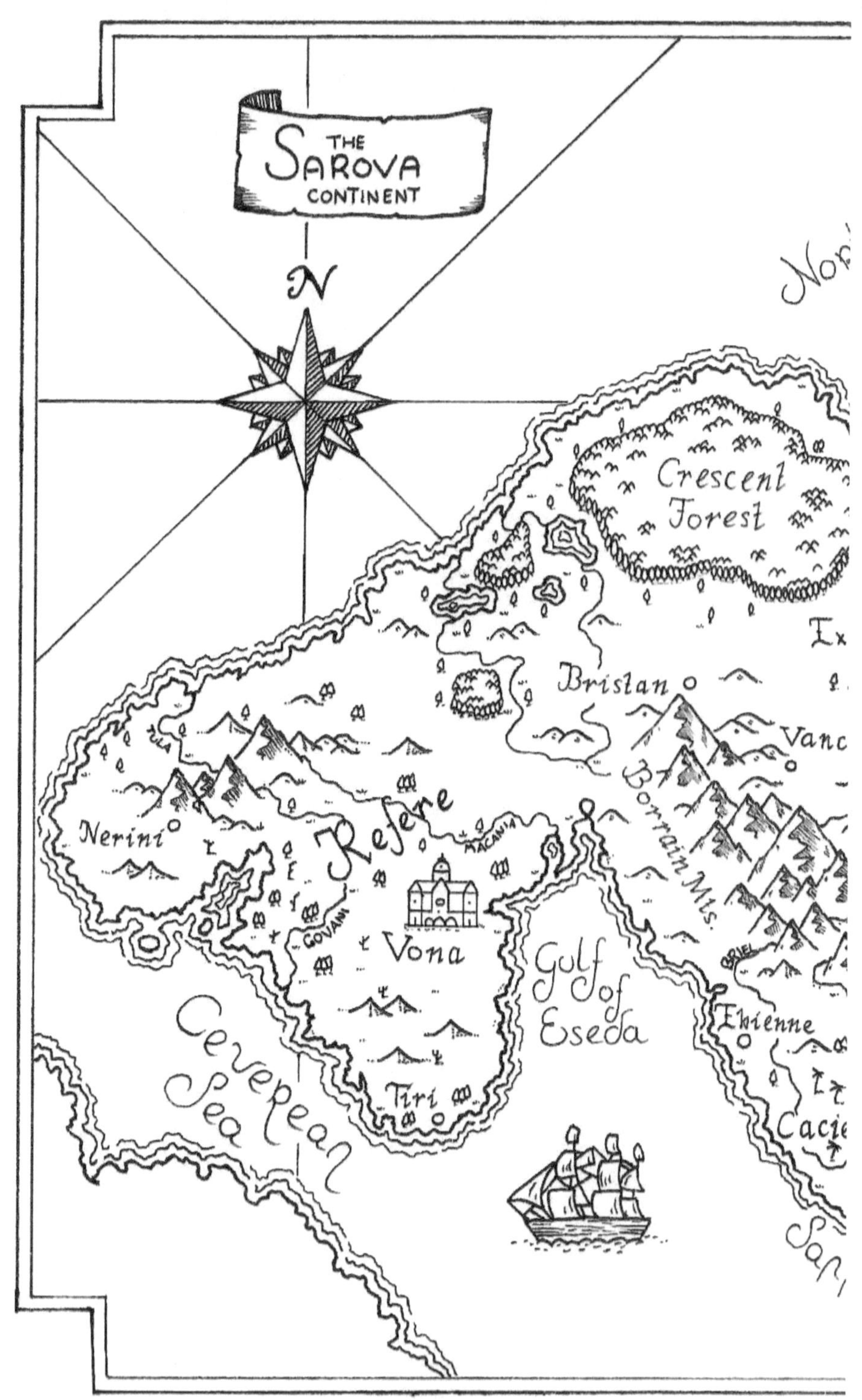

THE SAROVA CONTINENT
N
Crescent Forest
Bristan
Nerini
Refere
MACANIA
Govani
Vona
Borrain Mts.
Gulf of Eseda
Etienne
Cereceal Sea
Tiri
Vanc
Cacie

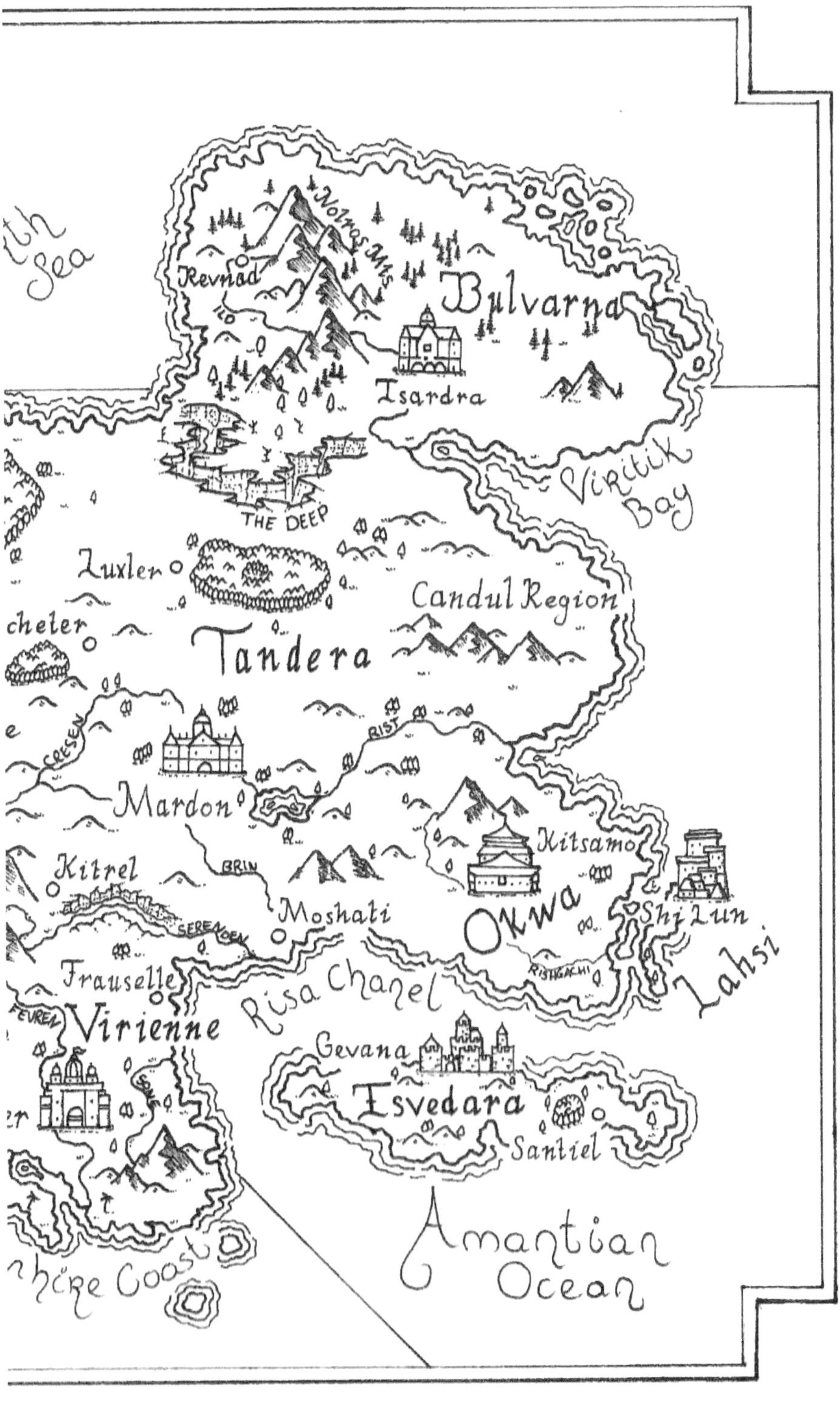

North Sea

Revnad

Nolnos Mts

Bulvarna

Isardra

Viritik Bay

THE DEEP

Luxler

cheler

Tandera

Candul Region

CRESEN

Mardon

BRIN

Kitrel

Moshati

SERENDEN

RIST

Kitsamo

Okwa

Shi Lun

Lahsi

RISHGACHI

Frauselle

FEUREN

Virienne

Risa Chanel

Gevana

Isvedara

Santiel

Amantian Ocean

...re Coast

1

RED

Doors didn't often bother Prince Frederick, nor did they give him headaches or drag him out of bed after a restless night. But this wasn't just any door. Of all five hundred twenty-seven doors in the palace, this was the only one he had not been permitted to enter. Ever.

Or rather, that had been the rule before Frederick's father died.

Working up the courage to say what he'd spent half the night rehearsing in his head, the prince, groggy and puffy eyed from grief, stared at the Royal Sorcerer's door. The shock of his father's passing was still a raw, wide wound, muddying his thoughts.

Today, when the world would turn their tear-stained faces upon the crown prince for guidance, when he had a million other tasks to accomplish, a million other issues to think about, here he was, trying for the hundredth time to open this door.

The gray wood carved with delicate patterns and covered in tiny shadows hinted at the magic hidden behind it, the magic that he'd once envied—the magic that should have kept his father alive.

Frederick swatted a curl off his forehead and checked the

corridor for watching eyes; he saw none but the silent faces on the paintings, then stepped closer to the knob. He lifted his chin and pounded his fist against the door; he was reduced to *knocking* on the door that, in his opinion, had kept him from his father far too often.

Many conversations with his father had ended at this door. As a child, he'd raced down the long palace corridors after the king. As he had grown older, he'd walked the halls alongside his father, discussing matters of state or one of Carolyn's new inventions.

Their talks had always ended here. *It is for your safety that you must leave the sorcerer alone, until it is your time,* his father would say, choosing, as always, the sorcerer's secrecy over his own son's curiosity.

Sadness, sudden and overwhelming, clawed at Frederick's chest.

No one in the palace—in all Tandera—had authority over him now, not even this door. The king was not here anymore to chastise Frederick for attempting a peek at the mysterious sorcerer.

Frederick shook away his sadness and knocked again, louder. "You can't shut me out now!" he yelled, his fist smearing down the doorframe with a pathetic squeak.

With his father's final breath, Frederick had inherited the throne of this nation, but his title as king would not be official until he was Bound to the Royal Sorcerer. However, as Theod would have it, the prince had been asleep when his father had passed and the country slipped quietly onto Frederick's shoulders, and despite the oaths he'd muttered, trembling in shock, one hand resting on an ancient copy of the *Verad* just after midnight, the reality of his new position hadn't really sunk in.

King.

King Frederick.

It didn't sound right. Not yet. This wasn't supposed to happen to him for *years*.

He wouldn't hold his first council meeting as king until after the Accession Ceremony, when he would publicly say the vows and hold the scepter and, at age eighteen, become one of Tandera's youngest sovereigns. But the throne was his, and with the throne came the magic of the Royal Sorcerer—the man who'd *killed* his father. Or let him die. Same difference.

The sorcerer, powerful enough to stop a bullet in the air, had not stopped the disease that had begun to drain Frederick's father's health three months ago. No one had expected it to take the king's life.

Bells chimed in the distance. The call to mourning had begun. All across the city, people woke to the news of their sovereign's death. Obediently, they would step out of their homes, open their windows, or stand on their rooftops, glass jars in hand, rattling the coins inside—a way of remembering the fallen king who had been a good leader, his reign a prosperous one for all of Tandera. The coins were the evidence. Even from the palace, nestled among its vast gardens, the sound was sublime.

As the noise coaxed up a fresh wave of tears, the prince couldn't help but peer out the window at the end of the hall. For the first day in a week, it was sunny, despite the early spring rains he could see hovering outside the city. The sorcerers of Mardon were performing their part in the ritual of mourning; it took a city's worth of sorcerers to hold back the rain.

Frederick clunked his head against the doorframe. Determination kept him from succumbing to the exhaustion of grief.

With a frown, he tried the knob.

It didn't budge.

The prince's face grew warm, his anger rising. The man who lived in these rooms—forever hidden behind cloak and mask to all but the king—had some explaining to do, and Frederick would speak to him, now, even if it meant taking an axe to the handle.

"This is absurd," he said into the empty hall. He understood, at least in part, being denied entrance while his father had still lived, but not now.

A creak behind him preceded Sebastian Thorin's deep voice. "Did you try the handle, halfwit?"

With a start, Frederick called out, with a hint of a smirk, "Yes, you idiot. What are you doing here?"

Seb strolled into the hall, still in his nightshirt, but wearing pants that looked as if he'd had them on for days. "Whole palace is looking for you." He grinned, his dark skin still sheet-creased.

A weight dropped in Frederick's gut. The entire country of Tandera was looking to him now, and he wasn't sure he could be who they wanted. They wanted to see his father, King Gevar, but they'd have to settle for Frederick.

"But those fools thought you might be in the garden or the solarium or some nonsense." Seb's bright smile lessened the weight inside Frederick. "No, I knew you were stupid enough to come here first. And you still can't get in!" Echoes of his cackling laugh bounced down the hallway.

Though anyone else would consider the day after the king's death the worst day to laugh at Frederick, Sebastian Thorin thought it was the perfect day for it, and this was why Frederick liked him better than the other young people who tiptoed around the prince like he had to be handled as delicately as a cocked pistol.

"I can have you hanged," Frederick threatened.

"Then who else would dare you to do stupid things?"

"Fortunately, no one."

"And that would be boring." Seb stepped up to the sorcerer's door. "Let's have a look." He never asked why Frederick was here instead of downstairs eating breakfast or rehearsing his lines for the public address he had to give later. "Hinges would be easy enough to blow. Want me to work something up?"

"We can't blow the door down. It's *magic*, remember?"

Seb shrugged. "Well, it's one thing we haven't tried yet, and I'm getting better at smaller explosions."

Frederick laughed. It felt wonderful. "You said that last time and nearly blew up half the garden." For the briefest moment, he forgot that his father would never wake.

"But those gophers got what was coming to them. No more tunnels under the roses."

"No more roses."

"Small matter."

The memory faded along with Frederick's smile. "Well, as long as you're standing here, of course the door won't open. Hiding just out of sight doesn't work. Tried it several times with Father."

Seb lifted his hands in surrender and walked toward the stairwell. "What will you say to him?"

Frederick had considered this in the silent hours after his father had died. "I'll demand an answer." Frederick cracked his knuckles. "A Reckoning."

Seb's easy smile faltered. "You think he's responsible, don't you?"

"My father should still be alive."

"Yes, he should." Seb had the decency to say nothing for a moment.

In the silence, the two stared at the nearest mural. In it, a vast, shadowy canyon stretched out before lines of soldiers on horseback. Shadows seemed to creep out of the earth, some in the shape of hands and others appearing to have eyes. At the head of the troops of mounted soldiers, a king rode atop a black horse. Beside him stood a masked figure in a white cloak—the sorcerer.

Finally, Seb said, "Brother, if you request a Reckoning, all that will do is prove you don't trust him—not a great way to start your reign. Maybe you could find out the truth without forcing it through a Reckoning. After all, their magic *comes* from the truth. Sorcerers don't tell lies."

With one knuckle, Frederick tapped the painting, right over the heart of the shadowy depths. "Some do."

Seb didn't argue that. Instead, he shrugged and scratched his day-old beard. "Let's make a bet."

Frederick waved him away. "Just leave. Please."

"Hear me out: If the guy has facial tentacles, I win. If he has warts or boils, you win."

Despite the tremor of fear in his stomach and the grief still clutching at his throat, Frederick forced a laugh. "That's a terrible bet. I never even said he *has* boils."

"He wears the mask for *some* reason."

"They all do. Now, please leave." Frederick's anger had subsided with Seb's presence, but the bitter reality was that his father's body was off to the mortician to be cleansed and dressed and prepped for his pyre. "Go. Tell Bernard and Yin and the others that I will be at breakfast shortly."

He watched his friend depart. When he turned back around, the sorcerer's door was ajar.

"Come in," a female voice said.

He was suddenly furious that the sorcerer had an *attendant* who was allowed in here. Frederick stepped in and shut the door behind him. The room, one he'd painted in his mind countless times, was nothing spectacular. No jars of preserved creatures like Seb had postulated. No bizarre apparatus to cage powerful men should they become unruly. All the theories, all the dreams, evaporated as Frederick observed a sitting room, complete with two leather chairs; a soot-stained fireplace; a vibrant rug; even a painting of flowers that boasted the signature of Umberto Yvesy, one of Tandera's most popular artists. So the sorcerer liked art.

Flowers? He'd not imagined a gnarled old man to appreciate a still of peonies.

Frederick glanced around for the attendant who had welcomed him. He opened his mouth to voice his annoyance when a woman suddenly *materialized.*

At a small desk by the latticed window, she shuffled papers, in a bit of a frenzy.

For several seconds he stared at her. She had not been standing there a moment ago. Bright sunlight painted a glow around her profile. She never looked at him, as if his presence were secondary to whatever was on those loose pages. She wore a plain red dress, belted, and was barefoot.

She turned a curious expression on him. Eyebrows lifted, head tilted, she waited for him to speak.

He could not. His gaze traveled to her feet, perhaps a little too slowly, and back up to her narrow, slightly freckled face.

She sniffed, annoyed with his examination of her.

"My king," she said with a sweeping curtsey, her voice now infused with adoration—mock or reverent, he didn't know. The look on her face when she straightened, however, suggested the former. She placed two hands on her hips. "Okay, stop gaping. You've seen me now." She waved both hands through the air in frustration or embarrassment. "Want me to be invisible again?"

The crown prince cleared his throat. "Everyone says sorcer*er*, not sorcer*ess*." He could not accept that this…young woman was the almighty sorcerer he'd imagined his entire life. He knew sorcerers could be women, but he had been *certain* Tandera's was a man. The broad-shoulders of the cloak. The rather manly phoenix mask. She looked *shorter* than the figure who'd stood by his father's side. Surely, the sorcerer was having fun with him on his first day. *Could the man change his appearance? He can make himself invisible, why not make himself look like an attractive woman?*

The woman walked toward him, her bare feet making small slapping sounds on the parquet.

"A woman can be a paint*er*; a woman can be a lawy*er*; a woman can be a cobbl*er*, a farm*er*, a hunt*er*."

"But—"

"*Er!*" she snapped, lips pursing at the syllable.

Frederick temporarily forgot he still thought there was a man somewhere underneath this disguise. She stood a few feet away, staring up at him, brown hair braided, her green eyes hard, her mouth a slim line. She had no jesting in her expression.

His shoulders sank with a breath.

"Have we come 'round?" She strode back to the desk strewn with papers and shifted more pages with long fingers.

Frederick stole another glance at the rest of her, his throat and his chest trying to shrink into one another.

This was not good.

How can this young woman be my sorcerer?

No. Not good at all.

How could she have been the sorcerer that served my father? The one who'd let him die.

All his questions slammed into him at once, but the most desperate one surfaced first. "Why?"

It was more of a croak than an actual word, but by the horrified look on her face, she'd heard him and understood.

Instead of answering, she pulled one paper out of the mess and held it against her for a moment, as if it contained a secret spell that, once revealed, would expose her true identity as some moth-eaten ancient corpse. Absently, she slid the paper down one side of her body, the *shh* sound of it drawing Frederick's eye.

"We have much to discuss." She adopted a more official tone and moved toward one of the two high-back leather chairs before the fireplace. No fire today, only a pile of gray and black ash. "Sit." She plopped unceremoniously into one chair and immediately pulled her bare feet into her lap, crossing her legs and arranging the folds of her dress to hang down around her. This made her look even younger. His age, even.

Frederick swallowed, still waiting for her to answer his question, and took a seat. He ran one finger around the collar of his tight jacket.

In a casual tone, she said, "Take that thing off if you like."

He gawked at her, then realized this wasn't that strange a

remark. After all, he could remove his jacket while in the presence of his family and closest friends. She was his secret body guard, his greatest weapon. No one else would ever join them in these conferences.

He left the jacket buttoned to the top.

"Your Majesty, I know you have questions. Ask away." She left the paper in her lap and spread her arms wide in a gesture that felt strangely intimate to Frederick, who was used to the women of court barely moving in his presence as they attempted to look poised. Only his sisters had ever made grand gestures around him.

For a moment, he panicked and wondered if she could read his thoughts. Better to know that now. "Can you read my mind?" he blurted, a little too forcefully.

She laughed. He wasn't used to strange women laughing at him.

"No. Magic can do many things, including invade someone's head, but it can't bring back what it finds there. And I have absolutely *no* desire to see what's in your head." She glanced down, possibly hiding a brief flush on her cheeks, as if nervous. "Next question."

He swallowed an unwelcome lump in his throat. "My father."

Fortunately, she seemed to have been anticipating this turn of conversation. She lifted the sheet of paper toward Frederick. He was alarmed to see she was fighting tears.

He began to read.

My King,

I know you are heartbroken over your loss. King Gevar was nothing but noble and deserved to live longer. From the bottom of my heart, I ask that you forgive me. I have studied my art for years, but nothing in my powers could save him. I tried.

I will miss him terribly.

There was no closing, no name. Frederick glanced up at the woman, who now swabbed at tears with both hands. She cried without sound. He sat there watching her, the letter of apology in his hand. She was *crying*. His sorcerer supreme was crying.

"You were…close with my father?" The venom in his tone did not escape her notice.

"Oh! Nothing like that! He was like a…" Her words fell away. "I never knew my father." For a moment, a shadow passed over her face. "Gevar was so kind. So strong."

Frederick nodded. "He was indeed. And he died before his time." *Thanks to your incompetence.* Frederick glanced back at the letter then again at his sorcerer. "You said you tried?"

"Yes, I tried," she snapped.

"But you're a sorcer*er*."

"Oh, and that makes me, what? Perfect?" She looked away, toward the ashes.

He didn't know how to respond. She was supposed to protect the king, to keep him alive. For three agonizing months some-thing had eaten away at his father's bones and organs to the point that Gevar had been in pain everywhere.

Frederick stood and tossed the apology paper onto the chair. "You expect me to accept that? Explain what—"

"Your father was cursed," she interrupted.

His mouth froze, half open.

She watched him, arms crossed, as if she wanted to hide behind them. "Yes. A death curse."

Inside of Frederick, his throat gnarled into a labyrinth, and his words could not escape. At last, he managed, "How can I trust you?"

She stood with a huff. Her face was narrow and smooth. She wore no color on her eyes or cheeks or lips like the women he encountered at court. Her green eyes were fierce, as if she too fought back buried anger. "Look, I know you blame me. I blame myself!" More tears filled her eyes. "But a death curse is different. There was only one way to heal Gevar, and he—"

"There was a way to heal him?" he balked.

The woman never faltered or stepped back. "He made me promise not to."

"I don't believe you."

"I tried to stop the curse. I *did* slow it, but once a curse like that is activated, there are only two known ways to heal a death curse. One is to cast it back into the sorcerer who created it—an impossibility in this case—and the other is to perform an act called siphoning." Her hands fumbled with the fabric of her dress. "Siphoning draws magic out of one person and into another. Papa made me promise not to do it."

Papa? Frederick's mouth hardened like clay in a kiln. She fidgeted with her pockets. *I called him Father. Who is* she *to have called him Papa?* Jealousy, furious and wild, roared within Frederick.

"You could have lied," he hissed.

"No!" Her face paled. "I couldn't lie!"

"You could have saved him! Just one lie and my father would be alive!" He'd taken another step toward her. They were close, breathing heavy. Maddeningly, she smelled lovely. Like lavender. Frederick was not backing down first. *She* was to blame for the king's death. She admitted it. She could not expect him to trust her.

Finally, she pressed her hands to her face and exhaled loudly. When she looked at him again, her eyes were rimmed in tears, but her mouth was hard. "Do you know what siphoning does?" Before he could respond, she continued, "Like I said, to perform that act, I would have had to take the curse into myself. I *wanted* to. I begged him to let me do it!" She shook her head. "But your father knew that if *I* became cursed, I'd end up like..." Her words broke off. She lifted her chin. "Like the sorcerers who trust the Deep. And he did not want to risk what would happen if someone like me became cursed with the Canyon's magic."

"So it's okay for a king to be cursed, just not you?"

Her lips pinched into a tight frown. "No, it's not okay, Your Majesty."

The title sounded strange to Frederick, and more so coming from this woman who'd been yelling at him a moment ago.

He stared out the window, breathing hard, his mind pinwheeling with this new information. A death curse. *Who would curse a king? Why?* This was the sort of news that could start a war.

As these questions volleyed in his thoughts, he became aware that she stood behind him, waiting. His skin prickled. She was going to try to Bind to him.

He'd known this moment would come. His whole life, he'd anticipated it. Binding his Truthwell to the power of the Royal Sorcerer was an action every king had performed—as ritualistic and predictable as the coronation ceremony. Yet he'd expected to Bind to a wizened old man. He'd expected to Bind much later in life. He'd expected…toss it all, he'd expected to *want* to Bind when the time came.

"I will *not* Bind to the person responsible for my father's death," he said, voice flat and firm as he whirled on her.

Her face was wet with tears, but she ignored them, letting them drip off her chin. In her eyes, a seething anger brewed. "You spoiled little…"

"Finish that sentence and you'll be finding a new royal to serve."

His thoughts buzzed with the stupidity of his words—she knew as well as he did that he couldn't *fire* the Royal Sorcerer. She'd served the kingdom for too long, knew too many state secrets, and had, by Theod's great design, been gifted with magic much stronger than the average sorcerer. But he couldn't back down now. He'd lost a father. She'd lost…her employer, regardless of what she called him.

In the wake of his words, her chest heaved up and down, her nostrils flaring as she discarded response after response that flashed across her face. Words weren't necessary to communicate what was on her mind. Rage. Offense. Hurt. Desperation.

He'd not expected that last one. To force himself to look away, he tugged at his jacket's sleeves.

Finally, after one long exhale, she said, "I know you don't trust me, but we have to do this."

That hadn't been what he'd expected her to say. She was capitulating—bowing out of the fight. He detected a note of panic in her voice.

"You're to be king now, and it's the only way to keep you safe." She offered a deferential nod.

"Wait." It couldn't be that simple. For a moment there, she'd looked ready to dismember him with her magic. He straightened his spine. "I demand a Reckoning first."

Her eyes narrowed. "How *dare* you." With a jerking movement, she spun toward the door, fumes of anger reeling off her like smoke from a freight train.

That was easy, Frederick thought, marching after her. "Right now?"

"Yes, right now." From a rack beside the door, she ripped down her white sorcerer's cloak and yanked her phoenix mask off a hook on the wall. "Ondorian is still in the palace."

"And how do you know that?"

Over her shoulder, she said, "I see everyone's Truthwell. I know his, just like I know your sisters', your mother's, and yours." She closed her eyes. "He's in the chapel. Let's go."

2

ALY

Heart beating madly, the Royal Sorcerer of Tandera walked down the hall before the young crown prince, fuming to herself in a tug-of-war between anger and grief. *How dare he! Oh, Papa, I miss you! This idiot thinks me a liar! But I did kill Gevar, didn't I?*

Though emotion warred like stray cats in her head, one feeling rose above the rest: desire.

For years, she'd wanted access to this boy's Truthwell. As dazzling as the sun and as perplexing as a vortex, this boy's Well had danced before her, untouchable, until today. Today, she would be Bound to it.

As she walked down the corridor, her steps machine-like as they traced a path she took every single day, she allowed her eyes to lose their focus, her senses to dull to the physical world around her. She opened her mind fully to the bright magic only sorcerers could see.

Eddies of light flickered and pulsed in the world around her. They waved from the flaming gas lights in the sconces on the wall. They called to her from the chandeliers, from the air that ballooned the hood of her cloak, from the wood beneath her feet and behind the paint on the walls. Those were mute calls, dim and immaterial compared to another source, the blinding light emanating from right behind her. The prince's Truthwell blazed against her senses, drowning out all other sources of magic.

And despite her years of practice and control, a sudden and overpowering yearning consumed her mind as she permitted herself to feel the energy of the prince's Truthwell.

Theod! I'm not ready.

She'd known this day would come. She'd never expected it to happen the way that it had. Frederick would only be the third person whose Truthwell she'd Pulled from to conduct her magic, but of the three, his was brighter the way the moon was brighter than the stars.

Her skin tingled beneath her cloak. Magic always called to her, the way light called to the eyes or heat to one's chilled skin. Now that Gevar was dead—*heaven forgive her*—there was no barrier keeping her from the infinite well of energy writhing and singing and drumming within the crown prince. It was *hers*, at least it would be after the Binding.

If he didn't do something horribly rash.

The prince—soon to be king, she corrected herself—had looked at her with pure loathing. The fears she'd buried six years ago rose to the surface, bulbous and ugly, a mushroom among her otherwise cultivated thoughts. For the first seventeen years of her life, she'd let magic drive a wedge between her and the rest of the world, believing that it marked her as forever separate from the lives of men. Instead, it bound her to them more inextricably than she cared to admit.

There was no turning away now. Her duty was to her king, forever.

Strips of light fell like pale gauze across the palace chapel's vaulted altar room. Empty choir benches lined the far wall, and only six rows of pews filled the intimate worship space. The stained-glass windows and the stone floor mimicked the architecture of Mardon's grand cathedral. The cool, sunlit room was small and unintimidating, save for the fact that the prince's Truthwell buzzed nearby like a million frantic fireflies.

Candles burned in the sconces, and a lone figure sat on the front bench, his bald head bent.

"Arthur!" she called, closing her mind to the alluring light of Frederick's Truthwell.

The High Priest's familiar face spun into view. His lips immediately pressed into his favorite, close-mouthed smile. Her feet, which she'd hastily crammed into a pair of heeled slippers, clacked against the stones, shattering the serene silence of the chapel. The broad-shouldered white cloak billowed out around her as she hurried down the aisle, the hood obscuring her dark hair and most of her masked face.

As she approached the priest, she ripped off her mask. The prince sniffed in surprise. He still thought of her as a ghost; no one was supposed to know a ghost.

"Alyana! I am so very sorry for your loss, my dear." Arthur Ondorian, High Priest in Mardon, lifted his arms and embraced her.

Frederick snorted. "You two are acquainted?"

She whirled around, eyes narrow and accusing, despite her efforts to keep her expression steady. *He's just lost someone too*, she scolded herself. She had no right to scowl at the man, but his condescension was boiling over, scalding her. *Or is that my own raw state, concocting offense where none belonged?*

Ondorian smiled at her and nodded. "Indeed. I aided Aly in her study toward Mastery back when she did not know magic for its true purpose, nor its true strength."

Aly smiled at her feet, recalling her first meeting with Ondorian, when he'd given her a copy of the *Verad*.

The prince's face pinched, then tilted in obvious confusion. "You aided her toward Mastery? How long ago was that?"

"What was it, Aly? Five, six years ago? It is hard for me to keep track of time these days," Ondorian said.

"Six," she confirmed.

The prince balked. Oddly, she enjoyed watching the stages of shock cross his freckled face. His eyes never left her. They traveled down, then up, then down again. Not in a hungry way, but in an incredulous way. His understanding was so limited. He'd never even known of the change of power six years ago when Augustus Penwater had died and Aly had taken his place. To the boy prince, then thirteen, nothing at all had transpired. He hadn't known a new person had walked under the sorcerer's cloak, wore the phoenix mask, and traveled everywhere with the king. A new person had been chosen for the position he now looked upon with distrust.

"Six?" he blurted. "How old are you?"

"Still think I'm ancient?" She couldn't help herself from poking, just a little, at his ignorance. His frown made her both regret and approve of the decision. "I'm twenty-two."

Prince Frederick took a step back. He removed his coronet and ran a hand through his hair. When he regained his composure, he stood with his body angled away from Aly, as if making an effort—conscious or unconscious—to avoid looking at her.

She could see in his expression that she was shrinking in his mind, tumbling down off of a pedestal of mystery that he'd built up over the course of his childhood, his adolescence, his endless hypothesizing with Seb over the years.

"I'm Aly, by the way. Alyana Barron."

He ignored her and turned his attention to Ondorian, who stood with hands clasped, waiting for the awkward exchange to end. The man's features were creased into a patient smile. "Right. Arthur." He tugged at his jacket hem, a nervous tick. "I came here for a Reckoning."

At his words, Aly's heart descended again into the mire of anger she'd left behind as she'd spoken to Ondorian. *He's annoyed that he doesn't know more about me, yet he demands a Reckoning like I'm some common criminal.* She shifted her weight, a hot breath puffing from her nose.

The priest's thin smile faltered. "A Reckoning, Your Majesty?"

"I want to know I can trust her magic before I Bind to her." He leaned in, knowing full well that Aly could hear, but choosing to whisper his next words. "I won't Bind to a murderer."

Aly, frustrated, lifted her arms under her cloak, turning herself into a tent, and spun around, marching toward the altar where she collapsed into a white heap of cloth. To silence the words she wanted to spew at him, she closed her eyes and began muttering snippets of the *Verad,* all the while letting her mind crash into the brightness of the prince's Truthwell.

It was this brightness, after all, that was the only thing keeping her from running away in pure shame. That, and the fact that she'd made her vows. She would serve the throne of Tandera as long as she lived.

"Strange creature," the prince muttered to Ondorian, staring at Aly.

That old prickle of fear snared Aly's navel. *He thinks you're not even human.*

Good. She needed that. It would make their interactions less awkward when they had to spend time alone or when she had to touch him to heal him or when she had to stand guard over him while he slept. With Gevar, there had never been any awkwardness. He'd been as kind as a father from the first day she'd served him until the last.

The thought of Gevar's last day brought fresh tears to Aly's eyes.

Ondorian's voice, though low, carried in the vaulted space. "As your spiritual advisor, I recommend you reassess your request for a Reckoning. She is a sorcerer. Her magic is built entirely on the power of the truth."

Thank you, she mused, abandoning her recitation and taking up instead the business of eavesdropping and fiddling with the hem of her cloak.

"You're saying you believe she's innocent in the matter?"

The cool air in the chapel did little to dispel the heat emanating from Aly's torso. After a quick spell to lower her body temperature, she ran a hand across the back of her neck to collect the sweat that had started there.

She wasn't innocent.

Ondorian knew it. If the prince maintained his demand for a Reckoning, he'd soon know it too. She glanced over her shoulder.

But the priest didn't know the true reason Aly's heart hammered in her chest right now, the reason sweat tried to pour from her body, the reason her hands shook at the thought of Binding with the prince. No one knew it. Except, perhaps, Augustus Penwater, the former Royal Sorcerer, before he died.

She might be wrong about Frederick. Some Truthwells burned brighter than others, that was a simple fact.

Ondorian peered at Aly. "I am saying, sire, that like the crown, the magic of the Royal Sorcerer passed to you upon your father's death. To dismiss one is to dismiss the other."

Frederick's face hardened. He darted a glance at Aly, made eye contact, then looked away again. "You assume I mean to dismiss her?"

"No. That is against our laws and the wisdom of our Maker, who gifted her with the magic she possesses. You are not as impudent as that. I assume that you intended this Reckoning as a means of providing yourself with an excuse to dismiss her *help*." Ondorian lifted a hand to indicate he wasn't finished. "If I may, as a member of your council and your spiritual advisor, inform you that you very much need her help and her protection."

Frederick pressed a hand to his temples. "All right, fine, but if she's telling the truth, then she wasn't strong enough to save my father." He dropped his hand. "I'm not sure I can trust her to keep me alive."

At the prince's words, a fresh wave of heat blazed down Aly's spine. She couldn't hear Ondorian's response. Frederick was right; she'd not been able to save Gevar.

If the same curse bespelled Frederick, she wouldn't be able to save him either.

He needed to know this.

With a deep breath, she smeared away her tears, stamped down her anger, and stood. She steadied herself and walked back to where the two men stood.

"Let him have his Reckoning." She nodded at the shocked prince. "I will wait outside, if you wish." *Don't say yes.* A part of her didn't want to be around to see the prince's face when the truth hit him. At least this way, the truth would be coming from Ondorian.

As if reading Aly's reasoning, the priest reached out a hand and squeezed Aly's shoulder once. "Ah, my dear, if it is the truth you wish for young Frederick to know, then I am not the one to tell him." He glanced between them. "A Reckoning is not necessary here." With his other hand, he reached for Frederick's shoulder, a bizarre connection that felt too intimate to Aly, who squirmed out from under Ondorian's touch. "Magic is a great gift from Theod. It is not, however, the very Maker himself. It has its limits. We are in danger when we begin to think of magic as a replacement for the Maker's hand." He lifted his face in reverence toward the ceiling and turned to go.

Both Aly and Frederick watched the priest depart.

When his form was gone, Frederick turned back to face her. "The truth?" he said, brows up.

Her gaze fixed firmly on her feet, Aly bit her lips before answering. Shame, sharp as briars, clung to her chest, her throat, threatening to silence her. "You were right," she finally said. "I am responsible for Gevar's death. Your father was cursed because of me."

3

RED

Frederick's breath quickened. Questions burned against his lips. Inexplicable rage abraded his ability to keep a passive face. The Royal Sorcerer was supposed to have the power to heal, to protect. She had nothing, not even the strength to hold down her own tears.

With a twinge of guilt, he recalled his own fountain of tears as word of his father's death had come to him in the night. *At least I hold myself together when others are around.*

He strode to a stained-glass window, but its opaqueness made him feel trapped, as if his world was morphing in front of his eyes. The world outside was waking to the news of their dead sovereign. The people of Mardon and, as news spread, of all of Tandera would collectively envision the face reflected in the shard of stained glass. Their new king. He wondered what they would think when Frederick's face came to mind. Would the thought bring with it a smile, a confident nod of the head, or would it bring a fearful glance or worse, a desperate cringe?

Behind his own reflection, he saw Aly's white robe mirrored over the fractured colors. The person designated to keep the king alive was the reason he was dead.

Staring at the floor, he rasped out one word, "Why?"

Aly moved and dropped, in a most unladylike manner, into the chair reserved for the choir director. Her cloak splayed out over the armrests, revealing her small frame beneath. "Because someone's been looking for me for a very long time." Her fingernails bit into the fabric around her upper arms, and she inhaled sharply before adding, "It's why I've been so careful to stay hidden. If he ever finds me…"

"Who?" Frederick spun around.

Her eyes bulged with savage fear. "My father. Dimitri Patrenko, the Royal Sorcerer of Bulvarna. The man who killed Gevar." She paused to let those words sink in. "So I'm really Alyana Patrenko, but I've never accepted that name. Barron was Renna's last name—the name of the woman who adopted me." She waved a hand across her face as if her words were a pack of gnats. "My father has wanted me dead since the day I was born —since my birth caused my birthmother's death."

"That's a long time to hold a grudge."

"He apparently never got over her death."

"Why did he kill my father then, and not you?"

By the look on her face, his question stung. "My father can only pollute my sources. He can't pollute my magic unless he directly curses me, which would take more than a cursed item. Also, he'd have to find me."

Red scratched his head as he considered her words. "So, he kills my father because he wants *you* dead, but he doesn't know where you are? Still doesn't make sense to me."

Appearing to retreat deeper into herself, Aly slumped lower in the chair. "He must have assumed I was a Royal Sorcerer." At Red's narrow gaze, she added, "He's an evil man. He Pulls from the Canyon. Who knows why he does what he does?" She fixed her eyes on the armrests of the chair. "He killed my mother when he was looking for me."

For several minutes, the two sat in silence. He lacked the

energy to pose another question, though several bombarded his brain. Nothing made sense to him anymore. His world and what he'd known had flipped upside down since entering the Royal Sorcerer's chambers.

A course of action, that's what he needed. He couldn't sit and ruminate on how his father had been smiling and joking days ago. Frederick couldn't return to the hope they'd shared for a cure. He couldn't bear to look at Aly while he allowed these thoughts into his mind.

"Well, then," he said, clasping his forearms behind his back. "Let's proceed."

Aly's face turned up, her eyes large. She gripped the armrests of the chair with white knuckles. "The Binding?"

He shrugged. "What else?"

Ondorian was right. There was one Royal Sorcerer in a generation, often for several generations. There was one Master Protector strong enough, devoted enough, and wise enough to serve the sovereign. History, tradition, and their religion said as much. Theod had chosen her for this role. He couldn't very well avoid Binding with her, distrust aside. If he was to wear the crown, he was to Bind his Truthwell to her magic. As all Royal Sorcerers did, she'd sworn her vows too—vows to serve Tandera's sovereign.

She hopped up, tangling a little in the cloak as it clung to the chair. He nearly chuckled in dismay. *This is my sorcerer. This. The legends he'd built in his mind were so wrong it was comical.*

When her flailing motions settled, she *humphed* and marched past him, tugging her mask down over her face.

"Where are you going?"

"Outside."

As crown prince, most people, even those of high rank, bowed to him before leaving his presence. She simply blazed on, as if the rules of society didn't apply to her. He supposed they didn't. She spent her life mostly invisible to the world. She lived apart, in her own little world of magic.

He ground his teeth and followed her. "Why are we going outside?" He hated having to ask.

One hand on the chapel door, she said, "Because I'm not really sure what will happen, and I don't want to burn down your house."

"Burn down my house?" he barked, stomping through the door and into the bright sunlight.

Clouds darkened the horizon south of the city. Spring rains normally dulled each morning for months, but the sorcerers, honoring the death of a king, were changing the world from dim to bright, in a strange reversal of the darkness he felt in his heart.

The grass, however, was still damp from the rains that had supernaturally ceased early this morning as the news of the king's death had spread.

"Every Binding is different," she said, still speaking to him over her shoulder, as if he was annoying her with his slow pace and persistent questions.

Frederick had heard his father speak of his own Binding when he became king, and he'd never mentioned that it was outside— nor that he'd undergone another Binding six years ago. That had been kept a secret.

As soon as they stepped into the garden, Aly vanished.

"That will get annoying," he said aloud.

"Get used to it," her disembodied voice replied.

The sensation of speaking to a ghost was surreal, and it grated against Frederick's already tenuous grip on composure. His father had handled it well enough, as had every other sovereign before him. Frederick would have to as well.

The ground squished under the crown prince's feet as they proceeded from the courtyard to the sprawling gardens. The palace walls looked a dingy brown when wet, the regal façade rising far above the nearest buildings. He and Aly descended toward the thin, gray Cressen River that separated the palace grounds from the rest of Mardon. Under the invisible feet of the sorcerer, small depressions appeared in the soft earth as they pattered down the gentle slope.

Evading the toxic grief pressing pain into his temples, Frederick instead thought of Aly's words about her father. He assessed what he'd heard of Bulvarna's Royal Sorcerer. *What do I know of the man?* Nothing at all, as was typical. For at least the past five hundred years, every crown on the continent had kept a sorcerer, but few sovereigns revealed the true power of their greatest weapon—that is, until a war arose.

Queen Kassia of Bulvarna, often called the Lady Wolf, allowed her sorcerer to be seen more than Refere's or Virienne's or Okwa's, and certainly more than Tandera's, whose sorcerer was so hidden that the crown prince himself had been completely excluded from any knowledge of the person behind the mask.

Four years ago, Frederick had attended a banquet in Bulvarna when he'd accompanied his father north. He'd seen the sorcerer then. Aly's father.

The man's cloak had been similar to Aly's, broad-shouldered and overly large to conceal his frame. His mask, however, had been memorable: a solid white owl's face. Somehow, the stark, expressionless mask, so unlike the colorful ones worn by other sorcerers, transformed the man into a living statue, a walking specter.

A chill ran down Frederick's spine as he walked in the damp afternoon air. Aly's father had seemed evil—perhaps from the rumors as much as the mask. Queen Kassia was long said to have been poisoned by the magic of the Deep, and who better to poison her mind than a man who could speak directly to it?

Glancing at the depressions made by Aly's feet, Frederick thought it strange to talk to an invisible person, but he couldn't hold in his questions. "Why couldn't you stop the curse? Is your magic not strong enough?"

Aly's hidden form stopped so suddenly that Frederick crashed into her. Alarmed and offended at the sudden contact, Frederick leapt backward, unsure what part of her he'd actually touched and troubled by this mystery.

She popped into view. The shoulders of her sorcerer's cloak stretched out inches beyond her frame, hiding her feminine shape. The red and gold mask hid her entire face. "Let me explain something to you," she said, her voice barely muffled behind the mask. "My magic is tied directly to the source I use to fuel it—the king. You know this, I'm certain, considering *you* are now my source—or you will be in a few minutes. *My* strength comes into play in knowing how and when and in what capacity to Pull from my source."

He recoiled. "Are you trying to tell me you couldn't heal him because *he* wasn't a good enough source?"

"No. Of course not! He was a powerful source." Looking away, she scratched her head under her hood. "As are you. You are…rather bright." He didn't know what she meant by that, but she spoke hurriedly before he could ask. "I tried everything I could think of to heal your father; however, even with all our research, the only known cure for a death curse is to siphon it out. It *will* kill someone. A sorcerer can live a little longer with it, but it corrupts, in essence dampening the Truthwell inside of a person until it snuffs out."

Frederick's brows rose. "So the curse made his Truthwell too weak for you to Pull from him to heal him?"

Aly's mask remained still for several long moments. "In a sense, yes. But again, the only true healing would have come from siphoning out the curse."

Frederick crossed his arms. He was ready for this day to improve. "Go ahead, then."

He was about to give this woman access to a part of him he didn't even understand, a part of him no one, save sorcerers, could even find. It was somewhat like trusting a surgeon to fix an organ no one else would ever see.

But there was no trust here. Tradition, perhaps, and expectation—but not trust.

Envisioning his father's bearded face, he asked, *Would you have chosen her if you'd known she would be the death of you?* His lessons on Royal Sorcerers came back to him: Theod chose them, not kings. Their magic was given to them, like a king's crown. However, like a king's ability to lead well, their magic was only fully realized through instruction and careful study. He didn't understand how this young woman had come to the palace, stronger and more fitted to the task of protecting a king than all the other more experienced sorcerers in Tandera.

Though she'd let one sovereign die, she was still the most powerful sorcerer in the entire country. If he couldn't trust her, at least he could trust the strength of her magic. "Trust the crown, not the person under it," the saying went. Frederick was now the man under the crown—or would be after his coronation—and he was facing a similar trial. Rule well and prove the crown well-placed.

He would trust her power. He simply hoped she would use it well and prove herself well-gifted. Only time would tell.

She closed her eyes to conduct the magic of the Binding, and a flash of pure panic bleached out all his other thoughts. Frederick's speculation about the Binding failed to prepare him for what came next.

A light grew in the corners of his eyes until he could barely see the world around him. The light persisted, and Frederick realized his own body was producing the glow. His clothes appeared lit from within; his bared skin shot beams of light into the garden.

His body trembled; the pulsing of his own blood was nearly unbearable. He wished he were sitting down. Willing himself to withstand the strange sensation without fear, he ground his teeth and spread his feet, knees bent, muscles taut.

Heat poured from the top of his head and down his spine, raced to his fingers, and flushed into his toes. Then, as the magic subsided, he felt the prickle of a heartache, which soon became a stabbing pain, as if he wanted the magic to remain, wanted it more than he wanted his next breath.

A small gasp escaped his lips. Surely Aly heard.

Despite his embarrassment, he was distracted by a new realization. This magic was *intoxicating*.

A terrible thought occurred to him: If the magic of the Royal Sorcerer was that overpowering, she could use it to weaken Frederick, perhaps even kill him. He wondered if, contrary to the *Verad* and history itself, sorcerers *did* lie. Then all her tears and grief could have been a ruse.

With a small grunt he hoped she couldn't hear, he shook off the euphoric feeling from a moment ago and squeezed his hands into fists.

Frederick was now Bound to this woman's magic. No other sorcerer could use his Truthwell for any reason, not even to save his life. It was a way of ensuring no other sorcerer could Truthstrip the one wearing the crown. Frederick knew all too well what it felt like to be Stripped, after an unfortunate incident several years prior. If he wanted the protection of magic, it would have to be from Aly, and her alone.

He took a breath, his heart still thundering like a startled horse. Last night, when his father had died, he'd inherited the crown. Now, with this Binding, he'd inherited the Royal Sorcerer's protection. As of this moment, all authority *and* power rested on Frederick.

They didn't have long before the world would crash down onto Frederick's shoulders.

To his horror, Aly reached under her mask to swipe at both eyes. She was crying. Again.

"I'm sorry," she blabbed, sucking air. "I'm sorry, I just—"

In that moment, she collapsed. Frederick's arms swung out as she fell toward him; the only means of avoiding a collision was to stop her trajectory.

"Aly?" He coughed, her weight sagging against him. "Um, Alyana?"

She burst to life, leaping like an offended cat out of his arms. Her hood fell back, exposing her mussed braid. Her mask had slid down, and she fumbled to right it.

He smoothed his hair, tugged his jacket hem.

"Apologies, Your Majesty. That was…most unusual."

"Don't call me that. It makes me think of Father."

"Everyone will call you that."

"Yes, which is why I wish you wouldn't."

She propped her chin with her hand. "It makes me think of Papa too."

Papa. There was that offensive word again. His nostrils flared.

"Then what am I to call you?"

He crossed his arms. "Something else."

"Red?" She pushed her mask up. Sweat lined her brow, clotting the hair at the edges of her face.

"My friends call me that."

Her brows lifted. "I see." She was not his friend. "But it's what I've called you in my head for six years."

Annoyingly, she'd known of his existence when he'd had no inklings of hers. He'd imagined a gnarled old man. She'd called him by his nickname. She already *knew* him.

The unfairness of it poked at him like a sore tooth. "Fine," he finally said. "But now I need you to show me some magic."

"Magic? Why? What is there that needs to be done?"

"Nothing needs to be done. I'm angry, I'm tired, and I want to see something that makes me not regret the fact that I just Bound my magic to the person responsible for my father's death." He cupped both hands behind his neck. Today will be a long day. He needed a moment before the well-wishers, the problem-solvers, and the sycophants showed up. He wanted a moment when his mind could relax before the maelstrom. "Can you really rip a tree out by its roots?"

"Sure. Want to see?"

"Yes."

"Come on then, Red."

4

ALY

Red stood behind her, his presence as ominous as a vulture's, his waiting gaze as hungry. The air was completely still. Aly's heart hammered as she lifted her hands toward a flowering tree on the river bank.

This moment would tell her what, for six years, she'd desperately wanted to know.

The Binding had been unspectacular. A puff of breeze on her skin, nothing more. With a Truthwell that bright, she'd expected to feel something. To *know*. If he was really a Beacon, and she was really the only one able to see it, there had to be a way to know for sure.

But now doubt flooded her mind, as well as a wave of relief more forceful than a tsunami.

Maybe I've been wrong this whole time. Augustus Pentwater had said the sorcerer who saw a Beacon would change the world. She'd never wanted that weight on her shoulders. She'd chosen to live in secret, in shadow, to not live in the limelight or the pages of history books. As long as she'd served Gevar, she'd been happily able to avoid thinking about the prince's Truthwell—and what it would mean if he really was a Beacon. The time of avoidance was over.

She'd always told herself that Binding with Red would reveal, once and for all, if he was a Beacon and she a Beholder.

It hadn't.

Surely not, she told herself, glancing over her shoulder at the prince—no, *king.* He was no prince now. He stood with arms crossed, his head cocked to one side like he was appraising an item he might bid on if the sight pleased him enough. *Wretched royal.* He wanted her to use magic for pure entertainment. After all, he was used to being entertained.

The power of truth wasn't mere fiction or fancy, and she hated to use it as if it were. *Ondorian uses magic to play his favorite symphonies. Yvsey uses magic to display his original artwork in other cities,* she reminded herself. Magic was often used to supplement artistic creation. She frowned and popped her knuckles with her thumbs. To do this for the king wouldn't demean her as Royal Sorcerer, despite how she felt about it. To be the king's Protector perhaps meant protecting his ego or his fragile emotions.

With that thought, she smirked and lifted her awareness toward his energy signature.

Her own curiosity burned within her, quickly plastering over his strange and spoiled request. To Pull from his Truthwell had been a dream she'd kept tucked away in the parts of her mind where her darkest secrets lurked.

Hands held high, she closed her eyes, felt with her magic, and *dove.*

His depths were sun-bright, electrifying. The current of his Truthwell surged around her consciousness, filling it—overtaking it. She'd practiced this, trained hard to overcome the bone-deep *want* that yanked her down into the infinite reaches of his energy. For a moment, she feared she would lose the battle and dive too deep, Pull too hard. The light of his Truthwell was mysterious and beautiful. Too beautiful to see and not desire.

The Master Sorcerer was one who could cut off the temptation to Pull until there was nothing left but a corpse. Reaching mastery wasn't about having the best or the strongest magic, though only the Masters could move and transmute rather than heat and cool; instead, mastery was about beating temptation. It was about *control*.

For a moment, a dangerous moment, she allowed herself to be fully immersed within the king's Truthwell before directing his energy toward a task. In that moment, Aly sensed her mind slipping into an abyss and reeled herself back.

Stop or you'll kill him too. Her reason returned and she yanked hard on his truth, and with it she uprooted the flowering tree by the bank as if it were a dandelion.

As the tree hung in midair, raining black dirt across the grass and the water, Aly stole a glance at Red. He still stood upright—a good sign—but the cocky tilt to his head was gone. He stared at the tree, a loose smile on his face.

Good, she thought, *I was getting tired of that scowl.* She turned her attention back to the suspended tree. At least the king didn't seem affected by her Truthpull. She'd yanked pretty hard, but he seemed unphased. His energy had come to her command so readily.

Even though she'd only ever Pulled from two other Truthwells, it surprised her to meet such little resistance this first time with Red. Maybe she was simply better now than she had been in the past. Her touch was, according to Gevar, completely imperceptible.

"Did you feel—"

"I didn't even feel—"

They both stopped.

Red continued first. "I did not feel a thing," he said, his frown returning.

Despite his face, Aly detected a touch of admiration in his tone. "I am the Royal Sorcerer, you know."

He *humphed.* "It wasn't a compliment. I don't like that I couldn't feel it. It seems so…wrong. You're using *me* to uproot that tree, and I can't even tell."

With a flick of her wrist, she righted the tree and sank it soundly back into the dirt, tucking in all the roots and replacing the two bird nests that had fallen out. No more than a smattering of white petals littered the ground as evidence of the tree's recent adventure.

When she'd finished, she whirled on him. "Would you rather I Strip you? Like that idiot from the Summer Palace? Leave you on your deathbed? Would that be better?"

His eyes sprang into horrified globes.

She clapped a hand to her mouth. "Sorry," she said then dropped her hand. "Sorry I…you make me say things." *Things I shouldn't say.*

"Oh, I make you prickly and irritable? Need I remind you that I'm standing here, fatherless, with a crown I had hoped to inherit much later in life, all because of *you*? And you have the gall to say I'm bothering you?"

His navy surcoat heaved with his heavy breaths, the buttons reflecting the sunlight above. He looked both regal and self-right-eous. He'd have to work on that if he wanted to rule Tandera well.

Insults rattled around in her head, but she pinched her lips and accepted his words. To her horror, tears bubbled up at the mention of Gevar. Once she'd collected herself, she saw that now was her best and sole chance to return Red's blow with one of her own. Wounded, she needed to hit him back—though she knew it was foolishness.

She drew her weapon—the truth—and aimed well. Through clenched teeth, she said, "Every time I look at you, I see him." *I see my failure.*

"Good," he snapped back, turning away.

Her heart shattered. The guilt was too much to bear, and the fragile shell of composure she'd erected to survive the day fractured and fell. She screamed, and the very earth seemed to recoil. The ground beneath her rippled like a disturbed pond. The king's hands shot out for balance as he searched the ground for any signs it would move again.

She hadn't invoked magic accidentally in years. She'd mastered her mind—the ring on her finger and the mask on her face proof of her accomplishment. Petty mistakes were in the past, or so she'd thought. But this boy king, this arrogant, hateful man, had poked at her guilt and had roused an anger in her she hadn't known she possessed.

And now she was Bound to him. For all her magic, she could only use his Truthwell, and his alone.

Despite the belief she'd once held that this boy could be a Beacon, the reality was that he was nothing special. His energy was bright and vivacious, but a Beacon and a Beholder were the stuff of legend—of myth. So rare were they that little had been written about them, and of what she'd found in the past six years, the writings all mentioned that the connection between a Beacon and Beholder was one ordained by Theod himself.

Their connection was certainly not the stuff of legend.

This—being Bound to King Frederick—was going to be a chore.

"Enough of this," he said, already marching away. "I need to tell my family about Father's curse. Then something must be done about *your* father." Then he stopped short.

At the edge of the garden, leaning against the last column of the chapel's portico, stood Sebastian Thorin. "Oy! King!" Seb pushed away and strolled toward them.

Aly was hidden from view, as her unnecessary display of magic had been, but Red had passed through her shroud and was now visible again to all the world. "Priest said you were down here. You have a room full of rich men waiting on you, and

I know from experience that rich men don't like to be kept waiting."

Red's shoulders sank. His council had been called from their homes by special messengers right after the king had passed early this morning. Ondorian was already present, which made five. The sixth seat was vacant until Red picked a replacement to fill his former seat.

Aly's heart stumbled. With all that had transpired in the past few hours, she hadn't expected to see the king's council today. One man, in particular.

Her memory flashed to the last time she'd wept like a child over the death of one taken too soon—the night she'd learned of her mother's death. With the memory, phantom hands wrapped around her shoulder. A familiar scent of polished wood and a man's scented beard oil ghosted through her nose. That night had been the night her life had truly changed, the event, or rather set of events, that pushed her to where she stood right now.

From behind Seb another figure appeared, silhouetted in his dark suit against the pale palace walls.

Lord Weston Grey.

At the sight of her former tutor, Aly's lungs shrank. Of all the people in the world she couldn't handle seeing right now, he was at the top of the list. After six years, and despite his long absence from her life, he still stole her breath.

A fire crackled in the palace library where Aly stood, masked and cloaked, in a shadowy corner between two ceiling-high shelves. She was accustomed to walking along the walls, standing in corners, and generally occupying spaces no one else would. Being invisible didn't make her mass disappear. She hated living in the corners and crevices of other people's lives, undetectable save when someone bumped into her and reacted as if they'd briefly encountered madness.

When she heard the library doors opening, she slipped under her shroud. Red's two sisters walked in, both clad in black. Seb's voice could be heard rattling away in the hall outside, even as the doors closed. Red had insisted that the council could wait another five minutes. He'd sent for his family, to tell them of Gevar's curse.

Aly respected his desire to tell his family the truth, even if it meant making the most important men in the kingdom wait a little longer. However, Aly was impatient to attend the council meeting, for reasons she didn't want to admit.

Lord Weston Grey had taken word to the waiting men that the new king would be along shortly. Aly had watched his eyes, which had remained fixed on the king the entire time they spoke. He never once glanced around, though he'd have known she was nearby. Ever the pragmatist.

The princesses, like so many in the palace, had been woken to learn of the king's passing. Their eyes were puffed and their pale skin had splotches, even under makeup.

The three siblings stared at each other. Elise dabbed at tears delicately with an embroidered handkerchief. With her jaw set, Carolyn walked over to her table, the one she'd helped their grandfather make, to check the secret drawer.

Aly smiled despite the thick sadness in the room.

Carolyn pulled out a note from the drawer and held it up with triumph on her face. "Yes!" She went about opening the note, lifting her arm to smear what was either tears or a running nose.

"Carolyn!" Elise scolded, watching her sister's crude manners.

"Oh, shut up, Elise." Carolyn brought both arms to her nose and dragged them dramatically across her face, one after the other. Then she read the note.

Aly knew what it would say. She'd written it the day before yesterday, but Carolyn hadn't come to the library, consumed as she was with her latest book, which had arrived from the press in Mardon merely two days ago. *The one who knows the time knows what everyone else wants to know.* It was a line from a book Carolyn had read. The young princess smiled at her note.

The inventor stuffed the note back in the drawer and scooted her chair up to the table, where sat her latest project: a clock she was building from the springs up.

Elise flowed gracefully through the huge room and sat down on a cushioned lounge near Carolyn's workspace. Red reached out a hand to muss Carolyn's hair. Her hair was the palest of the three, only noticeably red in the sunlight.

"Brother, you might now be the king, but I promise you this: Touch my hair and you *will* regret it."

Elise rolled her eyes, and Red suppressed a snort. Not everything had changed.

Aly was grateful to see the sisters composed and upright, a contrast to the way they'd been last night after the news had come. Weariness tugged at their eyes, but otherwise they looked every bit the princesses they were. They, too, lived behind shrouds of expectation.

Aly's attention shifted to Red. Pity for the sisters meant pity for him, and she was still mad at him for the way he'd looked at her, the way he'd spoken to her. But he *had* just lost his father. She felt the same pain he now felt. He couldn't understand how close she had been to Gevar; if he ever did, he'd hate her all the more.

I took their father from them. The sting of guilt cut like glass.

"I have something to tell you two," Red said. "Where is Mother?"

Carolyn put her hands in her lap and looked up. "Mother is not coming. She said not to wake her today unless the sky falls in."

At least she already knows, Aly mused. Gevar had not kept the truth from his beloved wife.

Carolyn tapped her feet and hands. She was nervous, as if any time away from her clock would put her dangerously close to breaking down in tears. She did not take sadness well. When her first pony had died two years ago, she'd disappeared into the woods all day, which had scared their mother half to death.

"Is it about Father?" Elise asked.

"Yes. It isn't good news." He looked at Carolyn, assessing her ability to take more bad news.

Aly, from her view in the shadows, had learned to read facial expressions. The twitch of an eyebrow, the tightening of the skin around the mouth, the subtle movements of a person's jaw—all could reveal so much. Elise's bottom lip twitched as she fought the onslaught of heavy sobs.

Elise, in addition to mourning their father's death, was still nursing a broken heart. She'd been certain—they'd all been certain—the Prince of Refere would offer her his hand in marriage, but for some reason he'd cut the relationship off. That had been months ago, but she'd only recently stopped coming to breakfast with red, tired eyes.

Now Red had to dump this terrible new information on them. There was no good way to share it, and Aly was glad she wasn't the one delivering this news. They would only hate her too, once they knew.

"Father may have been cursed," Red said bluntly. The princesses gasped. "At least the sorcerer claims it to be true."

Claims? You toss wad! Aly surprised herself with the childish insult. *He really does make me say stupid things.* Fuming, she crossed her arms and began to pace along the bookshelf. He'd said that simply to annoy her.

The fire snapped, helped along by an unwanted burst of energy from Aly. A log broke and tumbled off the irons, coals nearly spilling out onto the wood floor. Red stared at the coals a moment.

Get a grip, Aly scolded herself. Accidental magic was extremely dangerous. Masters weren't supposed to make mistakes like that.

Like letting kings die.

Aly mentally slapped herself and stood still. Guilt would only push her deeper into a writhing pit of uncontrollable emotion.

Carolyn stood, her chair scraping. "I told you! He was perfectly healthy, then all of a sudden he's sick and no one can fix it and… It sounds like a curse to me. You said the *sorcerer* told you?" Her face lit up. "You're Bound now, aren't you?" She glanced around the room, that innate curiosity taking over her features as she searched for any sign of the hidden sorcerer.

Elise's face remained prim and impassive, as usual. "And you believe him?"

Red glanced in the general direction of where he knew Aly had been standing. "Ondorian does. I…do too."

Well, that's a relief! Aly frowned and dug her nails into her upper arms.

Red cleared his throat. "Disease or curse, the sorcerer failed to save Father. Lying about this doesn't make him look any better."

Him. Aly pondered why Red had used that word. Was he preserving her anonymity? Was he lying merely to keep his sisters from asking questions? Other people could lie so easily. The fire popped again.

Looking at Carolyn, he asked, "What gave you the idea? None of the physicians thought of a curse."

Carolyn walked over to the bookshelves and crossed her arms, scanning titles. She tipped one book out and marched back to Red. "Here. It's a story about a—"

Elise made a small huff.

"What? Just because something happens in fiction doesn't mean it isn't real. Anyway, a witch curses a king in this book. The king dies. You asked what gave me the idea." Carolyn returned to the case and shoved the book onto the shelf.

"Did something happen in the book that *looked* like what happened to Father?"

Carolyn frowned. "In the book, the curse sort of made him turn to ash."

Aly glanced down at her ash ring, the sign of her Mastery, which curled around her finger in endless swirling patterns.

Carolyn walked over to Red and leaned her forehead against his shoulder. "In the book, the curse was given to the king via a poisoned note. I guess we'll never know if Father ever received a cursed item like that. There are probably a million other ways to curse someone in the real world, anyway." She lifted her head and returned to her table, where she immediately picked up a screwdriver and began affixing a tiny screw to the inner workings of the clock.

A knock sounded at the door.

"Come in," Red called. He moved toward the exit. "That was what I needed to tell you. I must meet with the council."

Aly stepped after him, silent as the dust falling all around.

In stepped Weston Grey. "We're ready for you, sire."

Sire. The word sounded odd addressed to Red, who was eight years younger than Grey. Yesterday, he'd been a prince.

In her moment of distraction, Aly walked into a small table holding nothing but an unlit reading lamp. The table wobbled, rattling the lamp. All eyes fixed on the table.

Aly's cheeks blazed under her mask. Grey couldn't see her, but she *felt* his eyes searching for her.

Why would he? Why would that lying, tricking, self-important —*oh, hush.* Calling him names didn't erase her desire to run up to him and loop her arms around him in a crushing hug.

A foolish thought.

After Aly had reached Mastery, Grey had deposited her here. For five of the past six years, he'd been serving at the border of the Canyon. His reputation as a killing machine had only grown stronger, making the ladies of the court even more terrified of him than they had been back when Aly had first accompanied him to the palace under the flimsy shroud of her early magic.

He was the first to look away from the mysterious noise, a smirk barely perceptible beneath his beard. He knew how clumsy she could be when distracted. *Toss it!* He knew why she was distracted.

Embarrassment and crippling grief threatened to break the concentration necessary to maintain her shroud. If she were to drop into view now, she'd hate herself for being so weak. Though no one could see her, she took a deep breath, lifted her chin, and stepped around the table.

Grey bowed to the princesses and turned to the double doors that led back into the hallway. He clasped his hands behind his back and waited for his king. His noticeably unencumbered left ring finger wiggled as Aly stared at it—almost like he knew she might glance at it.

Cursed idiot. She tried to shake off the memories, her stupidity. *It was* one *dance. One!* But she could still imagine the impression of his hand on her waist. To him, it had been nothing.

To her, it had been everything.

5

RED

Seb, in a crisp suit and shiny shoes, snapped his book shut and hopped up from a plush chair to follow Red and Grey as they exited the library. Mirrors reflected the warm light from burning sconces and the cool light of the spring morning pouring in from tall windows along the hall.

Presumably, Aly was somewhere nearby. Red couldn't quite shake the feeling that she was glaring at him from the shadows.

He didn't like it.

He also disliked the knowledge that the Royal Sorcerer of Bulvarna was responsible for his father's death. That was tantamount to an act of war. Though tempted by the thought of vengeance, going to war with the Queen of Bulvarna was not a foregone conclusion. Especially not on his first day as king.

Red knocked his knuckle against the book in Seb's hand. "Think you'll need that during the meeting? In case there are any dry spells?"

Seb held up the book. "Never leave my room without one, unless dancing is on the menu, of course."

"Not sure the men will appreciate you reading under the table while we discuss the future of this country. Consider this meeting a trial run. If you say nothing at all, I'm sure there will be no objections to you filling the vacant spot on my council." His voice lowered. "Still feels bizarre to call it *mine*."

Seb turned and started walking backward, grinning. "I could always make fun of Alexander. That'd make them all like me."

Grey shook his head, stepping up to enter the conversation. "Alexander has been on that council longer than any of us. My advice is not to offend him in Frederick's first meeting."

Red glanced backward at Grey, his brow slightly raised. "What are you reading, anyway?" he asked Seb.

"History of the shipping industry from the Kir Empire to modern times." He spun back around. "*Fascinating* stuff."

"Yawn." A real yawn punctuated the king's word.

"You look awful, man. If I'm allowed to say that."

"Great," Red murmured. "Wait, show me that title again." When Seb raised it, a confused smile crossed Red's face. "What language is that?"

"Kirish."

"Since when do you read Kirish?"

"Since you started sitting on your father's council. Had to do something to pass the time." He shrugged. "Kirish was the language of business for four hundred years before Tanderan. If I ever want to take over my father's role, I'll need to know it."

"You're telling me you actually *want* to be the Chancellor of Trade? What happened to opening a tavern on the beach?"

Seb tapped him on the shoulder with the edge of his book. "Have you *seen* what my father does? All he does is drink wine and eat the best imported olives he can buy. I can do that from the seashore as easily as he does it from here. Chancellor of Trade *from a tavern on the beach*."

They rounded a corner and walked halfway down another long hallway before pausing in front of the council chamber.

Red said, "If you want to be chancellor, remember that *I* have to appoint you, you toss wad."

Right then, Lord Alexander poked his head out of the council chamber and stopped short at Red's childish remark.

Red's ears turned pink. "Alexander, nice to see you. Perhaps you heard? I appointed Sebastian Thorin to my council." It had been a snap decision, but he didn't regret it.

The tall lord gave a curt nod.

When Alexander proceeded into the council room, Seb flashed Red a wide-eyed wince, followed by a conspiratorial grin. "We never made that bet." Only Seb could find so many reasons to smile on a day like today. Red was grateful that one person wasn't full of tears and condolences today, though he could tell Seb's smiles were bracketed with caution, as if he wasn't sure how much humor was too much.

"Grey," the king said, dismissing him with a small nod. Grey bowed and walked into the council room. Red turned back to Seb.

"Okay, here's the bet. If you—" Seb shoved the prince's shoulder "—mess up your lines during your accession, I win."

Red forced a chuckle. "Easy." The Accession Council would take place the following day in Mardon's cathedral. The men would discuss this and the funeral arrangements in the council meeting today. Then he was set to have lunch with his widowed mother and appear before the courtiers in the evening to receive their condolences. What that really meant was the richest and most influential people in Mardon would be falling over each other to be first to speak to Tandera's new king. He wouldn't have much time to practice his lines.

"If you so much as *stutter*, Your Royal Fanciness."

Red stood up straighter. "Fine."

Seb stepped closer, his chest puffed out. "Fine."

"What do I get when I win?"

"You mean, when you lose, what do I get?" Seb said. "If you lose, you introduce me to the sorcerer."

Red snorted. "You know that won't be possible."

"Fine. If I win, at least *tell* me what he looks like. Boils or tentacles. Come on, *something!*" Seb looked around, as if he'd catch a glimpse of the Royal Sorcerer. "What was it like, the Binding? At least tell me that."

Aly would be able to hear whatever he said next. Hot humiliation flooded his cheeks at the recollection of how much he'd *craved* the feeling of magic coursing through his body. "Ah, it was nothing really." His headache pulsed, as it often did with lies. Seb pointed at him, calling out his fumbled words. Red smirked. "If I win, you have to dance with Leeta Merrythorne at the ball."

A smile broke on Seb's face, easing some of the tension that had crept in. "It's a good thing I'm not going to lose, then." He shook with a fake shiver. "Leeta. Really? She's had you on her horizons since she could walk."

"That's why you'll have to dance with her. Most girls fall in love with you with just one dance. Isn't that what you say?"

"I'm not sure if that was a compliment, but I'll take it as one." After a moment, Seb chuckled, then stuffed his hands in his pockets, digging. "Got to seal it with something. Got anything?"

Red glanced down at his clothing and dug his hands into his pockets, searching for something that could act as the seal for their bet. In the past, they'd used everything from a shoe to a belt to a ring. But Red wasn't about to give up one of his shined black shoes, and his pants had grown a little loose over the past three months of watching his father's decline; he'd be needing his belt. With his thumb, he spun the signet ring on his right hand. He couldn't take that off, as he'd received it in the wee hours of the morning, after his father passed.

"Nope," he said.

"Ah," said Seb, drawing his hand out of his pants' pocket. In it was an earring. A large pearl with tiny diamonds around it.

"That's cute."

Seb flipped it up toward his ear. "I know, right? This should work."

"Who's it belong to?" Red's brows lifted.

"It's Josephine's. It, uh, fell off last night. I saw it this morning and grabbed it so I could return it. But this is better." Seb shoved it toward the prince.

"Josephine, as in Elise's atten—?"

Don't touch that, a voice snapped in his ear. He glanced around, startled. *You're through taking items that are handed to you.* Aly's voice was as clear as if she were standing a foot away—which, perhaps, she was. He knew sorcerers could communicate without speaking, but the sensation was off-putting, as if he were going mad.

Red ignored her, not sure why she'd burst into the conversation so rudely. As he lifted his hand to take the earring, his limb froze in midair.

Aly was using her magic *against* him, to keep him from taking the earring. How dare she!

"Yes, so what?" Seb said, a confused look on his face as he watched Red struggle.

Red wished magic allowed him to speak directly to Aly's mind, but it went only one-way. Unfair. Right now, he wanted to scream at her. He'd known her merely an hour—how dare she insert herself between him and his best friend? A small part of him whispered that she was merely doing her job, but he'd dismissed her ability to do her job properly as soon as Gevar had died.

Seb ran a hand over the back of his neck, apparently interpreting Red's hesitation for complete disgust at his choice of women. "It wasn't like that. She was fixing her hair or something. It just fell off. She *left.*"

"Right." Red stopped fighting Aly's magic and fisted his hand at his side.

"Come on, you know me better than that, Brother."

Red frowned. Seb was free to behave however he wanted; he would never inherit a throne. At the same time, it annoyed Red that Seb had been occupied in such a manner the night before the king's death.

Red turned away, feigning a reason to refuse the earring. "Give it back. It looks expensive."

"She said Elise gave them to her." Seb crammed the jewelry back in his pocket. "Apparently, Elise gives Josephine a lot of fancy things she doesn't need. What will we use, then?"

With a frustrated sigh, Red shrugged. "I don't know. We don't have to seal it with anything." Aly, as much as it disturbed him, wouldn't let him take anything anyway. Kings never accepted items handed to them by strangers, but this was a bit extreme. Seb was his best friend.

Though Red had expected the bet to grant him a welcome feeling of normalcy, something about it didn't feel right, as if the passing of his father and the events it set in motion transformed the triviality of a simple wager into a grievous offense.

Seb nodded, the levity from a moment ago on fragile ground. He flashed one more smile, returning to his unoffended self. "I'll be watching you." He turned to the council room door. "If you even say *um*." He disappeared into the room, whistling what Red assumed was a victory tune.

Before the dawn light had fully lit the city, Red stared at his ceremonial white and red suit, the suit of a king, freshly steamed and hanging in a large armoire in his bedchamber. With a grunt, Red folded his arms over his bare chest as Aly spun away from examining his clothes.

"It's clean," she announced to him, Bernard, and three other attendants, who'd stopped their ministrations when the Royal Sorcerer had barged into the king's rooms demanding to see the wardrobe for the day. Her gaze bounced off his undressed torso and roved the room for something else to look at.

"Of course it's clean. It was just laundered."

"Clean of insidious magic, Your Majesty," Aly corrected, her tone sharp.

Red rolled his eyes. "Doing our job now, are we?" The words slapped her and she recoiled. He bit the inside of his lip but did not retract the harsh statement. *If she'd done her job with Father, he'd still be alive.* A vision of the Bulvarnan sorcerer's white owl mask flittered through Red's mind. *Or would he?*

She turned toward the bed, which was strewn with the king's clean underclothes. He'd been preparing to bathe just before she'd marched in. Fortunately, she hadn't arrived two minutes later.

"Will you wear these today as well?" she asked, lifting her hands toward the clothes spread out on the bed.

"You're not seriously going to check those too?"

She scowled. "Want me to do my *job*?" Her hand waved over the undershirt and with it a small current of light.

Before she could examine any more of his underthings, he stepped forward and grabbed her arm. "Okay, that's enough."

Beneath her mask, her green eyes flashed. This close, he could read in her wide stare the disdain she felt at him for stopping her magic. Then her eyes betrayed her and flickered again to his chest. He smirked.

"Am I making you uncomfortable?"

She jerked her arm out of his grip and stormed toward the bedroom door. "I'll see you for the ceremony. And remember, don't touch *anything* the people try to give you."

"How could I forget? I might die just like my father if I do."

Above the packed square towered the spire of Mardon's cathedral, draping half the crowd in shadow. A lane had been carved through the center of the mass of people, where the chancellors, priests, and royal family now proceeded on horseback, the ladies in a carriage. Red's high collar chafed against his throat as he swallowed his nerves and his grief in rapid succession. The sorcerer, visible today in her mask and cloak as tradition mandated, followed behind him, the symbol to all present that the power of Theod was behind Red's accession of power.

Hands reached out from the crowd, handkerchiefs floated in the air toward the pavement. Flowers fell at the horses' hooves.

Don't touch anything, Aly commanded in his head for at least the dozenth time. *There's evil here, I can feel it.*

He clenched his jaw behind his false smile as he waved to his people. *His* people. Atop his horse, he pulled his shoulders back a little more.

Whistles and jeers jammed Red's concentration as he tried to focus on his lines. The whistles were for his mother. The people of Mardon adored Isabelle, dowager queen consort and one of their own, raised on Market Street in a small flat, whisked into the palace by a man in love. She was the epitome of hope, the fairy tale come to life. Many of the people lining the square didn't understand why she wasn't the one saying the accession vows today. They disliked Red for taking what they thought was Isabelle's rightful place as sovereign.

But people followed their hearts, not their histories.

He dismounted, waved to his people, and approached his sisters and mother.

"Long live the queen!" one man shouted.

"Don't listen to them," his mother said from beneath a black half-veil. She was radiant even in her mourning attire. Today at least, the only symbol of her recent loss was the small black veil. Her dress was fit for a celebration, pale gold with beads that sparkled in the sunlight. After the ceremony, however, she would resume her black garb. Briefly, she placed a hand on her son's cheek. "They will love you as they loved him."

Looking back over the past few months, even the past few

years, Red could see that his father had been trying to prepare him for this moment. Gevar had appointed Red to the council, insisted Red travel with him on diplomatic tours, even taken Red to the Canyon's edge twice to witness the fight against the Deep. Red had appreciated the closeness with his father, the trust his father had laid on him at such a young age. Now he knew why.

Trumpets shredded the little bit of Red's composure as the procession halted in front of the cathedral's doors. That tune, the funeral lament, unsettled his stomach and made him regret the sugar dusted beignets the palace staff had shoved at him with apologetic smiles.

His father would never laugh with him again. Never hunt with him again. Never teach him anything again. The knowledge that his father had been priming Red for kingship tainted his memories with a stench of deception. He hadn't picked Red for his council because he trusted his son's advice or valued his opinion. He'd chosen his son because he'd known he was dying.

Grand stone buildings buttressed the square, and faces peered down from every window, every balcony. The city's bakeries and florists and apothecaries, shuttered for the day of mourning, produced none of the familiar smells of the city. Everything stopped for the death of a king.

Except the beggars. Sadness for a dead monarch did not reach their outstretched hands or their hungry bellies. One thin boy, not much younger than Red, had cloth tied around his uplifted hands that soaked in places from oozing wounds. His face looked angry as he made eye contact with his future king. Red looked away.

Aly had been adamant that no item handed to him, gift or otherwise, could touch him. That was how Gevar had been cursed—he'd picked up a magnifying glass to examine a map during a meeting with his generals at the Canyon's edge. The magnifying glass, they'd learned, had been purchased in Bulvarna after the one belonging to General Daniels had mysteriously cracked. Slipping a cursed item to a king was not easy, but it was not impossible.

Though vexing, her constant reminders not to touch anything were at least proof she didn't want him harmed. She *was* trying to do her job. He just couldn't quite let go of the rage he'd bottled toward the sorcerer, intensified under the pressure of his grief. Though if Bulvarna had anything to do with it, Aly wasn't solely to blame.

The cathedral doors opened and the procession filed inside the chilled, dark space. The heavy silence of the cathedral's nave was more disquieting than the buzzing crowd outside. Now Red had nothing to distract his thoughts from what was about to take place. He was officially taking up the mantle his father had abandoned two nights ago.

Pews were filled with Mardon's wealthiest men and women. Crisp suits and fine silks whispered as the people all turned to look at their new king. Red scanned the faces, hoping for a glimpse of his grandparents, probably the only people in the audience not born to wealth and luxury.

After Gevar Windon had swept Isabelle Carrington off her feet and into the royal family, amid much fanfare from the people and objections from the nobility, the parents of the queen, a carpenter and his wife, had been elevated to Baron and Baroness, but they never liked those titles. Ethran and Margaret, or Pop and Gran, were the sole names Red had ever heard them accept, which had merely disgruntled the nobles forced to share table space with them at state dinners.

Red was glad they were here to witness his accession.

At the head of the nave, Arthur Ondorian paused, his white robes stark against his skin and the dark gray of the stone. His priestly robes resembled the Master Sorcerer's attire in color but not in shape. There was no hood, nor was there a mask to conceal his identity. Around his neck hung a gold-threaded stole that depicted a flame rising on both sides. The eternal flame of truth. He picked up a copy of the *Verad* and spun to face the crowd.

The muted rustlings of the people fell away as Red stepped up to place his hand on the book and say his vows, his bet with Seb entirely forgotten. The weight of this moment had pressed all other thoughts aside.

It is safe to touch, Aly said.

As if he needed her permission. He laid his hand on the smooth leather.

The official coronation ceremony would take place in four months' time. It would be the end of summer by then, and would allow enough time to invite the necessary guests, arrange the necessary security, and prepare Red for the task of leading a country. It had been clear enough on several of the chancellors' faces yesterday that they weren't quite ready to see Red at the head of the council table, where Gevar had sat. Whether he was ready to lead or whether his council was ready to follow, Red was now the king.

Ondorian stared at the king with urgent eyes. He'd been speaking, but his words had stopped. Red wasn't sure where he'd left off. His mind flashed, unbidden, to the sight of his father's still body stretched out like he was asleep in bed. One word bounced around in his head: *murder*.

From where he stood to the king's left, Lord Benedict Alexander cleared his throat. The small gesture rung like struck crystal. Red stiffened, his mind clambering for the words he'd hastily memorized. Was this the part where he said *I will* or *By Theod's grace* or where he declared his intentions to rule justly? What had Ondorian said?

You say, "I will."

A voice in his head drowned out his own fretful wondering. It was Aly's voice. Though not audible, it still sounded like her. She had a twitch of annoyance in her tone, as if she were rolling her eyes at his stupidity.

Tightening his jaw, he resisted the urge to tug at his hem and said, "I will."

Ondorian's face relaxed and they proceeded through the rest of the short ceremony.

After the ceremony, Red had one small gesture left. An act suggested by his council as a way to win the hearts of the people.

As Chancellor Benedict Alexander had suggested, on the steps of the cathedral, in plain view of all the people, he turned, pulled a handkerchief from his pocket, and handed it to his mother with a small bow. It was a symbol that she could now, officially, mourn Gevar's death, having passed all authority and responsibility to her son. It was a display of thanks and of love, to honor the widow; according to Alexander, it was a way to display Red's compassion and kindness toward the sweetheart of Mardon. Red thought it an odd, albeit good, suggestion coming from Alexander, considering the man's initial disapproval of the king's marriage to a commoner.

But instead of the expected smiles, murmurs and looks of horror spread across the crowd. Red wondered if they were muttering at his flushed cheeks or his too-stiff movements.

Above the rest of the crowd, he heard Elise gasp sharply.

Then he noticed what everyone else already had. The handkerchief he'd handed his mother, the one he'd pulled from his pocket, was soaked with blood.

6

ALY

Aly's heart dropped out of her chest at the sight of the bloody cloth. Desperately, violently, she hoped Red was bleeding somewhere under his suit.

Because the other option was one she could not stomach. She'd checked every item in the church, every stone along the way. She'd even checked his jacket.

But he had stopped her from checking his undergarments. The handkerchief would have been laundered and pressed along with those items. *Irrational sense of propriety! Look where it got us!*

No point admitting, now, that she had been grateful he'd pushed her away from his underthings. The awkwardness of it had been more than she could bear, standing there, in his bedroom.

She dove for his Truthwell, her magic unguarded and unbridled. As she proceeded down the cathedral steps behind her sovereign, her balance faltered as her consciousness was swallowed by the blinding brilliance of his Truthwell. She pushed a wave of magic through his body, an assessing spell, and a much stronger one than was necessary.

His head snapped up, but he refused to turn around. Her

magic washed through him and found nothing. He was not injured.

We need to talk. Now, she demanded above the din of excited spectators. It was a long walk through crowded streets as they made their way back to the palace.

"My dear boy, what in Theod's name were you thinking?" barked Benedict Alexander as the chancellors and the royal family entered the semi-privacy of the palace's grand foyer. The vast space felt empty in comparison to the crowded streets, but the palace buzzed with people, permanent staff and additional hands hired to help with the preparations for the upcoming accession ball, to be held the evening after Gevar's funeral at the end of the week.

Aly's pulse pounded like cannon fire in her ears, and dread weighed her ankles down. Questions, doubts, fears, and rage thundered in her head, and she was grateful to be walking without her shroud. Even the small amount of magic necessary to maintain it would be a challenge with her mind in turmoil.

The workers bowed as Red led the group across the marble tiles toward the sunlit Hall of Mirrors. Aly had been glad to leave the streets, with all the pointing fingers and hands hiding whispers in the crowd. They rarely saw her. Gevar had been kind to keep her in the shadows—it was what she'd wanted. She couldn't risk her father finding out where she lived or whom she served.

But he had anyway.

"I said *chivalrous* not *disastrous*." Alexander's words made Red turn to him.

Aly thought he might combust, judging by the look on his face. His Truthwell writhed and glittered and pattered its fast tempo against her consciousness. Grey's Truthwell hummed nearby, as did the Wells of every person in the room.

Aly, groping for something to take her mind off of the bloody cloth, let her magic wander to Grey's Truthwell. She couldn't Pull from it anymore—she was Bound to the king. Besides that, Lord Weston Grey had hired a new Protector. The cloaked figure walked behind them, and Aly wished she could tell if, under the guise, the sorcerer were a man or a woman. *Does he have another young woman as his Protector?* she wondered. *Will he bring her to the palace in ballgowns, too?*

Stop it, she said, jerking her focus away from Grey's profile. He'd slowed down a little as the company marched across the foyer. She wondered if he was hanging back because of her.

What did it matter now? The cloth—it was all that mattered. Until she knew for certain why it was stained, she could not entertain any other daydreams.

But her magic swept almost entirely past Grey's Truthwell, as if it barely registered the once familiar pattern. She paused, unable to prevent her eyes from flittering to Grey. He, already watching her, locked eyes with Aly.

Behind the large mask, Aly's face began to steam like a garden after a summer rain.

With a small tug on Red's Truthwell, she decreased her body temperature until her fingers were cold and her cheeks no longer burned. She broke eye contact first.

"Your Majesty," Alexander began again, his voice taut, as if calling Red by this title strained him. "I assume there is an explanation? Some people think that it might have been a prank. A *prank*, Your Majesty."

Red stopped walking, the entire party behind him halting with him. He kept his gaze pointed down the grand hallway. "I assure you, Alexander, it was no prank. While I may be no more than a boy to you, I am not in the habit of *pranking* my widowed mother as she mourns."

Alexander stiffened. Red continued his walk down the chandeliered hallway, the light dazzling as it reflected off a dozen mirrors.

"My king," said Edgar Wyndall, Duke of Luxler and another

of the king's councilmen, "how are we to respond to the people's questions?"

Red let out an annoyed breath. He slowed his pace and spoke over his shoulder to Wyndall. "Tell them I had a bloody nose right before the ceremony, that I gave myself a papercut when I was reviewing the language of the oaths. I don't know! Be creative."

Alexander gasped, either at Red's brazenness or at the king's use of a contraction. Red had never fully bowed to his mother's wishes to speak with the formality expected among the older nobility. She'd grown up speaking the lax language of the middle class, and her queenly training had instilled in her the necessity of speaking properly, to be accepted by those who looked down on her for her lack of status. Red didn't have to worry about that. He was Gevar's son, after all, and rightful sovereign of Tandera.

Wyndall nodded, lagging behind as they approached the palace library. Red hadn't told anyone where he was headed, they all just followed, like ducklings.

He paused before the library doors and turned to the small crowd. His councilmen, his personal bodyguards, and his two sisters. His mother was only halfway down the hall, walking slowly beside her attendants, so she hadn't heard their comments about the handkerchief.

"I would like to speak to my sorcerer. Alone. Please." He sounded so childish. Kings didn't make requests, they made demands. His father had said as much and had made Red practice. Not enough, apparently.

Aly hurried into the massive library and veered toward one of the adjacent reading rooms.

Red stepped in behind her. The king's personal bodyguard, Veeter Yin, knew enough to remain outside the room.

When they were alone, she ripped off her mask and rounded on him. "I think you might—" But she couldn't finish the sentence. Sobs burst from her mouth. She spun away, hands clamped over her lips.

Silence from Red. Then, a few footsteps. Sunlight streamed in through the diamond-paned windows, highlighting the ghostly look that had entered the king's features.

No part of her was able to process the fear inside her head. Words formed and failed as they jammed in her throat.

"You're scaring me," he said.

The crown on his head caught the sunlight. A small gold band, etched with feathers and flames. A reminder of the phoenix, Tandera's symbol of the persistence of truth.

She hiccoughed, reeled her breathing in, and pulled her shoulders back. After two tries to clear her throat, she said, "Unless you have a good explanation for that handkerchief, I believe you may be cursed."

Red reacted to the words with blank incomprehension. Finally, he blinked. "Excuse me?"

Aly, pushed by shame and anger and by a blackness that was clouding her vision, stumbled toward the king. "Show it to me." Without reason or explanation, she reached for his pocket where he'd crammed the offensive item.

Please, no. Please, no.

Red handed her the handkerchief, recoiling away from her.

As soon as it touched Aly's fingers, she dropped it with a muffled cry. The nightmare she'd feared was true.

The cloth was cursed, and so was the king.

Retreating into the comfort of invisibility was childish, and she knew it, but facing Red and the expression on his face was not something her eggshell composure could handle. She ignored his shouts and fled the small room. She needed air.

She needed a new reality.

Maybe, if she could run far enough, fast enough, she could avoid dealing with the fact that Red had just touched—and thus absorbed—a curse. It simply couldn't be true.

But a sorcerer could never really run from truth. It governed her magic, fueled her power, and shackled her choices—in the best way. Or so she believed. The truth that Red might be facing the same fate as Gevar was a truth she wished she could destroy.

The library's eastern wall opened onto a high terrace adjacent to the lower, larger terrace off the grand ballroom that was often used for spring teas and intimate gatherings. Today, the terraces were mostly empty, but for palace staff scrubbing them for the upcoming ball.

As she burst from the library, the glass door clattered shut behind her. Cool spring air wafted over Aly's shrouded form. She leaned against the railing, heaving. *Thank Theod for invisibility.* But being invisible didn't mean she could abandon her duties.

Within minutes, Red had found her, following the sound of the closing door.

Before extending her shroud to cover him—for she would not have this conversation in the open, with ears nearby—she stared at his face. His eyes searched for her, in the annoyed way one searches for an irritating fly. In his fist, he carried the bloody cloth.

He was handsome and young. His looks had always bothered Aly because she knew one day she would have to Bind with him, only to remain his closest armor until he withered with age and passed from the world. She, however, would remain, more or less, in pristine physical health until at last her time was up and all at once her magic would dwindle and she would no longer be strong enough to put off the effects of two centuries of age. No, serving as his sorcerer would be much easier if he were unattractive.

So, after that first day she'd noticed he was no longer a boy but a man, that first day she'd noticed the inward curve of his cheeks and the rigid line of his nose, Aly had forced herself to look away. Lying was not a viable option for a sorcerer, but there were other ways to ignore the truth. Hating Red for the way he'd spoken to her, for the way he'd made her *feel,* made it even easier to overlook the way his red curls lifted in the breeze, the way his throat bobbed as he swallowed, the way his brown eyes were bellows to her inner flame. Now, staring at him with unhindered eyes, she explored his freckled features and wished she could ignore the screaming in her gut.

With a deep breath, she pushed her shroud out wider, enveloping him in her shell of solitude.

He charged forward as soon as he saw her. "What on earth is wrong with you?"

She hadn't expected that. She stormed toward him. "What is *wrong* with me? I just watched one king die and now this?" Her nose pointed up at him, nostrils flaring.

"Tell me what is going on!"

"That handkerchief is cursed. Who put it in your pocket?" Faces, names, motives all flashed before her eyes, but her mind stopped on one man. Her father. *But how? And why?* There had to be another explanation.

"You do not get to badger me with questions! I will ask the questions. What do you mean, cursed?"

"Cursed! As in, your body will decay and you will die." *Like Papa.*

Her words slapped him, and he stepped backward.

For a moment, she thought about rewording her statement if only to erase the horrified look on his face; however, there was no way to rewrite the truth. Perhaps she'd been too harsh in her delivery, but there it was.

"And you can't keep me alive, can you?"

Impaled by his words, she stared blankly back at him. Finally, she blinked and looked away, wilting under the weight of guilt. If this was the working of her father, she could never forgive herself. Two kings dead, because of her.

He's not dead yet.

She stomped like a petulant child. "I warned you! You should have let me search your *entire* wardrobe."

His gaze narrowed. "How dare you call this my fault."

With the heels of her palms, she covered her eyes and fought back the screams that climbed in her throat. *It is my fault! It is my fault!* She dropped her hands and, seething, said, "We need to know who is behind this. Who put it in your pocket?"

"I don't know. Bernard might know. Clara? Francesca? They usually prepare my clothing. The only other person to touch the handkerchief would've been the girl who ironed it yesterday and perhaps whoever else carried it to and from the laundry. It was, in case this needs to be said, most certainly not bloody when I put it in my pocket."

Aly lifted both arms. "It wasn't even in your pocket this morning—I checked your suit. How am I supposed to protect you from cursed items if you *put them in your own pocket!*" she yelled.

"Toss me, woman! Do you ever admit your own failings? *You* allowed this. I am—I am cursed now because of you!" He swallowed, then his voice dropped. "Will I die like him?"

Several moments passed as they faced this awful question; Red's chest heaved, and Aly's eyes flooded with tears as they stood there, staring at one another.

As she stared at him, her heart clattered to the terrace like a dropped plate. "I—don't know."

"That's comforting." He paced away and leaned against the balcony railing.

"Red, I know you are angry, but we need to think through this. It was Lord Alexander who first suggested you give your mother the handkerchief, right?"

"Could he be responsible for this?"

"Anything is possible." She knew who was behind it, but she could always hope.

Red sensed her doubt. "You think it was your father again. Why won't he come down here and fight you, if he wants you dead so badly?" She scoffed. "And all because you killed the woman he loved over two decades ago?"

Aly wanted to be mad at his harsh words, but there was too much truth in them. If her father had taken his rage out on her years ago, Renna and Gevar would still be alive, and Red would not be cursed now.

"I'm sorry," she said, all defiance dispersed out of her like the last few wisps of steam from a once boiling pot.

Her apology startled the king. He leaned against the terrace railing and peered at her for several seconds. "How long do I have?"

His calmness frightened her. Rage, she expected. Fear made sense. But the eerie resolve in his tone chilled her bones. "I was able to keep your father alive for three months once he was cursed, and he wasn't as young or healthy as you. So, three, maybe four months? Unless we find a cure."

"Wait, what?" He hurried toward her, a ferocity in his eyes. "You said a death curse can't be healed."

"Yes. That's the common belief, but there are a few ancient texts that suggest otherwise. With Gevar, we ran out of time to investigate them all."

His hands gripped her shoulders. They were trembling. His composure wasn't as rock solid as she'd imagined. "We?"

"Arthur Ondorian was helping us research a cure. We read through all the Canticles, all the first-hand accounts of sorcerers that we could find. We never made it to fiction and poetry, though. If we're going to find a cure, Red, we need more help. We don't have much time."

His gaze snapped up. "I happen to know two girls who love to read."

"Your sisters."

He nodded. "If it's fiction that can save me, Carolyn will know where to start. And if it's poetry, Elise can help us there. Theod knows, Lordan sent her enough of it."

"Then go. Now. We can't waste any time."

7

RED

The solarium was one of the princesses' favorite haunts. Before Red had inherited more responsibility and a chair on his father's council, he'd frequent that room with his sisters to read or study. Elise liked to paint in the well-lit area, while Carolyn would tinker with her latest invention or practice breeding new plants, imitating the work of the scientists in Mardon's university.

"You seem bothered," Elise said with a small lift of her pale brows as Red approached. She sat at her watercolor and peered around the canvas at her brother. On a busy day, Elise still found a few moments for her paintings.

It was now late afternoon, and the light was growing warm and golden. An uncomfortable meeting with city officials regarding the funeral had occupied Red's early afternoon, and he only had a few moments before they would all be shuffled off to dinner in the Summit Ballroom.

Gevar would never again dine with his family.

The king slumped against the windowed wall of the solarium. The river below, as it dipped out of sight behind the buildings of

Mardon, reminded him of Aly standing on the banks, lifting the tree as if it were no more than a drumstick.

A mere few hours had passed since his accession ceremony and already the weight of the crown threatened to be more than he could handle.

"Frederick?"

He opened his eyes and stared at his sister. "Where is Carolyn?" They needed to hear this together. He couldn't bring himself to tell his mother, not a day after she'd said goodbye to her husband.

Elise pointed with her brush. "Down there."

Carolyn lounged on a couch at the other end of the bright space. Music hummed, spilling out the latest symphony of Xavier Orara.

"I still can't believe she got that thing to work. Everyone in Mardon will be wanting one."

"She is certainly incredible. If she can create that at fourteen, what will she accomplish when she is twenty?" Elise smiled as she shook her head, looking at her sister. "She will be the one to figure out how to make a carriage move without magic."

Red leaned onto his elbows. "You're probably right." Carolyn was capable of anything, and all without magic. She was proving, slowly, that her mind could do much of what people paid sorcerers to do. *But will I live to see it?* he wondered.

His sister tapped her brush against the side of the canvas, drawing his attention. "I know it will not be easy, but you were born to rule this country. You will do well."

A small laugh escaped the king's lips. Since their mother had given birth to a son first, no one expected Elise to ever have to worry about ruling. They might all have been wrong. If he died, she'd take the throne.

"We'll see."

Elise sat straighter. "Now, stop that. You have been nothing but gloomy these past few days. No," she held up a hand to stop him, "do not say it is because we are mourning or because you acquired a throne earlier than you planned. You are *king* now. Your country—and your family—needs you to act like one."

Her words pricked him, threatening to spark his anger and sadness again. But she was right. He was not acting like Gevar, and that only made him simmer with even more frustration. *Will I ever be good at this?* Only if he survived this curse and had the chance to try. He swallowed. "Elise, I need your help with something." He stood. "Come on, I want Carolyn's help too."

Elise gingerly set down her brush.

"Does she ever go anywhere without that thing?" Red asked as he walked toward Carolyn.

"No. Silvanus carries it everywhere for her. She thinks it's her best invention. She can bring the symphony with her."

Red glanced back at Elise. "Did I just hear you use a contraction?"

"Don't tell Mother."

"Your *Majesty*!" Carolyn said, jumping up. She offered a dramatic curtsey. When she saw Red's face, she stood straight. "What is it?"

With a sigh, Red told them. "It looks as if I've been cursed." Over Carolyn's gasp, he added, "Like Father."

Elise blanched. Carolyn's jaw fell open.

"Like, cursed in what way?" Carolyn crossed her arms.

"A death curse, Carolyn. That handkerchief at the ceremony? Turns out it had a curse in it."

Elise pressed one hand to her mouth as her face darkened. Carolyn dropped back onto the couch, dismayed.

"Who would do this?" whispered Elise.

Red had hoped they wouldn't ask. The truth was, he didn't know for certain. Aly seemed convinced it was her father. "Very possibly, Dimitri Patrenko."

"Who?" asked Carolyn.

But Elise had recognized the name. Her hand fell from her open mouth. "Bulvarna's sorcerer?"

"The man who killed all those people?" Carolyn yelped. "He keeps foxbloods for pets!"

No one knew if the Bulvarnan sorcerer really kept Canyon beasts for pets or whether or not the mysterious deaths in the north were actually of his making. Nevertheless, Bulvarna's sorcerer, while cloaked in rumor as much as fact, was a terror.

"You can help me. The sorcerer thinks there might be a way to heal me. A forgotten cure." Elise was shaking, and Red placed one hand on her shoulder. "I'm not giving up. We can find this answer. Arthur Ondorian thinks there might be some hints in novels or poetry. Can you—"

"I've got the novels." Carolyn jumped up. She'd changed into a simple, elegant blue dress suitable for the dinner they would attend later. "Elise, you can take the poems."

Elise's now haunted face stole some shadows from the air. "What is that supposed to mean?"

"You have, I mean…" Carolyn began, searching for words. "All that poetry he…?"

Nearly snarling, Elise stepped forward. "Yes, all that poetry Lordan sent me. You think I want to *reread* any of that? Think again."

Both Red and Carolyn recoiled and shared a look. Elise was never like this; but Lordan had hurt her, and they'd just lost their father, and her brother had told her he'd been cursed. She had the right to be harsher than usual.

"Okay, you can search the novels," Red said, eyeing Carolyn to make sure she wouldn't argue. "Maybe start with the book Carolyn mentioned that spoke of curses?"

Elise pursed her lips, her eyes averted and filling with tears. "But what was his motive? Why curse you? And through a *hand-kerchief*? Where did the handkerchief come from?"

Red shrugged. "All good questions, and I plan to find the

answers. That's why I need your help with the reading. We might have a war on our hands if I come to the wrong conclusion about this." *A war, Elise, that you may have to finish.* Her eyes bulged, almost as if she'd registered this silent fear.

"Will the Bulvarnan ambassador be at the funeral?" she asked.

"I assume so. It would look bad if she misses it. In any case, I'll have a few choice words for her."

Carolyn rubbed her hands up and down her arms. "We will find this cure. We *will*."

"Yes," he said. "Thank you both. When you're reading, look for anything that mentions an alternative to siphoning for healing a death curse."

Five days later, the sight of his father's dead body, decked in ceremonial attire and surrounded by white lilies, exacerbated the tingling sensation in the base of Red's skull. Ever since Aly had told him of his death curse, every twitch, every random flicker of pain seemed to be evidence of his body's demise.

He'd slept little. The research was slow, arduous, and as precise as birdshot. They had few ideas about where to look or what they were looking for.

Murder.

The word repeated over and over in his mind as he rode along, silent, behind the pyre that would soon drift over Lake Corinel and lift his father's remains to the sky. He'd not once considered that his father's sickness had been caused by a person and that now his own life might be taken in the same way.

The sorcerer hadn't stopped it. What was worse: a sorcerer who couldn't heal disease or a sorcerer who couldn't stop an assassin? The Royal Sorcerer was supposed to be the most powerful person in the entire kingdom.

What a lie.

Aly might have the ability to move trees or propel carriages, but she hadn't been able to help his father when it mattered most. Perhaps to tip the scales a little in her favor, she'd barely slept this week, passing hours in the library each night, searching.

She walked the road beside him, visible once again, a rarity considering her typical absence from the public eye for months at a time. More people pointed at her than at their new king as they moved toward the banks of Lake Corinel.

At the edge of the lake, he dismounted and swallowed the knot in his throat. After he delivered his poorly rehearsed lines about the heroic and selfless life of his father, the torchbearer lit the wood and gently pushed the floating barge away from the pier. It helped that Seb wasn't nearby to make fun of Red's fumbled words. They still hadn't resolved the bet Red had lost at the Accession Council. Seb, it seemed, had enough heart not to pester Red about it, given the ruckus surrounding the handkerchief incident.

In moments, his father's body disappeared beneath bright flames. The fire removed that which was not eternal, leaving only that which would endure forever—Gevar's soul. And, strangely, his teeth. An awful mental image littered Red's mind as he turned to the crowd, that of a pile of dead kings' teeth caked in algae.

"I visited the university library," Elise said as she stepped up beside him. The cool breeze blew Elise's profile into relief behind her mourning veil. "They have an entire room of pre-Canyon texts." She sniffed, the sole sign she was crying beneath her veil.

"Yes, but they're all in Kirish or Edrean."

"I am getting better at reading Kirish."

Red eyed her with respect. He'd never mastered the ancient language.

Tandera's anthem began. Carolyn sang loudly despite her

clogged nose and sob-choked throat. His mother remained still and silent under her veil.

As the crowd turned to disperse, Red bowed to the visiting sovereigns of Refere and Virienne, Tandera's closest allies. They had come despite the short notice. Among them stood Lordan, tall and smug in his pale blue tails and sash. Red frowned at Lordan then glanced at Elise, wondering why the Referen prince had bothered to come at all, given his recent behavior that had left his sister in a weeping, heartbroken heap.

Elise kept her gaze on the crowd and said, "Lordan said he wishes to speak with me. Should I let him?"

"Why?"

"Why should I or why does he want to speak to me?"

Red could hear the snap in her tone, though he couldn't see her face. He did not want to add to her pain today. He sighed. "Do whatever you want, Elise."

He meant to say it in a kind way, but it came out annoyed and grumpy, as if Red were somehow offended. Elise huffed under her veil.

"How is Carolyn?" he asked as they moved back toward the road where Red's horse and the princesses' carriage waited.

"She stayed up all night working on the clock." Elise walked away, to where the Referen prince stood next to his father.

Red steeled his features and stood taller as people, ready with condolences, moved toward him.

Behind the first row of faces, he spotted them; a man in a dark suit, jacket unmerciful over his middle, stood beside a slender woman with black hair as long as her waist, pale arms at her sides. She wore a brooch that spoke of royalty but no crown. Ambassador Anastasia Vitnona. Behind her loomed a masked Protector.

This was his chance to glean what information he could from the Bulvarnans. If their Royal Sorcerer wanted him dead, perhaps Red could convince them to slip in a confirmation.

There are two known ways to heal a death curse, Aly's words repeated in his mind. The research for a third way was taxing and slow; futile, considering he had months left to live, if that. If he could figure out who planted the curse, there was the chance they could employ the *other* means of curing a death curse: casting it back into the one who set it.

Stepping forward, the ambassador inclined her head, the movement graceful and much used. Though aged, she had the advantage of elegance and beauty—something his father had warned Red about. Never trust a woman simply because she was beautiful.

Aly's face flashed through his mind as he bowed curtly back to them. In his periphery, Aly's white cloak stepped closer.

A headache dulled his other senses, so be barely registered the cool, snakelike breeze that slithered over him. In the back of his mind, he recognized that someone was invoking magic. He hoped it was Aly and not the ambassador's Protector.

"Your Majesty," began the man. "We bring gifts to honor your father, from the court of Bulvarna."

Red bristled underneath his social mask. A king did not reveal his emotions to the enemy. *Stay calm.* "My thanks," he said. "Does Kassia wish to honor him, despite her refusal to meet with him before he passed?" He'd been trained to speak to other heads of state, other kings, other ambassadors, but now that he wore the crown and his words truly mattered, he wondered if he'd erred by bringing up a fragile subject.

But they were in his home, his palace, his country. He could say what he wished. *Right?*

No. Red realized he'd never be able to say *whatever* he wished ever again. He now spoke for the entire country of Tandera.

The woman lifted her chin, eying the king with a strange watchfulness, as if she were able to descry his thoughts. "We are aware of our intrusion on your good graces, but Bulvarna plans to make up for our former aloofness with the news we bring."

Her thin lips curled at the ends like dried parchment. "Queen Kassia wishes to relay a message to you."

This was it. The woman was about to admit her own sovereign had initiated an act of war. Right here, at his father's funeral.

The ceremonial sword hilt at his waist called to Red. He had a weapon, should he need it.

"Our Lady the Queen has specific intelligence that suggests you are in danger." Vitnona paused to absorb Red's poorly concealed look of shock. "And she would like to offer you her protection."

Heat broke out across Red's back and chest, scrambled up his neck, and blasted pain into his forehead, fanning the flames of his headache. "Is that so?"

The ambassador lifted her chin and nodded. "We were sent here to tell you this in person. Queen Kassia's sources believe the threat is one very close to you."

They mean Aly. Her words all but confirmed it was Aly's father behind the curses. *But why would Kassia try to warn me about Aly if her own Royal Sorcerer had already placed a death curse on me?* The political strings were too tangled for him to parse out right away.

"I have my own guards," he said. "And my sorcerer."

"Of course." The ambassador glanced at Aly. "My queen does not doubt the ability of your guards or your sorcerer, merely she wished to add a helpful warning in the case of an unexpected attack."

"Attack? Tell me plainly, what does Kassia know?"

The ambassador could hardly contain the satisfaction on her face. This was her goal—to hear those words. Red was now directly at Bulvarna's mercy, or so it appeared to this woman. He'd walked right into this trap. Among monarchs, knowledge was often as powerful as armies.

"We know nothing of specifics, only that our queen believes the threat comes from someone who lives inside the palace."

"How does she know this?" He intended to leverage the situation. They came here to hold this tidbit over his head, assuming that he was unaware of Aly's father's hand in all this. For Kassia to claim knowledge of his household that exceeded his own hinted that they thought him incompetent. Then again, Red had knowledge of one in Kassia's household. As always, it all came down to who held the truth.

The ambassador's face grew cold. "How a queen comes to know information is not of my concern. It is my duty to believe her."

Blind faith. Red wasn't sure if this equated to devotion or stupidity. "Then at least tell me this, Ambassador. How does your queen intend to protect me from so far away? Use magic? Perhaps she could send an enchanted item." He shoved as much anger into his eyes as he could manage, disregarding his father's advice to remain cool in the heat of conflict. Bulvarna had killed one Tanderan king. It would *not* kill another.

Anger, it turned out, could be alchemized into hope.

He now had as much proof as he needed to set his next steps in motion. He would not sit and wait around for a mythical cure to arise—Aly's advice be tossed! He had other plans.

The ambassador lifted her chin, a small gesture that meant Red had hit home. She knew now that he, too, held important information. If it surprised her that Red knew where his curse had originated, she hid it well; however, the conversation had shifted, and she was no longer the one in control.

Perhaps she'd expected this, for she quickly bowed her neck and said with a menacing smile, "We came as soon as a threat was detected, Your Majesty. We offer nothing but our help to mitigate the danger you are now in."

In his veins, a snapping fire kindled. Heat shot to his extremities. In contrast, a forceful breeze licked around his ears, his ankles. Aly was attempting to cool his temper, which instead stoked the embers. *She will not manipulate my emotions. I will remain sovereign over my own decisions.*

"I am most grateful for your offer," Red said, taking up his kingly duties. "The crown of Tandera extends the hand of peace." He pressed his palm against his chest, then offered it to the ambassador, who took it gently. He'd heard his father call himself the crown of Tandera, but it felt strange and clunky on his own tongue, as if he were role playing.

Politics were a strange game, and he had to remain in possession of all the winning cards. "I would be pleased if you would join us at the accession celebration the day after tomorrow." Though these two had come bearing threats, he had to win the upper hand. He'd allow the people see the Bulvarnans at his palace, let the world believe he and Kassia were working toward true peace. It was all a game of lies because the Lady Wolf had refused for decades to sign a peace treaty with Gevar, but if she agreed to play Red's game with his rules, he might just find a way to win.

Any bit of peace or cordiality, even if feigned, between their countries, might buy them time before reality had to be faced: Bulvarna's sorcerer, for a reason he didn't entirely believe, wanted to dismantle Tandera from the crown down.

The ambassador smiled, her restraint bulging a vein in her neck. "We are pleased to accept your invitation."

Red kept his face calm, but inside he smirked. He'd won this round.

As the woman and her escorts turned away, Red's lips curled in satisfaction.

With the chill of a receding breeze, from right over his shoulder, Aly whispered, "You idiot. What have you done? You've just invited the enemy to dinner!"

8

ALY

"How am I supposed to keep you alive? My enchantments at the palace only work against *unwanted* guests." Aly hissed as she walked beside him. They headed toward the waiting line of horses and carriages that would carry everyone back to the palace. "At this rate, three months was a generous estimate."

He stopped short. The fury in his brown eyes seemed almost comical considering the situation. If she weren't on the brink of more accidental magic, she'd laugh at him. She missed Gevar for a hundred reasons, but she'd not anticipated missing his common sense. This new king seemed aggravatingly apt at inviting evil into his life.

"Do not tell me how to run my country," Red snapped, his voice rasping.

She wondered if that was shame buried beneath his bravado.

As he leaped onto his horse, he wheezed. A tiny sound, but evidence of how much he had cried in the past twenty-four hours. She sighed. Of course he was making rash decisions—the young man had been tossed a crown and had no idea how to wield it.

He's going to die, and his blood will be on my hands too. Her night-marish thoughts drowned out the sound of weeping onlookers and whispering courtiers. Something had to be done. Books might hold the answer, but that only mattered if the relevant text was found in time.

The words of the ambassador floated through Aly's mind. *Someone who lives inside the palace.* They were trying to prod Red's distrust of those around him, to turn his skeptical gaze inward so he'd shoot himself in the foot.

She stepped up close to his stirrup and said, "We need to practice." The squeaking of leather at her shoulder obscured his grunted response. *His arrogance could chisel marble.* Fine, she would make this about her. "I need to practice Pulling from your Well. All newly Bound sorcerers have to practice, to discover the depths of our new source. It's to ensure your safety, Your Majesty."

He shifted in the saddle. "The day is full. So is tomorrow."

"You want to live long enough to find a cure, don't you?"

Another grunt. "I meet with my council tomorrow morning. If that ends quickly, we can do it then."

"Council meetings never end quickly." If the Bulvarnans were coming to the ball, they had to be ready. While she could techni-cally Pull from his Truthwell at any time, what she planned could potentially knock him down, and they couldn't have him falling off his horse during the parade or slumping into his pudding at dinner. No, she would have to wait until they were alone.

He pursed his lips. "The day after that I meet with the heads of the unions and lunch with Seb's father to hear about the state of our trade. I believe the next day I'm to take a tour of Mardon, meet some local business owners. Tonight we have a dinner with the chancellors and their wives and don't ask me to stay up late. I haven't slept in two days and I fully intend to tonight."

The short parade back to the palace stretched on eternally.

As they walked, she ignored the crowd. *Fine, I'll practice a little*

Pulling now. She pressed her magical awareness out to its boundaries, searching for threats. If the Bulvarnans were planning something, perhaps they had some evil magic lurking in the city somewhere.

With Red fueling her, she found she could reach farther than she could with Gevar. Her senses noted all the glowing Truthwells across the city, the Wells of the people brighter than those of animals, which were in turn brighter than the Wells of plants and stones. There were plenty of Truthwells swirling with darkness, some almost entirely dimmed by lies. Using a small bit of magic to keep her floating just off the ground—not enough for anyone to notice but enough to keep her from tripping in her state of extended awareness—she zipped her magic over each of the darkened Truthwells she could sense.

Within seconds, she'd identified twenty-seven Truthwells dark enough and twisted enough to present a threat, and that was only in the crowd they now passed through.

Her toe stubbed against a raised cobblestone and her focus shrank back to her immediate surroundings. She steadied herself with a quick whispered spell and began walking again.

Red glanced down at her. "What is it now?"

"I tripped."

He snickered. The noise shot arrows into Aly's veins. She blasted herself with cool air and used it to push Red's hair into a rather ridiculous standing position. Her mask concealed her smirk.

As sorcerer, her place was not to govern the country, but it was to keep the king alive. Her failure with Gevar left her with the constant sensation of being dangled over a deep ravine with nothing more than the strength of her grip to hold her aloft. Eventually, her fingers would slip and she would plummet.

"Can you, perhaps, leave me alone this afternoon?" he muttered to her from his saddle. "Your presence irritates me, and I would like a moment of not being irritated."

That idiot! In her head, she conjured insults and pelted them at him as she walked beside his horse toward the palace, ignoring all the people pointing at her and whispering behind their hands. "Fine."

Night had fallen by the time dinner concluded and the guests of the royal family were dismissed. Aly, who hadn't eaten, hid under her shroud and waited outside the palace's door, under the portico where a line of carriages waited.

When Lord Weston Grey exited the building amid a flutter of wine-enhanced laughter, she stepped forward to follow. Sebastian oozed out of the palace after Grey, his breath reeking of wine. Grey had never, in Aly's short time with him, consumed too much alcohol, but in the few months he'd been back from the Canyon, she'd witnessed enough of his late-night chats with Seb to know that Grey was no longer the man she'd known six years ago.

His carriage was, however, the same. She slid in, undetected, behind Grey, careful not to let her cloak touch his leg. Seb stood on the palace steps and waved to Grey. Fortunately, Seb lived at the palace and wouldn't follow Grey to his large manor house outside the city. Grey's Protector exited the palace and climbed onto the driver's seat of the carriage, where he would propel the coach to Grey Manor without need for horses.

When the carriage door was pushed shut by a palace doorman, Aly extended her shroud around Grey, enveloping him into her world of invisibility.

He choked on a cough, his eyes watering as he tried to recover with dignity.

"Aly."

"Grey." She Pulled wave after wave of cold air into the carriage, hoarding it around her face and pushing it through the open collar of her cloak. She could only hope it was enough to quell the blush rising in her cheeks. She removed her mask.

Six years dissolved, and she felt like she was again in a silver dress, unmasked, looking across at a younger, less tired Lord Weston Grey.

She shook the memory away. "He found me."

Grey was the sole person on the continent who would understand exactly who she meant without her having to say another word. The comfort of this fact eased the tension in Aly's shoulders.

The darkhaired lord leaned forward. The carriage began to move. "I'm so sorry. What can I do?"

Her heart twanged. "Still trying to protect me?"

He half-smiled. "You're right. I guess the better question is what will happen now?"

Aly opened her mouth but no words came out. She trusted Grey, but he was not the man he once was. She also had no real reason to tell him of the king's curse. She'd come here with dual purposes; one she could admit, the other she tried to bury.

"Will he come for you?" asked Grey.

Is he, too, thinking of the night I learned the identify of my father?

"He seems to be waiting for something, but he is active. I think he's trying to draw me out. The palace, as you know, is enchanted. He can't attack me here."

"Thanks to your ingenious magic." Grey smirked. He looked entirely too handsome with that expression.

Averting her eyes, Aly shook her head. "My magic is only ingenious because of you, you know."

Why am I complimenting him? Mentally, she slapped herself. Grief and anger had driven her to near insanity. Grey was a ghost. A figure of the past. An impossibility.

"You speak too highly of me," he muttered, "considering what I did."

Her gaze snapped back to him. She'd wanted to blast him for

his cruelty for *years*, but now that she had the chance, now that he was inviting the conversation, she could not. Her throat clamped shut, and she blinked in shock.

He sat back with a sigh. "Aly, I should have apologized. I should have never—"

"Never what?" Her pulse thundered louder than the wheels on the cobblestones. *Don't answer that*, she pleaded with her eyes.

Fortunately, he didn't. He rested his chin on his knuckles and peered out the window at the passing city.

Never what? She needed to know but didn't want to know. His answer could reinvent her pain in ways she wasn't ready to handle. Better to leave her understanding of the memory as it was. His affection for her had been a mistake; that was what she'd told herself, and it was the sole option that made sense.

"I need you to do something for me," she said.

"Anything."

"Don't be like that."

"Of course. I simply meant—"

"I need you to convince Red *not* to go to Bulvarna."

"Red?"

"Did you hear me?"

Grey stroked his beard. "All right. I won't ask questions, and I'll do my best."

"Thank you. I'm not sure he will listen to me." The determination on the young king's face after speaking with the Bulvarnan ambassador had been unmistakable. He set his mind to travel north; Aly was sure of it. She should never have mentioned that the death curse could be cast back into the one who created it.

He nodded in response. She slipped her mask back over her face and shifted toward the door.

"At least wait until we've stopped," he said. "It will look strange if my moving carriage door opens."

She couldn't decide if he was trying to keep her here or if he was applying simple logic. Or maybe wine was muddying his reason. "Fine, but I can't be away from the palace long."

"Grown attached, have we?"

She scoffed. "Says the one who put me there."

The rest of the ride passed in thick silence. At Grey Manor, Aly leapt out of the carriage and was flying through the night before Grey could even wave goodbye.

More now than before, Aly needed to dive into the king's Truthwell and surround herself with its light, because the light of another Truthwell was beating against her mind, one she no longer had access to.

9

RED

The council table appeared much longer from the head than it had from the side. High windows at the back of the room cast soft light on the smooth wood, on the faces of the men at his command, gargoyling them like the faces peering out of the great cathedral in Mardon.

Red took his seat in his father's old chair, avoiding the grim faces and fixing instead on the elaborate stitching of the red and gold table runner.

Aly, in her sorcerer's cloak and mask, stood with arms crossed beside him. Gevar had never had his sorcerer stand guard during a council meeting, but after the handkerchief incident, Red did not trust all the men at his table, and he wanted Aly's presence to remind the traitor that he would not be able to kill the king without incurring the wrath of his sorcerer. Red removed his hands from the table and placed them in his lap, leaving finger-shaped sweat marks to evaporate from the polished wood.

Seb now sat in Red's old chair, just to the left of the king's seat. Of all the faces, his alone smiled, though Red knew it stemmed from either sheer force or oblivion to the situation. He smiled back at Seb.

Red cleared his throat for the opening of the meeting. "May the Maker guide us."

"And His means provide us," Arthur Ondorian replied, the only man in the room to ever complete the traditional phrase. As priest-Reckoner, he sat on the king's council much the way a paperweight sat on letters; he kept the kingdom from flying off on wild and heretical tangents as, history would have it, kingdoms tended to do, but he offered little advice when it came to statecraft.

As soon as the Bulvarnan ambassador had confirmed that it was Aly's father who set the death curse, Red had made up his mind. Travelling to Bulvarna was the sole option. If Aly's father created the curse, he was their only hope in removing it. Red simply needed to come up with a decent reason for departing for Bulvarna and to convince these men that it was the right course of action.

Shoulders shifted, throats cleared, hands scratched and rustled. The short night of rest left Red's headache throbbing and his eyes puffy.

"Your Majesty," councilman Edgar Wyndall began, his bald head shining in the pale light, "the agenda today begins with a discussion of security measures for the ball. I move that we dismiss this item, as we are all aware of the protective measures to be taken."

"Second," said Grey with a dismissive lift of his hand.

"Motion passed," Red muttered. He loosened his clawed grip on the armrests of his chair.

Wyndall continued, "My lord, it has come to our attention, as of last night, that some people have claimed sighting an unbranded animal in Mardon."

Red's attention sharpened. "Has it been captured?"

"Not as of yet," Grey admitted, his gaze drifting toward Aly.

"This is unacceptable!" barked Lord Alexander. "We have Watchers in place for this sort of situation. On the heels of a monarch's death, the city should be on full alert." He directed these words to Red, as if the new king were somehow responsible for a lack of effort among the city's Watchers.

"But Tandera was purged of all lyths," Wyndall said, nodding at Alexander. "Since then, the Watchers have been lax."

Alexander grunted. "Perhaps that is why we face this threat again."

Red lifted a hand to silence the men. "Watchers can only do so much. Some animals are much harder to catch or kill. It's the Protectors who should have the answer to our query. If it is truly a lyth in our city, which I highly doubt, then the sorcerers will have felt it."

Aly's cloak moved as she shifted her weight. A few men glanced at her.

Some lyths can mask their Truthwell, Aly whispered to him.

As if he'd heard Aly's words, Grey said, "We can't forget that not all lyths can be detected by magic."

Alexander leaned forward to look at Grey. "Are you referring to the incident several years ago where that creature transformed into a man? That was one. One out of thousands. Surely that was a beast designed solely for that attack. We cannot assume that indicted a new pattern."

"On the contrary," Grey said. "The Canyon is always at work, twisting reality into nightmares. Believe me, I've seen it."

No one could argue. Of all the men at the table, Weston Grey had spent the most time at the Canyon's edge, the most time fighting the beasts of the Deep. His medals proved he had the highest authority to speak on the topic.

Arthur Ondorian cleared his throat with a small cough. "For as long as it has existed, the Canyon has been twisting the creatures of earth. Wolves became woodwolves. Foxes became foxbloods. The lyth was the pinnacle of the Canyon's twisted creation, because it could take any shape, save a human's. However, the evil of the Deep has not rested from its work. Nor shall it ever. It should not surprise us that a lyth can shift into a man."

"Perhaps," said Riode Liere, the Referen consul, "that is how the lyth avoided extermination these past years." The one foreigner at the table, his words were few but meaningful. The Referen consul, a man chosen by Refere's King Lucien and approved by Tandera's sovereign, was a permanent chair on the king's council, offering the advice of a trusted ally in all matters that were not considered strictly confidential.

The table fell silent. Aly shifted her weight, offering a stiff nod.

Alexander's expression still brimmed with skepticism. "I refuse to believe that all the faces I meet in the street could be a Canyon beast," he said.

Grey inched forward, his eyes on Alexander. "Refusal won't make the truth go away." He glanced at Aly and leaned back.

A noticeable rustle moved through the men.

"Danger returns when we forget our past," Ondorian mused.

No one responded. Seb, who'd been entirely silent and transfixed by the conversation, now concealed a small eye roll.

"Alexander," Red began, "to your point, we do not have to fear everyone we meet. As with their animal forms, a lyth can only take an unknown face."

Alexander snorted. "Are you suggesting we brand all our people now too? I am not sure that will be met with approval."

Red sighed and did not dignify the man's words with a response.

Fortunately, Grey stepped in again. "Human lyths must be very rare. In all our years of eliminating the creatures, we never once found another capable of this, save for that one at the wedding in Virienne. A few perhaps could have already been in the cities, hidden well enough that our sorcerers could never find them. We know from that night that the human-shifting lyth could shroud its energy signature. Perhaps the others can as well, making them *very* hard to find." Again, he looked at Aly. "But I do not believe there are myriads of them out there, living among us."

"*One* is enough to fear, Lord Grey. You, of all people, should know." Alexander's words rung like a bell. Grey's face darkened. Wyndall shifted uncomfortably.

Aly's arms uncrossed and fell to her sides. Everyone at the table knew of Grey's efforts against the Canyon. His reputation was legend, his feats heroic. Lord Weston Grey had killed more Canyon beasts than some soldier-sorcerers. Some said it was an unhealthy obsession. Others said it was why he was so hard-hearted. Though he was the wealthiest man under thirty in the city of Mardon, women feared him. Even his own sisters and mother chose to live in a townhouse in the city rather than the enormous estate of Grey Manor.

"Enough," Red said. "What we need today is unity. We must choose a path forward and execute it. You are my most trusted men." He scanned their faces, looking for any sign of the betrayal that he assumed lurked within one of them. *Which of you had the handkerchief replaced with a cursed one?*

At that moment, when the king's blood hammered his temples, a stiff knock on the door preceded the arrival of Aldrich Letz, messenger to the king. In his hand was a letter.

Red knew from his time on the council that any letter brought during a council meeting brought only bad news; he wasn't ready for more bad news.

What he read stole the little composure he had left. He crumpled the letter in his fist and slammed it on the table. "A foxblood was spotted outside Luxler." He withheld the fact that it had reportedly killed a field worker, leaving a sickening mess for the farmer to find.

Silence fell. Even Seb's typically jovial face fell into a grimace. Foxbloods, a distorted version of the shy red fox, preferred to shred their victims and leave them for the crows. These creatures crept out of the Canyon and preyed on remote homes, not usually visiting more densely populated places. Luxler was the largest city in northern Tandera.

Ondorian broke the painful silence, his fingers steepled in front of him. "Things appear to be changing. History tells us that when things change, it is either because we have learned something new or because we have forgotten something old."

"Poetic," snarled Alexander. "It appears that our defenses are weakening." He flung this accusation toward Red, as if he had something to do with it.

"Or Queen Kassia has, as we've long feared, forgotten the evils of the Canyon," offered Grey with a shrug. "There are two sides of the Canyon, after all. We only defend one."

Wyndall spoke from behind a hand that cupped his bushy chin. "The beasts grow bold again. If Kassia will not help us, we will never be safe."

Alexander scratched his cheek, a convenient way to frown without looking rude. "Queen Kassia avoided your father's requests for a summit for months. She knew he was ill, yet she still refused to meet. That seems tantamount to her outright rejection of the terms set forth in your father's proposals."

If you knew she was behind Gevar's death, you'd understand why she refused to meet. If he truly doesn't know, perhaps he wasn't the one to set up the handkerchief curse. That, or he's a good liar.

"We need her support," Liere said. "Neither Refere nor Tandera can operate without her coal."

"Not to mention we cannot fight the Canyon on our own. No matter our efforts, if Bulvarna fully withdraws from the fight against the Canyon, we will all lose." While Ondorian remained erect, his words had the effect of a throat-kick to everyone else in the room. The man had a way of speaking brutal truths.

"I understand your concern, Alexander," Red said, trying to hold down the volcano before it blew. These men needed reassurance, not a reason for increased fear. He avoided Ondorian's face to keep from scowling at the high priest. "But remember that the containment efforts, though a tradition for the past two decades, are not law. She is not rebelling against anything or anyone, merely disregarding a long-held expectation to hold the Canyon beasts at bay."

Liere scoffed. He met the king's gaze the way a wolf might meet a deer's. "Long held, Your Majesty? The *tradition* you speak of was bought with the blood of my people. Yours too. What your grandfather and father built in the seven kingdoms was unprecedented before their reigns. *Peace* among us, three of the continent's seven kingdoms, was something our ancestors never dreamed could be possible. All that was known before your grandfather took the throne was hatred and bloodshed, thanks to the evil of the Deep. Then Leopold forged a peace between Refere and Tandera, and Virienne soon followed, as she does, and like searing a bleeding wound, our swords pressed the beasts back into the earth. The bond never failed after that." He placed a fist on the table. "I will not see that peace tossed so lightly to the wind as mere *tradition* or *expectation*." He leaned forward over his fist. "Refere's sword weeps along with her people if that is the case." Leaning back, he added in an under-tone, "This cannot be what has become of Leopold's and Gevar's work."

Red bit his tongue hard enough to feel pain and kept silent for a moment as uncertainty at this disastrous situation rolled through him. *Toss it.* Wyndall needed confidence. Alexander needed reassurance. Liere needed calming. He had to regain control of the room. *If I can't lead these men, how can I lead Tandera?*

He had a plan, two-fold and fledgling, but he dove at it. "I will travel to the Canyon myself."

That captured Liere's attention. Aly stiffened at his side.

"I will meet with the soldiers. I'll find out why the beasts are escaping." *And that will buy us some time to come up with a plan for casting this curse back into Aly's father.*

Wyndall nodded approval. Grey stared at him with surprise. Liere's firm brow held, and Alexander still scowled, dissatisfied.

Red continued, "We will make our lands safe again, I promise." *Does that sound too desperate?* He couldn't retract the words now.

"And if Kassia is letting the beasts out? Our efforts will be pointless." Liere's words unmasked the true fear behind all the faces in the room. "You *must* convince her to guard the Canyon as diligently as we do."

"Tell her of your trip," blurted Wyndall. "She missed the funeral—she will not refuse to welcome a king who shows up at her doorstep, no matter how busy she may claim to be." The duke, clueless to the real danger his king faced, looked so hopeful at his suggestion. He couldn't be the traitor. That optimism seemed too genuine. But then again, he'd just proposed Red and Aly travel into Bulvarna.

Which was exactly what Red intended to do.

"Wait," Grey said, leaning over the table as if suddenly remembering something. "Don't go to Kassia." All eyes turned to him.

"No, I think he should," Liere said with a firm nod. "I will speak to my king. He may desire to accompany you. A great idea, Wyndall."

"Yes. Tell us, Lord Grey, why should he not take up Gevar's work and attempt a peace summit with the Lady Wolf?" asked Alexander.

"Be-because," he fumbled with a quick glance at Aly, "she is untrustworthy. What if she's sending evil our way, trying to draw our king out of his protected palace?"

Red noted that he didn't say *beasts*. He said *evil. Could he know of the curses?*

Alexander's mustache twitched. "Nonsense. You are perhaps poorly affected by your time at the Canyon's edge. Our king will be safe enough on a diplomatic trip north."

Grey's eyes darkened but he offered no rebuttal.

"It is settled then," Alexander said. "You will travel north. Your presence at the Canyon will certainly improve morale for the soldiers there, if nothing else. And I look forward to the progress you will make with Kassia." No small gauntlet had been thrown.

Aly cleared her throat. Grey glanced up at her.

Is that a small nod Grey gave her? Red's ears burned. Under the table, his knee jiggled; he was grateful the men couldn't see this and ask prying questions that would reveal the fact that the Royal Sorcerer of Bulvarna wanted the Royal Sorcerer and the King of Tandera dead. Red's entire hope for survival hinged on facing the man who was trying to kill him.

"Your Majesty?" pressed Alexander.

He swallowed. "I will request a meeting with Kassia."

Liere's posture finally relaxed. Alexander smiled.

"Then we will begin the preparations for your journey immediately," Ondorian said. "May the Maker guide us," he said, closing the meeting.

"And His means provide us."

They were going to Bulvarna.

The door to Red's study burst open.

"Nice to see you still exist." He tipped his fountain pen up and sat straighter at his father's old desk.

Aly stormed into the room, hair like a rainstorm around her face, mouth a hard line. "You can't expect me to be happy with this!"

"No, but I can expect—or I thought I could expect—my sorcerer to answer when I knock, or respond when I leave a letter stuffed in your door. Exactly how am I supposed to summon you when you insist on being invisible?"

Her knuckles cracked at her sides. "You think marching up there will solve this? Solve anything? What about me?"

He tossed his fountain pen, splattering his book on Bulvarnan grammar. "You? You're the one with magic! You can hide when it's convenient and avoid confrontation whenever you please. This trip to Bulvarna should not worry you."

Instead of the retort he expected, she said, "I'll be marching right into his hands." She wrapped her arms around herself and dropped her gaze to the floor. "And you might not care, but he does want to kill me. Which will make all this worthless." She lifted a hand in his general direction.

"All what worthless? Protecting me? Serving Tandera?"

His desk lamp threw shadow and light, drawing every texture into fine detail. The bookshelves held deep shadows; the crown molding cast a bright line around the room. Aly's face reflected the warm tones of the kerosene flame, but as her hand continued to rise, stopping before her nose with palm facing in, her face fell into darkness. The light now illuminated her black ring.

"No. This. My promise to myself." She lowered her hand. "I wanted to be strong enough to face him, when the time came. But I'm not. I can't even practice Pulling from you because you're too tossing busy." There was something else there, beneath her words, something she wasn't sharing.

Red steepled his fingers, trying not to be offended at her answer. "Then let's practice." Her shocked expression hit him like a physical slap. He shoved backward and stood, hands on the desk. "Why are you so convinced you won't survive meeting him?"

Fists at her sides, Aly took three loud, heavy breaths before answering. "He has done horrible things." Her words were faint, and Red automatically stepped around the desk to hear her better.

"Flooded a village, destroyed a coal mine. I've heard."

"No." Her eyes flashed. "You've heard what Kassia wants you to hear."

From years of watching his sisters hide what they really meant, Red spotted Aly's tight mouth, her darting eyes, and her fidgeting fingers. She was used to being invisible, and as such was terrible at hiding her body language.

"And you know more." He crossed his arms.

A slow inhale preceded her next words. "While in Bulvarna with your father, I did not show myself in the palace, for obvious reasons. Instead, I polled villagers living outside of Isardra, asking them about magic. The stories they told, the things they said…" She bit her lip.

"Tell me, Aly. I have a right to know, too."

"In Bulvarna, sorcerers are required to register at the palace. They must present themselves as soon as they discover their abilities, upon threat of death."

Red scoffed. "How can Kassia know if a sorcerer *doesn't* register? Seems a bit of an empty threat."

The shadows gathered on Aly's downturned face. "In every village I visited, several magical children who'd attempted to hide their powers had died within months of discovering their ability. The people there *fear* the Royal Sorcerer. They believe he has a way of detecting new sorcerers, and they have enough evidence to back that up. Children *died* because of him." Red's arms fell to his sides, but Aly continued, "From what Gevar's spies indicated, few Bulvarnans believe there are any unregistered sorcerers in the country. What they don't know is that he likely set up that whole process as a way of finding *me.*" She brought the heels of her hands to her eyes. "Those kids died because he was looking for me."

Red's ears flared with heat, betraying the flicker of fear coursing through him. His unbuttoned vest breezed in a welcome bit of cool air. "You are not responsible. He's wicked. Do not burden yourself with this." Though he could see she did. *And now we're going to meet this maniac.* He understood why she was afraid. A man who would strike down children was certainly not going to fight using the standard rules of war.

Red leaned against the desk, tired from a late night in the library and the bustle of activity surrounding his preparations to leave for the Canyon. "You know why I want to go," he said.

"Foolish. It's a mad hope."

"I'm okay with mad hope. That's better than certain death."

She looked at him with piercing eyes. Within them, a fracture in her resolve revealed a flash of what might have been empathy. "I want you to live, too, you know."

"You make it difficult to tell sometimes."

She scoffed.

"We're going to the Canyon first to see about the lyths and to encourage the soldiers. Let's focus on that. On the way, let's find a cure for this curse. Then we won't have to worry about your father. Assuming Kassia even agrees to meet."

"We can't bring the whole library with us."

"I'm the king. If I say I want to bring a giraffe with me, someone will sail to the outerlands, capture one, and have it brought along. With your magic, we can fill an entire carriage full of books if we want."

The hint of a smile toyed at the edge of her mouth.

"And if we don't find a cure and Kassia does invite us to her palace," he said, "I'll give you permission to Truthstrip me, give you an extra boost of power. Whatever it takes to beat your father. At least that way, one of us will live."

Her mouth fell open.

"It was a joke," he said. A far-off look had entered her eyes, and he wasn't sure she'd heard him. He sat back down to his ruined translations. "Goodnight, Aly."

With a whirl of fabric and loud footsteps, she turned and left.

He closed his books and, against all reason, felt a flicker of hope. Mad hope.

10

ALY

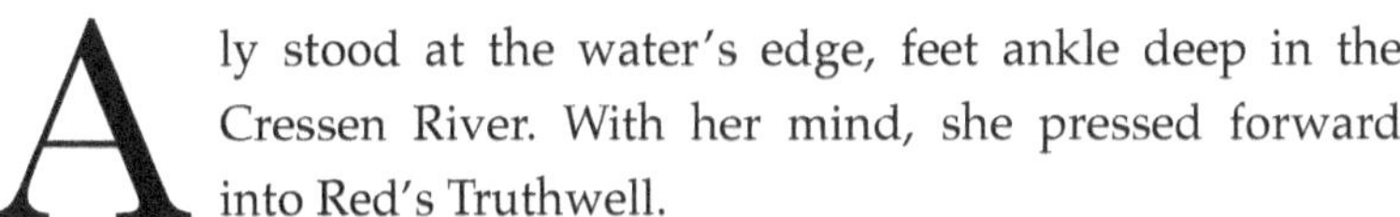

Aly stood at the water's edge, feet ankle deep in the Cressen River. With her mind, she pressed forward into Red's Truthwell.

"Make me believe you can keep me alive," he said to her as dawn rose over Mardon.

Leave it to him to say something to ruin this moment. She ached to reach into his Truthwell, to learn of its infinite light. Practice was the only way to know the patterns and crevices, the secret places where more light lurked beneath the shadows that clogged every person's mind. Aly hadn't detected too many shadows in Red's Well until the moment the death curse entered his body. He had shadows of lies and doubts and fears, as did all people, but his was still the brightest Well she'd ever seen. She wondered if she could do *more* magic than she could do with Gevar, if she could but discover the depths of Red's Well.

She scowled at him. "It'll be easier if you keep your mouth shut. *Majesty*," she added hastily at his glower.

With her magic submerged in the king's Truthwell, not even the sun itself could steal her eyes away from his light. Using the technique she'd mastered at Grey's instruction, she looped her will around the swirling light, as a rider would grip a horse's mane. Then she Pulled.

Maybe there was hope. Maybe they really could find a cure. She hated to think of it but also yearned for it to be true—that there was a missing piece of information, an elusive cure. If there was, Gevar hadn't benefitted from it. But she wanted it to exist, more than she wanted anything.

The water pressed into a ribbon, clear and crinkling, and began to loop around her, rise, and shoot, fountainlike, up toward the sky, where it arced and crashed back down around her. Water was a favorite medium of hers. It moved with such little coaxing; but because of that, it wasn't much of a challenge, either. She'd come out here to search the depths of his Truthwell, to dive deeper, to feel the infinity at her fingertips.

She dropped her arms, and the water fell like an impromptu rain shower.

He stepped backward to avoid the flying droplets. "What's it like? To conjure magic?"

Aly closed her eyes, recalling the first time her magic had been truly challenged—when she'd learned to stop a bullet. It had been the moment she'd learned to blend the words of the *Verad* with the energy inside of a person's Truthwell.

"It's like art. Like math. Like dancing." The water flowing around her ankles swirled into a twisting, rising pillar. She scooped her hands through the air, as if molding clay. "A painter takes colors and creates something only his or her mind can see. Math reveals the truth of the world, the truth that's underneath everything. Dancing," she smiled to herself, "makes art of us all and reveals the truths inside us, truths we often can't say aloud." Her breaths were loud, and her torso expanded and collapsed quickly. When she opened her eyes, she caught Red staring at her with a strange expression.

"But you asked what it's like, not what it is. Conjuring magic is like anything else. It takes some effort at first, but becomes easier with practice. I grasp the energy inside of you and tell it what to do, guiding the truth of the world to a certain purpose. Like this."

She squatted down, hands on the grass. "You may want to sit down. I'm going to Pull pretty hard."

Amusement flickered through her mind as Red sat in the dewy grass.

She stood and rubbed her hands on her hips, and Red's eyes followed the movement. "Sweaty," she said in explanation. "Magic cools the air, but it makes me hot."

His eyes bulged and she caught him staring at her hips. She looked quickly away, making the moment more awkward than it had to be.

This time, she wanted to test the power inside him. It was infected with darkness, the mark of his death curse. So far, the tendrils of black had only begun to leech light at the edges. His Truthwell was perhaps more resilient than Gevar's. But it *was* weakening as the curse crept ever closer to the center.

If he was a Beacon, she could not let his light go out.

Her eyes popped open. He stared up at her, elbows propped on his knees, expectant. *Make me believe,* he'd said.

No matter who or what he was, she could not let him die. She would not.

With all her might, she yanked on his energy and, with the words of the *Verad,* commanded the earth to rise.

Underneath her feet, the ground moaned. Then the grass breezed against her bare feet, tickling her skin. The earth resisted being moved. The words were true, and the earth could not deny their truth, but something about the spell wasn't holding. Aly knew that the ground beneath them was at her command, ready to rise, but the surge of power from her source, while strong, was not continuous, as if she were pulling on a sheet with holes darted through it.

Red held his head in his hands, eyes bulging.

Aly dropped the spell and fell to her knees. "Did I hurt you?" Her magic had never once Stripped anyone. She'd never imagined she *could*, given the only way to Truthstrip someone was to intend harm.

His scrutinizing eyes held hers a moment. "No. I have a headache."

Relieved but still disturbed, she moved to replace her shoes, which sat a few steps away in the grass.

Red stood and stretched. "What was that last one? What were you trying to do?"

She pulled her hood back over her head and lifted her phoenix mask off the ground. "Trying to move the earth."

He chuckled. "Moving heaven and earth, are we?"

"It didn't exactly work."

"I noticed." His eyes narrowed.

She hadn't given him much hope. Instead, she had more bad news to share. "Your Well…it's turning darker. It makes conjuring magic harder. Less consistent."

"Oh."

For a moment, he stared out over the river, then he stormed back toward the palace. Today was the day of the Accession Ball. In two weeks, they would leave for the Canyon. Aly only wished, now that they were going, that they could leave sooner; the more time that passed, the more the curse would spread.

And the weaker her magic would become.

If they were to face her father, she needed to be as strong as possible.

It was still an hour until the midday meal, and Aly had been dismissed by Red earlier for some *quiet time to think*. No time to waste. Aly rounded a corner onto a wide hall, and in front of the library doors, a guard stood sentry.

"That's odd," Aly said, her voice confined to her shroud.

The palace guards knew of the enchantments she'd placed on the building. Every entrance, including windows and secret passages, were spelled to alert her to an unwanted presence. No spell could fully protect the royal family from lies, the ultimate weapon of the Deep, but she could at least detect those who brought them in.

With the guard present, she couldn't walk in unseen. With a huff of annoyance, she retraced her steps around the corner, removed her shroud, and approached the library. The guard snapped to attention and stepped aside.

As Aly stepped inside, she replaced her shroud and saw the reason for the guard. In one of the reading rooms, a warm light burned. Elise sat at a reading table, a stack of books beside her, her back to the library.

"Elise," Aly said with a smile.

The princess did not look up. The ache inside of Aly at not being noticed was so commonplace she barely registered it anymore. Aly had only ever been a masked mystery to the residents of the palace. Save the king.

She had to be grateful for Red's condescending glances and arrogant scoffs. He was the sole person she knew, besides the High Priest and Lord Weston Grey, who were rarely at the palace.

Grey was a difficult topic for her mind to handle.

The library door opened, startling Aly. Red charged in, spotted his sister, and beelined for her. Aly ghosted along behind him.

Without looking up, Elise said, "Shouldn't you be preparing for tonight?"

He yanked a chair out and sat. "I'm not the one whose hair takes two hours." He turned her book toward him.

"You mean this," she swatted at his hair, "does not take hours? I would never have guessed." Elise glared at him.

"Brother, if your life is in the balance, fixing my hair is not really a priority right now."

She's right, Aly said to Red, privately. He jumped, and Aly smiled to herself. The king scanned the room for her, a silly habit.

Elise's narrow eyes watched him. "I am reading that book Carolyn mentioned. I have reached the part about the curse, but so far there is no mention of a cure. I scanned the ending. The king dies."

Red's frown deepened. "I'll go look for some poems."

"Perhaps you should rest before tonight, and I will keep reading," Elise suggested, tilting her head.

A yawn delayed his answer. "No. Like you said, if my life is in the balance, rest isn't a priority."

Red moved into the larger library and grabbed a book, seemingly randomly. Aly followed. She used magic to reach the book that was next on her list, and came to sit, unseen, in the reading room with Elise.

Not fifteen minutes later, Red dropped his book on the table and rubbed his face. "I think I'm going to dream in verse tonight."

"Nothing?" asked Elise.

"No. Not unless you count the lyrical description of a flower growing on cursed soil or the ballad depicting the opening of the Canyon."

Elise glanced at the title of the poetry book and flipped to the inner cover. "Wesson wrote his poems in what years?"

"About a hundred years ago."

Shaking her head, Elise stood. "I think, if we're looking for a hint about a cure for a death curse, we need to look a lot further back."

Aly's mouth quirked up. Elise was right.

"Was that a contraction?" asked Red, teasing her about how their mother often corrected them.

Elise glared at him. "My brother is dying. Toss grammar."

Red cracked an impressed smile at her mild curse. "The princess of propriety uses the word *toss*? Since when?"

"I'm about to *toss* this book at your head. This is life and death! It's not a time for jokes."

"It's a perfect time for them, actually. Didn't you say we needed to look further back?"

"Yes. Because if no one alive knows of a way to cure a death curse, save siphoning, and none of the histories show it, then it must be from something very old—so old that most people forgot it had ever been written. I bet it was an obscure reference, otherwise people would not have missed it. A cure for a death curse is a big deal. If someone wrote about it, the whole world would know."

Aly stepped forward and dropped a book onto the table, sliding it out from beneath her shroud. Elise yelped. Red jerked in surprise, then frowned in Aly's general direction. He grabbed the book. "Not if the book was destroyed."

Elise, with a careful glance into the corners of the room, circled around and stared down at the book in her brother's hands. "*The Ballads of Kanto*. Kanto was a heretic."

"According to the king at the time—can't remember who— that is why all his books were burned. Nearly a thousand years ago. But maybe that king had it wrong."

A smile grew on her face. "I always wondered why the royal library contained a copy of all the banned books from throughout the ages." She reached for the book. "Let me, Brother. You know I am better with poems."

"You are better with poems," he agreed. "And I bet that one is written in old Tanderan or something."

Opening the book, Elise shook her head. "Looks more like Kirish or some version of it."

Very good, Aly mused.

"Great. That'll take forever to translate."

"I can do it," Elise offered.

Gevar had wanted his daughters to be as educated as any man, and Aly smiled with pride at the thought of him. She needed Elise's expertise in the language. Growing up in Kitrel did not equate to a noble education. Aly was lucky her mother had taught her to read.

Aly moved toward the library door, her task here completed. She was grateful Red had included his sisters in this search. Many of the ancient writings were not translated into Tanderan, and Aly had been forced to avoid them in her earlier research.

"All right," Red said, incredulous.

"You doubt me, Brother?" Elise said with a small smile. "I don't like when people underestimate me or disregard what I can do."

Red chuckled. "Whoa, there. Sounds like someone is ready to exact revenge on a certain Referen prince tonight."

At the reading room door, Aly paused to listen.

Elise laughed, a small sound in her nose. "I am not so petty as to need revenge." Then, with a more serious tone, she said, "Go, Brother. I will translate the first poem before tonight. It's the least I can do. However, since you invited the Bulvarnans, I think we all should be on alert tonight." At Red's frown, she said, "You were the one who told me they were behind the curse. Then you invite them *here*?"

"Does no one assume I can make wise political decisions?" snapped Red.

He is rash in his grief. We all are. Aly wished she could sympathize with him, but the masked face of her wicked father hovered in her mind's eye and all sympathy fled. Aly walked on, their words carrying across the library.

"Brother, I fully trust you will be a wise king. One day."

"The Bulvarnans won't be able to hurt us tonight. The palace is protected," he said.

Thinking magic will solve all our problems, are we? Aly turned to look over her shoulder at Red, framed by the doorway to the small room. He had much to learn, if he lived long enough to learn it.

Elise lifted her brows. "My understanding was that the palace was only protected from *unwanted* evil. You, dear sir, invited them."

1 1

RED

In the mirror, his white tails had looked every bit as regal as his father's had, every bit the bright, happy celebration attire of a new king. The medallion noting his status as king and commander of armies hung at his chest; his newly forged king's coronet nested in his curls, a small, constant weight reminding him of what now rested on his shoulders. Minutes before he was expected to waltz into the accession celebration banquet, Red stood in the rain-dampened back gardens.

Aly, her cloak open and breezing with her movement, paced back and forth along the edge of narrow stones that marked out the rose garden. Her shroud covered her and Red from the eyes of the guests already congregating on the nearby terrace.

The hood of her cloak was down, and he stared absently at her hair. Her braid, even messier now that the damp air pulled it into little ringlets around her face, hung halfway down her back. Red uncrossed his arms, never really disappointed by a braid before, and feeling somewhat silly for it, but annoyed all the same.

Despite her vehement gestures, the sorcerer never faltered, never wobbled, as she paced along the narrow stones. "If my father knows I am Tandera's Royal Sorcerer—which he does, officially, after that handkerchief debacle—then he won't let us come near Bulvarna without attacking. The two people he wants to kill are heading *toward* him."

"Yes, you have made that quite clear."

She snapped narrow eyes at him. They stood beneath a pergola draped with blooms of purple flowers that hung like grapes. Red could never remember flower names, except for roses. His father always said to know two kinds of flowers: roses, for the first time he gave a woman flowers, and the woman's favorite for every time after that.

"What do you want?" Her arms shot out by her sides. "We have two options: wait for him to come to us or run. Either way, the curse will…the curse will…"

Red scratched his head. "Kill me?"

Her chest heaved a few times before she lowered her arms. "Yes."

"The ball begins in half an hour. Elise said the first poem in that book you gave her was a ballad of a seafaring man. Useless. Unless you have something *else* you wanted to talk about, I am required inside."

Aly closed her eyes in frustration. "Fine. No, Red, I have nothing else of value to add."

"Don't be a grouch."

"Oh? You realize that the people you invited tonight could bring wickedness with them? And because they are here at your invitation, it will be much harder to detect. Elise was right."

For a few seconds he thought of all the words he could snap back at her. Finally, he sighed and said, "You're the Royal Sorcerer of Tandera. Theod gifted you this role. That should mean something."

The frown on her face loosened into an expression of mild shock.

He shifted his weight, avoiding her stare. "You've got five

minutes. Enchant me—or something." The phrase made his ears burn and Aly, glancing down, scratched beside her eye. Why were words so ambiguous?

With a gulp, she lifted her hands. Whispered words and strands of light filled the space. Like the sun glinting off falling dust, the sparks of light danced in the night air and clustered around Red's chest before swarming over his arms, his legs, his hands. Lifting his arms to watch the magic engulf him, he bumped Aly's hand.

"Sorry," he muttered, but she didn't seem to hear him. She was lost in her spell work.

As his hand touched hers, the light pouring over him intensified.

The air beneath the pergola began to glow a pale golden color, clear as champagne, almost as if dawn were breaking right where they stood. A cool breeze descended upon him as the magic drained the warmth out of the evening. The purple flowers released all their petals at once, filling the space with violet snow that hovered and swirled and twisted into shapes. Aly stood with her eyes closed, her hands raised like a priest in prayer, and her jaw tilted skyward. Her fingers curled and bent in small, fragile motions.

The magic was beautiful and mesmerizing to watch, but his eyes drew back to her hands, her arms, her unmasked face.

Breaking the strange moment, he said, "Great. We can survive with flying flower petals."

Her eyes remained closed, and her brow furrowed as her mouth turned down.

This is part of my protection for the evening? When she'd said she wanted to place protective spells around him, he hadn't envisioned flowers.

As the petals danced in the air, his eyes watched Aly. Though so thin and mild-looking, this young woman had power in her hands that moved the very world around him. Without thinking of it, he shifted his weight closer to her, his mind begging her to be strong enough to save them.

Suddenly, the tiny purple petals swirled into the shape of a phoenix and burst into flame.

Her eyes popped open. "What did you do?" She glanced at his feet and took a step backward.

"I didn't do anything." Warmth seeped back into the air.

She brought both hands in front of her face and flipped them over, examining them. "You did something." Her eyes bored into him. "I never meant to burn them." Her hands scooped into her hair and yanked, making her braid lop over to the side. "Now all these poor flowers are dead."

"You were the one who ripped off all the petals. I only watched."

"I did not *rip* the petals off. I was building an enchantment with…with…" She trailed off, peering at the bare branches in dismay. "Magic doesn't direct itself. It obeys my thoughts. That's how it *works*."

"So now you've confused yourself? That greatly increases my confidence in you."

She frowned. "My magic moves objects. Theod gave sorcerers a little of his Maker-ness when he gave us truth magic. We can move and build and reshape, we can even dismantle, but we don't destroy without cause. We don't just burn stuff." She shook her head. "That's what the lies do. They distort and destroy. They can even change our perception of reality." After a few seconds of silence, she said, "It's been five minutes. Go to your ball."

"Fine." He'd wanted hope; she'd given him more reason to panic.

Her lips pursed. "Fine."

He turned to go.

"Wait," she said. "I'm sorry. I know your life is on the line here." She chewed her lower lip. "Maybe we can still find a way to cure you."

"Maybe?" He lifted his crown and ran a hand through his hair. "I was hoping for more than *maybe*."

To his alarm, she said, "You're right. I'm sorry. Again."

She was always apologizing. He'd not expected the Royal Sorcerer to do that so often, or to need to.

She sniffed and continued. "I'd say we *will* find a cure, but I can't lie. Lies weaken my magic. Lies can make you believe really awful things."

"I think there's room for optimism here. Aly, I *need* you to be optimistic about this." He leaned his face toward her, forcing eye contact. "Three months ago, life was pretty great. Since then, I've lost my father, inherited a throne I'm not ready for, and learned I will die before I hit twenty. If I need to believe a lie for a bit, a lie that says I'm going to *live*, I'll take that lie. Mad hope, remember?"

A frustrated sigh burst from Aly's lips. "I know! I'm just not able to do that. Lies, when we believe them, can *change* us. My magic is based on *truth*, and I can't afford to believe a lie."

"Rigid, huh?"

Aly's eyes narrowed. "Honest," she corrected. "You need to go. But remember, if you're in a place and can't talk openly to me, you've got Ondorian to Reckon the truth when you need it. He can't invoke magic, but that man can spot a lie a league away."

Red scoffed. "That man is strange."

Aly looked offended. "He's a priest. He knows the *Verad* better than anyone. Better than me, and I've studied it relentlessly for the past six years. Trust him, Red. He's a Reckoner, which means he can use the *Verad* in ways most men can't. He can set you straight if you ever think you've been tricked by a lie, and I'm here to help you fight the magic of lies, remember? But I want to make sure you know enough truth to spot the lies for yourself, or find someone who can."

He pointed at the flowerless branches. "What was that, then? Truth or a lie? You said you can't destroy things."

Aly stood stone still a moment, fists by her sides. "I don't know," she admitted with a frown. "But when I was Truth-pulling, I felt my magic flicker or something. Like there was a little extra burst of power that I wasn't expecting."

"So you're saying that fire was somehow my fault?"

"No, that's not possible. What happens with magic is based on me, not you. And we can't simply dive in and grab up all the beautiful light we see inside of a person."

Her words frightened him. In a way, the best sorcerers were also the most dangerous. They alone had the power to Strip a Truthwell bare.

Red grimaced. "Yes, I know. I've had the privilege of enduring a sorcerer's lack of restraint."

Aly slapped her forehead. "Toss me! Sorry! I remember. I was away with your father—they picked someone they didn't know well—it was awful and I'm glad he..." She stopped, finger tapping her lips.

"Glad he what?"

Crossing her arms, in the way she did when she wanted to hide, she mumbled as she continued. "Glad he trusted me to heal you."

Red's brow rose. "I was hours away from my parents. From you."

"Your Truthwell is...bright enough that I can sense it from a long way away. Papa trusted me. He knew I could heal you, even from that distance." Then she squatted down and brushed her fingers against the pebbles of the pathway. "Red, look."

This woman had been the one to bring him back from a death-like state after nearly being Stripped by an amateur sorcerer, a man hired to protect the royal children while the king and queen were away. It had been the first and last time they'd hired a Protector they didn't know personally. Then this woman, who'd been halfway across the country at the time, had somehow healed him. He owed her more than he knew.

He squatted beside her and saw tiny green stems peeking out between the stones. They were soft and cool to the touch and grew as he stared down at them.

Aly gasped. She cupped one hand over her mouth and used the other one to steady herself by grabbing Red's shoulder. They stood at the same time.

"Looks like you didn't destroy the flowers." Already, a few purple buds had appeared on the stems.

"But how?" She knelt again, brushed the flowers with her fingers before picking one. "It's definitely real, but it's not the same kind of flower. These are irises." She rose and handed it to him.

"So you turned them into irises. It's magic, right? What's so odd about it?"

"It doesn't make any sense. My magic doesn't do that." She was so excited—or possibly agitated—that she shifted her weight back and forth as she examined the flower in his hand. On one sway, she bumped into him, then hopped awkwardly out of the way, as if she'd touched something foul.

Red shrugged, not sure these flowers warranted her overreaction. "I have to go. You really won't show yourself at the ball?" He hoped she didn't interpret his words as disappointed. He couldn't care less if she was visible or invisible—though if the Bulvarnans were really a threat, he hoped she would stay close.

In the distance, musical chords sounded, indicating the opening of the ball.

She nodded, eyes scanning the flowerless vines above them. "Oh, I'll be there, but I'll stay hidden. With your special guests on the way, I certainly can't leave you with only your guards! That wouldn't be very safe."

Fuming, Red tapped his foot against the wooden dais at the head of a packed ballroom. The wood beneath his body, albeit cushioned, felt wrong, as if the overstuffed velvet had compressed in the shape of his father's much larger frame, leaving Red sitting on a throne he didn't fit.

On the dance floor in front of him, dresses and suits blurred in his vision. His headache made it feel like all the clicking ladies' shoes danced on the backside of his eyeballs, which was not improved by the gold band pressing just above his temples.

Desperate to run a finger under his too-tight collar, he instead gripped the arm of his throne and the shaft of his scepter a little harder. As he did so, he remembered his mother's advice not to fidget.

This night was meant to celebrate Tandera's new start, but he couldn't help thinking of the dark magic that was slinking through his veins, undetectable for now. Three months. That was all the time Aly could give his father once he'd been cursed.

The Bulvarnan ambassador and her escorts hovered in the crowd near the dais, their dark clothing a smear among the spring prints and white jackets of his own people. He hoped he'd made the right choice inviting them. Just as funerals meant the end of something, and black signified the end, so his ascension meant the beginning, and white was the color of beginnings. The king's white gloves stood out against the deep honey stain of the throne. He alone wore the bright red medallion of Tandera on his chest and a red sash around his shoulders. A spark amid a sea of white ash, the phoenix in rebirth.

"Breathe, Son," his mother said, leaning over from her seat a few inches to his right.

"Yes, you look rather miserable," Elise added from her seat to his left.

Carolyn sat on the other side of Elise, absorbed in watching the milling courtiers. Everyone in the room, save for their mother, wore celebration attire, white with small bits of color as adornment. For Isabelle alone, the mourning period would not end for another month; someone had to wear the color of smoke, the color that reminded the world what fire could do. If Red was like the spark to start the blaze anew, his mother was the charred remains of what was left behind of the old Tandera, the Tandera of Gevar.

Red glowered at Elise. He'd wanted to smile, to make a silly face like they used to, but a frown—an expression he'd felt too often today—came first and easy, like a breath after being under water. Except for that moment in the garden with Aly, when they'd seen those strange new flowers, he hadn't smiled much that day. Realizing this made him frown deeper.

Elise's expression faltered for a moment, then she turned a beaming face back on the celebration. "Brother, we will find a cure," she whispered, careful to keep her tone low.

He was the king; he was in charge; he was the one people would come to for advice. He was supposed to lead Tandera for decades, to leave a legacy. Though the circle of gold on his head didn't mean he'd leave a *good* legacy, he'd at least hoped for enough time to try.

His back stiffened. The purpose of the sorcerer was to give him the chance to live long enough to lead his country.

Where the blazes is she?

"Looking for someone?" Elise asked.

His sister was lovely tonight, and Red didn't want to bother her with his worries. She needed a distracting evening, something to take her mind off the boy she should have been dancing with—the tall, blond Prince Lordan of Refere, in pale blue tails and ivory sash to match his father's. Lordan currently was sipping wine and chatting with a young woman, his face prominently visible from the dais. The Referen king sat at a table laughing with Duke Wyndall. Though a powerful king, he always appeared at ease, as if the world waited for him. Red wondered how a man with a country to run could ever relax like that.

Red and his family had to preside over the room as his guests ate from the overstuffed buffet tables and mingled with the foreign dignitaries come to offer their congratulations. After his guests had eaten their fill, he would join them, a symbol of his gracious deference for his people's needs.

"You are terrible at hiding your feelings. You probably should work on that."

"He will learn," their mother interjected, surprising them both that she'd been listening. "All kings must learn this. I, too, had to learn it." She turned a faint smile on her children.

Elise toyed with the curled ends of her long hair. "How are you getting on with the sorcerer?" She'd meant it as a means of changing the subject, but instead she'd hit Red with the most bothersome subject of all.

"Things with the sorcerer are—" *frustrating, horrible, annoying,* "—awkward," he finally said.

Elise dropped her gloved hand into her lap. "Sorry to hear that, but I am not surprised."

"Why not?"

"He is the most powerful man in our country, yet he stays hidden from everyone. I would think he would be a bit awkward. I am certain it will become easier with time."

Their mother stifled a small chuckle, then shifted her weight and her gaze as if to withdraw herself from the conversation.

Red scrunched his face a little at every use of the word *he*, but he forced a nod. Elise was right. Aly spoke like no one he'd ever met. She simply said what she thought and didn't couch it in pleasantries.

His fingers slicked beneath his gloves as he gripped the scepter. By the end of the next waltz, he'd be able to relinquish the heavy staff and join the party. He wasn't sure he was ready for that either, considering his headache throbbed and the dreary Bulvarnans skulking nearby offered him no comfort. The ambassador never traveled alone, and at least four other people had entered the palace with her, according to Red's guards, who'd been instructed to watch them all closely throughout the evening.

Mad that he couldn't speak to or see Aly, he inadvertently began to tap the scepter several times on the dais. *Thunk, thunk, thunk.*

"Stop that," Elise said, glancing over. "You look impatient."

He ground his teeth. "I am."

From the crowded ballroom floor, a man approached Elise and, with an ostentatious bow, asked for the next dance. She accepted with the typical lift of her chin that only Elise could manage and not look haughty. She wouldn't like him, just from that hideous bow, but Red was glad she had been asked. Elise's beauty was the kind that people might walk past and not notice at first, but on second glance would wonder how they'd ever missed it. She possessed a soft beauty, the way a candle drew the eye. Not a hearth fire, like Carolyn. At only fourteen, Carolyn was too pretty to allow the queen any peace.

A bold young man stepped up and asked Carolyn for the next dance. She blushed and giggled, then politely nodded.

The first song ended, the couples clapped, the music resumed, and his sisters stepped down from their thrones, gloved hands lifted gently by their eager partners'.

Before the dancers had taken one full spin about the floor, Bernard, the king's personal attendant, stepped up to the king and bowed; while bent low, he offered to take the scepter away. Red tried not to look too gleeful as he handed it over, placing the scepter across the man's open hands. Now he was free to enjoy the evening, as much as might be possible.

When he pushed up from his throne, the entire room stopped their movement, bowing or curtseying, and then carried on. As he descended the dais, he blinked in shock as his eyes landed on Aly, dressed in a simple white dress with black beads vining up the hem, visible to all the world.

She stood at the edge of the crowd of dancers. A daring choice, black on white. She was, in a way, both the old and the new Tandera. The ash and the rising phoenix.

His breath caught; he nearly tripped. She looked stunning.

She walked away, toward a table draped with food that smelled of smoked meat and aged cheese. He followed, shoes clacking in heavy annoyance at this bizarre chase. Every head he passed dipped low in reverence.

As he approached the table, he nodded toward a couple who wore matching silver-white silks. They seemed embarrassed to be picking at food with their king watching, so they offered a deep bow and a sweeping curtsey before abandoning the table to shuffle off into the crowd.

Stepping up behind her and pretending to be eyeing the food, he whispered, "I can see you. Can they all see you?" He stood close enough to her that he saw all the hairs on her slender arms stand to attention at his words.

A dozen questions swam in his head, but the tempo of his heartbeat drowned them all. She'd been lying to him when she'd led him to believe she'd be invisible tonight. *And she claimed she couldn't lie! Toss everything she's told me!*

Her head whipped around, a simple silver headpiece dangling over her forehead. Her cheeks surged with a blush much too deep to be rouge.

Then, in an un-ladylike fashion, Aly picked up a cluster of grapes and yanked one loose with her teeth, turning her shoulders away from him. The dress was made of fine silk, tailormade, he noticed as his eyes roamed. *No one else can see her. No one else can talk to her. All a load of lies.* Someone took her measurements to make that dress.

When she turned back to him, a grape stopped halfway to her mouth. "Red, you're scaring me."

Anger bent him closer, but something hotter than anger—betrayal he couldn't explain—flamed his cheeks. "All these people can see you, and all this time I've pitied you thinking you lived entirely alone in your secrecy. My whole life really, I've thought the sorcerer stayed invisible because he—she, whatever—*had* to for some epic reason. But it turns out you come to our parties like anyone else. All dressed up and fancy and—What?"

Eyes of the people nearest them watched them closely.

He shifted his shoulders toward the food table, slamming a strawberry onto a plate to appear occupied. A server fluttered over to attempt to fill his plate for him, but he shooed the man away. He let Aly drift away down the table until the people directed their attention elsewhere.

"But this whole time you've been lying!" he hissed, stepping closer.

She whirled on him. "Oh really? You think I'm stupid enough to lie?" Her nose wrinkled as she scowled at him.

"You said no one can see you. You said that you never spoke to anyone besides my father and Ondorian—for six years!" A huff of air bull-snorted out of his nose. He squared his shoulders with the food table again, trying to appear interested in its display.

Aly mimicked his stance, her fingers drumming against the white tablecloth on either side of her crystal plate. "Simply because I am visible doesn't mean anyone looks at me."

Cheeks hot and chest full of tambourines, he guffawed. "How could you possibly think no one here will look at you?"

She held his gaze a moment. "Stop talking to me."

The tambourines in his chest disliked that answer. Rattling like mad, they jangled so loudly he imagined she could hear them. "I'm the king, or did you forget? You can't order me around." He meant it in a jesting way, but it came out brisk and domineering. He swallowed hard, forcing down the acute desire to apologize or add something to lighten the mood.

"Is that so? Well, you may not know, Your Majesty, but women without a title are as invisible as the servants in this room. To these people, I'm *nobody*." Her last word sliced like a knife. "Believe me, I know what invisibility feels like."

Pursing his lips, he snatched a piece of cheese to toss in his mouth, hating the twangy taste and the slow chew, but sensing the need to end this conversation and move away from her before too many eyes discovered them.

"Then why are you dressed like that?"

The grape she'd just released fell out of her open mouth. It bounced off Red's shoe and rolled under the table. "Because no one else knows who I am, but they will if you keep talking to me." She walked away.

He turned to face the party, forcing himself not to watch her. Oddly enough, his headache had subsided, despite his throbbing blood.

"I thought everyone wanted to be king," a familiar voice toned from a few paces away. Seb walked up, glittering white waistcoat reflecting the bright smile on his face. "But the way you're looking, it's a job no one wants."

Seb's imitation of the king's expression mimicked the haunted masks for sale at the weekly market. A laugh bubbled out from under Red's scowl.

"That's more like it. That young woman you were just talking to, eh? Eight? Nine?"

Instantly, Red's temples turned into hot cooking plates. Seb had seen him talking to Aly, and had *rated* her. Red didn't know if he should correct Seb—she was definitely a ten—or be glad that Seb hadn't thought her the most beautiful woman in the room. Because if he had, Seb would ask her to dance.

Wait, when did she become a ten?

But Seb drew Red's mind off of that conundrum when he said, a little sheepishly, "Your *Majesty*," as if testing whether or not he had to use the term.

Red knew, suddenly, why his father hadn't had many close friends. The ring of gold on his forehead might as well have been a viper poised to strike. No one could get close, not to a king, not even the person who'd once climbed into the decorative suits of armor with him as a dare and who had accidently set the curtains in his royal bedroom on fire.

"Seb," Red began, voice thick all of a sudden. He needed his relationship with Seb to stay the same. The laughter. The jokes. He needed a friend. "You don't have to do that."

Seb looked up, his eyes a bit wide, a bit of mischief there. Then they shrank and Seb's posture lifted. "Yes, I do, Your Majesty." He drew up into a soldier's stiffness. "You are my king now."

Maybe not for long. Even though he itched to tell Seb of the death curse, he wanted to try to enjoy the evening. Seb also deserved to have a good time. No sense unloading the bad news on him now. The more people he told, the more real it felt, the less hopeful that they'd find a cure.

Behind Seb, Red caught sight of Aly hovering close enough to a group of courtiers to make it appear she wasn't alone, but clearly not talking to anyone. Her eyes darted away when he spotted her.

Seb elbowed him. "You might be king, but you *did* lose the bet. Thank Theod, because Leeta Merrythorne is over there giving you the come-hither eye." He slapped the king once again on the shoulder and walked away.

Red laughed, his knotted muscles relaxing a little.

A woman with a lily-pad face approached, bent in an uncomfortable angle, as if trying to walk while beginning her curtsy. Red knew he wouldn't be allowed to enjoy the party by talking to his best friend, not now that the crown rested on his head. He sighed and stood up straighter.

Otto Dumar, the man responsible for introducing every

important person the king met, hurried up behind the woman and introduced her with his boulder-rolling voice.

The woman curtsied. "I wish you wisdom from Voire and much happiness."

Voire. He'd studied the gods of the continent, memorized them as best he could, though he didn't understand why each country worshipped something different and called it the only right way to worship. Voire was a god of the Virienne people, a people prone to good wine and good times and really excellent pastries.

"My deepest thanks, madame."

The woman was already backing away with her head low.

"Your Majesty, might we return to the dais where you can receive your guests more comfortably?" suggested Dumar.

Red grunted. "I haven't eaten." But people were beginning to line up to speak to him. "All right, fine." If he was really going to be the gracious king they all wanted, he could prove it by waiting a little longer to eat.

Walking behind Dumar, Red spotted Aly's silver headpiece near the wall to his right. She was talking to someone, but he couldn't see who over the heads of the dancing couples. People bowed as he walked by, but his attention was wholly on who might be talking to his sorcerer. She wasn't supposed to know anyone other than Arthur Ondorian, and the priest was seated at a table near the dais. The dancers twirled away and Red caught sight of who Aly was speaking to: Lord Weston Grey.

Now what are you up to? Red wondered. He couldn't see either one of them very well, but he could tell how close they were standing. A man as rich and as single as Weston Grey didn't stand that close to a stranger in a ballroom full of gossiping nobles.

His secret sorcerer, a person whose identity he'd spent his life trying to discover, wasn't as secret as he'd believed.

Red took his seat on the dais just as another fluttery woman approached, this one flanked by a stiff-coat with a burgundy ascot all billowed out like the neck of some exotic lizard. *Were these some of the people who'd entered with the ambassador?* He thought he remembered the strange attire.

Dumar began again, "Your Majesty, may I..."

His words drowned out in a sudden burst of pain behind Red's eyes. The king's hand leapt to his forehead.

"All right, sir?"

Red had missed the names of the people in front of him. *How can I lead a country when I can't even make it through a ball without headaches blocking the names of guests introduced?*

He blinked, trying to ignore the pain, and stared at the couple, hoping Dumar would reintroduce them.

"The Deep, O King, blesses you," the man said in a thick Esvedaran accent.

Red bristled. The Deep, or the Canyon as most people called it, represented all that was evil about the world. Esvedara, the southern island right off his own coastline, was a rich country, one often conquered for its strategic location in the gulf. Tandera had once possessed it, but had granted her independence some two hundred years ago after a bloody conflict. Then, sixty years ago, Bulvarna took the island and established a presence there, essentially bookending Tandera to the north and south. If Red knew anything about the islanders, though, it was that they claimed little loyalty to whichever country officially ruled them. They were their own, they always said, no matter the flag flying above them.

The islanders were some of the most superstitious people on the continent when it came to the Canyon. How this man had come to use the Canyon's name as a source of *blessing*, Red could only guess.

Not wanting to become embroiled in a theological debate, he simply replied, "I am pleased you could attend tonight's celebration." He wished he'd heard their names. *Nothing makes a person feel more important than a king greeting him by name.* Advice from his father.

The twang of sadness in his throat cinched the headache tighter.

Trying to remember all his father's advice was hard enough now that he was gone. Every time he thought of his father's bearded face, the pain came, the headache worsened.

His eyes traveled the room for Aly, who was nowhere to be seen. Nor was Weston Grey. *Grey bowed to her in the council room,* Red recalled. He'd thought it was simply a gesture of respect. But what if Grey, against all odds, had known who stood beneath the mask and cloak?

The next person waiting in line to speak to the king pressed against the backs of the Esvedarans.

"Pleased to speak with you, Majesty," said the man. "May the Deep bless you. Always."

This man, whoever he was, worshipped the *Canyon*, the scar that bled darkness into the world from a place lost in shadow. In his nightmares, Red had been tossed from its edge too many times to count.

His lips plummeted into a scowl. Mentioning the Canyon—the Deep, as this man called it—in a positive way amounted to a direct insult. The Canyon stood against everything Tandera had been founded on, everything it believed in. Some Bulvarnans no longer feared the Canyon, but Red had never heard of people worshipping it until now. He shuddered.

Before Red could respond, an invisible hand gripped his wrist, yanking him out of his throne.

And just in time.

A light flickered and his throne burst into flame.

12

ALY

The chandelier overhead was now dark, every bulb extinguished.

"Magic!" someone shouted.

Aly's magic was muddy and slow, her mind a bramble patch —thanks to Lord Grey and those bizarre words from Red. He'd looked at her with a strange fire in his eyes of mingled anger and attraction. He was confusing and difficult, and she didn't have time to be thinking about him.

Distraction was hazardous for a sorcerer, even a Master. She slapped away the childish thoughts and yanked on the king's Truthwell. *Are there more shadows in his Truthwell tonight, or is this just my own distraction dimming his light?*

Horrified, she feared her father had come. If the Bulvarnan sorcerer was here, they would all be dead by morning.

Stop that! she chided herself.

A scream followed when another bright spark shot toward the king. This one came from a wall sconce, now burned out and black.

In a flash almost too fast to be human, Veeter Yin tossed a plate in front of the king, perfectly timed so that the tiny flame hit the crystal. The dish shattered as the magic-amplified fire hit it, crashing to the ballroom floor in a spray of fragments.

But Red was already halfway across the room, lifted from his throne by Aly's magic. She grabbed for all the light inside of him, voracious and keen as a cat about to strike. With her mind again focused on the present, she placed Red in the saferoom at the back of the ballroom, and attempted to move the rest of the royal family to safety. The energy it took to move three humans was astounding, but Red's Truthwell poured power into her hands. Despite the shadows licking at the corners of his Well, she was able to move the royal family to safety.

A gunshot ripped through the room, followed by another flash of magic.

People scrambled toward the double doors along the east side of the ballroom that led into the palace's grand foyer.

Aly ran for Red, extending her shroud over him.

Red stumbled into the golden wallpaper of the saferoom, the dusty scent of thick, painted cloth filling the air. Woven flowers reflected the bright light from the ballroom, but the sconces on the walls remained unlit.

He spun and knocked into Aly's body. Her eyes bulged, her hair a falling mess.

"Aly!"

"*Shush!*"

He looked about ready to reprimand her for shushing him, but she lifted her hands and pressed her palms against his chest, hard. Her eyes narrowed, then closed. Her breath undulated in her body, so close to his.

A chill burst through the small room. He gasped. Then almost instantly, heat bloomed under Aly's hands as she checked his body for any additional curses.

"What was—?"

"You're fine." She glanced over her shoulder.

The room behind them was still in chaos. Courtiers cowered

in the corners or under tables, the ladies' dresses too bulky with petticoats to allow them to squat down. A few men were starting to stand, glance around, and assess the danger.

"Is it your father?"

She shook her head, still looking out at the ballroom. "No. Something else." Her fear was rising, but she couldn't voice it—not yet. "I had to check," she added, snapping her gaze back at him. "If that magic had infected you, even only a little bit." She quivered. "But you're clean."

Red stormed back into the ballroom, ripping a toppled chair out of his way.

"Where are you going?" Aly asked, darting after him.

"My family."

"Already safe," she said.

Red took a few more steps before he realized what she'd said. "Where?"

"In the Emerald Room."

Correcting his course for the Emerald Room, the king spun on his heel toward the farthest of the double doors leading out into the foyer.

"They're *safe*, Red." Her footsteps clicked quickly compared to his. "Trust me; I set up the barrier myself. But *you* need to come with me. Now."

"Can't they see you?" He waved a hand at the milling courtiers as they rose from their hiding places.

Aly shook her head. "And they can't see you right now either."

Red stiffened. "Your shroud."

She nodded.

His face brightened. "It's gone! My headache. You healed it."

Aly snorted like a disgruntled horse. "I pushed a wave of clarity through you. That's all. It's not medicinal." She picked up her dress and hustled toward a door. "These idiots," she grumbled as they wove between members of the king's guard, rifles desperately searching for a target.

"My men?"

"Yes, idiots. They think bullets will help against a lyth." Her feet stopped. She hadn't meant to say it aloud. The fear rose up like bile. No sense standing around. With forceful arms, she shoved between two men, causing them to stumble apart, bewildered by the unseen source.

Red stopped. "Did you say *lyth*?"

"Lyth. Yes. Shapeshifting nightmare. Let's go. The beast hasn't left the palace yet." Aly blasted several chairs out of the way with a flick of her wrist.

Red followed her, shrouded in invisibility, out of the ballroom, down a smaller hallway lit only by sconces.

"Curse these lights," Aly said as they passed another wall sconce that had been snuffed out by magic, judging by the black stain on the wall. They turned off the main hallway, darted through a door discretely set into the trim in the wall, and took off up a winding staircase that creaked at every step, a staircase the king probably hadn't used since his boyhood days of chasing Elise through the palace in grand orchestrations of hide-and-seek.

They rose to the level of the royal family's living quarters. This hall was lit by wide chandeliers, but all lay quiet and still. The endless paintings that lined the walls depicted horses at spearpoint, shields lifted against falling arrows, and the gnarled heads of foxbloods, the beasts that climbed out of the earth to eat the forests bare of every living creature. One tapestry wove the gray wolves into the story, the wolves who, legend had it, came to the aid of their long-hated rival, the humans, to defeat the foxbloods.

Aly lifted a finger to her mouth.

"I thought we were shrouded?"

She nodded. "But if they are sorcerers, or if even one of them is, then it won't matter. They can hear through the shroud like I can."

Aly paused before his bedroom. Her hand lifted to the carved wood.

"In here? Why would they be in here?"

She shushed him again.

A quick survey with her magic told her only one man was within the bedroom. Exactly what she feared. A lyth could hide its energy signature.

With a grunt, she pushed the door open and burst in.

A fire flickered in the king's huge hearth. Footsteps rustled in the next room, the king's bedroom. Lunging forward, Aly drew from Red's Truthwell and lifted the flames from the hearth. Crafting the fire into a shield before her, she stormed into the bedroom.

A feral scream exited her mouth when she saw the snake in the Esvedaran man's hand. He dropped the snake on the king's bed and lifted his hands toward Aly.

Wood from the fourposter burst free, a hundred tiny shards darting her way. The fire destroyed them in a whirl of ash.

A flying object zoomed past Aly's head. *Was that a bird?*

No, simply a statue. It *thunked* against the hardwood, making a large dent.

Her awareness of Red's Truthwell told her he was approaching from behind. "Stay back!" she demanded. Her eyes roved for the snake. It had to die.

The fire in her hands rolled into a massive, swirling inferno. She hurled it at the bed. Within seconds, the entire four-poster was engulfed.

Aly yanked the rug out from under the fleeing man. With a crash, the man with the burgundy ascot toppled over one of the chairs by the mantle. Blood bubbled from his mouth and whisps of crimson smoke swirled up from his palms. Aly screamed and brought her hands down, commanding crackling strands of fire and light to land on top of the man. He struggled against her magic a moment, but the scarlet curse leaked through his cage of flames like spilled ink on parchment.

He was no trained Master. His magic, fueled by the objects in the room, would not hold against hers. He knew it, yet he refused to yield.

As the sorcerers battled, the air turned cold.

The man's blood-red curse seeped through the flames that were destroying his body. He would maintain the spell until he died, Aly realized. He was going to keep pressing until his curse broke through her enchantment.

"Go!" she screamed, hoping Red listened.

Then, in a bit of a gamble, she moved the flames off the man, surrounding him in a cocoon of smoke instead. She tossed the flames back on the blazing mass that had been the king's bed. As she's assumed, the man's curse, free from her enchantment of flames, wiggled through the smoke and shot, arrowlike, over her shoulder.

Aly leaped, and as she did, she called up the bird statue into her raised hand. The movement took less time than a breath. The curse shattered the statue, spraying Aly with stone dust.

The man, still caged by smoke, coughed and blinked and cursed against the swirling ash. His magic was running low—he'd drawn all the energy he could to conjure that curse. The smoke was inhibiting his concentration.

In the anteroom, the sound of the boots of approaching soldiers indicated the guards had finally come.

"Tell me quickly, witch," Aly said to the man. His face, half-concealed by smoke, contorted at the insult. "Who sent you?"

She knew, but she had to *know*.

Red appeared beside her. That deaf idiot.

"My guards will not give you a second chance to offer anything useful." The threat in the king's words came out heavy and sharp.

Her time was out—she conjured her shroud around her just as the soldiers discovered the flaming bed.

"I'm no witch." He stared at where Aly had been. "Not like that one. *She's* the reason for your curse."

Red's stance faltered. "What do you mean?"

"Protect the king!" a loud voice behind them boomed as heavy boots rushed into the room.

Armor-clad men marched in a circle around Red, backs toward him, weapons facing out. With a flick of her wrist, Aly doused the flames on Red's bed. With a second wave of her hand, the ash and burned material rose in the air before shrinking into a tiny, fist-sized ball. With her other hand, she pointed at a tall window, opened it, and hurled the ball of wreckage out into the night.

The soldiers gaped at the strange sight. All that was left behind was a charred scar in the hardwood floor and a smoke stain on the ceiling. Easy enough to fix with a few more spells or some paint.

"Your Majesty, let us take you to a saferoom." Gavin, the head of the guard, spoke in urgent tones.

As the soldiers gathered up the injured man, who was no longer surrounded by Aly's smoke cage, Aly Pulled every bit of smoke, ash, and fire stench out of the king's chambers. She pushed them out the window, into the breeze.

But when cleaning up the king's bedroom, she didn't find a snake carcass.

The beast had escaped.

She debated telling the soldiers of the missing lyth. *What can they even do?*

No. It was her task to find and kill the lyth. The lyth that, she was fairly certain, had come to the party dressed as an Esvedaran courtier.

She's the reason for the curse, the man's voice replayed in her mind. Her father had sent the man and the lyth. *But why?* The curse had flown over her shoulder—it was heading for the king. *If Red was already cursed, why bother with another attack? What am I missing?*

"Yes, yes," Red lifted a hand, quieting the guards. "My family?"

"Safe in the Emerald Room, sire."

Red followed his guards out of his bedchamber. The apprehended Esvedaran was in handcuffs and headed toward Mardon's prison to await a trial that would not end well for him.

Aly disappeared down the hall, intent on finding the shapeshifting snake—which could just as easily walk *out* of the palace on two legs as it had walked in.

13

———

RED

The king's bedroom had been cleaned and put back together, not a picture crooked or a book out of place. Red followed Bernard and Yin into the room and surveyed the shining tables, the pristine floor, the flickering fire. He'd only been out of the room an hour, which had been long enough to speak with his family and consult his guards about his wishes for the prisoner.

"That will be all, Bernard. Thank you."

The man gave a small bow and departed. Yin remained silent, hands clasped at his waist.

Red knew the Esvedaran man from earlier could be of use. He knew something about Aly, or so he'd claimed. *Had they truly been sent by her father?* He still couldn't believe that part. *Why another curse? Is there some other enemy out there, trying to kill me* before *the death curse kills me?*

Being king had not started out well. *How did Father do this?*

He thought of the handkerchief. He still did not know how the cloth had been swapped and put into his coat. Amid all the other duties and dilemmas of the past two days, neither he nor Aly had discovered who was behind that act of betrayal.

Someone in the palace was working with the Bulvarnans—and because of their aid, Red now had a curse.

A small dent in the floor caught the king's eye—the single sign that a fight had occurred here. To his surprise, the stone falcon had been replaced on his mantle. He'd *seen* it explode into dust. The bird, wings extended as if to take flight, had been a gift from the Virienne king years ago, and had always been one of Red's favorite pieces. Yet now, he recognized the fierce anger in the bird's eyes, anger at never being able to release his branch and soar.

Sleep was not on the king's mind. He wanted answers and confirmation that the snake would not feast on his brain while he slept.

To Yin, he announced he wished to see the sorcerer. His guard trailed him as he made his way to the stairs.

One hollow knock filled the hall on the fourth floor. A sentry at the stair one floor below, a measure taken after the attack, had nodded at the king on his way up, but no one guarded the sorcerer's hall. She didn't need it.

Unfair, he mused.

Yin posted himself by the top of the stair, facing away so that he could not see the sorcerer.

One more hollow knock.

She couldn't be sleeping. His blood still pulsed in his veins, the threat on his life not easily forgotten. He hoped she had found the snake and that the palace was now safe.

He grew impatient. A king should not be kept waiting, in a cold hallway in the small hours of the night, no less.

Lifting his hand for a third pound on her door, his jaw fell open as he heard the muffled tones of a man's voice. Then silence, before the knob turned.

His breath caught.

The door swung open, revealing Aly in a long silver dressing gown that was sashed at her waist and swallowed her body in folds of fabric. Her hair was loose.

"What couldn't wait 'til morning?" She groaned and stepped away from the door, leaving it open for him.

For some reason, he'd not thought about this being the place she slept. He suddenly felt unwelcome, as if he'd stumbled into a ladies' dressmaker hoping to have his sizes taken; all the rules of proper society melted away when he stepped in this room. The king kept conference with the Royal Sorcerer. That was simply the way it was, despite the fact this sort of late-night meeting would sully even the best reputation among normal men and women. But Red and Aly were anything but normal.

"Who was that?" he asked, eyes scanning the firelit room behind her, searching for the owner of the voice he'd heard. He left the door open so that he felt less alone with her, dressed as she was. However, she wasn't alone—he'd heard someone in here. A man.

Aly rubbed her hands down her face. "No one." She glanced toward her bedroom.

His eyes followed her gaze and an inferno roared to life inside Red's chest. "You've got someone *with you*?" Without under-standing why, he stormed toward her bedroom door and opened his mouth to chastise whomever he found waiting there.

I'm dying, a lyth just escaped in my house, and she's got a man in here? His mind immediately went to Lord Grey.

Chest heaving, he searched the room. The fourposter bed was empty—a tangled mess—as were the corners of the room. He bent down, no one under the bed either.

"What are you doing?" she demanded, fluttering up next to him.

An iron spiral staircase led up through the ceiling. He growled and stomped to the bottom of the stair. "I know you're up there!" With one foot on the first stair, he felt Aly's hands grab his wrist and yank him around.

"Do not go up there!"

He ripped his hand free. "Stop me." Two more steps up and his body lifted away from the iron steps, slamming hard into the wooden floor before he could so much as yelp. Groaning, he rolled to his side to see a fuming Aly, fists by her sides.

"Never do that again," he muttered, unsure why he felt so angry, why she'd body slammed him with magic to keep him from discovering her secret lover—or why he cared that she had one. Rubbing the back of his head, he stood, grabbed the iron railing, and scowled at her. "You've been lying to me." He had no right to care, yet the seething inside him did not subside. "And you said you never lied."

Maybe this was why she hadn't been able to save his father. She'd weakened her magic with too many self-serving lies.

With deliberate steps, he climbed. She whimpered but did not stop him.

"You won't like what you find," she said as she followed behind him.

He was certain of that. The betrayal roiling in his abdomen made him forget the real reason he'd come to see her: to ask about the shapeshifting creature who might still be loose in the palace.

The small room above held only a small table and a thin mattress draped with a thick quilt. On the table sat a wooden box. No one was there.

"Where did he go?" Red glanced around for windows, hidden doors, escape hatches of any kind.

She stepped up beside him, placed a hand on his upper arm— a gesture that lit his mind and rage on fire again—and strode to the small table. "He's right here." She picked up the box with both hands and turned to face Red, eyes wide and full of an alarming sadness.

"Pardon?" He shook his head in confusion.

Squeezing her eyes and lips shut, she opened the box. Words began to pour into the air.

Red nearly choked.

It was his father's voice.

"What magic is this?" he bellowed, lashing out for the box.

She spun, snatching it from his reach. "Calm down!" She closed the box and the voice silenced. Gently, she set it on the table. "It does what Carolyn's music box does. It captures sound and plays it back, but with magic." She pressed her knuckles against her mouth, then spoke around them. "Your father said these words before he died, when he knew he wouldn't be able to..." She trailed off, fingers held against her lips as if to prevent vomit from spewing. Her shoulders began to tremble. A sob burst from her cupped mouth.

Startled, Red stepped backward, nearly losing his balance at the top of the stair. "All right," he said, trying to sound comforting but instead sounding condescending. He still wasn't over his rage from moments ago.

"Your father would—it's silly really—he used to—sometimes —read to me before bed." Her confession spilled out in fits and jerks. After several beats of awkward silence, she fumbled for more words. "He started when I first came here. I was seventeen, had just lost my mother, and felt very alone. It's hard...some-times...I have trouble sleeping, and he would read and it helped." Her head hung low. "I would come up here on the nights I felt afraid and he'd sit right there on the floor and read until I fell asleep." When she raised her head, her eyes were puffy. "He was a good man. He recorded this for me when he was no longer able to come up here and read."

Confusion, shock, and needling cords of jealousy wove among Red's racing thoughts.

Fortunately, Aly said, "You don't have to say anything, but now you know how pathetic I am. I think we can go downstairs and talk about whatever it is you came here for." She slipped by him and padded down the iron steps.

Father used to read to her... The thought tumbled around in his head as he descended behind her. Shame, like the spire of Mardon's cathedral, rose above his other thoughts. His anger from a moment ago felt so childish, so unforgivable now that he knew the truth.

I haven't given her a single reason not to hate me.

Downstairs, instead of sitting by the fire, he stood with hands in his pockets by the window, staring out at the slivered moon. Mental images of his father reading to her kept bombarding his thoughts and preventing him from asking his questions about the snake.

He had to know. Over his shoulder, he said, "What makes a sorcerer feel afraid?"

A sigh preceded her answer. "More than you know, but mostly, being alone."

He rounded so fast that she jumped. Her hands were tucked under her arms, her back to the warm hearth. Nothing about her —about this sorcerer supreme—had been what he'd expected.

"Oh." Needing to change the subject, Red thought back to the events of the evening. He recalled her trembling while she'd held the Esvedaran captive with her magic. "Does it wear on you?" He searched for the right words. "Conjuring magic, I mean?"

She shot him a look that suggested he'd asked if rain fell down from the sky or up from the earth. "No. I've got you."

He lifted his brows. "My Truthwell, you mean?"

"Yes. Didn't I tell you how bright you are? Your energy, it's so tangible, so..." She reached out a hand as she spoke, then jerked it back as if appalled he'd caught her reaching for him. "The hard part is concentration. Holding back, really. It's a mental fatigue more than anything."

"You're saying you could Strip me?" His own words had a peculiar impact on him. Despite the inappropriateness of it, he couldn't hold back a chuckle, though the topic of Truthstripping was anything but funny.

Aly did not laugh. Instead, she hung her head. "It's always a temptation," she said. "But Masters have learned to ignore it, or rather, to use magic despite the feeling. That's why using words and phrases from the *Verad* makes it easier. A sorcerer who uses lies can't possibly have the same ability to withstand the draw of a Well."

She'd just admitted she had the ability and even the desire to Strip him. *The snake. I need to ask about the snake.* But he wanted to know what she meant. "Bright, you say?"

"Brightest one I've ever seen."

"Some are brighter than others." He wasn't sure why it mattered.

She stared at him a moment. Something brewed behind her eyes. She was contemplating, perhaps deliberating, what her next words would be.

"What?" he asked, prompting her.

With a wave of her hand, she dismissed his query, confirming that there was indeed something she wasn't saying.

"It's not *so* bright that I can't turn away." As if to prove her point, she turned around. "But that doesn't matter now. I'm Bound to your Well. So, to answer your question, no, magic doesn't make me physically tired."

"Right," he said, his brows working as he stared at the back of her head. Whatever she wasn't saying, it was bothering her. The crossed arms, the fidgety movements. Was it embarrassing for a sorcerer to admit their own weakness—their own insatiable desire to Truthpull? "And the snake? What of it?"

She covered her face with her hands and spun back around.

"Aly?"

With a groan, she pulled her palms down her face, dragging her skin in ugly ways. "It got away."

His tongue froze, his chest constricted.

"Lyths are good at hiding, okay?"

The words sawed into Red's composure. "You left it in my *house*? You're supposed to be a Protector."

Aly's eyes rose to his with a look of mixed repulsion and anger. "Sorry I am not your perfect dream of what a sorcerer should be. Lyths are hard to catch and harder to kill. Believe me, I know. However, it *left*, Red. It's gone."

He folded his arms. "And that's meant to comfort me? A lyth —which were supposedly eliminated in the purge—is now wandering the streets of Mardon? One with the ability to shift into *human* form, no less. The only other one known to be capable of shifting into a man was at a wedding I attended six years ago in Virienne." He leaned closer. "You were there, weren't you?"

"Yes." She blinked slowly, perhaps at the memory of that terrifying night. "I was still training to become a Master, but I was there."

"Serving whom?"

"Lord Grey."

Red's mouth fell open. *So they do know each other.* Suddenly, he wasn't sure if that made their closeness in the ballroom more or less surprising.

He lurched forward without thinking. "Is there something between you two? I saw you at the ball."

Aly's brow bunched and her mouth parted in what was either confusion or shock. For a moment, she studied Red, her expression melting back into perfect placidity. "No."

She's not supposed to lie, but there's more to that word than she's revealing.

"About the wedding," she said, carefully drawing the conversation back to more pertinent information. "I killed the lyth that night." Red's brows rose, impressed. "Not long after that, I was appointed Royal Sorcerer. Even then, my father had been searching for me, but when I came here, my trail went cold. Until three months ago when he cursed Gevar. Since I kept your father alive long enough to arouse suspicion about whether the curse had worked, it wasn't until your ceremony, when *your* curse activated in such a public manner, that Dimitri could be sure it was me serving the Tanderan crown. Both times, it was *my* magic that activated the curse."

He stepped toward the fire but didn't sit. Cooler air drifted in through the open door, dousing the heat in Red's cheeks. "Why does he want us dead *this* badly? Because your mother died giving birth? I don't buy it. That was twenty-two years ago."

She sat in the chair by her mantle, pulled her legs under her, and wrapped her arms around her knees. "As far as I know, that *is* the only reason he's hunting me. My mama—the nurse who raised me—never told me my father's identity or the fact that he wanted me dead. I think it was her way of protecting me. She died before I could ever ask her about it. Ondorian believes my father's grief poisoned his mind. He thinks Dimitri may have become susceptible to the Canyon's darkness after my mother died, and he never came back to the light."

A twinge of dread pricked in Red's stomach, a portcullis cranking down, pressing iron teeth into his once promising future. He didn't know what to say, so he simply watched the glowing coals, letting his mind drift as the light pulsed and faded among the logs.

Aly, sensing his racing thoughts, asked, "What is it?"

"Nothing."

"Nice try."

"Okay, what does your father think killing you will solve? It won't bring your mother back. And why kill *my* father?" The still-sharp grief over his father's death weighed on Red. He dropped into the chair opposite Aly. "Why kill me?"

Aly's chin rested on her knees. "I don't know, Red," she whispered. "I don't know."

"What would happen to you if you siphoned the curse?"

Her head popped up. "No. You can't—"

"Aly, I'm *dead* if we don't figure this out. My father? You watched his body rot! I don't want—I'm not ready—"

His words cut off as she moved out of her chair onto the floor before him. She squatted, her eyes pinned on him. One hand lifted toward him.

"Light overpowers the darkness," she murmured. Warmth tingled through his legs, rising toward his chest. "It's easier if I touch you. Can I?"

Dumbfounded, he stared at her. Gentle and light as a silk sheet, her hand rested on his knee. With her touch came a burst of heat into his entire body—both from magic and from her hand on his leg. Not an uncomfortable heat, but the heat of a bath, the warmth of total relaxation. He melted into the chair.

"Better?" she asked, slipping carefully back into the seat behind her.

For a moment, he fought sleep, the magic nearly sending him into a dream state. "Yes," he finally muttered.

"That was a little truth to fight against the darkness inside you. I can keep it from spreading. For a little while."

After the way he'd stormed in here tonight, the rage he'd displayed so foolishly, it was a wonder she had any compassion left for him. He stood. "Thank you." He cleared his throat. "And thank you for keeping my family safe tonight."

She nodded and followed him toward the door.

His leg still burned from where she'd touched him. *Or is that simply my imagination?* His mind reeled. To force his brain back to the situation at hand, he said, "I have one more question."

"One more. Then bed."

Her words, unexpected, spiraled down into his navel and exploded. She meant *she* was going to *her* bed, of course.

He coughed. "Do you ever tire of being invisible?"

A small frown pushed a little annoyance into her sigh. "You had one more question to ask, and you want to know if a woman tires of never being looked at?" Her green eyes narrowed. "Waste of a question."

He stared down at her, mouth fixed in a mortified scowl. He wanted to slap himself but found that her nearness changed everything he thought he would say or do.

"I—"

"Bed, remember? You had your question." She started shooing him toward the door with both hands. "Not my fault you wasted it."

He shuffled toward the door that would send him back into the mirrored halls, back into the world where he had to pretend not to be cursed—the world where Aly did not exist, where she was only a cloaked figure with a sorcerer's mask.

"When do I get to ask more questions?" For an inexplicable reason, he tried to think of a way to extend this conversation a few moments longer.

"That was a question, Red."

He fought a smile. "Right, but I'm the king, so I can ask questions whenever I want, and you have to answer them." He stared at her without moving until her eyes began to dart and look anywhere but at him.

Magic might inhabit her veins, flow from her mind, and strengthen her arms to uproot trees, but in that moment she looked broken, fractured by a world she hadn't created or wanted for herself, but one she found herself in day after day.

For the span of mere seconds, neither of them stepped away. The small space between them might as well have been the Canyon itself.

"Goodnight, Miss Barron," he said and walked away.

Preparations for departure had begun immediately after the council meeting, though the royal convoy would not leave for at least a fortnight. Red battled round after agonizing round of headaches while Aly remained out of sight for the next two days, searching the city for the lyth and demanding Red remain on palace grounds while she was away.

Magical communications as well as formal letters had to be sent, returned. Travel arrangements had to be made, security measures put in place. King Lucien of Refere, via Riode Liere, had heard of Red's plans and had offered to accompany him to the Canyon to assess the threat there and hopefully secure a meeting with Queen Kassia. As the kings of Tandera and Refere would be traveling to the most dangerous place in the world, the entire city of Mardon, and likely Refere's capital as well, was in a tizzy.

People clustered around the palace gates to catch a glimpse of the new king, who was rumored to be bold, brave, rash, or immature, depending on who was speaking. The priests presiding over weekly services in the churches of Mardon and the surrounding villages had started offering prayers for the king's protection as well as for protection from the lyth. Somehow, ludicrously, word of the lyth had slipped into the city streets like an injection.

Brand checks were up. Stray dogs and street rats, once a nuisance, vanished amid the intermittent increase of gunshots. Mardon felt tense, as if bracing for something it couldn't yet see coming. The price for a Protector skyrocketed, and all known sorcerers in the area were coerced by these higher paychecks into the homes of the city's wealthiest, while the charlatan sorcerers, not powerful or schooled enough to be Protectors, charged astronomical amounts for petty magic that wouldn't keep a curse at bay any better than a spiderweb could delay a train.

When Queen Kassia's message of acceptance came, Lord Benedict Alexander seemed as happy as a cat in a window box. He, along with the rest of the king's council, would also be accompanying Red to the meeting with the queen.

Red's sisters, however, pleaded with him not to go.

"Kassia is evil," Carolyn blurted, her face more freckled with her afternoons in the spring sun. She'd been building a functioning, miniature trebuchet in the back gardens, with Seb's help.

Elise sat in a nearby chair, Kanto's poetry open in her lap, a parasol held over her head by her personal escort, Jacobs. Elise's two female attendants lounged in the sun on low couches, pretending not to listen to the conversation. "Can you not wait until we have solved this?" she asked, gesturing to the book in her lap.

Part of why he was going was because they *hadn't* solved the problem. If Aly could cast the spell back into her father, all their problems would be solved. Red needed to convince Aly that facing her father was the right move.

Red sighed, shaking his head. "Kassia refused Father's invitations to talk for months. She's accepted mine. I can't turn her down, nor do I want to." He might not be king for long, but if he could secure an agreement with Kassia to protect the borders, his kingship wouldn't be for nothing.

Glancing at his sisters, Red asked, "If you two were offended by something I said or did, what would be the best way to apologize?"

Carolyn picked up a hammer and tapped it against her palm. "You're awful at being cryptic, Brother. Who do you need to apologize to, and what did you do?"

Elise snorted without looking up from her book.

How does she always know? Red shifted his weight. "None of your business. I am king, I have plenty of people I offend on a daily basis."

"But kings don't apologize to just anyone," Carolyn pointed out.

"If you must know, I'm asking how to appease *you*, Carol. You don't want me to go north, but I am. How can I win back your most coveted affection?" He hoped she bought the lie. It was half true anyway. She didn't need to know it was Aly he needed to appease.

He wanted Aly to come on this trip without feeling forced. He hoped she would *want* to come, want to save him. If she *wanted* to save him, perhaps she would find the strength she felt she lacked. Magic, after all, obeyed her mind. He needed her to be confident —otherwise, he would fall to the fear that kept him up at night and fed his headaches with fury.

Carolyn squatted beside her trebuchet. For some reason, Elise had been taught to be a lady, never sitting with anything less than perfect posture, rarely speaking with anything less than perfect grammar. However, with Carolyn, his parents had been less strict. He smiled and watched her hammer in a peg.

"You could always help her with the trebuchet," Elise offered with a wry smile. "Why not aid our sister in the creation of tools of war?"

"That's Seb's job," said Red. "If it's destruction you want, he's your man. Where is he, anyway?"

"Off on an errand for his father," Elise offered, eyes still on her book.

Carolyn placed another nail. Their mother would be furious if she saw the dirt on the princess's hands—though the former queen had grown up with dirt on her fingers. "He was supposed to add the counterweight to the machine today."

"What will you do with this?" he asked.

Smearing a bit of sweat off her brow, Carolyn peered up at him. "I want to use melons first. Seb's father says he can have some shipped here by next month. Then I'll try potatoes. A sack of flour."

"He's rubbing off on you."

Elise snorted. "I still cannot believe you agreed to this," she said to Red.

"Me?" Red pressed his fingers to his suit jacket. "Don't blame me. She's the one who went to Seb directly. I had nothing to do with it." He flashed her a smile. "I'd like to see that sack of flour." He mimed a big explosion.

"Then don't go over that bridge," Carolyn demanded, arms folding.

The bridge that spanned the eerie depths of the Canyon, though only completed these last fifteen years, had a mythology all its own. Most believed it to be cursed or at least bewitched. Some said it took people into an alternate world.

"We'll be fine."

Elise looked up. "People vanish from the bridge every year."

"Thanks for the vote of confidence," he muttered. "Listen," he eyed the attendants nearby. "You know I need to make this trip. You know I can't just sit here and wait." He didn't say for his own death. "And if this meeting with Kassia goes well, I might make a difference for you two. For your futures."

Carolyn dropped her hammer in the grass beside her project. "*Your* future too, Brother. Can't you go around the Canyon?"

Going around the Canyon added three weeks and no less danger, as the journey along the edge added ample opportunity for Canyon beasts to sneak out of the depths and make a meal of the travelers. He didn't have that kind of time.

He shook his head. She seemed to catch his meaning and looked quickly away.

"Elise, where are you with that?" he asked, nodding at the book.

"Not very far. Translation is slow work, especially when it is poetry."

Turning around, he tried to hide his sigh of frustration. They hadn't found an answer yet. Not in any stories. Not in any poems. The death curse was eating him alive, though he couldn't feel it—a fact that almost made it worse—and there was no way to stop it. Behind him, the book flopped closed.

"I will go with you," Elise said. "I will keep translating."

He closed his eyes. When he turned back around, Elise was

standing. Her face was set. Carolyn might be the impulsive one, the unpredictable one, but Elise was determined and immovable once her mind was made up.

Despite Carolyn's outburst of protests, Elise's gaze did not break from Red. In that look, her resolve burned brightly. He needed her help. His Kirish was terrible, and translating poetry required a person much better suited to the task than him.

She would be one more person he was putting in danger.

"You understand the risks?" he asked.

She nodded. "I do not fear the Canyon."

"Fine," he said, though he doubted she truly did not fear the place where evil dwelled.

Elise nodded again, satisfied.

"Now you *both* have to buy me something to make up for leaving me," Carolyn blurted.

"Buy you something?"

"Yes," she lifted her chin at her brother. "You asked how you could appease me. Buy me something pretty."

"So you can shoot it with your trebuchet?"

Carolyn's eyes narrowed. "No. Simply because I like to blow up stuff doesn't mean I can't enjoy a new ballgown or maybe a custom diamond bracelet?" She tilted her head at the last suggestion.

"You're ridiculous," Red laughed.

"I will not be buying you any diamonds, Carolyn," Elise said, tipping her nose down over her translations again. "But she's right. If you need to apologize to someone, perhaps a gift is the right idea."

Was he really that bad at lying? Both his sisters saw right through him. But they couldn't know about Aly. Not yet. After all, she was still a secret, in more ways than one.

14

ALY

The gutters ran with last night's rainwater. The stench of Mardon's livestock auction mixed with the twangy smell of wet streets to make a bouquet that reminded Aly of home. Her nose flared at the smell. Kitrel had been home for seventeen years, but it had been a place of shadow and silence, a place of ignorance and a freedom that had cost her mother her life. Renna's choice to hide Aly from the world hadn't made sense at the time; it had angered Aly and cultivated assumptions that were difficult to overcome, but at times Aly yearned for the quiet of her mother's cabin, the oblivion to the world's problems.

A cat slunk into a side street, and Aly snapped back to the present. She sensed the animal's Truthwell as it trotted along the side of a stone building. Not the lyth. The animal's brand was burned into its side anyway, declaring it someone's pet.

The brands were a necessity, but it didn't make them any less gruesome or fun to administer. A cattle brand was one thing. A dog, a cat. Those were worse. Most people, when they came across unbranded cats or dogs, simply eliminated them rather than inflicting the branding process on the animals.

There were entire organizations dedicated to branding street animals while others were dedicated to the extermination of them. In all ideologies, there were competing viewpoints and rarely much ground for discussion.

Aly was glad the cat had a visible brand. Maybe it would survive the next week. People in Mardon were unloading pistols at all manner of moving creatures. Rats were handled mostly by the extermination fanatics, but the ones missing a brand were poisoned or shot by the rest of Mardon's lyth-frenzied populace.

I'll find it, Aly told herself for the hundredth time. If the creature had been sent to hurt Red, it was her responsibility to kill it. She didn't think it would return to the palace, her magic had at least sent it away injured, but she wouldn't rest until it lay dead at her feet. And it couldn't reenter the palace, not now that its invitation had been revoked.

I can't believe he invited a lyth into his house, Aly thought for the dozenth time. *He let the stupid thing in!*

Her mind wandered back to the way he'd stormed up her bedroom stair. To the way his eyes had widened when he'd seen her in her nightgown. To the way he'd stood close when she'd shooed him out of her sitting room. Red was stubborn and a fool for wanting her to cast the curse back into her father.

But he was a handsome fool. His fear of death was making him do stupid things. *Stop this!* She tossed away the distracting thoughts and focused.

Walking under her shroud, she hugged the walls of the buildings in the streets that already bustled with activity leading up to Mardon's weekly market. Wagons wheeled down the streets, some carrying goats, others chickens or pigs. The smaller animals had tiny brands or ear tags. The chickens had bands around their legs.

None of these animals were the lyth, but what an excellent place to hide a shapeshifting creature. Aly was certain the beast would be hidden among the auction animals. Too easy not to.

Or perhaps, that was the very reason it wouldn't be here.

A man, impatient at the slow progress of a pair of enormous oxen, bumped his wheelbarrow full of potatoes up onto the sidewalk and bustled toward Aly. With a whisper of a spell, she lifted herself into the air and clung to the gutter as the wheelbarrow trundled past.

Her feet touched down quietly. The king was still at the palace, though from this distance, she couldn't tell if he was in the garden or the library or his personal study. At least within palace grounds, he was safe.

Pulling from his Truthwell was as easy at this distance as it was when she was near him. With Gevar, and likewise with Grey, she had needed to remain near them to Pull from their Truthwells, not because a Truthwell's power lost strength when it moved away, but because they became harder to see when distant. Red's Truthwell, on the other hand, burned like a bonfire, always on the horizon of Aly's magical sight.

This was more evidence that he was, indeed, a Beacon.

However, the evil of his death curse crawled in, dark and fingerlike at the edges, casting shadows on his brightness that would one day encompass all his light. But a Beacon couldn't be snuffed out. Surely.

Thus, as the curse grew, it was more evidence that he was not a Beacon, and she was not the Beholder.

The streets were becoming too crowded. With a deep breath, she gathered up more energy from Red's Truthwell and jumped straight up, cloak billowing, and landed softly on a slanted rooftop dotted with chimneys. The smell was cleaner, crisper up here, save for the occasional whiff of soot.

In a squat, hands anchoring herself to the tiles, she pressed her consciousness outward like she had after the funeral. Red's Truthwell responded. Her awareness grew, blanketing the city.

Thousands upon thousands of Truthwells called to her. The magic inside them was almost eager to be directed. Like water over stones, her magic passed over them all, even those choked with darkness, looking for one that would present itself as entirely black.

A lyth could hide its Truthwell, but only when it sensed someone was searching for it. She had a limited amount of time to scan the city before the lyth would suspect it was being hunted and shrink into nothingness.

How the creatures did this, no one could explain. Only one other lyth in history had managed it—the one she'd killed at the wedding six years ago. The night everything had changed for Aly.

Grey!

She could feel his Truthwell in the city. He was leaving the city, headed north. He was heading home, at this early morning hour.

Still undertaking late-night business? Curiosity, and perhaps a need to be mad at *something*, drove her toward his familiar Truthwell. She used very little magic as she scampered over the rooftops, dropping silently into a deserted street several blocks from the city market.

With her magical awareness still stretching, she sensed something flicker, then disappear.

Her muscles froze, all attention lightning-focused. There had been a murky darkness, then nothing.

It was the lyth.

"Toss you, Grey!" she screamed into the silent street. She'd been thinking about Grey, and the lyth had slipped by her.

She reeled her magical awareness back in and tried to recall exactly where she'd felt the lyth's presence. It had been to her right, maybe six blocks?

With all her speed, and a little extra from magic, she bolted down a street that wound to the right. She cast her magic out in waves, hoping to catch the beast off-guard again. The pulsating awareness of hundreds of Truthwells made her nearly dizzy as she ran, but fear and determination and rage drove her onward.

After several minutes of running, her lungs ached and her heart felt ready to burst. The concentration it took to fly only allowed her to maintain one or two other spells, but she had to do it. She couldn't let the beast escape again.

Above the horses, above the carriages, above the streetlights, Aly tore through the air, cloak battling the breeze. With a hand, she held down her mask so it wouldn't fly away. She'd never flown so fast. The energy she drew from Red's Truthwell almost sizzled in her mind. *It won't run out*, she reminded herself as she arced up over a building to cut a corner.

When she reached the place she'd sensed the beast, she slammed back down, not taking the energy necessary to craft a perfect spell for landing. For a moment, she dropped all enchantments and simply breathed, bent double, on the sunlit street. A few people rounded a corner and stopped short.

With a grunt, she shoved her shroud back around her. The people yelped and scurried away.

The beast was gone. She knew it, but she wasn't ready to give up.

From her shroud, she pushed her mind outward, knowing the beast could be in the building beside her and she'd never sense it. She had to try something, but she had no other ideas.

"I know you're here!"

She looked around. She'd come to the edge of town. The main road out of Mardon was directly ahead, and she could see carriages passing by. One of them was Lord Weston Grey's carriage.

She'd caught up to him.

Then a woman screamed and glass shattered. A horse whinnied. Aly's heart thudded inside her chest.

If the lyth was here to harm the king, harming one of his councilmen might be a pleasing alternative.

Darting out into the busy street, she saw that Grey's carriage had stopped. A few people stood staring up at the lord's carriage, pointing. Then she noticed the glass in the street. One of his carriage windows was busted.

One leap put her atop the carriage. She peered inside, prepared to see blood, a small animal gnawing on Grey's neck, or some other horror.

All she saw instead were empty seats.

He had a Protector. Of course, the man had shrouded them.

Aly swung down to the street and searched with her eyes for any animals. Then all the hairs on her arms and neck rose as a thought slammed into her. The lyth could be standing right behind her, an innocent pedestrian staring from the sidewalk.

Standing slowly, Aly rounded on the onlookers.

Heart pounding, she backed toward the carriage. If Grey was shrouded, he'd still have mass. She opened the door and climbed in, ignoring the gasps from the small crowd as the door appeared to open of its own accord.

Her face bumped into something firm and soft, something that smelled like cold stone hallways and varnished wood.

She pushed her shroud around the interior of the carriage, thus revealing herself to anyone inside.

After a short pause during which Aly sensed a warm body scooting away from her on the seat, Grey dropped into view. His sorcerer had released him from his shroud.

"What happened?" she blurted.

Grey stared at her a minute. "What are you doing here?"

"I'm on the king's business! Answer me!"

"A man threw a stone at my carriage window."

Toss that. "The lyth is here."

He stiffened. "You're certain?"

"It was here five minutes ago."

Grey nodded at something Aly couldn't hear, some silent

communication from his Protector. "Thank you for the information. I will be safe. You may go."

How dare he dismiss her like that! She sat back, dumbfounded. "You want me to leave?" The other night at the ball, he'd seemed less inclined for her to leave, despite the way she'd harangued him for letting Red decide to travel north.

His eyes closed slowly. "No, Aly. But you must go hunt this beast. Kill it. You're the best hope we have against it."

The compliment startled her. It flung her back to a previous life, when she'd served Lord Weston Grey as his Protector.

"Says the man people call Beast Slayer."

He smiled. It was awful. It reminded her of what was lost.

Aly slid out of the carriage, needing to escape the feeling of being trapped. She hadn't meant to repay his compliment with one of her own, but she'd done it anyway. *Stupid, stupid.*

When she'd closed the door, Grey leaned out. "Aly." His voice was urgent. "My sorcerer just detected the lyth. It's Well disappeared, but it was moving toward Wyndall's estate."

15

RED

Visions of foxbloods and shapeshifting lyths darkened King Frederick's mind as he strolled down a market street in Mardon. Aly had vanished again to hunt for the lyth, and he'd happily not interfered. With her gone, it was the perfect opportunity to visit the city without her knowing.

Red was hunting something specific, an apology gift for Aly, but he wasn't sure what it would be. *How do I apologize to a magical, invisible, maddening woman whose very existence is the reason for my father's death and my own curse?*

He strolled through the city accompanied by Seb, Bernard, and three guards. He paused in the lane as a carriage rolled by. When he thought about why he was out here, endangering himself for the sake of a woman who made his very blood boil, he contemplated returning to the palace.

No, she needs to want to travel north with me. His mind was made up. To heal him, Aly would face her father—and his job, his entire aim, would be convincing her to do just that.

The city buzzed with news of the lyth in Mardon and the foxblood in Luxler as Red and Seb, amid stolen glances and rude finger pointing from the citizens, strolled through the aisles of Mardon's weekly market.

A lane of kiosks begged them to buy feathered masks, hand-carved pipes, imported teas, and stained leather pouches. The smell of oolong competed with the heady scent of cowhide; the crisp freshness of cut wood drowned out the sharp tang of drying glue as the mask maker finished adding a bouquet of peacock feathers to a painted blue beak.

The mask maker stood to bow to his king. Down the street, the words *foxblood* and *lyth* rose above the chatter and the bustle. Luxler was on the way to Bulvarna—they would have to travel through it. Red had sent messages, via the sorcerers stationed at the border, to the men at the Canyon to increase patrols and to send out hunting parties for the wandering foxblood. Fortunately, the creatures usually traveled alone.

"Think she'll be there?" Seb lifted a brow and the corner of his mouth.

Red's mind jumped to Aly, but he reminded himself Seb didn't know Aly existed. "Who?"

"Kassia's niece. Lady Mira."

Oh, her. "Let's hope not." Red was glad he'd appointed Seb to his council, but he now regretted that his best friend would have to march straight into danger with him; his advisors would travel north with their king for the summit.

An elderly woman sat at a table filled with tiny, knitted scenes of Tanderan folk tales. One fabric square depicted Gevar's marriage to Isabelle. In the image, Red's mother had little wings peeking out behind her back and hovered, barefoot, over the crystal surface of Lake Corinel.

"Fine work you have here," he said, nodding at the woman, who immediately cupped her face with her hands and began trembling in glee.

"Look, I've been telling you your face scares people," Seb

said, knocking Red with an elbow. "There's proof." He lifted a hand toward the woman.

A week ago, Red would have laughed. Now he simply felt like those words were vinegar tossed over his otherwise good meal. Wanting to make a point, he said, "Mira better *not* be there, in fact."

Seb snatched his fingers back from a fox-fur hat. "Why not? Think you'd still go all water-knees on me?" Seb had been thrilled with the notion of traveling to Bulvarna. Even though he'd moved to the palace nearly a decade ago, he'd never had the chance to travel outside of Tandera. That would change now that he was on the king's council.

Red rolled his eyes. He still hadn't told Seb about the curse. Telling Seb was tantamount to admitting his own impending death. "No. I'm certain I care nothing for her now." The one time he'd seen Kassia's niece, he'd been young, and she'd been as beautiful as the dawn. That was all. Seb hadn't let him forget it.

Seb chuckled. "Okay, sure, but what if she is there? She's the queen's niece. I mean, wouldn't a marriage with a Bulvarnan *make* Kassia sign the agreement?"

Red stiffened. "That will not happen."

The gravity in Red's tone surprised Seb. "All right," he said, lifting two hands. "All right, but you'll have to marry someday, King. That's a pretty powerful institution—marriage. You'll have to use it well. For Tandera," he added at his friend's scowl. "And any girl would want to marry a king."

Seb stated this like it was enviable.

But, straighter and faster than his arrows, Red's mind shot to the one person he did not expect to think about right now.

He wasn't sure Aly *could* marry, given that she'd outlive anyone except another Master Sorcerer; she'd outlive him by decades, if not an entire century. Also, she was Bound to serve the king, which meant meeting another sorcerer would be unlikely. Why she was on his mind right now, he didn't know. He shoved the thought away.

To his left, a bent-double man teetered proudly behind a table of knives. The smooth blades reflected the brown and burgundy kiosk rooftop and the gray slit of sky between the stalls.

"Fine blades," Red said, more to shift his mind away from Aly than anything else. Marriage was always something he'd wanted to look forward to, despite his father's warnings that marriage, especially to a commoner, was a difficult river to swim, albeit worth it for Isabelle. But right now, Red merely needed to live to the end of the year.

The man muttered an incoherent response, snatching up one knife and twisting its hilt out toward the king.

"How much?"

"Like you don't have enough of those already," Seb quipped, stuffing his hands in his pockets and leaning over a smoking tray of incense in the next stall.

Bernard paid the man, and Red smiled his kingly best as he walked away. "No, I may not need another knife, but that man can now say he sells to the king. Think of how many knives he'll sell now. I just paid for his next year's rent, his daughter's dowry, and probably his grandchildren's education." The look on Seb's brow puzzled Red. "What?"

Seb shook his head, then nodded. "You'll make a fine king."

"If the Maker allows." His father had always used that phrase, and Red felt the need to pawn off any success of his own on someone greater than him. Because there was no way he'd turn out to be a good king on his own or even live to *be* one for very long.

The tunnel of market stalls stopped abruptly at the end of the narrow lane, opening up into Mardon's main square. On market days, the square held livestock auctions. The smell of hay and fur and dung wafted down the small lane.

"Can we not?" Seb asked, turning back the way they'd come,

halting before running into one of the three guards that trailed the king.

Red laughed, glad for the impromptu mood change. "Oh, look, Seb! Goats!"

Stretching out his lower lip, Seb wheezed in disgust. "Nasty things!"

"You and goats. I'll never understand it."

"They creep me out!"

"But I haven't found what I'm looking for yet." He doubted Aly could make use of any livestock, so he turned to walk back the way they had come.

"Tell me what you're looking for, and I'll help you look," Seb pressed.

Since the attack at the ball, Protectors, though rare, were out in number, standing in shadows and against walls, their white cloaks and colorful masks standing out against the drab clothing of the commoners and the dark suits of the nobility. The Protectors as well as the Watchers, men and women designated to check every living animal for a brand, were only a small comfort to Red as he and Seb strolled away from the auction, glad to be moving away from the animals.

The lyth had still not been caught, unless Aly had disposed of it in the last hour.

A dog barked nearby, and Red jumped.

"Everything all right?" asked Seb.

"Fine." He glanced around for Veeter Yin, who walked a few paces behind them. "I still need to find that gift."

Red ran a hand along the edge of a table stacked with spices in bowls. The warm scent of cumin wafted up to his nose, blissfully obliterating the smells from the auction behind them.

"At least tell me who it's for. Elise? Carolyn?" Seb's easy demeanor crept back over him. "Carol would love a mask. She'd prance around in it to breakfast."

Red chuckled. "She would."

"Elise, then? Okay, what about… Oh, what does Elise even like? All she does is paint."

"And read," Red added.

"Oh, buy her an Yvesy! All the ladies love his stills of flowers. It's like buying an eternal bouquet," he said with his hand lifted wistfully to the sky. "But you wouldn't want to purchase that for your sister, so never mind." He dropped his hand.

A painting was a good idea, but Aly already had an Yvesy hanging in her room. In fact, it *was* a still of flowers.

"You really won't tell me who you're shopping for? Something's changed in you, Brother."

Deep between his ribs, Red appreciated the closeness he felt with Seb, the closeness he hoped could remain despite the circlet now resting on his own brow and the bows and curtsies he received from everyone they passed. Wanting to show Seb that he considered him his best friend, Red decided to share a partial truth. "It is for a woman, just not my sisters."

"Wait, seriously? Okay, now you've got some talking to do."

Instantly, Red wished he hadn't said *that* particular truth. "I can't tell you much else. Not right now."

"Whoa, whoa." Seb lifted two hands. "The king is buying a gift for a secret girl? *This* is news!" He looked around, almost as if he wanted to call the shopkeepers and traders in to hear the gossip.

For a fleeting instant, Red feared he would.

"But okay, okay, no more questions. What're we hunting? A nice fur? A fancy dress? Jewelry?" He hung on the syllables of this last word like they were the rope of a church bell that would wake the whole town.

Ignoring Seb, Red turned toward a table of small ladies' purses that he'd purposefully avoided moments before. What would an invisible sorcerer need with a dainty little purse?

"One of these?" Seb asked, hopping over to peer down at the bags.

Red smiled at the woman behind the table but shook his head and stepped away.

"What's she like? Right, no questions!" Seb cocked a wicked grin.

Hoping to dampen the grin on Seb's face—and pry his mind off the questions Seb must be thinking about him and Aly—Red offered one more bit of information. "The gift is an apology."

"Well, well," Seb began, turning to the wares on his side of the street. "Now we've got something." After a few minutes, Seb said, "When I was seeing Corinia, and she caught me kissing Lilac, I bought her a diamond bracelet. It seemed to work pretty well."

"But you're not still seeing Corinia."

"Good point. All right, fine." Another few minutes passed in silence. "Okay, how about a good book? I can never get enough of those."

"That's what *you'd* want as a forgive-me gift, and maybe Elise. But not her."

Seb shrugged. "Merely trying to help. You don't seem to be finding anything."

He was right. What does one buy for a woman capable of transforming flowers into flames and welding water into shapes?

What did she want?

He gulped. He didn't really know, except that she wanted freedom from the threat of her father. Instead, Red was making her march straight toward him.

Suddenly, sweat bubbled up on Red's temples and chest. The first pulse of a headache thrummed, a beast waking. *Not now!* He had gone the whole morning without one, after Aly had pushed some more healing magic through him.

He paused before the table of masks. Sweeping black feathers nestled against one another on a mask that scooped low over its cheekbones and fanned wide above the forehead. Two gold-rimmed eye slits made the mask appear alive. Beautiful and disguised. A way to see and not be seen.

Aly's father already knew she served the Tanderan king. As soon as they arrived in Kassia's palace, he would know his daughter had come. Her sorcerer's mask would make her an even easier target. What if she came in as a guest? She could slip in as a courtier traveling north with the king and his men. No one knew what she looked like, her father included.

Red picked up the mask and paid the merchant.

Queen Kassia had not only accepted their offer to discuss Canyon security, she'd already scheduled a masquerade ball for the final night of the negotiations.

"Really?" Seb asked, looking down at the mask as they walked. "I'm sorry, dearest, but here's a mask you can wear so I don't have to look at your face." Seb inhaled, dropping the Referen accent. "Should work!"

Before Red could snap back a response, shouts and the sound of galloping hooves filled the narrow road. A man on horseback broke through the crowd, already swinging down from his saddle.

"Your Majesty," he announced, bowing while still holding the reins. Slightly out of breath, he fumbled through his next words. "You must return to the palace at once, for your safety. The lyth has been spotted on Duke Wyndall's estate."

Their horses thundered toward Duke Wyndall's ivy-covered mansion at the edge of town. A few surprised marketgoers had lent their horses willingly at the request of their king.

Where I go, she goes, Red thought, clinging to the reins and a wad of horse hair.

It was madness to be heading *toward* a lyth, especially one ordered to harm him. But Aly had killed a lyth before, and she would do it again. When she did, Red would have ample fodder to support his argument that she could face her father.

With all the available Protectors headed toward the duke's estate, Red ignored a flicker of fear that told him he should have returned to the palace. To Red's surprise as he, Seb, and his guards galloped through the front gate, people in day dresses and spring suits scattered like chickens.

"You all must leave!" he bellowed as he rode down the long drive.

Women covered their mouths with lace gloves, and men swept into hasty bows as they recognized who spoke.

Wyndall's estate was one of the oldest in Mardon. Built centuries ago, the main house, constructed in the Rothman style, was a tourist attraction among Mardonians. Wyndall and his wife enjoyed the attention and didn't mind complete strangers strolling through their gardens and touring their art gallery.

Aly would be here by now. Surely she could sense the danger. He didn't know how he was supposed to summon her when he had no way of contacting her. *She* could contact *him* from anywhere, but the magic didn't work the other way around.

"Why haven't you cleared the grounds?" demanded Red as the duke scurried out to meet him. Red swung down from his horse and turned toward the butler, who remained in a half bow. "Get rid of all these people!" he shouted at the man.

Seb called down from atop his mount. "I'll round them up." Yanking the horse around, he kicked his heels and rode away.

"Tell me of the lyth," Red demanded.

"Sire, it was a kitchen girl. You can take her word for what you will." Wyndall sounded apologetic, as if all the fuss wasn't worth it.

"Take me to her."

"No need, sire. I can relay her impression."

Red lifted his brows at the duke. "I will speak with her." To the butler, he now ordered, "Fetch the girl."

With a nod, the man departed.

"Where was it? *What* was it? And do you not have Watchers here? Good lord, man!" Red marched toward the house after the butler.

Wyndall followed. "She was in the dining room, my lord, serving breakfast to the duchess. Said she saw out the window a funny looking shape lumbering across the lawn. Said when she looked closer, it was a *bear*. A bear! Here!"

Inside the marble foyer, their voices stretched out into echoes. "That would be the lyth, then."

"But can you be sure she really saw a bear? I sent my man for your sorcerer, not for you, Your Majesty." Wyndall waved away a man in livery holding a silver tray and beckoned the king into a sitting room. "Please, sit."

Red remained standing. "You do realize that my sorcerer goes where I go?" *For the most part*, he mused, thinking of the market.

Wyndall nodded, wringing his hands as he looked out a tall window.

The butler returned with a thin young woman in tow. She paled at the sight of the king. Her entire body went rigid, which made her curtsey look painful.

"Tell the king what you saw," barked Wyndall.

Red, his blood still hammering from the ride, stared at the girl. She was terrified. She might have been fourteen, if that. His own mother had been only a few years older than this girl when the king had noticed her and decided she was fit to be a queen. It was strange how a single glance could change the entire course of a person's life.

"It's all right," he said. "I'd like to know exactly what you saw." He perched on the edge of a couch, to better allow the girl some room to breathe.

She stuttered through her sentences, starting half of them over again. Finally, Red gathered that she'd seen a black bear; she'd sent out a fellow servant with a pistol to do away with the bear, and the man had not come back. Too afraid to send anyone else after it, she'd alerted the duke that she'd spotted an unbranded animal on the grounds.

Red nodded. "You did right."

"But it could very well be nothing! Perhaps a passing shadow. The girl could have seen anything—the way the fear of this lyth has warped people's minds."

Glancing out the window, Red saw people fleeing toward the exit. "The tourists weren't that concerned, were they? Busy day on the estate." He looked at Wyndall. "Fear only shapes us when we let it. I think *your* fear is shaping your ability to trust this girl's —I'm sorry, what was your name?"

She gasped so loudly that Red tried not to laugh.

"It's Margaret," Wyndall said. Then he scratched his head. "It is Margaret, right? Yes, yes. Margaret. I believe she's new."

"Well, Margaret, thank you for your time. You may go."

The girl, face splotchy with blush, curtseyed again and darted from the room.

As soon as the girl left, Red heard Aly's voice in his head. *I'm here. Outside, by the woodshed. I've found him.*

"My sorcerer has found the bear," Red announced.

Not the bear, the body.

16

ALY

The man's body lay beside his pistol.

Aly knelt in her massive white cloak, her mask hiding her from Wyndall and Seb and the other men gathered around. Among the crowd was Wyndall's sorcerer, also wearing the customary white cloak, but this man's mask depicted the stripes and mouth of a tiger.

The duke turned his face away from the blood and pressed the back of his hand to his mouth.

Aly could sense Red staring down at her, but her task was before her. The man was dead, that was an unchangeable fact. Magic couldn't help him now.

Grey, who'd insisted on coming, stood beside Seb. All the people who most needed to be protected from the lyth were here, where the lyth had just made a kill. With a spell, she closed up the man's still-bleeding wounds.

"The tracks lead this way," Grey pointed out.

"Those aren't bear tracks," Seb said, squatting down. "Cat. Those look like cat tracks."

Wyndall shuddered. "Tiger?" He inadvertently looked over at his sorcerer, whose mask resembled the very beast they sought.

Grey shrugged. "Or leopard. Or cougar. Hard to say."

"All of the above, right?" said Seb, standing again. "This creature can change into anything."

Yes, it could. The beast's magical presence had again disappeared. Aly couldn't sense it at all, which meant it was the human-shifting lyth.

Aly stood too. All eyes watched her, as if her words alone would decide the next steps.

Aly said to Red alone, *Ask if Wyndall personally knows all of his staff.*

Red looked at the men around him. Seb. Grey. Wyndall. A half dozen of Wyndall's men, most of them guards. He turned to Wyndall. "Do you personally know all of your staff?"

Wyndall fumbled his answer, his composure slipping as he registered the real reason for the question. "I, yes, I believe so."

It's still here, Aly said to Red, turning to head into the house. As she thought about it, it made sense. Though she couldn't sense the beast, it had killed here. Lyths only had bursts of magic, enough to shift perhaps a dozen times before needing to crawl away and hide as they regained strength. To kill involved shifting multiple times, to confuse the enemy. The beast had likely shifted while fleeing Aly's search and was nearing its limit for changing. They had to locate it before it turned into a mouse and slipped away into a hole. Just because the creature could act human for a time didn't mean it had the mind of a man. Attack. Survive. These were among its instincts. Reason and strategy, fortunately, were not among them.

"Split up," Red said. "Wyndall, take the grounds with your men. Grey, you and Seb take the lower floors. A—I and my sorcerer will take the upper floors."

Watch it, you almost said my name.

His lips pursed in annoyance.

Aly vanished, making Wyndall jump. A few of the men cursed under their breaths. The groups departed.

When Aly and Red entered the house, Aly pushed her shroud around Red, absorbing him in her private world. "You were reckless to come here." Her tone was clipped.

"I came so you would."

She glanced at him. "I was already on my way."

Red nodded. "I suppose I should have assumed as much, but I had no idea where you were, what you were doing, or how to contact you. I rode here as fast as I could, knowing that somehow you'd find me." His brow pinched a little, as if he was digesting the way those words had sounded and didn't like the taste. "I don't care how powerful or qualified those other Protectors are, you're the best chance against this threat." His brow remained pinched as Aly stared at him in mild shock.

That was a compliment, she mused.

She scampered up the last few steps of the large stone staircase and said over her shoulder, "You have to stay out of the way. I can set an enchantment and leave you here while I look."

"That's idiotic."

"That's my job." She stepped forward, finger pointed at him. "*You* have to stay alive." His eyes widened. "And don't bother with the chivalry thing, because it is completely irrelevant to our relationship."

"Chivalry is never irrelevant." His mouth twitched at the corner.

"The beast is here. I think it may be in human form. Wyndall doesn't seem to have much of a clue about who is working for him."

"True words." They set off down a hallway.

Duchess Wyndall had been evacuated with the tourists, as had everyone of rank who had been inside the house. The only people left behind were the servants.

A startled woman dropped a basket of laundry at the sight of Aly and the king.

"You should leave," Red said to the woman. "It's not safe

here." At the woman's bewildered face, he added, "On second thought…" He glanced at Aly. She shook her head. "Okay, you may go."

They had searched three bedrooms when they heard footsteps thundering down the upstairs hall.

"Sire." Grey was out of breath. "Come quickly."

Downstairs, a man's screams cracked the stillness, echoing off the stone floors and walls. Smells of drying meat and fresh bread wafted through the narrow hall.

Aly ran ahead of Red and Grey. They burst into the kitchen to find Seb cradling his arm, pistol drooping in his fingers. As soon as he saw them, he collapsed against the wall.

With a shout, Aly pelted pots and kitchen utensils toward the fleeing form of a girl. In the girl's hand was a kitchen knife.

"Wait!" Red shouted.

The girl had no discernable Truthwell—she was the lyth. Aly raced after her, the pots exploding at Aly's command. A shard of an iron skillet sank into the lyth's back just as the creature was transforming into something with fur. The transformation halted. When the girl faceplanted against the stone, she stayed down. Still.

"Help Seb," Red ordered Aly as he whirled on the duke.

Aly checked the lyth for a pulse, then, satisfied, darted to where Seb slumped against the wall.

Behind her, Wyndall said, "I had no idea!"

"Of course you didn't. That's the *point*. You had *no idea* who she was," snarled the king.

Grey stepped past Red and the duke, behind Aly, toward the fallen creature. Two men rushed forward with him. The small space was crowded and hot.

Wyndall continued, "But I've never even seen that one."

That one. Was he using that phrase because the girl was really a beast underneath or because he felt like servants were interchangeable objects—*this one* or *that one*? Aly reached for Seb's wound to heal it, but he slapped her hand away. With a wave of dread, Aly pushed magic through Seb, then recoiled. She tried again, to be sure.

Oh no, she thought as her magic sense brushed against what felt like a barb.

"But a young girl? I would have never—" said Wyndall.

"Exactly," said Grey from a squatted position beside the lyth. "You would have never suspected a petite young girl like that to be a beast from the Deep." His eyes flickered across to Aly.

"Oh, I suppose you would? The expert on all things beastly."

Grey's features turned icy as he stood. "No, much simpler. Unlike you, Duke, I'm not in the habit of employing girls barely old enough to leave their mother's house." His eyes closed momentarily, as if remembering something.

Aly glanced up at him from where she knelt by Seb. *That's right, Grey, I was seventeen. Does that make it any better?* Aly's heart twanged a little but mostly she just felt angry. Angry that this beast was here. Angry that Red had come and put himself in more danger. Angry that even if he survived the attacks hurled at him by his country's enemies, he'd die anyway if they failed to find a cure. And she sure as sunrise wasn't going to cast his curse back into her father. Red had no idea what he was asking for by heading toward Bulvarna.

A small part of Aly admired the fact that Red was going to attempt to talk sense into Queen Kassia. If the Lady Wolf did not increase her patrols at the Canyon's edge, more beasts might seep out into the world. Someone had to try to persuade her.

Seb groaned. Aly grabbed his ankle, shoved her healing spell into him, and released him before he could kick her away. Red rushed to his friend, but Aly leaped up and stuck out her gloved hand, holding him back.

"What on earth?" he hissed through clenched teeth.

"He was bitten," she whispered, quiet enough that only the king and Grey could hear.

Red blinked, not comprehending. Grey, however, turned slowly toward Seb's slouched form. On Seb's right arm, above his elbow, was a small, curved set of thin puncture wounds seeping blood. That was not from a knife. It was a *bite*. A human bite.

Cold fear blanched Red's face. "Heal him. Do it now."

I healed the wound, but the infection is...resisting.

"What?" he snarled.

The look he gave her chilled her blood. Right now, she imagined she was not fitting into Red's preconceived ideas about what a sorcerer could and could not do.

She'd *tried* to save his father. She'd *tried* to apprehend the lyth in the palace. She could almost hear his accusations flying from his closed lips. Her cheeks burned and she was grateful, once again, for the phoenix mask that hid her features.

Red shoved her hand away and dropped down in front of Seb's boots. Aly lurched and grabbed his shoulder, attempting to hold him back. "Brother, how are you feeling?"

Seb fisted his hands by his sides. "You killed her." He glared up at Aly, ignoring Red's question. Aly pressed an enchantment around her king, Pulling deeply, crafting a wall she hoped was as strong as the stone beneath their feet. But as she Pulled from the king's Truthwell, she felt a little hitch, as if the Truthwell were simply sluggish today and didn't want to participate.

She'd *flown* with Red's energy earlier. This strange new sensation, more than the lyth, more than Seb's bite, stole her breath. The death curse was affecting her ability to Pull. *No. It's too soon.*

"That *girl* was the lyth," Red said, stepping backward.

When Seb turned his eyes on the king, he lost all recognition as a new and deeper malice entered his eyes. Aly muttered a line of the *Verad* and wove a spell to keep Seb seated. His body relaxed against the stone wall.

"Come on," Grey said, pulling the king away from his best friend. "Let's get you home. All of you." He pushed Red, gently but firmly, toward the door, and turned to help a dramatically weakened Seb to his feet.

Aly darted forward, stepping in front of Grey to reach Red. Did her back press against Lord Grey's chest?

She cast a quick spell to keep Seb's lips frozen shut. He wouldn't be passing his infection along while Grey helped him. Canyon beast bites worked like any other infection. They could be mild and result in nothing more than a few days under the weather—or rather, under the influence of lies. However, they could also be a nasty, fast sicknesses that twisted the minds of the infected until they became consumed by darkness.

Sebastian Thorin was now a threat to the king, and her magic was struggling to resolve that threat.

17

RED

U p, up, up. The king's legs burned by the time he had made three revolutions in the tight turning stair that lifted him to the sleeping quarters of the palace. He'd dismissed Bernard as soon as they'd entered the palace. Yin knew enough to remain out of sight as the king headed toward the sorcerer's chambers. After the events of today, Aly would not hide from him all night. He'd wait at her door, pound until morning if need be.

As he rounded the stairs and came to the landing on the fourth floor, he became aware of footfalls behind him.

Whipping around, he faced Aly, her eyes big and her sorcerer's cloak billowing open to reveal that she wore a white shirt tucked into pants, like a man. She had not intended to be seen tonight.

They both started shouting at once.

"What hap—"

"What did—" She scowled, waiting for him.

"What happened earlier? Why couldn't you heal him?" Accusation buzzed through his words like a swatted wasp.

"Do you want to hear the truth, or do you want to stay mad?"

He inhaled sharply but did not respond. She matched his gaze, staring up at him with an ire of her own. "My magic—with the curse, it's…getting weaker." Her gaze fell to her hands.

A thousand reckless, angry words threatened to burst from his mouth. *What good is a sorcerer who can't do magic?* He opened his mouth to say these words aloud, but the look on her face silenced him. It was a look of pain, of defeat, almost as if she could sense what he wanted to say and was wounded by his words before he ever spoke them. He recalled Elise's words to him; he needed to act like a king. Finally, he said, "Then what must we do to make you stronger?"

Her eyes widened. "The curse is darkening your Truthwell. As long as I'm Pulling from you alone—as I'm Bound to do—my magic will become weaker as you do."

That was not what he wanted to hear.

"What's going to happen to Seb?"

Aly's shoulders sank. "The magic has infected him. Usually, with a Canyon beast's bite, the infection affects the mind first. It kills our ability to detect and dismiss lies, but eventually, if left untreated, it turns physical. Vomiting, shakes, bowel trouble. Basically, he'll get so sick he won't be able to eat. If I can't heal him fully, his mind will turn darker and darker."

Red's resolve faltered. He took a step back.

She closed her mouth and stepped around him to continue onto the floor that held the king's quarters. He turned and followed.

"Wait," he said. "Why? Why did it target Wyndall's? You said it wouldn't come back." His attempt to keep the accusation out of his tone failed.

"I didn't exactly get to question the creature, but my guess is Dimitri, or maybe Kassia, *really* doesn't want this summit taking place, but Kassia couldn't outright refuse it. So, she thought she'd infect one of your council members, maybe bespell him to persuade you not to come. Maybe she wanted to infect Wyndall, but Seb was easier." At Red's horrified expression, Aly lifted her hands. "I don't know, okay! I have no idea why the lyth went to the duke's and then bit Sebastian. Once it left the palace grounds, it couldn't very well come back here, unless you invited it in *again*."

Red waited a moment for his temper to cool. "If your father wants to kill you, why keep us from traveling north, right to where he lives? Toss it all. It doesn't make sense."

"I agree. It doesn't make sense." In the candlelit hallway, she turned. Her cloak was so large it pooled on the floor around her bare feet. In one hand, she carried a pair of muddy shoes. The shoulders of the cloak swept outward, hiding her tiny frame. Her mask hung around the back of her neck, lost in the folds of her hood. "At first, I assumed you'd played right into their hands with your little decision to visit the Canyon and Bulvarna. However, it looks like they *don't* want us going there. To tell you the truth, that frightens me more. Why wouldn't they want us heading toward the most dangerous place on earth?"

Confusion and anger summoned a few more phrases to his lips, but he held them back. He'd wanted to give her an apology gift; now it seemed like a dumb idea. He'd sent the mask back to the palace with a courier while he'd ridden to Wyndall's estate.

Guess I'll give it to Carolyn after all.

Outside his bedchamber, she stopped, spun, and waved an arm at his door. "I have escorted you to your chambers, Your Majesty. Will there be anything else I can do for you this evening?"

An asp-like venom dripped through her words. He'd wanted to apologize but could not bring himself to say the words. He leaned past her and opened the door to his rooms, his shoulder pressing into her broad cloak.

He paused, hand on the golden doorknob. Without looking at her, he said, "If you can't heal Seb, then I'll find someone who can." It came out worse than he'd intended, and her face lit with rage.

Aly's breath was close enough that he could smell it—fresh as mint, as if she hadn't eaten a bite all day. When *did* she ever eat? The poison of his guilt began to sting even more.

Red turned now, his arm against the open door, his body only inches from hers. If the moment had lasted merely a second, the closeness would not have been strange. Now that he paused there, so close, he felt it was too much. He stepped into his room, widening the space between them. He still felt like a bull in a pen with Aly as the sole target.

She stormed in after him, moving across a tiger rug toward the hearth. This was the third time she'd entered his private rooms. Then again, he'd barged into hers, too.

"Listen to me!" she shouted, tossing all propriety and respect out the tall windows.

Shock at her brazenness silenced him long enough for her to begin.

"In the garden, I had hope," she said. "Hope that your Truthwell was…different."

He rubbed his chin and frowned. "Sorry I'm such a disappointment."

At that moment, Aly looked dangerous. Her ability to use any item in the room as an explosive device or to set his hair on fire with the flick of a wrist made him regret—nearly—his last words. He chucked his coronet, a little too forcefully, onto a nearby table. It slid off and clattered to the floor.

Aly squatted down to her ankles, again her strange movements evidence of her years of invisibility. Her cloak puddled around her. "Take your eyes off yourself for one second and you'd see that—"

"What? That now my best friend is going to die too? I *see* it, Aly. But I thought I had a sorcerer who could prevent all this."

They glared at each other. This entire day had been a train wreck.

And now Seb was infected with Canyon magic. Aly's power was waning. Red was dying. Elise had agreed to ride north with them—putting her in danger as well. He'd been stupid to agree to her demand. That poem could very well be a dead end. There was no guarantee it held the mysterious cure they sought. But they were running out of options.

"I'll tell Elise to stay. As a member of my council, Seb will ride north with us. He can work on the poem. He reads Kirish."

Aly shook her head. "His mind won't be right. Even if he stays lucid for a week, two weeks, his ability to translate will be lessened."

Red slammed his fist on top of his mantle. "Then find another sorcerer to heal him! Grey has one. Since you know him so well, why don't you ask him?"

The stillness that fell over Aly made Red fidget even more. "Yes, he does. We can see if Grey's Protector can heal Seb."

"If? Isn't it a simple spell?"

Aly strode toward the door, which was still open. "I'm beginning to think none of what's happened these past few months has been simple. Maybe we're only just discovering the tip of what my father has been up to for years. What's this?"

She stood looking down at his breakfast table where a box sat open, displaying the king's purchase from earlier. A black feather mask.

"I. Um." He sounded like a monosyllabic troll. *Why did they leave it there?* "I bought you something." It sounded too personal. He should have worded it differently, but it was too late to change that.

She lifted the mask.

"So you can show yourself at Kassia's ball and not be seen." *Too rehearsed?* He'd thought through what he'd say about the gift, but now that he'd said it, he felt like a court jester tossing lunacies out like juggling pins. "Queen Kassia said she would host a masquerade in honor of our negotiations. For once, everyone else will have on masks too. I thought you might be safer if you attended as a guest rather than my sorcerer."

"Oh."

What does that mean? Red rubbed his fingers together at his sides for lack of anything else to do with them.

"Toss me," she muttered. She kept her eyes on the mask. Was it shaking?

Before he could ask what she meant, she turned and darted from the room.

"That did not go as planned," he said to the empty room. A marble phoenix statue beside the door peered its white eye at him, as if laughing.

The whole evening had not gone as planned. In fact, not a bit of his kingship had gone as planned.

As he rolled in bed, fighting his headache, he wondered if the trip to Bulvarna was the worst decision he could have made.

The morning of departure came with a quickly dissipating fog and the sun intent on proving it was nearly summer. A dread the size of Mardon's cathedral set in Red's stomach.

Two woodwolves were spotted—and fortunately killed— outside of Mardon, and the letter bearing this news had arrived with the king's morning tea. A last-minute addition of guards was assembling.

It appeared Aly was right. Someone really didn't want them traveling north, someone with the ability to direct creatures of the Deep where to hunt.

Aly had been distant since the night she'd found the mask. Was it because every time she looked at him, she saw his darkening Truthwell? Or was it because he'd decided to march straight to where her father lurked, as if handing the man his own decades-long revenge?

Whatever the reason, Aly wouldn't meet the king's gaze, even when they spoke in private before leaving the palace. She'd cast her protective spells around the palace and also around the princesses and Isabelle. He had to hope they were strong enough to hold off any threats should they arise.

Seven carriages in all departed from the palace. A king never traveled alone.

The king's council, made up of several of his chancellors, Seb, and the High Priest, was coming. Also coming along were Elise, a handful of attendants, a guard for each carriage, and two sorcerers: Aly and Grey's Protector. Lord Alexander's wife, to Red's displeasure, was coming with her husband, insisting on seeing the great country of the north.

To make the situation worse, Lady Alexander was towing along the young Leeta Merrythorn, who was a close friend of the Alexander's. Her parents hoped the trip would afford her a chance to get to know the king on a more personal level. Baron Merrythorn had no idea what he was agreeing to, sending his daughter toward the Canyon with nothing more than a false hope of spending time with a king who had no more interest in her than in a passing butterfly.

In his carriage, the king sat opposite Elise, her nose bent toward a copy of Kanto's poems. She was nearing the end of the text. He'd attempted again to convince her to remain at the palace, despite Aly's words that they needed her translation ability. However, as his successor, should the death curse have its way, Elise had more reasons for coming than she or Red admitted. He wasn't sure how many more weeks he had left to live, should they fail. It was good to spend those weeks with at least one family member.

He remembered the days before he began traveling with his father. When the king was out, the palace relaxed. He remembered the days of racing the halls with Seb and requesting tea at all hours, just for the crisp cookies that accompanied it. Elise would not be able to enjoy that laxity this time.

Red's carriage breezed with cool air as it rattled along with no horse pulling it—thanks to Aly's magic. If Red's Truthwell hadn't been cluttered with shadows, she could have pushed all seven coaches northward without a problem. As it was, Grey's sorcerer was pushing three of them. According to Aly, thought magic was too taxing for a task that large, so she employed a series of word magic spells, which were much more powerful than thoughts, to move the carriages along.

As they left the chimneys and spires of Mardon behind, Red wondered at Aly's motivations. Now that her safety was compromised, Red wondered why she didn't simply up and leave, taking her stores of wealth, given by years of serving as Royal Sorcerer, and plant herself far from her father's reach.

There was something keeping her there, beside him. He didn't have any illusions that it was mere duty.

This far north, spring mornings held an icy tint, a reminder that winter didn't fade until the solstice. Elise hadn't said more than a dozen words since the trip began, and Red wondered why. She was not the sister who withheld prying questions. She'd been so quiet since Father's funeral. He eyed her with a pointed gaze, waiting for her to look up.

Vast stretches of verdant pastureland and freshly tilled fields rolled by the window, promising another year of well-fed children and happy mothers. Another harvest sent by the Maker's goodness, many would say.

Red hadn't slept more than a few hours in days. His headache had dulled, thanks to his herbal tea, but the pressure on his eyelids grew as the carriage rumbled over uneven country roads. Though it disturbed him and he'd tried to talk her out of it, Aly rode somewhere on *top* of his cab. She'd claimed that a seat on top of a carriage was normal for her, like her strange, invisible chair in the corner of the state dining room. He had no idea how she held on or how she managed to sit still. Perhaps by magic.

Eventually, Elise placed her finger in her book, shut it, and raised her eyes. "Yes?"

Now that he had her attention, he didn't actually know how to tell her what was on his mind. He didn't really want her to know all the threats, the fearsome possibilities, of what they were driving into, but he felt she had the right to know.

"There's more going on than you realize. I don't think it wise to tell you all of it, but I'm not the only one in danger from a curse anymore." *Aly. Seb.* Their names rang in his head. He still had no idea how Aly planned to heal Seb, but he poured all his resolve into believing she would.

"Ah," was all Elise said. She looked out the window for several minutes.

Red kept back the truth about Seb. He'd be healed, cleansed, purged, whatever it took. Aly could do it. She *had* to. Any doubt he still harbored about her he shoved away, not capable of processing what would happen if she failed. If it was a mad hope, he didn't care. He had to believe she could do it.

After their heated discussion the night Seb had been bitten, Aly had gone to Lord Weston Grey's estate and begged his sorcerer to heal Seb. Red had suggested it himself, so he couldn't explain why he was mad she'd acted exactly as he asked. The bite, since it was from a lyth and not a woodwolf or foxblood, required an extraction spell that would take time. Grey's sorcerer had agreed to perform the extraction spell as they traveled, but that meant Seb would be riding north without being fully healed.

Elise slipped her finger out of the book and gripped it tightly with both hands. "So, how's it going with the sorcerer? Still awkward?"

Red jerked his gaze out the window. A thatched roof cottage sagged in the middle of a cow pasture. These people did not have the luxury of Comforters to heat their homes or city pipes to draw water in from the rivers. A well stood beside the house. "Not the best."

There was a small *thunk* on top of the carriage. Elise looked up, but Red ignored it.

"Can you talk about it?"

He glanced at the tome in her lap. "No."

Elise lifted the top of the book. "In this one section of a poem, Kanto says that rivers bend the earth, not the other way around."

"Hmm."

His sister huffed in the most ladylike manner possible. "You wanted to know what this book was about."

With a sigh, he ran a hand through his hair. "Anything useful?"

Her eyes narrowed. "I am trying, Brother. I have read two thirds of the book. He writes about nature, about law, about nations. He even has a bit in here about a bat going on a journey. Or at least I think that was what happened. My Kirish is good, but his poetry is strange. He likes to talk about nature as if it has more power than we think it does."

"He wasn't a Theodist?"

"No, he was. He believed Theod created everything, but he believed there is *creative* power in nature too. Like the rivers making the earth move, thus making new habitats and national borders, things like that." Elise glanced out the window. "I mean, when I think about it, the border between us and Bulvarna is the Canyon. Before the Canyon existed, there was no natural boundary there. So, in a way, nature forced the two nations to stop at the edge."

"But magic made the Canyon, not nature."

Elise shrugged. "True." She reopened the book, her attention once again absorbed in the pages. "This poem is about the Black River."

"The Black River? Are you comfortable reading that?"

"I am not so easily persuaded as to be turned heretic by a poem." Her eyes darkened.

"Of course," agreed Red, still uncomfortable that his sister was reading about the river whose waters had polluted the world for centuries. Some in the stricter religious sects believed mentioning the Black River was tantamount to inviting its evil into one's life.

"Kanto seems to have thought of the Black River as powerful, but his language becomes difficult to interpret in this section here. It is as if he is saying the river can give and take life itself, but we know that power is Theod's alone."

"True, but death curses take lives and healing spells give life, the same way a bullet can take a life and a natural doctor can heal with herbs. We have many ways in which to give and take life. Perhaps it isn't farfetched to think that a river could as well. I mean, people drown in the Cressen every year."

Another clunk on top of the carriage drew their attention. Red cleared his throat.

"The Black River is powerful," he added. "It's the fount of wickedness."

"Perhaps that is why his poems were banned. It was once unlawful to mention the river at all."

After a half hour of the gentle motion of the carriage on country roads, Elise closed her book, rested her head against the cushion behind it, and closed her eyes.

As soon as her chin lolled sideways, a hand reached down and through the open window to tug on Red's sleeve.

"Finally, she's asleep. Come with me." Aly flashed a smile as gnarly as a bramble patch.

"Now?" He glanced at his sister, whose queenly mouth hung open in a sleep-frown.

"Ever flown before?"

Gaping, he shook his head.

"First time then? It's usually a bit uncomfortable. Let's go."

18

ALY

The king's body lurched up and out of the open carriage window, bumping and scraping the frame. Aly Pulled from his Truthwell to carry them both a short distance from the caravan, her shroud hiding them.

Her mind wavered, struggling to remain focused on the magic necessary to keep them aloft. Instead, her thoughts kept veering back to Elise's words. *Focus!*

When she glanced over at Red, she burst out laughing.

Red pinwheeled his arms for some sense of control as the ground dropped away. He let out a scream that would have fueled Seb's jokes for weeks, if he could have heard it.

She cackled. By the time she flopped him down in a wooded grove, her face shone with tears of laughter. She crumpled over on the ground, hands in the dirt, heaving for air.

"It really wasn't that funny." His cheeks were bright red, as were his ears.

Standing, she brushed grass off the knees of her traveling pants. "Come on."

"I thought you said magic doesn't make you tired."

"I'm not tired. Your face made me laugh so hard it was difficult to concentrate." At his frown, she added, "At least I didn't drop you!"

"Glad to know my fear was entertaining to you."

With one finger, she shoved his chest. "I have a dying king to keep alive and a whole *army* of important nobility to protect—" she waved a hand back toward the carriages "—as we approach the world's most dangerous place, and, oh yes!, then go visit my murderous father so you can have a little chat with an evil queen. Laughing felt *good*."

"Does Grey know? About the curse, I mean."

Blindsided by the question, she furrowed her brow. "Yes. What of it? You *told* me to seek his sorcerer to heal Sebastian. Naturally, he asked why it was necessary."

"And you can't lie." He shook his head, clearly annoyed. "Yet *you* wanted to keep the curse as secret as possible. Admit it, Aly, you care for Grey."

Aly froze. She had no mask to hide her expression now, no cloak to conceal her arms as they wrapped around her torso. "He is only a friend."

Red laughed and turned aside. "You're not a good liar."

Storming back into his line of vision, Aly fisted her hands. "It is *not* a lie. Grey never... He taught me how to Truthpull, that's all." Aly's eyes flickered restlessly, as old memories replayed. *Was that a lie? And why do I care so much if he understands?*

"That was all, was it?"

Aly's fists relaxed. She lifted a hand toward the canopy of branches. Wind swirled in the leaves, then light focused, as if through a magnifying glass, on the tip of her finger. "Sometimes people are put in our lives for a reason. We cross paths, and the entire course of our existence is changed, leading us toward a future we never expected but were always meant to have." The light collected into the form of a butterfly. "Grey was that for me. He bent my path in a new direction." Her eyes leveled with his.

"Toward you." Her hand came down and the shape diffused, a fleeting ethereal glow lingering on her skin.

Air became scarce, like they'd summitted a high mountain peak. She waited for his reaction. More than his stone-still face, she feared her own internal response to what she'd said. Behind her ribs, her lungs tightened, her heart flipped. Red was the *king*, but she'd just made it sound like she'd been waiting for the day their paths had met. In a sense, she had been.

Finally, Red shifted his gaze and said, "All right, Aly, why'd you haul me out here?"

"To discuss what Elise said. She said the poem describes the river as being able to give or take life. Maybe that's our answer."

"Yes, but so can *you*."

She stared up at him for a brief moment, then broke away. "In this case, I can't. That's why we're here, to find a way to keep you alive." Behind her, she felt Red step closer. He breathed loudly enough that she could hear him and feel his warm breaths push the hairs beside her ears. *What's he thinking about?* "Also, we need to practice." She whirled around.

"Practice what?"

"Whatever happened in the garden that night. You said it yourself, an extra boost. That butterfly I made? It was no more real than a dream. I need to be able to recreate, like I did that night. Because if I can do that, I could take any weapon my father uses and turn it into something else. A sword could become a spoon. A shard of glass could become a cloth."

"Or you could make a weapon."

Her lips pursed. "Yes, or that. The problem is, I have no idea what that magic even was. I have no way of replicating it, unless we practice."

Without further warning, she lifted her hands and twirled them in the air. She kept her eyes on Red, but he averted his gaze to a squirrel scampering up a nearby tree. He shoved his hands in his pockets and peered back at her out of the corner of his eye.

After a long two minutes, she dropped her hands. "Well? Did you do it?"

"Me? Do what?"

"You did something that night. *Think*, Red. What was going through your mind while I was conjuring magic?"

His Adam's apple bobbed twice and he cleared his throat. "I don't know."

He was hiding something. "That's helpful."

Then again, she was hiding something too. If Red really was a Beacon, she should tell him. But what use was it if he was dying? They would only have a few short weeks to change the world—with his Truthwell darkening every day and her own magic suffering as a result. "We must keep trying. I've…uh, read some ancient texts about this sort of thing. The boost thing. I think it's possible." Her eyes darted away from him and her cheeks pinked. "We have nothing left to lose."

"I imagine you'll tell me what you're hiding when you decide I need to know it." Startled by his assessment, she gave herself away as a small gasp left her lips. "In the meantime, simply tell me what I'm supposed to do."

Her green eyes blinked at him. "Stay alive."

"You really do want me to live." He said it like it had just dawned on him.

"Of course," she breathed.

For a moment, he held her gaze. The man behind those brown eyes was not the boy she'd met the morning after his father's death—helpless, reckless, and angry. These were the eyes of a king—powerful, determined, and hopeful.

A deer darted through the thicket behind her, startling them.

She muttered her healing spell, her eyes drooping shut as she worked her magic, her hand extended toward him. She sent the warmth of healing through his body. When it was over, he stumbled forward, as if drawn by her healing touch.

She watched her extended fingers, transfixed with the possibility that he might bump into them. He did not. She lowered her hand.

The forest pressed in on her, the new green of the leaves was both mockingly cheerful and aggressive in its growth. These leaves would die and return again, year after year. In a way, they were the real phoenixes of the world.

"Aly, we've got to start being optimistic here."

Chided by his words, she bit her lip and nodded. "I think Elise is getting close. There is an old saying among sorcerers: *Give and take, but never break.*" A rock lifted from the forest floor and floated into her downturned palm. "Theod has given us the power to change our world. I can break this rock into a million pieces, but we can't step outside the boundaries he set—hence, we cannot break the order he's established. There are limits to what we can do. Lies make those limits a lot harder to pin down." The rock burst into dust. "I can merely do what the truth says is possible. I can't turn that rock into a bird, but I could make the dust fly. I can't *alter* nature. Only Theod can do that."

"What about those flowers at the ball?"

"I've been thinking about that." She paused.

"Go on," he urged, crossing his arms.

Birds chattered above, oblivious to the woes of the world.

"What if, like the flowers, there is more we can do, more that can be done, than we've fully realized? What if, over time, even those who know the truth have begun to believe lies?"

He rubbed his jaw. "Which would hide the truth from us and weaken our magic."

"Yes." She found it odd that he'd called it *our* magic, but he was correct; it was not just hers. Using his Truthwell, she called one droplet of water from the air to hover over her upturned palm. It glistened with the greens and blues of the forest and sky. "Rivers hold great power. Perhaps they can take it as well as give it." Her eyes flickered up to his.

"You think it could take the curse?"

"I think it is a possibility, one we must look into." It was hard not to smile back at him.

He stuck his hands in his hair and turned halfway around. "But the Black River? To go there is to die."

Aly shook her head. "Some have done it."

"And they came back so muddled in their minds that they were as good as dead."

"Let's not jump to conclusions. Let's see what the poem says. When we stop for the evening, I will join you and Elise, and we can review the poem."

His face was speckled with the moving sunlight filtering through the trees, as if the light and shadow were dancers and his skin was the stage. Since that first day they'd met, she hadn't admitted to herself how handsome he was. Now their lives had gone so terribly downhill and here she was staring at him with a flicker of heat in her chest.

"Anyway, I think we're getting close," she muttered, turning away from his stare. Her words echoed in her mind, redolent with double meaning. She extinguished that foolish thought.

"Aly." He touched her arm. "We wondered why your father and Kassia would try to keep us from going north. What if there *is* something about the river? Something they know and we don't?"

This close, she could see the tiredness around his eyes and the wild desperation in his gaze. No, not desperation. Hope. Mad hope. Like a wildfire, it leaped from him, igniting her.

"It's possible." She rubbed her hands against her sides, breaking his grip as she wiped away nervous sweat. "Go on, then. I'll catch up. Or I can fly you back?"

"No, thanks." He scowled and they both laughed. "I'll walk. Feels good to move."

Aly watched him for several minutes as he picked his way through the underbrush back toward the road. He glanced back once.

At his glance, she smiled. Stupid and foolish it may be, but she did not want to hold back that smile. She wanted him to have hope. She needed him to believe he would survive. If she appeared optimistic, then perhaps they could forge a new kind of hope, built from the ashes of despair.

19

RED

Her smile, it had transformed her face. The hope written there was enough to spark a new determination in him. Somehow this ludicrous plan they were forming was the solution they'd been looking for—a way to avoid her father and rid Red of the curse.

But to go to the Black River in search of a cure was possibly the stupidest thing he would ever do. *Definitely a mad hope.*

The second time he turned around, she had her back to him, arms raised for spell work. With a twitch of her wrist, she lifted up a swirling current of dead leaves and dirt from the forest floor. She Pulled on his Truthwell for this demonstration, but he felt nothing.

Red watched as she swirled the cloud of dirt and leaves and moss around and caused it to worm in the air before her. Her movements became quick, harsh. The detritus lurched through the spaces between the trees, a twisting, writhing mass.

He stepped back, the magical display turning almost violent in its thrashing. The veins in Aly's arms began to bulge at her exertion. Then it made sense. For a woman who'd been wrapped in invisibility for six years, *this* was her form of expression, of coping. Magic was her art; like Elise painted, so Aly used magic as her brush and nature as her medium.

Suddenly, the magic became almost too painful to watch. Red pulled a hand down his face, struck by the tangible emotion flowing in the strange scene before him. In her orchestration, he saw fear, but also anger, loathing, and maybe a bit of longing. *What does she long for, beneath all those other emotions?*

Safety? Survival? A second chance to prove her ability? A way to bring justice for Father's death? Lord Grey? She'd said she wanted Red to live.

Like his father, Red faced an early death. She *could* survive, perhaps. He, unless they found a cure, would not. Watching her magic, his own deepest desires spilled into his mind.

His father's company. The carefree days Red had left behind. His best friend's healing. Love. A family. A happy future. A chance to prove he could be a good king. Safety for his people and his family. Survival.

He stared at Aly. They wanted many of the same things—her spell made it obvious, though he couldn't explain how he knew.

They were not so different.

"I wish I could keep you safe," he muttered, though she couldn't hear. He'd thought a silly mask could hide her from her father. He'd been wrong about too much in his short kingship that he wondered if he'd ever have the chance to get something right.

The carriages had stopped on the road. Red increased his pace across the field that separated him from the caravan. Elise was running toward him.

"What is it?" he asked, dashing to his sister's side.

Her eyes were wide. "I think I found it."

"Found what? Is everything all right?"

"Yes, yes. I would like someone else who reads Kirish to see if I have the translation correct, but, Red, I think I may have found the answer."

By the time Weston Grey's carriage rolled into view at Lord Abrim Indegwa's country estate, Red's headache pressed the world into a tight tunnel around him and fuzzed the edges of reality. He leaned against the moss-covered stone wall marking the front garden of Indegwa's manor. He sipped a cup of herbal tea that had been brought out to him by Lady Indegwa herself, buttoned into a gown much too ornate for the occasion but which complimented her dark skin.

Elise had come across a difficult line about the Black River in the poem, and they needed someone else who could read Kirish to take a look at the passage. Seb was the only other person in the group familiar enough with Kirish to read the poem, but he was also the only other person in the group infected with Canyon magic. According to Aly, his mind wasn't sound enough for the task. Even if he could translate the words, what he might say aloud could be an utter distortion of the true meaning of the text.

Despite Seb's infection, Red had made up his mind to ask his friend for help. Aly had asked Grey's sorcerer to heal Seb, but the spell was apparently tedious and slow. If descending into the Canyon was anything short of certain death, Red would drive all his energy, all his hope, into this mission. But they had to know for sure, and understanding the poem was critical.

In the yard beside the house, Lady Alexander and Leeta Merrythorn were admiring a trio of golden puppies tripping along before their slow-moving mother. Leeta's giggles screeched like a beginner violinist, rattling Red's brain. He was not oblivious to her frequent glances, but he kept his eyes on the approaching carriage, the one carrying Weston Grey and Seb.

The railways in Tandera all led west and south, not north, thus, making any journey north slow and bumpy, though magic carried them much faster than any horse team could. Now Red wished they could all disappear and reappear at the Canyon's edge tomorrow and be done with this curse of his—if, of course, their fledgling plan could work.

"How is the tea, Your Majesty?" Lady Indegwa's dark eyes shone with kindness, but her hands trembled slightly as she handed him the sloshing cup of tea.

"Just fine, thank you."

His words disappointed her, he could tell, but he had bigger issues to worry about than the hostess' anxiety right now. His teacup broke as he set it down on the stone wall a little too forcefully.

"Oh, I am very sorry." He moved to pick up the pieces, but Lady Indegwa fussed at him to let her take care of it.

Veeter Yin, following the king inside the house, walked out from the shadows into the thin evening light. "Grey will be all right, Your Majesty," Yin said. "The magic will not have spread simply by sharing a cab."

Red stared wide-eyed at Yin. "How do you know about Seb?"

Yin dipped his chin. "I follow you everywhere, sire. You do not often speak quietly."

"Right." *I don't even know the man who follows me around every-where.* He'd watched Yin follow his father around for years. Yin was a legendary fighter, dangerous with his twin Okwan blades; the stoic bodyguard; the foreigner who'd pledged his life to protect Tandera's king. Like Aly. Here was a man transplanted from his homeland, dedicated to serving Tandera to the death. *My father inspired that in others*, Red mused. *Maybe one day, I will too.*

The manor house, built some two hundred years ago, smelled like refinished wood and hot bread. The Indgewas, after learning that the king's party would spend one night with them, had apparently redone the entire downstairs of their house and the room Red would be sleeping in.

Paintings of their ancestors adorned the walls of the dining room where two long tables had been crammed in to make room for everyone. Diamond-paned windows stood open overlooking a pond and distant stables. Crickets trilled their happy song as the diners complimented the Indegwa's masterful chef.

"He hails from my island, Contiba," Lord Indegwa said. "Of course the food is good!"

"How goes the trade in Contiba? Do they have paved roads down there?" asked Lord Alexander.

Indegwa twisted the stem of his wine glass and winked. "The islanders prefer the slow life. They do not rush, and paved roads make life much faster." He chuckled.

"Hmph," Alexander muttered.

After dinner, Lord Indegwa raised his glass. "Our king has had a long day of travel. You shall all rest well tonight. My wife has seen to it! New linens for everyone!" Deep laughter rumbled through his chest, and the faces around the table smoothed into smiles.

I won't sleep well until I know what that poem really says.

The party left the dining room for the two withdrawing rooms, men to one and women to another.

Red approached his best friend. "Up for reading a little poetry?"

Seb's usual smile was absent.

In his mind, Aly snapped. *No! Don't let him read it. We couldn't trust what he'd say.*

Ignoring Aly, he said to Seb, "Elise has it, actually." Red turned toward the room the women had entered. Elise was sitting at a small table, already reading by candlelight. Seb shuffled along behind him. He was their only option. They had no other choice but to hear his interpretation of the text.

Silence from his best friend was stranger than if he'd said something harsh or hurtful. Red chose to ignore this and asked Elise to show Seb the passage. Lady Alexander peered at them over the back of the couch she occupied, and Leeta Merrythorn pretended to be absorbed in perusing titles on a bookshelf against the wall.

"You really need me to read you poetry?" Seb almost smiled. "Man, let me read it to Elise; she's at least pretty. You're just…an ugly brute."

Red warmed with the insult from his friend. This was more the Seb he knew. Perhaps the Canyon's magic wasn't taking his entire mind. Elise blushed crimson as she handed Seb the book.

Seb's fingers traced down the lines, his face inching closer to the text as he read. He tilted his head back and forth a few times before looking up.

"Want me to go for it?"

Elise stood, her hands also moving down the text. "We do not need you to read the whole poem. Here." She stepped around, leaned toward Seb, and found the line she needed. "This one."

Red tensed a little at his sister's closeness to someone infected with Canyon magic, but he told himself to let it go.

Seb glanced at the princess and then back at the poem. "Rise and fall, the current produces—no, gives birth…" He fumbled through the awkward translation. "Gives birth to life and brings forth death. The earth twists…no, bends and the world breaks as the river gives. Inhale, river, and take death. Exhale, waters, and make life cease." He shook his head and pushed away from the book and his closeness to Elise. "Makes no sense."

Elise turned to Red. "That is what I could not figure out. Those last two lines. The sentence structure…"

"Tricky," Seb agreed. "But see here, I knew he was talking about the river inhaling because he used the word *trisak*, which is a poetic way of shortening the Kirish word for river, *trisakav*, to make the meter work. Poets do weird stuff like that."

When she looked again at Seb, Elise's eyes were round.

"The village idiot knows his poetry," Red said, taking the book from them and tucking it under his arm. "Thank you, Brother."

Seb blinked, and a shadow coursed over his face. A frown settled on his dark features. The Canyon's magic was still there. Aly needed to heal Seb. Tonight. But first Red wanted to talk to her about this passage and his dangerous new plan.

The room designated for the sorcerer was beside the king's, adjoined by a small door tucked under an eave. Lady Indegwa thought that might be convenient, but it only made Red sweat with the knowledge of his sorcerer's nearness as he bathed in the in-room clawfoot tub. Not that a closed door meant much to someone who could be invisible. He dismissed Bernard and clambered into a clean undershirt and pair of pants as quickly as possible, stuffing his hem in before knocking on the little door.

The lock clicked and the hinges creaked. Aly peeked her head under the short door frame, brows raised. For a moment, neither of them moved. He wasn't sure, given this new location, whose room it was more appropriate—or less inappropriate—to chat in.

"Fine, come in," he said, sweeping a hand and stepping into the alcove by the latticed window.

He'd opened it for the breeze and the moonlight, though the air would become cold before morning. For now, the chill helped him fight the tea-kettle-pressure in his head and the heat blooming up his chest at the sight of Aly.

She ducked and walked in. "Nice," she said, eyeing the large room, the wide bed piled with entirely too many white blankets and pillows, the scrubbed floors, and the cluttered surfaces crammed with all manner of expensive trinkets. Her eyes flitted to the bathtub, which still had water in it. She spun away and crossed her arms, looking out the other small window. "We can't trust his words."

"He didn't twist them. He pointed to the words and told us

what they meant. Elise's understanding was pretty much the same, give or take a phrase."

Aly peered back at him. "You want to hedge your bets on the word of a man infected with Canyon magic?"

"What other option do we have? No one else reads Kirish."

She deflated and turned to face him. "I don't know."

"We are so close. The river has to be part of the answer."

"I think it's possible," she admitted.

He shoved both hands into his wet curls, his headache surging. "We need better than *possible*. This is madness. If we're wrong…" He couldn't find the right words.

"I know," she said. Her hair was still knotted, still windswept. She had not changed out of her traveling trousers and blouse.

"Have you eaten?"

She stared blankly for a moment, apparently caught off guard by the sudden question. "I eat after. Most of the time it's once you've gone to sleep."

"That's terrible."

"It's simply the way it is. I have to be your Protector, which means I can't be distracted with something like food. Plus, I'm not invited to your dinners."

"Perhaps we can change that."

His words must have startled her, because she recoiled as if a mouse had scampered across her feet. *It's not that outlandish an idea*, he thought.

Stepping across to the trunk at the foot of his bed, she sat. "The river *takes* death? That's what it says?"

"Exhales and takes life. Inhales and takes death. Something like that. Elise wrote it down." He grabbed the piece of paper Elise had written on and handed it over to Aly.

Her fingers tapped against her lips as she read.

"What if you could cast the curse back into the *water* instead of Dimitri?"

"That…is exactly what I was planning to say."

One side of his mouth curled up. She bit her lip, hiding her own smile. He crossed the space to her in two strides. Her eyes closed slowly.

"What?" he asked.

"Let me speak to Ondorian. This is potentially more dangerous than facing my father. We don't even know what's down there."

He wanted to grab her shoulders, shake her into a straight answer. "Can it be done? Can we survive a trip into the Canyon?"

"You know I cannot lie."

"Aly, I know you can do this. If the river can take the curse back, if that's possible, then you can do it."

Her gaze lit a fire within him, that flame of unreasonable hope. It was no longer a farce, crafted to make her *feel* more confident. This was the woman who'd saved his life, and his family, at the ball. She'd saved him before he'd ever known she existed. She could kill a lyth with a single spell. She could shape the world to her liking or dismantle it. In her hands was the power to save him. He stepped closer.

Aly looked down, fiddling with the loose folds of her manlike blouse. "I will try to heal Seb again tonight."

Red rubbed one hand down his stubbly chin, aware that his closeness had made her uncomfortable. For good reason. He had to remember their roles.

"Good. Perhaps my Truthwell isn't so dark yet that you can't perform the spell you need. Or maybe you can find a way around it if it is." *Whatever you do, don't turn to Grey for help.*

She looked up, brows high. He'd wanted to blame his woes on her lack of skill. It was easier that way—or so he'd believed. "Also, we never found out who put that cloth in my pocket. If it was one of my councilmen, then we've brought the traitor with us." Pain lanced his forehead and he wobbled forward an inch before catching his balance.

Aly leaned onto her knees, her legs wide like a man's. She was so unlike the courtiers; it no longer annoyed Red. Instead, it was refreshing to see someone so utterly unshaped by the world's expectations. "You're right. Whoever put that handkerchief in your pocket that day knew you'd be using it at the ceremony, knew it would be *after* the Binding, and knew what it would do when it touched my magic." She pushed forward again and stood. "That can't be very many people. Your council, or someone they told. Someone working with my father. Perhaps when we arrive in Bulvarna, I can spy out the traitor. Surely, whoever it is will be contacted by Kassia."

Red nodded, still uneasy that a man on his council might be in league with Kassia. "So, Seb will be okay? He won't come murder me or anything?"

"Shouldn't."

"That's comforting."

"I'm right there," she lifted a hand to the still open door between their rooms. "He wouldn't get past your door without me feeling it. I'd be here before he could touch you."

Red snorted, suddenly uncomfortable, and turned away, hoping the dim light and his wet, drooping curls would hide the pink fire leaping up into his ears. "You make me sound so weak."

Enough seconds of silence passed that Red turned around to see what Aly was doing. She stood in the middle of the room, barefoot on the hardwood floor, arms by her sides. "You are not weak."

He laughed. "But if danger comes in the night, you'll be there to save me." She scoffed, but he kept talking. "The little king with murderous headaches, a knack for stupidity, and no charm whatsoever."

The words were out before he'd even realized what he'd said. In their wake, pain surged.

She lifted a hand and rested it against her chest. When it fell, she beckoned him, "Come here."

"What?"

Worry creased her brow. "You're full of lies yourself. Come here."

"Canyon magic?"

Shaking her head, she stepped up to him, reaching for his shoulder. "No, no. Simply a bunch of garbage you've been telling yourself, and it's making your headaches worse." Her eyes looked both mad and merciful. "When we believe lies, it makes us all weaker, not only sorcerers."

"Are you saying I'm not stupid or that I do have charm?"

She sighed. "You're not stupid." She pointedly didn't say anything about his charm. "You could have told me the pain was that bad. I can fix it." She rubbed her hands down her hips and stepped closer. "Actually, sit. It'll be easier. You're kind of tall." She nodded at the trunk beside the bed.

He sat.

Standing before him, she lifted both hands toward him.

He realized what she was doing and stiffened as her hands met his head. The way her fingers felt as they slipped into and under his hair, the cool lines traced by her fingertips on his hot skin, made his entire body shudder. She felt his tremor and clamped her hands around his skull, her magic already beginning to seep in.

The knots in his shoulders, neck, back, chest, began to loosen almost immediately. He couldn't even tell she was doing magic, but he felt the pain ebb. His head tipped forward even more, her strong hands holding him steady. The crown of his head hovered merely inches from her stomach, and every part of Red could feel those inches like they were the last few steps between a thirsty man in the desert and a pool of clear water.

The blood flushed to the knotted areas in his body, melting the tension and seeking the places that had been closed off for too long. He heard himself whimper. As his muscles gave way to her magic, he felt sleep beginning to creep up from his toes to his torso. He was going to fall over and sleep right there on the floor.

But for a moment, he fought the tiredness, not wanting to cut this moment short. Her fingers twitched slightly against his skull, the sensation electrifying on top of her closeness and the magic surging through his body. He did not want it to end.

Unexpectedly he wanted only one thing: to cross the distance between them.

He tipped his weight forward, closing those last few inches until his head pressed into the soft but firm wall of her abdomen, right above her hips. He breathed in, tension trying to rise in his muscles again. For a moment, she pressed against his head, a short, staccato laugh falling over his shoulders as she tried to pry him away.

"All right, that's enough." She pressed her hands against his head, lifting his face up and away.

He peered up at her with both adoration and fear. In that moment, he believed she could do anything.

With a huff, and most certainly a flush of red, she turned away and looked out the window. "Did it work?"

Red stood, walked toward her, his mind pinwheeling. The narrow look she threw over her shoulder slowed his approach but did not stop it. He stepped up behind her, his body close enough that, though not touching her, he could feel her warmth.

"Yes," he said.

"Good." She coughed, turned, and hurried from the room.

His blood thundered in his veins as he stared at the small door to her room. He went as far as putting his hand on the knob, but no farther. Her quick exit had been proof that his actions had offended her.

Then why couldn't he shake the feeling of her hands in his hair?

ALY

That night, Aly planned to heal Sebastian after allowing herself a few hours of sleep. Her senses would be keener, her mind sharper, and she needed every advantage she could muster, because not only was her magic weakening with Red's progressing curse, someone had muddied her mind like a country road after a summer rain.

Her hands felt hot as she lay in bed staring at the slanted ceiling, knowing that Red slept under the same ceiling, merely a wall away. The small door no longer seemed convenient. It was entirely distracting, her eyes finding it every few seconds, keeping her from sleep.

With a small Pull, she crafted a spell to wake her up after an hour. Her magic was built on truth, but because of that, it tended to fall apart when she cast a spell she didn't fully believe in or when she couldn't keep her thoughts organized and controlled. So it took a while, once she started dreaming, to realize she wasn't seeing reality. Part of her was aware she was asleep, but when her mother rode through Lord Weston Grey's dining room on King Gevar's horse, she tried to grab on to the dream, to hold it a little longer, to hold onto the pieces of the people she'd lost.

She only startled from sleep when she discovered she was clutching Red's jacket as he lay on the floor, lifeless.

The next morning they woke to find Lady Alexander's carriage ripped to shreds. The door was chewed and raked with slash marks, and the cushions inside were ribboned by claws.

The soldiers had never caught the foxblood spotted outside Luxler weeks ago, and it had been silently picking off those who wandered too far from civilization. Though this animal had been attacking in the Luxler area, this was the first attack so close to a home. It was as if the creature had been emboldened.

Lady Alexander and Leeta Merrythorn, visibly rattled, were reassigned to other carriages. Lady Alexander would ride the rest of the way with her husband. Leeta Merrythorn, to her instant delight, would ride the rest of the way in the king's carriage, since an unmarried woman couldn't travel alone with men, and Elise was the only other female on the trip to act as chaperone.

Red, to Leeta's visible disappointment, announced he would be riding with Arthur Ondorian, on account of propriety. Aly smirked to herself, thinking of their conversation last night, alone, in his bedroom.

She recalled the way he'd stood awkwardly at the door to his bedroom, in his shirtsleeves, unsure if he should invite her in. He'd flushed crimson when she'd spotted the tub. Back in Mardon, he'd left the door open to her anteroom while they conversed, forcing her to have to keep up her shroud to hide their words. Propriety between them was a strange, subtle thing. If Leeta Merrythorne knew that Aly had spoken to the king in his bedroom last night, she would turn purple.

Aly's own cheeks heated unexpectedly as she shuffled through these memories. She pressed her fingers against her lips to hide a sudden smile.

What am I doing? she forced the smile off her face and lifted herself to the top of Ondorian's coach.

Ondorian's carriage, much simpler than the king's and with less comfortable seats, accommodated Red and the priest with plenty of space. Aly, who perched on top, couldn't determine a way to insert herself into the small cab without physically bumping into either Red or the priest. Her fingers twitched as she pressed them to the cool, damp top of the carriage. Ever since she'd healed Red, she couldn't forget the way it had felt when his head had tipped against her. It was as if in that one touch he'd lit a fire and, from the ashes, raised something new—bright and burning and rising quickly.

She'd seen the look in his eyes when he'd peered up at her.

After she crafted a spell to move all the carriages onto the road, she thought back to the way Weston Grey had looked at her once, years ago, the night they'd shared a dance. His gaze had sparked her young heart into a fast flame. But six years of solitude had made that flame a bitter memory.

Then the king had looked at her and awoken a part of her she'd thought was buried for good.

She peered down into the carriage. Ondorian sat with his eyes closed, back erect and chin not bobbing. Aly assumed he was praying. She hated to interrupt, but this was as good a time as any to barge in.

She gripped the top of the doorframe then turned the glass window to a hovering wad of sand. Her feet entered first, then her legs and torso, and then she was stepping all over Red's lap as she bounced down to the seat. Red yelped in surprise. She flicked her wrist and replaced the window, solid as ever. When she glanced at the priest, he was staring at her with the hint of a smile.

As soon as he saw her, Red asked, "Seb?"

Aly's shoulders sank. "I'll explain later."

"He's *still* not healed?"

Aly turned intense eyes on him. "No. Now, let's tell Ondorian what we planned. I will try to heal Seb when we're finished."

Red tore his wide eyes from Aly and cleared his throat. "What do you know of the Black River?"

Ondorian's bald head and dark suit gave the man a crisp and unfriendly facade, until his warm smile broke out and softened his appearance. But the smile disappeared in a flash. "The Black River is the conundrum of existence."

With effort, Red did not roll his eyes. "Sorry, sir, but I need specifics."

"Very well. We know it was buried deep in the earth until Usrich split the world apart and unleashed its darkness. From that time, it has been corrupting all the creatures who drink from it. As a source of magic, it corrupts any who Pull from it. Though it is but a river, it has reach far beyond its banks."

"And it's the source of all curses, isn't it?"

"Magical curses, yes."

"There are other kinds?"

"Oh, a great many. Drought. Sickness. Death. Loss of loved ones." He nodded at the king. "Not all ill that befalls us is the result of dark magic."

Ondorian believed the truth without a waver of doubt. That made him at times blunt and at other times too poetic, but Red respected this man's knowledge of the *Verad* and his commitment to it.

He swallowed and asked, "Based on your recommendation, we found an old poem that suggests the Black River can give and take life."

Ondorian narrowed his eyes. "Be wary of any words, poetry or otherwise, that venerate that place."

"You recommended we look at poetry."

"Indeed. Look at is not believe. You speak of Kanto's poems, do you not?"

Red nodded. "One line said that the river inhales and exhales death."

Ondorian smiled, softening again. "Ah, the poet's sympathies are not always Theod's truth. But they can offer some helpful ideas we had not considered before."

"Arthur," Aly said, "Can the river take *back* a curse?"

The priest rubbed his chin. "An object can hold a curse, for a time. Like that handkerchief did."

"But a death curse, once it's in a person and—" she glanced at Red "—killing that person, it can't be put back into an object."

Ondorian made a thoughtful face. "True."

"And only manmade objects can hold curses like that. Items without natural Truthwells," Aly added. "Any item with a Truthwell in it can't hold a latent death curse. Smaller curses, maybe, but not death curses. On that reasoning, the river couldn't take back the curse."

"You said the poem claims the river takes death?" asked the priest. Red and Aly nodded. "Hmm. That does make it sound as if the curse could go back into the water." His gaze intensified. "It is a lot to risk on the words of a poem."

Red glanced at Aly. "Sir, it's that or I die."

"Actually, sire, I believe you are wrong. If I may be so bold, if you fail to rid your body of this death curse, I fear it will result in the death of *both* of you. You from the curse, and Aly from Pulling from a corrupted source." Aly's face paled. "I am no magic man, but I imagine, as your curse grows within you, your Truthwell will darken, making it harder and harder for Aly to use it as fuel."

"It is darkening, sir," Aly confirmed.

"I believe this, more than anything else, is why Dimitri cursed the kings you serve, to make you too weak to ever defeat him."

The clouds outside had little to do with the gloom that settled over the king and his sorcerer. An impossible choice stood before them: descend into the Canyon and siphon the curse back into the river—and likely die trying—or die anyway.

Though this was the more dangerous path, it was the only one they had left. To wait and face her father was to face him with her source of magic greatly diminished. She'd crafted her ash ring to remind her that one day she would face him, and on that day she'd have to be the strongest sorcerer in the world to defeat him.

That day would not come as long as Red was dying of his death curse.

My father was always going to win, wasn't he? she wondered to herself.

To Aly's shock, Red reached out and grabbed her hand. She was too dumbfounded to yank it back.

"We will do it, sir," he said. "We will go to the Black River and rid me of this curse." His eyes found Aly's. They were full of hope. A wild, mad hope. He squeezed her hand.

With that glance she found she did not want to let go.

Three days had passed since their conversation with Ondorian. With every hour they crept closer to the Canyon, Red's condition worsened. Aly, perched with her legs folded atop the High Priest's carriage, poured over her small copy of the *Verad*.

The spells would have to be perfect. In the Canyon, there would be no margin for error. Descending to the river could be deadly. Her magic, weak as it was becoming, would have to be worded seamlessly, her concentration unwavering.

In the Canyon, she couldn't expect to be able to Pull from any object, no rock or bush or river. That meant Red alone would be her source of power while down there. Though her source was dimming, the words of the *Verad*, which shaped and gave meaning to her magic, would never fade or change. She had to rely on them as she never had before.

Glancing at the forest, Aly scanned the shadows for any signs of movement. Her magic skimmed outward, searching for danger. A half dozen deer, a myriad of birds, and the pale glowing Truthwells of a thousand trees were all she detected. For a moment, she relished the sensation of all the magic around her. It was beautiful. Theod had crafted such a lovely world. She only hated that not everyone could see the beauty she saw in it.

Unexpectedly, a slithering black Truthwell scampered through her magical awareness. She focused all her attention on it. It moved with agility, but it did not vanish. No lyth then, but a beast of the Deep. Foxblood or woodwolf. She lifted both hands out by her sides and conjured a boundary spell to prevent the animal from coming any nearer.

A relieved breath wheezed from her lungs as she finished the spell. *Glad I spotted it before it got closer.*

Again looking with her magical gaze, she noted the flashing shadows of Red's Truthwell. Amid his blinding light, the darkness was so much deeper. She focused now on him. He was in pain—at least she assumed so by the angry twists and violent shuddering of the shadows within him.

They would stop for lunch soon, and Aly would need to cast protective enchantments around the group. Peering over the side of the coach, she glanced through the window at Red. His head lolled against his chest. Since they'd left Mardon, he'd slept more and more each day, his body taxed by the curse. A line of drool hung from his open mouth, soaking his ascot.

Embarrassed for him, Aly muttered a quick spell that dispersed his drool and dried his clothes. At least no one but Ondorian had seen the king in this state.

Aly swung over the side, her weight rocking the cab. A quick spell removed the window and another propped her body up with a focused blast of air. She reached her hand in through the now-open window. The king's cheeks were flushed.

Her hand traveled to his shoulder, but at the last moment, it settled instead on his cheek. His skin was hot. His body was beginning to fight the curse as it might a winter cold. Little good it would do.

It was strange to be perched on the outside of a moving carriage, but stranger still to have her hand resting against the king's face. His skin was prickly from two days without a shave.

She uttered a spell to ease his pain, then uttered a different one to push back the darkness, as much as she could. It was gaining ground, and she needed to know exactly how much. When they stopped for lunch, she would conduct her daily dive into his Truthwell to search out how far the curse had spread. To rid the king of the curse, she would have to know how far down it reached.

The process was not enjoyable, considering Aly had to run headlong into that which she craved most but could never possess. It was dangerous, even for a Master. But it had to be done.

When Red's sleeping face relaxed, she felt satisfied that her magic had eased his discomfort. With one last spell, she cooled his body and removed her hand from the carriage. Under the privacy of her shroud, she watched him a moment longer than was necessary. Sleeping, his face lost all the harshness it normally harbored.

Guilt at Gevar's death ate away at Aly every single day. Staring at Red, she determined that he would not meet the same end.

"I will save you," she muttered, then hopped down from the carriage.

With her arms lifted, she slowed the caravan and eased them to the edge of the road.

In the long stretch between Luxler and Caridan, the military camp at the Canyon's edge, a flower-dusted meadow beside the road provided the ideal picnic spot. As soon as the carriages stopped, Aly flung enchantment after enchantment around the meadow: one to alert her should a creature of the Deep approach, one to deter any other people or sorcerers from crossing the grassy space, and one to block any spoken curses.

The entire party had been on edge since leaving Luxler, and the councilmen waited in the carriages as the attendants hustled about, propping up table legs, snapping out fresh linens, wiping crystal goblets free of fingerprints, and uncorking wine that had been brought from their homes in Mardon.

This spot would have to work—they were running out of time.

Aly needed space, a *lot* of space, to practice the magic they would be using in the Canyon. Once comfortable with her protective enchantments, Aly stalked off into the woods, blasting the leaves and twigs out of her way to leave a trail for Red to follow. This would be their last chance to practice.

Tomorrow, they'd reach the Canyon.

RED

Red's head snapped up when the carriage stopped. He'd been dreaming. A cool hand had reached for him in the darkness. He felt refreshed, and his headache had subsided.

Aly.

He'd known, since she'd put her hands in his hair three nights ago, that it was her magic keeping his pain at bay. Despite her efforts, the headaches were growing worse, evidence that his curse was spreading faster, taking Aly's power as it grew.

He should tell her to leave, to break their Bond and flee to safety.

If he did, he would surely die. It was selfish of him, but he couldn't stomach the thought of allowing the curse to take its course. His father had been braver than he was.

Red had grown up living in the rich legacy of Tandera's good fortune, but he'd always enjoyed the woods, the meadows, and the palace gardens as much as any grand ballroom or gilded drawing room. His father had seen to that.

Though a king, Gevar never lost his love of the woods, and Red cherished the times they'd spent waiting behind taut bows or riding through the King's Wood well past the chimes for supper.

A few startled birds dispersed as Red stepped out of Ondorian's carriage into the verdant meadow. A strong spring sun brought clouds of gnats to hover over the dense grass.

Bernard hurried up to Red. "Does Your Majesty require anything?"

Red placed a hand on his attendant's shoulder. "I require a walk. All this sitting is making me stir crazy." He needed to find Aly. This was their last chance to practice in a secluded place before they would arrive at the Canyon.

"Sire, I beg you, remain with the caravan."

"Bernard, thank you for your concern, but I will be fine. I'll have Yin with me…and the sorcerer," he added, to appease the concerned look on Bernard's face. "And after lunch, I require a round of Hearts. I'm on your team, of course. I don't feel much like losing today."

Bernard smiled. "I'll find us two more players, Your Majesty." They hadn't played cards in weeks. Red offered the man a half-smile, then turned toward the woods.

Yin, who had ridden beside the driver all morning, stepped forward to follow. "Given the circumstances, I request that another guard join us, Your Majesty," Yin said from behind him.

By "circumstances" he meant foxbloods. Red shook his head. "We should have all the protection we need." Aly's enchantments, even if weakened by his own curse, would be enough to protect them. There was no sense going into the Canyon if they didn't know exactly what spells they would need once they arrived, and Aly had said practice was the only way to know for sure.

"As you wish." Veeter Yin slipped into the forest behind the king, making no more noise than a doe in a hunter's wood.

So far, Aly had not been able to fully heal Seb, though she'd said the infection was weakening with each of her attempts.

Oddly, Red felt responsible. If not for his own deteriorating Truthwell, Seb would already be healed.

Everything depended on that one poem. If it was leading them astray, they were heading toward certain death; he supposed they were anyway.

Though death was hovering all around him—inside him—the king was glad for the blade and bullet kind of protection Yin offered as they strolled into the forest. However, it was not Yin's blades or bullets that had saved him the night of the accession ball, and it wouldn't be Yin saving him in the depths of the Canyon.

Aly's path lay before him in the woods, her magic making it easy for him to find her. For years, her magic had made it impossible to find her. He smiled at how that had reversed.

As he searched for a path around a bramble patch, he looked back at Yin, who waited as the king chose his steps. The guard hardly ever spoke. Or maybe it was simply that Red never talked to him. Yin was paid to keep the king alive, but Red knew so little about the man.

In Red's memory, Yin was a legend. Red and Seb had made up stories about what nasty and glorious deeds those twin blades had performed in the service of the previous king. Yin had always frightened Red a little and had always seemed more warrior than guard.

He waved Yin forward. "Tell me, sir, what first brought you to Tandera?" He'd always wondered why a man so skilled would leave his own country for another.

Yin stopped several paces away. "Your Majesty, you do not need to refer to me as sir."

"Old habit."

Yin offered the faintest smile. "I came to Tandera after the death of my father. He was a strong Okwan general."

Red waited, assuming there would be more to the story, as he looked again for a way around the brambles. "Tell me about Okwa." He picked his way forward.

"Ah, she is a beautiful woman. Awake, she is mesmerizing, but fall asleep and you will ruin your life."

"Um, all right."

"A saying among those of us who have left."

"Is it popular to leave Okwa?"

Yin stepped lightly over a fallen tree. "No. Not popular."

"But you did."

"I did. Those who pray to Theod are not tolerated in Okwa. Most of us eventually leave, seeking shelter in Tandera or Refere."

Red had a vague knowledge of Okwan religion. "You said your father was a general. Did he follow the truth?"

"No." The shortness of the word, and the fact that Yin began to march forward into the forest meant the conversation was over.

The next quarter hour passed in silence.

Red trudged up a steep incline beside a small stream. Above the sounds of trickling water, his and Yin's footsteps, and the rustle of a squirrel in leaves, he heard someone else's footsteps up ahead. *Finally.* He was beginning to wonder how far he'd have to walk to find her.

On top of this knoll, there's a good place, Aly said into his mind.

Red lifted a hand, miming for Yin to wait where he stood. He felt somehow worse about this gesture now that he'd spoken to the warrior about his personal life. Giving orders made it hard to feel close to anyone—another reason kings had few friends. Red pointed up toward the top of the knoll in what he hoped was a friendly gesture to Yin, indicating where he was going to talk to his sorcerer. Yin nodded, narrowing his eyes almost in protest.

Pressing his hands to his knees, Red clambered to the top of the slope in a few quick steps.

"Aly," he hissed, hoping his voice didn't carry down to Yin's post by the stream.

She dropped into view a few feet away. "We need to be quick. I don't like being this far from the group." Her quick eyes darted among the trees.

"If there's a foxblood out here, will you be able to feel it before it gets close?"

"Probably. Unless I'm too deep in your Well."

That's comforting. Red rolled his shoulders, his gaze flashing toward every shadow, every snapping twig. Aly walked up to him, her sleeves rolled, her hair tied back. Determination hardened her brow.

She began at once. Hands lifted, her spells fell out of her mouth. Some of the words Red knew, and some were in Edrean, the original language of the *Verad*. As usual, she hadn't explained what she would do, only that she would be searching his Truthwell for the curse—to see how far down it went. Why she needed space for this, he wasn't entirely sure.

Aly's face went through a series of perplexing expressions. Her brows crinkled and pinched. Her mouth flattened. Her cheeks grew red, then a paleness washed over her and her entire face sagged. He stood, puzzled, watching the leaves swirl around their feet as an icy breeze rushed in.

Her hands found his chest, her touch as light as a ray of sunshine. She was inches from him, but leagues away. There was nothing personal or enjoyable about her hands on his waistcoat, but he stared at them the way he might stare at sunlight on water. Eventually, her eyes drifted closed and her mouth clamped shut. Around her fingers, light rose. Looking down, Red couldn't tell if the light was coming from him or from her. He hoped that whatever she was doing, it would help them at the Black River.

Then, with more strength than her tiny frame should possess, she shoved him, hard. He fell backward onto the moss-covered ground. A burst of energy pulsed outward, rippling over the forest floor, rattling the nearby trees.

"What in the—?"

She crumpled to the ground before him, knees bent, hands cupping the sides of her face.

"Aly?"

At her name, she seemed to come out of a dream. Her eyes focused. "I'm sorry," she whispered.

"What happened?"

"It's very difficult." Her eyes looked everywhere but at him.

"What is?"

"To dive into a Truthwell. It's like you've been starving for weeks, then you're ushered to a bursting banquet table and told not to eat anything. When I first encountered the light inside someone, I craved it."

"Grey. You mean Grey." A small thorn pricked at his hand.

Her eyes stopped darting. "I didn't think I'd ever master that craving, but I did." Finally, she met his gaze. "Just then, I felt like a novice again."

Processing her words, he remembered the way the Binding felt. Intoxicating. Was that how she felt when she Pulled from the energy inside him?

"Did you, er, do what you needed to do?" He stood up, brushed himself off, and offered her a hand.

She stood up without taking his hand. "Yes and no. I dove as deep as I could. I dove until there was no more darkness." She cringed. "It goes very deep, but I did find the end of it. And… that's when I pushed you. I placed that spell on myself before we began, so that if I entered your Truthwell and didn't want to let it go, I'd push you down, break my concentration."

"Interesting choice." He picked a small twig from his sleeve.

"Truthwells are infinite, you know, and yours is…particularly extraordinary."

"Extraordinary, eh?"

"Oh, hush. Theod crafts us. We can't take the credit. It took *years* before I could pass by you and not be drawn to the energy inside you." She was pacing, so she failed to see how far Red's brows rose as she spoke. "The sorcerer prior to me, his name was Augustus; he helped me understand why it was hard to ignore your Truthwell. Now I'm supposed to search out the depths of what was, for years, off limits to me."

"Off limits?" His words were so quiet, he didn't think she heard them. "*I've* been off limits to *you*?" he said, a little louder. "All this time, I've wanted to know who my father's secret sorcerer was, but you were off limits to me."

They stared at each other for a long moment. In his mind, memories of peeking around the corner nearest the sorcerer's door tangled with imaginative scenes of Aly watching Red from her shroud. For the past six years, they'd *both* been held back. From each other.

Her features revealed nothing of what she was thinking. Magic had kept them apart, and now magic Bound them together —in a strange, twisted dance toward death.

A twig snapped. Red whirled, drawing his knife. Just in time. A snarling red foxblood bolted out into the clearing.

The beast had found them.

Its fangs parted. Fur raised on the foxblood's oversized neck. The telltale black eyes of a Canyon beast glinted in the sunlight.

Red flung his knife as the beast lunged. It grazed the fur at the neck, but the beast only shuddered and kept coming.

"Move!" Aly's arms shot out and the air grew cold. The entire forest floor seemed to rise as leaves and rocks and twigs leapt into the air and swirled around the foxblood's face and paws. Confused, the animal growled and snapped at the debris. Aly leaned forward, shoving her hands toward the beast. A gale force wind slammed the beast down on the ground where she attempted to bury it alive under a mound of dirt.

Loud stomping drew the king's attention to the top of the

knoll before Yin burst into view. Never had he heard Yin move with so much noise.

"Sire!" he panted as he ran up.

Aly had disappeared from sight. Yin spotted the thrashing animal under the still-swirling debris. He lunged for it—and knocked right into Aly.

She plunged into view as her body lurched and lost balance. Yin grunted at the unexpected impact. Her scream as she fell toward the beast was lost under Red's own scream and the beast's snarling.

In the moment she lost concentration, the foxblood scrambled free of the piled-on dirt and sank his teeth into Aly's right arm.

As Aly snarled in pain, Yin drove a blade all the way through the animal's throat. It went limp.

Cupping a hand over her arm, Aly stared at Yin as she scrambled to her feet. "Leave. Now."

He bowed at her and turned to go, glancing at his king for orders. Red gave a curt nod, then he rushed to Aly's side.

With one stiff hand, she shoved him away. "You have to leave me. Now." Her head shook in small, disorienting twitches. "I'm done. I'm infected. You have to go."

He balked. "Can't you heal yourself?"

She whimpered and looked up at him. "It doesn't really work that way. I can heal the wound, but the magic is in me now…and it'll twist the magic I already have. It's not like Seb's infection; it's more like yours. With a sorcerer, it can only be siphoned out."

"Do it."

"What?"

Red grabbed her shoulder. "Do it. Siphon the magic into me."

Her head shook several more times before she said, "I can't."

"I command you to! Look at me!" He tried to memorize her face, the way her eyes were both green and amber when the sun hit them. She had more freckles on her nose than her cheeks, but she'd sprouted more in the past few days. "Get it out of you, now."

She looked back at the wound, which seeped blood under her pressing fingers. "Frederick."

"Don't call me that. You're going to be fine."

She inhaled sharply. "The magic will make me horrible. I'll be like my father."

"That's why you have to siphon it into me, before it turns you into a raving, mad monster, or whatever it does."

"Thanks for that, but I won't put this evil in you."

He picked up her bloody hand and pressed it against the buttons on his coat. "Yes, you will. I'm already cursed, what difference does it make if you add more? Then you can heal me. I know you can. I need you." He coughed. "As my sorcerer. I need you to be my sorcerer. I can't cross the Canyon and travel to Bulvarna without one." He shook his head. "Without you."

The way she looked at him sent his blood into a frenzy. He'd fumbled those words and wasn't sure if she heard the right parts or the wrong parts.

"Red, I don't—"

"Stop." He refused to release her hand. "You can heal me. It's the plan, remember? When we reach the river, you can Pull this magic out and dump it back where it came from."

After a long pause, she nodded.

"You can do it."

"This will not feel good." Her fingers wiggled between the buttons of his coat, then his shirt to find his hot skin.

This felt nothing like the warmth she'd sent through him at the accession ball as she checked for dark magic, or the way his muscles had melted the night she'd healed his headaches. Where her fingers touched his skin, shards like broken glass shoved their way into his bloodstream. He groaned, then panted through clenched teeth. He reminded himself that he'd asked for this.

Soon, it felt like she was trying to kill him. The pain was too intense. He tried to push her hand away, but his strength had fled.

Then it was over, and she let go. He swatted her hand away when she tried to touch him again.

"Red." Her voice was a whisper, her eyes wide. "I need to touch you one more time."

He backed away, wondering how long he could stand the needles coursing through his entire body. The world around him teetered, and at his next step he collapsed in the leaves. Before he could roll over, Aly had a hand on the back of his neck, holding him down. Her body dove on top of his. She was pinning him! She would kill him now that he was down.

Rage gave him the strength to wrench his body around, but she kept him pinned with some effort and an elbow in his throat. Her hand flattened against his face and instantly he felt cold sink into his body, then heat. He'd felt this before.

Words tumbled from her mouth, hurried and desperate and foreign. She looked up and down his frame, frantic. The heat pushed all the pain away, replacing his muscles with the most extreme exhaustion he'd ever felt. With one last deep breath, she released him and sat back, her legs tangling with his. She extracted herself and leaned against a tree beside him.

Sprawled on the ground, he stared up at the branches for several minutes, calming his heartrate and recalling the events of the past quarter hour. Of all that had transpired, the memory that stood out above the rest was the recent pressure of her body against his. "Thanks," he finally said.

She smacked his shoulder with her uninjured hand. "I can't believe you made me do that!"

He rolled to his side and propped on an elbow. "I didn't make you do anything. You knew as well as I did that you'd be worse off with that magic in you." When she didn't look up, he added, "So, it's all gone?"

She nodded, arms around her knees. "It's gone. I felt...

stronger somehow. Like my magic had…" She tapped two fingers against her lips. "It felt like it did that night in the garden, when you made me burn up all those flowers." He started to interject but she kept going. "I can heal Seb too; I know I can now."

Red sat up, not yet ready to stand, feeling an undeniable tug toward her. "Okay, so heal him now—fly yourself back now."

"I'll have to touch him. Healing like that works so much better with physical contact." She shuddered a little as she said this, rubbing one hand down the outside of her arm to disguise the movement. Then she lifted her injured arm and, eyes closed, muttered a few words that made her blood lift off his shirt, off her arm, and out of her wound, then the bite mark on her arm glowed a bright white and was sealed. Her eyes popped open. "I can only shroud sound and sight, not touch. He'd feel me if I got close. Not likely to get away with that."

He couldn't help but remember her hands in his hair, her fingers on his chest. "Why can't you shroud the sense of touch? And why do you have to? You stayed hidden so your father wouldn't find you. Now he has found you. Just walk up to Seb. He's wanted to meet you as long as I have."

Aly dropped her chin onto her knees. He craned his neck to look at her face.

A hawk circled on an updraft over the valley. Red recalled a statue in his room of a falcon taking flight. He'd often felt like that bird, nearly able to soar but forever frozen to the ground. Aly too was tethered, perhaps in even more ways than he was. She had enough power to lift boulders and reroute rivers, but she had to live her life as a security blanket for a foolish king. In his stomach, he felt a weight drop.

She stood. "How are you feeling?"

He laughed, a bit surprised, and pushed himself up. She hadn't answered the questions, but he didn't reiterate them. He walked to the dead animal and retrieved his dagger. "I need a nap."

"As for shrouding," she continued in a somewhat defensive tone, "touch is so much less subjective than sight and sound. People *think* they hear things all the time, even think they see things. It's much easier to drape magic over those senses than it is touch. That's why I can't shroud touch."

A thought occurred to Red, and without any ruminations into the consequences of his next actions, he simply stepped forward and placed one hand on Aly's face, fingers straddling her left ear, thumb gently brushing against the tiny hairs at her temple. She froze, mouth parted in shock.

He leaned forward, just a fraction, a leaf's width, but the movement was as pronounced as a formal bow. She withdrew, her face sliding out of his grip, a few of her hairs tugging out as they caught on his signet ring, as if a tiny part of her didn't want him to let go. At least he hoped that was the case. Her horrified face suggested otherwise.

"You said touch was not subjective," he said, a wilting smile on his lips, a circus in his chest.

"What *was* that? Seriously?"

"I thought I'd prove to you that touch *is* subjective." The confidence he felt a second ago breezed off of him. He dropped his gaze to his feet, kicked a few leaves. "I thought if you realized touch was subjective, you'd figure out how to shroud it." He snapped his head up, determined not to look the coward. "But I'm no sorcerer, so what do I know?"

She glared at him, face purpling in either rage or embarrassment; he couldn't tell.

"Don't ever do that again," she said, voice soft.

"Fine."

As he turned to descend the hill, he was once again alone.

❧

"What is the matter with you?" Elise asked as Red tromped back into the sunlit clearing.

He snuffed air, annoyed that he hadn't managed to calm his reddened face during his walk back to the caravan. But Aly's face, her comment, her *outrage* had crawled under his skin like maggots and eaten away at his composure, mixing with his fear of the foxblood, the memory of evil in his blood, and his worry over Seb's infection.

Elise stood, brushing off her dress even though it hadn't even touched the grass, and moved toward her brother. Her hand caught his arm and jerked him around. "Look at me."

Red rolled his eyes and turned toward her. She knew him too well. "I'm fine, Elise."

"Do not lie to me. I may be a subject of the king, but I am also his sister." She looked him up and down, her eyes pausing at his rumpled appearance, even though there wasn't any blood left on him. Her eyes snapped up. "Who is she?"

Mutinous heat flared in Red's ears and throat. Seb's dark skin never gave away embarrassment like this. It wasn't fair.

Elise cracked a huge grin at this discovery. "Someone traveling with us! You went off to cavort with her in the woods!" She punched his shoulder. "Frederick!"

He looked anywhere but at her. Was Aly nearby, listening to all this? He wished more than anything that he could shroud his mortification right now.

"It's not that," he grunted. He had to lead Elise off the trail. No one could know about Aly. Ever. Except now Yin knew. Red hadn't stopped to talk to Yin as he stormed back to the road. Red considered telling Elise of the foxblood, but that would simply scare her, and the animal was dead now.

"Uh-huh." Elise propped her hand on her hip, tilted her head. Today her braid hung down her back, swinging like the pendulum of a grandfather clock. "Okay, I will take that as a challenge." She flashed a conspiratorial grin. "By the time we reach the border to Bulvarna, I will solve this mystery! There're only two choices: Leeta or Josephine! And I can't imagine you'd fall for my handmaiden, given Seb's recent interest in her."

Red waved a hand at her and stormed away. Elise could *not* discover the truth. No one could.

The truth was that his sorcerer had bewitched his heart.

2 2

A L Y

Soft as a breeze, Aly dropped onto Grey's carriage. She sat there, listening to him talk to Seb. The gritty lilt of his voice took her back to the first night she'd slept in a four-poster bed, the first time she'd seen the palace, the first time she'd worn a ballgown, the first time she'd attended a symphony. Without Grey, her life would have been so very different.

She had no right to eavesdrop, but as she prepared her spell to heal Seb, she listened. They spoke of the trade from Esvedara. Ships carrying rice up from the island had been ferrying illegal goods hidden inside the bags. Aly *humphed.*

Her time at Grey Manor had been short, but it had transformed her and catapulted her toward the king she now served, whose chest had been hot beneath the pads of her fingers, whose head had tipped against her stomach as she'd eased his pain, and whose Truthwell had fueled her magic like nothing ever had before.

But she'd made herself a promise to never again let herself fall.

Besides, I'll outlive all these people by a century or more. She frowned at the thought. *Alone, I'll always be alone.*

Dismissing these gloomy thoughts, she conjured her shroud around her body, her voice, and—she hoped—her touch, as she reached her arm down and found the edge of Seb's shoulder through the open window. But as she drew from the king's Truthwell to fuel her magic, she couldn't shake the tingling in her fingers or the impression of Red's hand against her cheek.

As her magic entered Seb, she sensed a change in him. When she checked him again for his infection, it was gone.

I've got to tell Red! Excited, she dove off the edge of the carriage, used a spell to spin in the air and land on her feet.

Shaking her head, Aly smiled and ran back toward Ondorian's coach. Red had been right. He'd known something about magic that she'd never figured out.

A sunrise later, the rip in the earth known as the Canyon rolled into view. Caridan, the tent city that served as headquarters for Canyon defenses, sat right at the edge.

The guards stationed at the entrance to the military camp welcomed the king's convoy with smiles, though their rifles spoke of the dangers that lurked nearby. Bullets may not work against magic, but they pierced Canyon beast flesh just fine.

As they rolled into the camp, Aly noted the sudden appearance of hundreds of Truthwells. The Protectors had enchanted the place to make it impossible for sorcerers on the outside to sense who lived within.

Aly wondered if their enchantments included a spell that would alert them to the presence of a cursed man.

In the distance, marking the entrance to the Canyon's sole bridge, stood two white columns, dim against the ever-present fog lifting out of the Deep.

Red shifted his weight back and forth as General Daniels, a quiet and bearded man who was aided by a tall lieutenant, briefed Red and his men on the search for the foxbloods that had slipped by recently.

True to their agreed upon word, neither Yin nor Red said anything about the attack in the forest yesterday. The soldiers would never let the king out of their sight if they knew, and Red and Aly were descending to the bottom of the Canyon, one way or the other. Time was running out, for him and for Aly.

As the tall soldier counted on three fingers the number of foxbloods they had tracked and killed, the men's faces fell. Seventeen deaths in the area, all attributed to the wandering beasts. In her mind, Aly added one more to the count of killed beasts.

The men, uniformed and armed, stood at attention as their king passed. The early morning haze had only just begun to clear and the rows of tents seemed to appear out of a void. Visible in her sorcerer's garb, Aly walked behind Red, followed by his councilmen. General Daniels led them through the camp, explaining the rotation of patrols and the need for more troops, given the unusual nature of the Canyon of late.

"Are you saying the Canyon is changing, General?" asked Alexander as they stood at the northern edge of camp. A sharp breeze rustled Alexander's mustache.

Daniels kept a flask at the ready. He took a sip from it. "Something down there is changing, my lord."

"What are you going to do about it?" Alexander demanded.

Daniels grunted. "My men are doing everything they can. While in camp, they're safe. Soon as they go out, they're in danger. But it's not against an enemy they know. Canyon beasts have their tendencies, as we know, but their behavior is no longer consistent with what we know of them." He scratched his beard with a thumb. "Foxbloods don't normally travel in packs. Wood-wolves don't normally come out in the daylight, nor do they often ascend in waves. Since the purge, we'd kill probably a dozen foxbloods in a six-month span, and maybe twice as many woodwolves. This spring, we've already killed eight foxbloods and twenty-seven woodwolves."

"Twenty-seven!" barked Seb.

Finally cured from his infection, Seb should be somewhere else recovering, not so close to the Canyon. Red had disagreed with her, wanting to keep Seb close in case he needed Aly's magic again. She'd lost that argument. Kings could be rather stubborn.

The general's eyes flashed at Alexander. "War dictates that we know our enemy. When we meet an enemy we can't predict, we fail."

Alexander bristled. "But you can hold them back, right?"

Turning to his king, the general said, "Right now, Your Majesty, we are rocks against a flood. My soldiers can't hold back the beasts for long. Eventually, we will be overcome."

That quieted the entire group. The six soldiers who accompanied them didn't so much as flinch at the general's words, but Aly watched the face of one young man, probably near her own age. As if sending an appeal, the soldier's eyes flashed toward the king, then, as quickly, to the sorcerer.

He was scared, and he looked to the sovereign and his sorcerer for aid. Little did the young man know, his two greatest hopes were about to plunge into the very depths that housed all his fears.

Night brought a flurry of activity around the military camp. Three cloaked Protectors walked the grounds muttering spells. They nodded to Red and Aly whenever they passed, but they failed to bow or salute as the others in the camp. As Master Sorcerers, they'd earned their prestige through talent and possessed the equivalent of noble status among sorcerers. They were subjects of the crown, but merely because they chose to be. They could easily walk—or fly—across the bridge and present themselves as Protectors to Kassia's soldiers or flee into the forest and live among the zealots—the sorcerers who avoided society.

Fleeing to the zealots had crossed Aly's mind more often than she cared to admit. She knew what the zealots were, misguided religious extremists who thought magic shouldn't be controlled at all. They were dangerous and reckless. But they had one thing going for them: their magic didn't have to keep anyone alive. Since leaving Mardon, the idea of escape had ignited in her mind, only to be doused every time she thought of Gevar. The guilt that plagued her daily would simply fester if she left Red to face a similar death. Now that they had a chance to heal him, she could not walk away.

Augustus Penwater's words about Beacons rang in her head: *They appear at pivotal moments in the world's unfolding.* That truth drove her toward a cure, toward her *father*, since that was what Red had chosen. But now, rising up from beneath her curiosity, her determination, and even her guilt was a reason for staying that she hadn't expected; she didn't just want Red to live because it was right, she wanted him to live so he could look at her the way he had started to on this trip.

She followed Red into a tent set up especially for the king, annexed onto the main camp by the extension of the wall and the sorcerer's enchantments. The sole indicator that this tent was different from the others was that it had a thin rug on the floor and two lamps instead of one. The soldiers here had little in the way of luxury, though they'd spared what they could for their king. Fortunately, this king didn't require a bed of furs or a hanging chandelier. Aly appreciated that.

"How exactly are we getting down there?" Red asked Aly, leaning on a shaky table inside his tent. Her shroud kept any listening ears from hearing their conversation.

"I have a way."

"Don't be mysterious with me."

She half-smiled, but it faded before she spoke. "You don't need to know right now. You'd only worry."

"*That* makes me worry."

"Oh, hush." She pinched her brow and fiddled with the string of her mask on the table.

The silence spoke of all they didn't say.

What if they failed?

What if they died?

What if they came back changed?

Red sagged against the table. "We need more time."

"We don't have it."

"Coming here was a mistake."

Her gaze snapped up. "No. It was rash, but it turned out to be exactly what we needed to do." She flattened her hands on table between them. "Interesting, isn't it?"

"What is?"

"That we were headed the right direction the whole time. I think you were right; my father knew the river could take back the curse. That's why he sent the lyth—he didn't want us to come north."

Leaning back, Red stared at her. "Now that we're so close, I imagine he'll increase his efforts to stop us. I'm not looking forward to seeing what he chooses next." For a moment, neither spoke, then Red asked, "Doesn't it bother you that we're hedging everything on a line of *poetry*?"

Her fingers curled into fists. "Parts of the *Verad* are poems. We believe them."

"But people have been studying those texts much longer and with much more insight than an old monk's forgotten poems."

She shrugged. "I suppose, but no one ever said the people who study the *Verad* always get it right."

"Seems a bit cavalier of Theod to let us get it wrong."

"Seems a bit foolish of us to lose the real meaning."

Red accepted her rebuttal with a nod. After a moment, he stood. "I'm fully aware that my life is likely about to end. No, don't disagree. I might not come out of that Canyon." He paced to the end of the table and clasped his hands behind his back. "I would like to do two things. First, I would like to take a walk. Alone." He raised a hand. "You can protect me from afar, remember?"

She sat back down. "And the second?"

"I think it would be best if I meet with Kassia before we attempt our descent into the Canyon." He lifted his hands to silence the protests spewing out of her mouth. "Hear me out. We came here to see what was really happening, to boost the morale of the men, but also to plead with Kassia to see reason." He straddled the bench and sat. "If I don't make it out of that Canyon, I'd like to have at least tried to talk sense into the queen. We're so close. Let me do this one thing. For Tandera."

Squeezing her eyes shut, Aly said, "You don't have to ask my permission; you're the king."

"Yes, and I'd be dead already without your magic keeping me alive. So, I'd like you to agree to this."

She opened her eyes. "But Dimitri—"

He leaned forward. "Four years ago, you didn't accompany my father to Kassia's palace. Don't accompany me either. Stay here with the soldiers, with the other Protectors. Nothing can happen to you here. You're safe."

She shook her head. "You…"

"They can't kill me. Not while Lucien and I are there by official invitation. It would be outright war. The worst they could do is curse me." He chuckled. "It's *you* they want, anyway. Sorry," he added at her frown. "But that means I'll be all right. I can go, have my talk with Kassia, and return here to go with you into the Canyon. Save the worst for last." He lifted his brows, expectant.

Aly sat close enough that her hand rested only inches from

his. When she pushed away from the table, her cloak brushed his arm. He followed her to the tent door.

Over her shoulder, she said, "Okay, Red. Go save the world. Then come back here so I can save you."

But she had no intentions of remaining peacefully at camp.

23

RED

The following morning, Red strolled through the military camp one last time. He nodded to soldiers and offered words of encouragement while his mind wandered to the bridge he was about to cross. He'd crossed it once before with his father. Though he'd survived that trip with no incident, it did not dispel the fears that rose as the carriages rolled toward the group waiting to depart the camp.

The lazy gray fog obscured the opposite side of the Canyon, though right above the trees the sun shone hot and bright. Red bid farewell to General Daniels and joined the rest of his party beside the carriages. Aly had been invisible all morning, but as he ducked into Ondorian's carriage, she sat waiting for him, in cloak and mask.

"We agreed you would stay here."

"Hush, I wanted to talk to you about Seb."

"You said he was healed."

She shook her head. "He's healed. You still don't trust me! But he needs to hear the words of the *Verad* often, especially as you drive over the Deep."

"Ondorian has a copy with him."

"Good. He can ride with you two." Scooting toward the door, she said, "Be careful. My father is a wicked man. There are many other actions he can take besides killing you. His goal is to weaken me, keep that in mind. There are many spells he can cast that pollute my source."

Resisting the urge to reach for her, his hand remained stiff as a scepter by his side, where it belonged. Then Aly vanished once again.

"You don't always have to disappear, you know." He fumed inside, mad that she kept shrinking away from the world, away from *him*.

A moment later, Seb's face appeared outside the carriage. "I hear I'm riding with you?"

The soldiers' horses whinnied and snorted as they were driven onto the smooth surface of the bridge.

Red felt as if the Canyon reached for him, as if a hand might slither out of the fog and into the window to grab him.

"If Carolyn were here," Seb said, "she'd be praying to see a woodwolf or a garland cat."

The carriages began to rumble forward once again, propelled by magic. This time, however, they were propelled by Grey's sorcerer.

Of course Aly had told Grey of their plan. It had angered Red at first, but her reasoning was valid. They had to ensure the carriages made it to Isardra. The way Aly's magic was weakening, though she could Pull from a long distance, there was no sense risking her magic failing and leaving them stranded, horseless, on the road. Grey's sorcerer would be moving the carriages, but Aly would still be the one protecting the king via spells cast from the relative safety of Caridan. Kassia wouldn't order a guard to shoot him or anything as brazen as that, so Aly's protective spells were crafted mostly to ward off other word magic.

One by one, the carriages passed through the two pillars at the entrance to the bridge and began the journey across. Magic had built this impossible bridge, back when Red's grandfather had first established friendly relations with Bulvarna; magic still sustained it, the spells cast a half century ago holding strong.

"She'd want to see a garland cat, you're right," Red said. "Since they're *fictional.* No one in their right mind wants to see a woodwolf. And Carolyn, she'd scream your ears to bleeding if she did."

Red blinked hard at Arthur Ondorian, then pointed his eyes at Seb as his friend craned his neck to look out the window. He mouthed the word *truth.*

Ondorian remained oblivious to Red's eye movements.

Frustrated, Red said, "So, you were reading me the history of the Canyon from the *Verad.*" He lifted his brows at the priest.

As if startled by the fact that he wasn't alone in his carriage, Ondorian jumped a little before answering. "Even though that is a lie, Your Majesty, I can certainly read the histories if you would like, but I need not read it to tell it to you."

Red cringed, annoyed that the priest had to call out his lie. He nodded at Ondorian.

Seb kept his eyes toward the opaque fog and the passing white pillars that meant their carriage had rolled onto the bridge. Red's pulse began to dance. In his dreams, he always made it halfway across the bridge before bad things began. A stiff wind would knock him off, or he'd approach the center and find that the bridge was falling apart from the other side, dropping into the blackness like fractured ice on a winter lake.

But those were the nightmares of a child. Soon he and Aly would be descending into the Canyon by their own choice. It was their only recourse, if he hoped to live. Although going into the Canyon was almost like welcoming death. At least by descending, they had a chance he could be healed. He closed his eyes and listened to Ondorian.

"In the fifteenth year of Queen Alina of the Varnans, ancestors of the Bulvarnans, the third year of King Josef of Refere, the earth split in a great quake as the two peoples warred. Usrich of the Varnans, sorcerer of the northern kingdom, lived two-hundred and seventy-five years, and died after diving into the Black River."

"Hmm," Seb muttered. "That's depressing."

Red agreed. It didn't offer much in the way of hope for their plan.

The air in the carriage suddenly felt thick, as if charged with the electricity of a coming storm. Red poured his energy into a fierce stare at Ondorian.

"Josef had one son, Nathaniel, who reigned for seventeen years. At his father's death, Nathaniel fled the presence of the Canyon, establishing his people far to the south. The Varnans entered the land and took possession of it. Alina reigned for thirty-one years, and her reign was full of evil."

Seb spat a laugh. "That's pretty blunt."

Ondorian did not pause. "Her son, Tomas, was fifteen when he took the throne."

"Hey, some kid younger than you!"

Red ignored the elbow jab, heart and head throbbing. The blackness seemed to be seeping in from beneath them, surrounding them, making the shadows in the carriage a little deeper, a little darker.

Seb continued, "I remember him. The guy who was king when the foxbloods attacked and ate everybody. He was pretty tossing bad."

Ignoring him, Ondorian pressed on. "At the age of twenty-two, Anson I of Tandera rode to war against Alina's son and took the land south of the Canyon as the nation of Tandera."

"Bulvarna had claim to our land before we did. Seems strange to be going there now to talk to the queen about how to keep our country safe."

Red leaned toward his window, straining to see the twin pillars that marked the other side of this cursed bridge, the end of the danger. Seb shouldn't even be here. Red never would have allowed him to come on this trip if he'd known the depth of the darkness lurking inside his best friend. He thought the *Verad* would work, like Aly had said. Maybe his infection wasn't fully gone.

Chills and sweat erupted all down Red's back and chest. "Ondorian," Red said, "enough history. Shall we recite a poem, perhaps?"

Seb burst into laughter and slapped Red on the shoulder. "You and poetry again. Man, that crown has changed you, Brother." He scratched his head. "You know, I recall you asking me to read a poem, but I can't remember what it was about. I feel like there was something I wanted to tell you about that poem. Odd."

Ondorian finally sensed the danger because he nodded at the king and opened his mouth in the rhythm of memorized verses of the *Verad*, the short concise sentences acting like little soldiers against the dark.

Seb's shoulders relaxed a little, and he leaned back, gaze fixed out the window once again. His twisted smile remained, but his buzzing fury of a moment before ebbed. A breath hissed from the king's clenched teeth. He could see the pillars marking the other side now, a shade paler than the fog.

On the other side of the Canyon, the Bulvarnan welcome party waited. It was a measure of respect and a measure of safety to send a party to greet visitors at the bridge. No peace summit should begin with the unhappy disappearance of either of the sovereigns of the guest countries.

Refere's King Lucien was only a few hours behind them, set to arrive at the military camp before noon, receive a quick update, and proceed across the bridge. Lucien would be arriving at Kassia's palace shortly after Red.

Solid ground rolled beneath them and a wave of relief doused the crackling fear in Red's gut. They were on Bulvarnan soil now. If in coming here Red had chosen wrong, he might never see his sisters again, his mother. He might never see his sorcerer again either.

As the white walls of Isardra came into view, hot anger and cold fear metronomed in Red's chest. His headache sharpened. The palace was minutes away, in the heart of the Pale City.

Seb's elbows rested on his knees as their carriage drew up the cobbled path toward the fabled palace of Isardra.

Kassia had begun her own renovations, as many monarchs did to their palaces, and hers were anything but modest. The north façade was covered in a cobweb of scaffolding, and men wove around the webs plastering pearlescent tiles to the stone. Red couldn't deny the beauty of Kassia's home. Her new renovations would change the fable-worthy palace to something more akin to sun-struck snow. She was coating the castle in sparkling white.

The home of kings long dead, Isardra's ancient castle still perched on the city's highest hill, a testament to this country's past strength. That castle had been home to Alina, the reigning sovereign when the Canyon was created. Some said magic kept the walls from crumbling down. Others said it was merely well-built. Its brooding walls had never once been taken in battle, only eventually abandoned for brighter, larger palaces.

The cobblestones had been taken from the River Ild, which flowed from the white mountains of Revnad to the Pale City. Bulvarnans loved their snow and ice, and felt the ivory hue of the Revnads proved their purity. The entire city, from royal residence to rented flats, had been built of the white stone of those mountains. A trick to the eye at first, the city rose from the dark earth toward the gray sky, almost as if the clouds had reached down to form Isardra. The shadows between the buildings and the flowing ivy that blanketed the walls were the darkest parts of the city. Stone rooftops, stone walls, stone streets all washed together in a jumble of white geometry.

"A bit monochromatic," Seb muttered, eyes scanning the city as they rode up one of its streets.

"But memorable," Red added. "And Bulvarna likes to be remembered."

"You remember Mira, eh?" Seb lifted an elbow.

"Mira Mirkova hasn't crossed my mind since the last time you brought her up. Maybe it's you who has the fixation."

"Fine. No need for anger." Seb leaned his head out the window and ogled the city.

Mira might have been an attractive face to Red once, but nothing more. Now the woman he couldn't stop thinking about was not available to him.

A month ago, he'd blamed Aly for his father's death. He'd wanted to hate her, to place the ugly weight of his grief on her. Nothing had turned out as he'd expected. Even though Aly's face populated his every waking thought, he would either die in a few days or, if he was lucky, a few decades from now. Aly would live for centuries. There was no denying that simple fact. More than the mask, the cloak, or the ring she wore and the crown he bore, *that* was the truth that built an unbreachable wall between them.

A cart paused by the side of the road for the royal procession to pass. A woman in a dingy gray cloak stood beside a small heap of potatoes and a few bags of rice. Her face wore deep wrinkles and a red tint that meant many hours out in the cold. The Bulvarnan blush, as many called it. Of course, Mira did not carry this poverty-pricked redness in her pale cheeks. For a moment, Red wondered if this woman might be a lyth, standing there as innocent as a tuber, ready to snarl into a crocodile or snap into a long-taloned hawk.

He couldn't trust anyone in this wretched country, and that attitude wouldn't serve him well at a peace summit.

"What do sorcerers do at summits like this? Do they stand outside and blow stuff up? You still haven't told me anything about our sorcerer." Seb wiggled his brows, like Red might disclose some intriguing tidbit about the person they'd hypothesized about for years.

"The sorcerer is back at the camp." The carriage rolled over a pothole, and Red's head knocked the side of the cab.

"What?"

"I promise, Brother, I'll explain everything you want to know on the way home from Bulvarna." *If I go home, that is*, Red thought.

When the palace rolled fully into view, Seb leaned out the window like a boy on holiday. "Whoa."

The Lady Wolf descended from the grand foyer steps to a flourish of reedy music from a dozen wooden pipes as Red and his party entered the palace. Suits of armor bookended the stairwell, reminding Red of Aly. She was his armor, and she wasn't here.

A stab of pain in his head accompanied the thought that Aly's father was likely in this room right now. Invisible. Inevitable.

Red glanced over at his sister. She carried herself like a sovereign; should their plan go south in the Canyon, she would be. That was the reason she was here. He offered her a small smile, then faced Kassia.

The queen floated on silent slippers, as if she had command even over the floor on which she walked. Her pale skin had been snowed with powder. She wore a bold dress of deep plum, shockingly garish against her chest and exposed arms. A chalky scent doused with the sharpness of pomegranate wafted forward.

"Dearest cousin," she cooed, lifting her hand to accept a hastily administered kiss from Red. He nearly choked on the powder that puffed into his open mouth from the back of her hand. He could smell the silver polish on her rings. They must have broken out these relics from storage for the occasion.

"Nice to see you again, Cousin." Their lineage had as much in common as butter and a butterfly, but he felt no need to break habits of old just yet.

"You've grown quite tall." Her dust-covered brows crinkled and fine white mist fell into her eyes.

Red tried not to smirk. "Much has changed since last I visited your great country, including the grandeur of this magnificent palace." He had watched his father speak with other kings and queens. Pour praise on an enemy, and it warmed even the coldest waters. He looked up at the domed ceiling painted with half-naked winged cherubs and pale princes. "You've quite outdone yourself, Kassia."

She blinked, perhaps also blushed, but he couldn't tell under the cherry-red dots painted on her cheeks. "You are kind like your father, dearest Frederick."

Once their names had been spoken, they could proceed to business.

But the mention of his father spiked a nerve in Red's chest, sending a small surge of pain up his neck to add to his headache. "He planned these negotiations, as you know, before the illness took him. I thank you for accepting the proposal to hold them here."

Kassia tilted her chin up, nearly level with his. "Long live the king." She watched his face with prying eyes before lifting both hands, gesturing at her silent attendants. "Come! Let us speak of brighter topics! I have planned a celebration to be remembered!"

Of course she has, Red thought. Anything to be remembered. "My thanks, Your Majesty. My companions are tired from the journey, and we wish to refresh before dinner."

The queen curled the edges of a smile into her plum-colored lips. With a dip of her chin, she dismissed the king.

Men in white tunics, embroidered with Bulvarna's royal crest of a snarling wolf, led the king and his men to their chambers in the palace. Negotiations would begin in the morning. The masquerade to celebrate their agreement—whatever it would be —was set for the night following.

As Red strode down a long, carpeted hallway toward the guest wing, he couldn't help but wonder if he would live long enough to attend the masquerade.

Tomorrow night, no matter the outcome of the negotiations, he'd be meeting Aly at the Canyon's edge.

The next morning arrived with steaming tea and screaming pain. Red's headache threatened to keep him thrashing in the bedsheets instead of descending for the first roundtable discussion of the peace summit.

He needed Aly's magic.

Guilt twisted inside his chest as he downed the herbal tea that helped numb the pain. *She'll be safe,* he told himself. Her father wouldn't attack four sorcerers and a camp full of highly trained soldiers. Besides, he would assume Aly had come with Red.

I'll have to convince him that she has.

He replayed the well-worn memory of her hands in his hair, of the magic of her closeness that night she'd chased his pain away. He needed the magic of relief that she alone could give, but he wanted more than that, which he hated to admit.

Breakfast was brought to his room on a tray soon after he pulled himself out of bed. Yin stood sentry by the door, but Red's nose followed the smell of Bulvarnan pancakes slathered in jam. A little cold from the trip up the servants' stair, but Red downed them with gusto, hungry after the poor food served at the military camp.

Red had to conduct these peace meetings in Bulvarna without

Aly by his side, without her standing guard, without her hidden presence giving him boldness and taming his pain.

He would have to do this on his own.

I really have been too harsh with her, he admitted, a barb of remorse pricking at him for all the times he snapped at her.

"They must know Tanderans have a tooth for sweets." Yin's voice cut into the king's thoughts.

"Come eat some. I couldn't eat this many pancakes if my life depended on it." The king paused and ate a bite. "Well, maybe if my life depended on it." They'd served coffee with the pancakes. Perhaps Kassia, despite her many spies, didn't know of Red's headaches. Even the thought of caffeine boiled the simmering pain in his skull.

Yin remained by the door, hands clasped at his waist.

"Yin, please. This food will be wasted if you don't eat it."

"I cannot eat off a king's plate."

Red grunted. "Yes, you can. You and I are no different." Yin had lived in Tandera for nearly two decades, but still he balked at some of Tandera's ideas.

"Your Majesty, that is entirely untrue."

"Just because I wear that thing," he lifted a finger toward the small circlet of gold resting on the table by the window, "doesn't mean I am a person who has to eat off of different plates and be treated like a diseased…" The words petered away as it brought back a flash of his dying father, an image of the man Red had once thought invincible, shivering under the blankets. He did not finish his sentence or his point, but instead dipped his head for another bite, then tossed the silver fork on the blue-patterned plate, a crescendo to his awful statement.

As the king rose, yanked his napkin out of his collar, and moved toward the window to slip into his surcoat, he noticed Yin step toward the breakfast tray.

His father had been a wise king. Red had spent his life wanting to be like his father, to *be* his father. Gevar had been cursed with magic, and rather than allow anyone else to be harmed, he had let himself die.

"Let's hope we make history today," Red declared. He tugged at his jacket hem, noticing that the tilt of the mirror made him look thin, teetering almost. Pushing at the mirror with one boot, he tried to angle the glass to show his real proportions. They did not make him look any stronger.

His strength was in a military camp across the Canyon.

No, he thought, *she's not my only source of strength.* Tandera, the phoenix surging up again and again out of its own ashes, was strong. Red represented Tandera. He would be strong because of Tandera.

This agreement, should Kassia sign it without butchering it first, would make history, even if no one ever remembered the signatures on it. The Canyon loomed large in his mind, but today he had the chance to protect his countrymen, to give those soldiers some real relief.

"I will not have it!" bellowed King Lucien of Refere, the golden lion of their seal roaring in sparkling threads upon the king's chest, a miniature of the man's face. His amber beard shivered as his lips fought to remain still.

Red hadn't said much since the deliberations began. His headache had not dulled enough to allow his full concentration. His chin sagged near his collar bone; his limbs felt heavy as timber.

These negotiations weren't proceeding as well as he'd hoped.

He stared at Kassia, whose powdered face seemed to have alchemized into marble. The lines around her beet-purple lips created small shadows of contempt. White gold dripped through her hair onto her brow in intricate snowflake shapes punctuated with diamonds. As soon as the queen had entered, Seb had leaned over and whispered that the diamonds clustered on her brow looked more like white pimples than signs of power. Since then, Red hadn't been able to look at her without a small urge to chuckle.

She lifted her brows, the snowflake jewels twinkling as they moved. "My decision is firm, cousin. The Canyon is not to be contained, and I will not be bullied into agreeing to your terms." The queen rested her wrists on the table and steepled her fingers.

Lucien frowned and rolled his head toward the tall windows at the back of the domed hall. Cherubs danced in the blue-painted sky above them, mocking their attempts at peace.

They spoke in Bulvarnan, a requirement of being in Kassia's house, and Red wished he'd spent more time pouring over grammar books, but he'd had other things to focus on.

Red wondered what sort of peace they'd be celebrating at Kassia's planned masquerade, if any. Two days, that's all she'd given them for these negotiations, and the palace preparations for the masquerade were all but finished. Before the ball, however, a river at the bottom of the Canyon was calling Red's name.

"The Canyon must be contained," Lucien growled, voicing Red's own opinion.

Kassia pinned Lucien with slit-eyed condescension. "What *must* be accomplished by me is of my determination alone."

"Indeed. But surely your renowned kindness extends beyond the wide borders of your own great lands," Red said, cutting Lucien off from what would surely have been a snappy remark, given the fiery hue on the other ruler's features. "The people of this continent look to you to provide the security they so desperately desire. They look to you to quell the nightmares at the source. They look to you to quiet the terrors that have so long plagued our lands and will again if given the chance." *Compliments,* he reminded himself. *Pour on the compliments. Make her feel like a hero.*

Kassia's brows sank, leaving her eyes hooded and lost in

shadow. The lines around her mouth twitched. As established by the three sovereigns before the meeting, none of the sorcerers were supposed to be present during this meeting, as a measure of respect and at least feigned honesty—but a sorcerer could still whisper silently to his or her sovereign from afar, and given their easy ability to be invisible, Red doubted if Lucien or Kassia had abided by this agreement. Aly, of course, was not present and had not said a word to Red since he left her in the camp.

He'd never thought he'd *want* her silent words in his head. Would he know if something happened to her?

"The problem with you two," Kassia said, flicking her eyes at Lucien and Red, "is that you believe the Canyon to be the enemy. I have tried explaining to you this morning that your understanding is simply wrong." Two of Lucien's men coughed, as did Lord Grey, but she blazed on. "The Canyon is our *blessing*. My scouts have found what they believe is a vein of copper running deep into the walls of the Canyon. Surely if we explore the depths more fully, we can discover other valuable resources. Not to mention this *power* Cousin Frederick is so keenly interested in."

Money and power; for some sovereigns, that was all that mattered. Red was surprised how deeply Kassia had taken to the lies coming from Aly's father.

"Whatever resources are down there, we are better off without them. The power I have been discussing is the one that transforms animals into murderous beasts and whispers lies into the world. It is not a power I desire, Cousin."

Just then, Seb's elbow jabbed him. He ignored it.

Kassia's cheeks pinched in a wicked smile. "Frederick is right. From the Deep comes worlds of power we never knew of before. Despite your words, you wish to claim it for yourself. There can be no other reason you want to keep us from it!"

Red's mouth hardened in shock. He glanced at Lucien, who

sat a few seats down, past Seb and Alexander. Lucien's blue eyes were friendly, but within them flickered doubt.

Turning his attention back to Kassia, Red caught a glimpse of Seb's and Alexander's expressions. Seb's eyes were wide, his mouth flat. He looked like he was about to burst to say something. Alexander, on the other hand, looked at Red as if the king had boils on his face that threatened to explode on the lord's good suit. Repulsion infused even his quivering mustache.

Do they believe Kassia? "I assure you, I want nothing to do with the Canyon," he said to Lucien, over Alexander.

"Of course he would say that," barked the queen. "At least I am honest. I admit I desire the riches the Canyon holds. For too long the world has feared what lay down there. Perhaps we have all simply been wrong."

Red snorted. "Do you call foxbloods good? Or do you think of woodwolves as *riches*? What about death curses?" At this last phrase, he broke into a sweat.

Again, Seb tried to get his attention with his boot.

Watching Red, Kassia tilted her head and tapped her middle finger. He'd all but admitted to her the one piece of information she'd not known until now: Gevar had indeed died of a death curse. He could assume she knew that Red was infected, which meant she also assumed he, too, would eventually die. As this information passed through Kassia's consciousness, her face moved from rigid and annoyed to soft and almost pleased.

He could have kicked himself, but the words had flown out of his mouth. Now Kassia assumed her opponent was beaten. Red would die like his father. The Tanderan sorcerer was clearly not enough to keep him alive, as the queen had planned. The corners of Kassia's mouth curled up.

"Death curses are only bad when you are on the receiving end, Cousin. If used properly, they could eliminate criminals with much less pain than a noose. As I have been a sovereign nearly as long as you have been alive, I can assure you that having an easy, clean way of removing unwanted people from the world is one remarkable benefit the Canyon offers us."

"You're talking about murder," Red snarled. Was he more aware of the ache in his bones, or was it nerves?

Kassia shrugged. "You may call it that now, but give yourself a little while under the crown. You'll see the advantage of a death curse. Isn't that right, Lucien?"

The Referen king's eyes darkened. He did not meet Red's gaze, implying that Lucien may have ordered people dead using death curses too. He was here to take a stand *against* the Canyon. Surely he was not employing its dark magic.

Angered by Kassia's boldness, which marched toward recklessness, Red had to act. These discussions were supposed to end with added protection for his people. For the Bulvarnan people too. The entire continent relied on the troops at the border to keep the Canyon beasts contained. But if the kings and queens of the continent *sought* the Deep's wickedness, the soldiers were no more than an inadequate afterthought.

"Cousin," Red began, forcing himself to remain cordial as he addressed the queen, "perhaps you have been persuaded of these ideas by someone else?" He had not seen Aly's father yet, despite the rumors that Kassia liked to show him to her guests. Had he left to find his daughter? Could he, like Aly, Pull from his source's Truthwell from afar? Staring at the bulging vein in Kassia's neck as his words stoked her rage, he wondered how there was any light left inside her to Pull.

What happened when someone's mind became darkened with lies? If a death curse dimmed a person's Truthwell, making it less powerful, what would a long-believed lie do?

If Aly's father had been darkening Kassia's mind with lies for years, perhaps his own source of power—the queen herself—was weaker than they all realized. Aly feared her father's strength, but what if *he* was not strong at all? What if, as Ondorian suggested, Dimitri wanted to diminish Aly's power by damaging her source—so that their power would be more *evenly* matched?

His heartbeat doubled. He had to tell Aly.

In the uncomfortable silence, Seb leaned over and whispered, "I remembered what I forgot about that poem."

"Not now," hissed Red.

"I misjudged a word. I said, 'inhale, river and take death,' but it really said, 'inhale, river, and *make* death.' I can't shake the feeling that you really need to know that."

Red's blood crystalized. *Are we about to make a huge mistake?*

With a delicate gesture, Kassia stood. "I will hear no more of your nonsense. Know one thing, boy, that I alone rule Bulvarna. Can you say as much of Tandera?"

Red, too, pushed back from the table, peace talks no longer on his mind. He needed to reach Aly. "Truth rules Tandera. Can you say as much of Bulvarna?" he retorted.

He'd had enough of this curse. It was time to descend.

2 4

ALY

The scent of fresh-cut firewood, rich and sweet, wafted over the field that abutted the small gathering of wooden homes barely an arrow shot from the Canyon's edge. Aly, dressed in a plain gray dress, walked toward the houses, pulse thundering in her temples.

It had been easy to leave the military camp. The guards, of course, couldn't see her, and the protective enchantments were built to keep people out, not in. Red had never directly ordered her to remain at the camp, he'd merely assumed she would for her own protection.

Bulvarnans did not give the Canyon the same wide berth as Tanderans. Several small villages stood within sight of the Canyon's sharp edge, a place no Tanderan would build. The people who chose to live in these communities were driven there by desperation, but Aly hoped their familiarity with the Canyon could give her the answers she sought.

She did not trust Seb's translation of the poem, and she had only one other idea for where to find out about the Black River before descending to its banks.

Called the Forgotten Cities, these communities existed alongside the Canyon in much the same way as beggars prostrated at the doors of churches. At the edge of the village, a bowl of meat had been left out, its stink wiping out all other smells as Aly walked closer. A circus of flies buzzed around it.

"Interesting," Aly muttered, making a face at the awful sight. These people were trying to attract the beasts of the Deep. Perhaps they didn't know that Canyon beasts only liked live bait.

Four years ago, when Aly had accompanied Gevar to Bulvarna, she'd spent her time questioning the citizens of this country, trying to learn everything she could about the ways of her father. That was the first time she'd heard of the Forgotten Cities. Four years ago, she hadn't had time to visit one.

If there was a way to see what happened to a mind fully twisted by the darkness, it was here.

The first home she passed had its windows open as well as its front and back doors. She could see straight through the one-roomed abode. It appeared empty. Weeds grew along the walls, peeking through the plaster in places. A shingle was missing, leaving a large hole.

Aly swallowed and walked toward the only house where a chimney smoked. She had a purpose in coming here, and she would not be disappointed.

"Oy!" someone yelled.

Aly turned around. From the seemingly abandoned house, a woman stepped out, her eyes squinting in the sunlight. She wore an apron that might once have been a pale color. Its front was smeared with enough grease and charcoal and something red that a look of disgust crept over Aly's features. The woman's hair was matted.

Speaking in seamless Bulvarnan, Aly said, "How do you do?"

The woman snarled.

"I simply want to know what I can do to be healed," Aly said, forcing a bit of pain into her tone.

For a moment, the wrinkled woman stared at her with narrow

eyes and an open mouth, displaying gaps where teeth should have been. Finally, she waved a hand as she walked off her stoop and up to Aly.

Her smell preceded her. "Ah, come to the light, have we? Come with me, child."

The woman shuffled across the dirt lane toward the house with the smoking chimney. There were perhaps a dozen buildings, nothing more.

With a stiff arm, the woman pushed the door open and barged inside. "Alef! Come here, we've got a new one."

When Alef showed himself, Aly nearly stumbled back against the bare wall. His face was dark purple and red, contorted in the ripples of skin that marked a terrible burn. He looked her up and down. She could barely hold his gaze.

"What's wrong with you?" he asked, his words clear and crisp.

"I seek healing." *It's not a lie. It's not a lie.*

"Indeed, but you look well."

"Some pains are inside, hidden from the world, yet no less painful." Her mind shot to Red. He was the one suffering. He was the one in pain. Her pain was in the mind. She missed Gevar. She carried the weight of his death on her shoulders. She worried for Red, for his comfort, for his survival.

That's why I'm here, she told herself.

"Ah, that they are." The man tilted his head. "Burdi here knows of that kind of pain. Come. Sit. We shall speak."

Aly followed the man into what amounted to a sitting room and sat on the edge of a chair with a cushion spewing strands of hay. In her mind, she uttered a spell to keep away bugs, a spell to steady her breathing, and one to knock her down should they attempt any sort of hypnosis.

"I want to know of your healings here," she began, hoping to quickly direct the conversation toward what she aimed to learn.

"When nothing else helped, I heard of these cities. Tell me, what is the secret to your miraculous healings?"

The man smiled, his lips stretching and creasing in strange ways from his scars. "We have found the cure. It is magic no one else is wise enough to see, and we have it all to ourselves. We live like *kings* here." He lifted his hands.

Aly's face muscles twitched as she controlled her expression. She reached out to the Truthwells of the two in the room and found them dark as mud. Their Wells raged and swirled, black muck clotting and reforming on itself in endless motion.

This is what it is to live a lie, she thought.

Trying not to sweat, Aly took a deep breath. "Tell me of the river." She had to cut to the chase. *What do these people believe about the river?* If they lived on lies, fed on them as their daily bread, she might not collect an ounce of useful information out of them, but if they trusted the Canyon, then perhaps they knew more of the Black River than anyone else.

The man's smile faded. "Our river is deep. It is strong. It rages against the darkness, sending its power out into the world to reclaim it for what it once was."

They think it fights against *the dark. They have been so warped that darkness is light and light is darkness in their minds.* "Its power?" she asked.

"Burdi, tell the woman of how it healed you."

The woman's voice rasped a few times before she began. "It took away all my pain. Nothing else could, but the river did. As it healed our Alef." She smiled toothlessly at the scarred man.

"I see," Aly said, nodding. "Do you descend to the river to find healing?"

"No," they said at once. Alef continued. "The river heals whom it wills."

"It doesn't heal everyone?"

"It kills the unworthy."

Aly pursed her lips. She was ready to leave this place. These people worshipped the Black River; they had no truth for her. "Do you have to physically touch the water?"

The two exchanged a glance. "Ay," said the man. "That is why you must have faith. If you step into the river for healing without believing, you will die. The river will Pull out all that is within you."

Aly's head popped up. "And that is why you are healed? Because you believed?" The man nodded.

Their healing is entirely in their minds. These people certainly came out of the river changed, but not in the way they imagined. *They know the river can kill. They've seen it.* That much was true.

Recalling decency, she thanked the two for their help, stood, curtsied, and explained that she needed to be on her way. The two appeared confused, tried to convince her to stay and descend to the river.

As soon as she stepped around the edge of the house, she yanked her shroud around her and disappeared, her mind pinwheeling with the notion that to heal Red, she would have to touch the waters of the Black River.

Maker above, don't let me end up like those people.

By the time she reached the Tanderan side of the bridge, her mind stopped racing. Though she'd never fully released her awareness of Red's Truthwell, she now focused her mind on it. It was swirling with death, but it was still luminous like a torch in the night. It was moving closer; he was returning.

Relief and fear tangled inside her as she ran to the camp gates.

It was time.

Nearing the edge of the forest, out of sight of the military camp, the mists of the Canyon rose like a moonlit wall before Aly and Red and Yin.

Yin had insisted on accompanying his king, especially after

Red told him the destination. Aly, grateful for the extra set of weapons and eyes, did not object.

The bridge lay far to their right, and the nearest patrol had just turned to begin another circuit. An eerie howl whispered in the night. Every twig that snapped in the darkness implied a foxblood coming to tear their flesh. Every hoot suggested a spy from the Deep.

Her shroud covered them from the eyes of men but not from the senses of the Canyon beasts. To the creatures, they would be as visible and as scented as any other human.

"There," she whispered, pointing up ahead. The trees stopped all at once, the ground simply falling away beneath them. The Canyon gaped, its mists like an exhaled breath.

"Seb's words, you really think that doesn't change anything?" His voice quivered.

The words of the Bulvarnan man echoed in Aly's mind. *It will Pull out all that is within you.* Lies, especially the well-crafted ones, twisted truth and warped the mind. The people living in the Forgotten Cities had been so deceived for so long that they lived in an entirely separate reality. Their crumbling homes were castles to them, their sores and scars a memory only.

Aly couldn't forget the hopelessness she'd felt in that man's home. He had abandoned reason, yet it appeared not to bother him. He no longer worried about the scar on his face or that it wasn't properly cleaned or treated. Lies had warped their understanding of the world. The magic of the Canyon was on full display in the Forgotten Cities, and it made Aly sick to her stomach.

"No," she said. "The river is the source of death. We knew that already. We're going down there to put the curse back where it came from. But I *did* warn you that Seb's translation would be untrustworthy."

She was now armed with the knowledge, albeit stripped from within a lie, that the Black River did both give and take, as the poem suggested. Kanto was right. Seb's translation had been wrong, but it didn't change their plan now. They just had to be certain not to touch the water after the siphon was complete.

As with any lie, if not mixed with some truth, it usually wafted away with the breeze. Perhaps that was also the case with the truth buried in Kanto's poem. It had been diluted over the centuries with lies. The Black River did not *give* life, as the people of the Forgotten Cities assumed, but if the river was the origin of death curses, it could receive them back by siphoning, as could the sorcerer who cast a death curse.

Aly did not tell Red where she had gone or what she had done. Her goal while the king was away had been to prepare for their task, which she had completed.

And now she knew that she would have to touch the water; there was no other way. As with her healing magic, the only way to ensure it was effective was to maintain physical contact. She left this part out, too, as Red and Yin peered down into the black depths.

The rest of the king's party slept peacefully at Kassia's palace, ignorant of their king's secret absence. The masquerade was still scheduled for the following night. Kassia would celebrate her victory, and the world would think they'd come to some sort of agreement.

If they survived this, Aly would return with Red to Isardra. She would, at last, face her father. She glanced at her swirling smoke ring, her constant reminder of why she chose this path. She'd chosen to serve as Royal Sorcerer to gain the strength necessary to one day defeat him, should he try to kill her. Little had she known he would attack her sources to weaken her first.

With Red fully healed, she would be as strong as her father. Maybe even stronger.

"Are you sure about this, sire?" asked Yin as he checked the chambers of a revolver.

"There is no other way. You do not have to come."

Yin stuffed his gun away, behind the hilt of one of his swords. "I will not abandon my duty merely because of fear."

Aly's brows lifted as she pulled items, ones they would need to descend, out of a satchel. Among them, one of her recent secrets from Red. She was impressed that Yin admitted to being afraid of the Canyon. His stoicism was unmatched. A true warrior felt fear, he simply did not let fear win. Aly nodded at the man in respect. He nodded back.

She'd left her cloak and mask behind. No sense wearing the garb of a Master Sorcerer into the Deep. Besides, Yin had already seen her face when they'd fought the foxblood.

"Aly," said Red, squatting down to help her separate three bundles of dark cloth. "If Kassia is as polluted with lies as it appears, how can your father still be strong? If you think there is any way you could cast the curse back into him, I think we should attempt that rather than the river."

Standing, Aly put her hands on her hips. "Having second thoughts, are we?" She glanced down into the foggy depths and exhaled. "I don't blame you. This is insane." A small pause punctuated her words. Then she added, "But the Canyon has its own strength. Even if Kassia's Truthwell is polluted with lies, I don't think it is weakening my father's magic." Mental images of Alef and Burdi populated her mind. "There is a magic all to itself in the power of lies. We know this. Don't let the Canyon's magic twist your mind before we even get down there."

Red did know it. History had taught it to him. His *own* history also had taught it to him, when he'd nearly been Stripped. He turned aside and flexed his jaw.

"We will heal you tonight, then we will see how strong my father really is."

He lifted a hand toward her, holding it out for her to take, if she would.

Shocked by her own movement, she placed her palm in his,

gripping hard. It wasn't a handshake, not when she spun her hand to clasp his, forcing him to step closer.

"When tonight is over, you will be healed," she said.

"Or I will be—"

"There is no '*or*.'" Her voice stayed firm. The way she held his hand, crushing his knuckles and making her heart pound, was foolish and unnecessary. Yet, there was more magic in this small gesture than she cared to admit. No time for that now. If they survived, if the world turned right side up, she could remember the way her fingers felt laced through his.

"Do you feel it?" Aly's hand loosened and let go. "The darkness?"

He shrugged and shook out his hand, reacting as if something inside him rejected her touch. The curse inside him was growing bolder. She could see the way it licked at the edges of his Truth-well, swirling into the light and spreading like blood in water.

Aly picked up one dark bundle and pushed it into Red's chest. He suppressed a startled cough as he took it. "What's this?"

"I never told you how we were descending."

Red unfurled the bundle. It was a cloak.

Holding out her own, Aly laced her arms into the fabric. "These will carry us down. Even more importantly, they will carry us back *out*, no matter what happens in there."

"You're kidding."

Aly tied off her own cloak at the wrists and ankles. "It's the fastest way. The safest, actually."

He laughed, a startled, panicked sound. "Jumping is the safest? That's a good lie, Aly."

She exchanged a glance with Yin. "It ensures we avoid the beasts on the way down. I constructed the magic myself. Not another soul has touched these cloaks. No one could have tampered with them."

"That's comforting." He bent to tie the cloak to his ankles. "These don't seem like strong ties."

"If you do not trust me, this *will* fail."

"Great. My entrails will decorate the Canyon floor forever, then."

Aly grunted, fists by her sides, a magical light hovering above the group. Stepping over to Red, she leaned forward and knocked him solidly in the chest with the heel of one hand. When he stumbled backward, she stepped with him, pushing a wave of freezing cold magic through him, then the heat followed and his mind cleared for a moment.

"Thank you," he mumbled, as if ashamed.

Aly inspected his wrist ties, holding his arm up near her face, the way a tailor might examine her completed work. "If something happens to me in there, I want to know you have a way out." She dropped his arm as soon as Red looked down at her hands. "This will bring you out of the Canyon in one hour, no matter what happens."

Red stiffened. "You didn't tell me that."

"Well, now you know."

Yin stepped up to look over the edge, perhaps giving them some space.

Red leaned toward her in the dim light. "You're wearing one, too. Will it bring you out? If you…well…?"

She crossed her arms at her chest, hiding her body beneath the cloak. "Not necessarily. I can't risk returning if I get infected down there. If I'm corrupted, then you don't *want* me to come out. My cloak will bring me out only if I speak a certain phrase, a line I don't think I'll be able to say if I'm corrupted."

"That's not going to happen."

"It very well might," she muttered.

"Tell me the phrase."

She shook her head.

Grabbing her shoulder, he pulled her around to face him. "Aly, I will not leave you down there. Tell me the phrase."

She rolled her shoulder, pushing off his hand. "No." Her voice was firm. "The river will be dangerous," she added, changing the subject. "From what I've read and what little is known about it, it sort of operates on different rules. Don't trust anything down there." Aly dropped her head. "Not yourself. Not what you see. Nothing." *Or you'll come out of there as twisted as Alef.*

"Don't trust myself? How am I supposed to manage that?" asked Red.

"Especially not yourself." Aly looked up at him, frowned, then took a deep breath. "Yin, thank you for coming. In the Canyon, remember what we spoke of earlier. Down there, you answer to me, not him. Not until we've siphoned that curse into the river."

Red opened his mouth to rebut this new imperative, but she cut him off.

"Remember," she said, "my father doesn't want us trying this. That makes me optimistic. Now, it's time to jump," she said.

And with that, she ran toward the cliff edge and leaped into the mists.

2 5

RED

R ed left his stomach on the rock ledge.

Air whooshed up his torso and rustled his hair. The fabric around him rippled fiercely, like a sail in a maelstrom. Adrenaline, panic, then nausea doused Red's nervous system. His living nightmare.

He'd just tossed himself into the Canyon, as if he were enacting the mild swearword used so flippantly by so many. He'd think twice about using that term in the future. If there was a future for him. As he hurtled down into darkness, Red was certain death was rushing up to meet him.

A scream cracked from his mouth until his lungs emptied. At that moment, the fabric around him stiffened, jolted, and cupped the air, knocking his body flat.

As his movement slowed and his open mouth scooped the cold air, he began to look around for the others. The darkness lapped up from the Canyon depths, the milky gray of the fog inking into jet. *Where are Yin and Aly?*

He heard a strange shuffling and scraping sound on the rocks behind him, and when he glanced, he saw three large shapes—wolves—running directly downward, like ants on a wall. They ran quickly, but not as fast as Red fell. Soon, they were far above him, scrambling down and loosing small rocks as they went.

"Your Majesty!"

Red turned his head, but with the movement, his entire body flipped over so that he fell face up. A small black star floated in the milky gray mist above him.

"Can. You. Hear. Me?" Yin's words came as individual shouts.

Red coughed and cursed and spluttered a yes. Yin was alive. He whirled back around and the cloak caught more air.

Beyond him, falling in the darkness below, was another cloak. Aly. She was farther away from the wall and would land a good distance away, unless he could figure out how to direct himself toward her.

The pressure of the wind on his face made it hard to see. Tears streamed from his eyes. The anger and fear twisting inside him collided with the feelings he had for Aly—a boxing match in his chest, his stomach, his head. They were here to cure his curse—a strange irony—but what if Aly needed saving too? The cloaks would save him and Yin, but who would save Aly?

A new thought slammed into his head, worse than all the rest, as he awaited sight of the ground.

Will there be a ground? Will I fall forever, dying of thirst as I drop into nothingness?

The answer came in the howl of a wolf.

The sound of a river.

The screams of a girl.

A pale gray light oozed up through the fog, which had grown even thicker and smelled of wet rocks. *How am I going to land?*

That answer came with a strange billow of air pushing up against him, against the fabric stretched between his arms and legs. He saw dark stones below him, an oil-black river reflecting only dim gray lines. The air seemed to press his body upright, tilting him with no movements of his own. He was a puppet, marionetted onto the Canyon floor by Aly's magic.

Somehow, that felt wrong.

He yanked the cloak off as soon as he felt stone beneath his feet. *Better. Now I'm in control, not someone else.* He hated to think of magic being able to control his body's movements.

An odd stillness met him at the bottom. *Where is Aly?* She should have landed already. But he'd heard a scream. *Surely that was only the howling wind.*

His eyes began adjusting to the dimness, a faint light beckoning from some place up ahead. Perhaps that's where Aly had gone. It was not firelight that lit the Canyon floor but something else, something unnatural.

Yin touched down nearby. He unfastened his belt, yanked it free, then wrapped it around himself and the cloak. "Sire, your belt. It will help keep the cloak out of the way until we need it."

Red snorted, ignoring his cloak on the damp stones.

Yin looked at him with both shuddering uncertainty and dogged determination. "Recite the *Verad*, Your Majesty. As Aly instructed."

Red waved a careless hand at Yin and stepped toward the light and the soft snarl of a hidden wolf.

Drawing his dagger, Red felt the hairs on his arms lift. Behind him, he heard the voice of his bodyguard reciting short snippets of the *Verad*.

He jogged forward, urged onward by a sudden memory, as if he'd nearly forgotten.

His curse. The river.

They had to find Aly and siphon out the curse. Yin jogged to catch up.

Urgency flooded his body, his blood. He had to reach Aly before the wolves tore her apart or infected her with evil that would change her forever.

The sound of their boots on stone echoed in the flat bottom of the Canyon. Gurgling water rushed nearby. In the gray light, the outline of a wolf stepped into view. Then another.

Red halted, Yin beside him with blades drawn. Blood thundered in the king's hot ears, but he fought the fear in his heart and remembered Aly as he faced the Canyon wolves.

"Where is she?" he snapped at the wolves, as if they could answer.

Their hackles raised; their ears tilted back. They stood at least as tall as his chest.

To answer him, the wolves lunged. Red stabbed one in the mouth with his dagger. The beast howled and shook him off, while another set of fangs launched. Yin battled behind him. Red could not spare him a glance.

The second wolf knocked Red to the ground, paws the size of tea plates pressing him into the rough stones. Drool splashed his collarbone. One forearm pressed the wolf's enormous face away from his own. The beast's teeth ripped into his arm.

A prickling sensation seeped into his arm from the bite. It felt like the magic Aly had siphoned into him only yesterday.

With a howl of pain, Red kicked his legs into the animal's underside. The wolf toppled off, but his jaws held on. Red rolled with the wolf, realizing it had him in a death hold. The animal would not let go, jaw frozen in place.

Blood now mixed with drool sliding off the wolf's tongue. With his right hand, Red plunged the dagger again and again into the fur. After four stabs, the wolf's body ceased struggling, but his jaw remained clamped. When the wolf lay still, half on top of him, Red pried the jaws out of his left forearm and scrambled away.

He cradled his arm across his middle and, spinning, saw Yin swinging a revolver between two approaching wolves. He hadn't known Yin to ever use a gun. He didn't even know the man carried one.

"Go!" he shouted at Red.

"Not a chance."

The wolves attacked simultaneously. One sustained a bullet to the chest. The other found Yin's left thigh, whose scream split the night. The revolver clattered to the stone, and Yin rolled out of sight beneath the wolf.

"No!"

Red held his arm against his ribcage and dove at the wolf as it ripped and snapped at Yin. *No, no, no!*

His shoulders knocked the wolf off of Yin. His dagger missed its chest, sinking into the skin beside the back leg. The wolf cried and slunk away, dripping blood.

Yin lay still, chest rising and falling, red everywhere. A tooth-marked gash across his torso spoke of worse injuries than the blood seeping from his thigh.

"Yin!"

He did not respond. The man's cloak was ripped in several places. Red's abandoned cloak spilled out from under Yin's body, where he must have tucked it away at his belt. Red yanked it free, Yin's limp frame wobbling each time Red tugged.

With a shout of rage, Red slammed his hand into the stone, dagger blade skittering away. He jerked a handful of hair with his good hand and stood. "Aly!" he bellowed.

He could not let Yin's injuries be for nothing. The sooner he found Aly, the sooner he could leave this wretched darkness and find help for Yin—as long as the evil seeping into his bloodstream didn't stop him.

With his dagger, he tore the hem off of his shirt and knotted it around Yin's thigh wound. There was nothing he could do for the chest wound. He would have to hurry, and pray the wolves left Yin's body alone. He grabbed the gun and took off at a jog.

An odd light diffused the air only enough to see. Beyond the light hovered shadows, from which came the sound of strange mutterings.

His arm throbbed. Black lumps, which might have been sleeping creatures, stood out against the damp stones. He did not look at them.

Red continued to shout for Aly.

Then he stumbled upon the source of the gray light.

A body hovered above the rocks, limbs extended but limp, skin emitting a pale gray glow. A muffled gasp clawed from Red's mouth.

It was his sister.

"Elise!" He ran forward, lifting his hand to feel her, make sure she was real. Her skin was difficult to look at directly, the light growing stronger the longer he stared. She was warm to the touch. He nearly wept to know she still lived, despite her still features. Spinning in all directions, he looked for who or what held his sister captive.

From the darkness he heard, "Leave her, Red. It's not real."

Aly stood at the edge of the river, dressed in her traveling clothes and cloak that rippled in the Canyon breeze.

"I can feel her! She's *alive*, Aly!"

She shook her head. "Remember why we came."

He grabbed Elise's hand and tugged. She did not open her eyes, and her body barely bobbed in the air where it hovered. "Elise!"

He had grown used to operating under the pain of his constant headaches, but as anger and fear began to clog his airway, his headache sharpened like an axe on a grindstone.

Aly must have heard his whimper, because she reached out a hand and beckoned to him. "We must remove that curse."

Whirling on Aly, he barked, "And why should I trust you? You convinced me to throw myself down here. All along, I believed you. I let myself *believe* we needed to come down here." He glanced at the river. It seemed closer, but he didn't remember moving. "When maybe there never *was* a curse. What if I've been fine this whole time, and you have been pouring the evil into my body every chance you could?"

Aly glared at him.

"And now we're *here*. You want me to die down here, don't you?"

"You know that's not true."

"Then you want to summon a curse, something stronger than what you could manage on your own. Something from that river." He chuckled, a jarring, off-beat note. "And then you strapped that cloak on me to carry my cursed self back out into the world. Clever."

He was glad he'd taken off the cloak.

"You were bitten. Again. I'm sorry." Her voice held a twinge of pity. "But I was a little busy." She nodded toward the dark shapes he'd seen lying around.

Bodies.

He squinted in the darkness at the nearest one. "Is that a *man*?"

Instead of answering, Aly lifted a hand, mumbled a few words, and a pulse of light shot from her hand toward the fallen body. As her light passed over the shape, the figure flickered from a man to a bear. When her light extinguished, the shape was again a man.

"A lyth," she corrected. "Dozens of them."

Dozens? He glanced around, then his eyes pinned on Aly. The pain in his arm burned. His head pulsed. He didn't stand a chance anyway. If he couldn't trust Aly, he was already dead.

He stepped toward her, nearly slipping on the wet rocks. *Is the river close enough to splash these rocks? Or is it still behind Aly?*

Aly?

Looking around, he could no longer see her. *Has she shrouded herself?*

Alone and in immense pain, he felt a sickening feeling in his gut, the kind that preceded vomiting. At once, everything in his body began to rebel against him.

First his headache surged until his skull felt like it cracked into tiny fragments. Light tricked him, weaving in and out like a turning kaleidoscope of warning. His balance faltered as the world started to flip as if he were a trapeze artist.

As he collapsed to the pebbled ground inches from the river's edge, one thought pulsed through his scrambling brain: *Don't let the water touch you.* He wasn't sure if the voice was his own, but he heeded it, squirming away from the water.

The river was hungry, reaching for him. *Or am I creeping nearer to the river?*

The world spun round and round about him, leaving him disoriented. His injured arm throbbed with heat and pain.

Nothing remained but to curl into himself, holding his knees and shutting his eyes against the madness of the tilting earth. Helpless. Once again.

The truth was, he'd always been helpless. Worthless.

Even if everything else he saw or felt was a lie, *that* was the truth. He had tried to be brave, facing his nightmare to cure his curse, but he'd been rash and foolish yet again. This time, he'd die because of it.

Great king he'd been.

With his eyes closed, Red became strangely aware that he was bashing his head against the stones with little, terrible thumps. As he stilled, horrified, a voice inside his head whispered to him: *Fight the lies, Red. Light the Deep.*

Those words were familiar. *Did someone just speak them to me or are they a memory?* His mind scrambled as if trying to climb out of the Canyon with nothing but fingers and frustration.

Fight it with truth.

He struggled to remember what was true.

You are the king of Tandera. That was true.

You are in the Canyon. Also true.

He opened his eyes. The Canyon walls rose like endless stone curtains, cutting him off from the world.

But the walls no longer tilted and whirled. His nausea lessened. He sat up. The rush of the river drew his attention as his ears once again registered sound. The water's edge lapped at his boots. He'd not been so near it when he fell.

He crashed backward onto his elbows, trying to scramble away from the river. Pain in his forearm stole his attention. Teeth marks oozed blood. He could barely remember anything, including what had happened.

His mind again began to tumble and reel.

Fight it.

Cold air washed over him.

"This will hurt," a voice said.

Do I recognize the voice? Is it just my crazed mind? Then something white-hot burned against his chest. He yelled and tried to shove off what felt like an iron brand. *I'm going to die.*

Now, Red! Fight the darkness.

He couldn't fight. He couldn't even breathe.

The white-hot brand on his chest would be the end of him. It would melt through his skin and plunge straight into his heart.

"You're not dying! Fight it, Red!"

Words he couldn't understand rolled through the darkness. *"Eranh hamma cortincamsa!"*

He opened his eyes. Aly knelt directly above him. He lay on the ground, his head lolling against stone. One of her hands was on his chest, the other was plunged into the river.

The river!

"The curse!" he shouted, suddenly remembering. His head slammed back against the rock as Aly shoved him down. Stars danced in his vision.

"Light overpowers the darkness! Say it, Red!"

He stared up at Aly. Her face was covered in sweat, so much sweat that her brow dripped onto his chest. The river sloshed and raged just inches away. Water soaked her hair and side, but not a drop fell on Red's outstretched body.

The pain in his chest, where her hand met his skin, stifled his words. He hissed out one syllable through shallow breaths, then fell silent.

"Light. Over. Powers. Darkness," he finally spat out through gritted teeth.

Warmth began to seep into his bones where Aly touched him, but the air around them was so cold that Aly's breath shot out in puffs of steam. Small ice crystals formed on her eyebrows, her eyelashes. Her nose turned red, and she blinked back tears.

Then it hit him. *This will break her.*

He sat up with a jolt, her hand still pressed against him. She bit her lip, shook her head, and pushed against him. She did not have enough force left in her to push him down. "No, you have to let me finish. There's no point if I don't siphon it all."

Her features contorted in pain. Red had not expected this. He'd not once thought of how this process would impact Aly, having been so focused on his own healing.

Then, with absolute certainty, he knew she would succeed. Despite his previous doubts and his recent plunge into near insanity, he knew that Aly would heal him.

He reached up and grabbed her hand, pressing it firmly to his chest. *Keep going,* he told her through determined eyes. It had to work.

The water hissed and swirled as it accepted the curse from Aly's hand. He hadn't expected the curse to have to go *through* Aly to leave him.

The heat from her touch lessened, and Red sucked in a large breath. "It's working. I can feel it."

Again, Aly shook her head. Her brow tossed a few drops of sweat, which seemed to turn to sleet before hitting the ground. She looked pale, save for her nose. She croaked out a sound, but then cringed and shut her mouth, as if in pain.

"What is it?" He held her hand against him. He would not let go until the curse had left him. *But what would this do to Aly?*

A pained growl ripped from her throat.

His grip loosened. He was losing her.

She looked up at him, eyes wide and red and rimmed with frozen flecks of ice.

Phoenix, she said in his mind.

Her stare was jarring, forceful. He blinked, ready to pull her hand off of him.

Phoenix, she said again, pressing her hand into him with what strength she had left.

"Phoenix? Like the bird?" He hated watching her cringe as if his words were adding to her pain. "Okay, okay. Phoenix. Um. Fire? Rebirth? Mythological creature? Scepter?" She blinked away tears. *What else rises?* "Truth! Truth will rise?"

She physically wilted against him, her hand slipping off his chest, her other barely still in the water.

"Aly!"

Her arm fell limp into his lap. He jerked her shoulders upward, feeling suddenly very cold. He couldn't tell if she had healed him, if the curse was gone.

"Aly!"

She was freezing. Her fingers, even the ones that had been sending fire into his body, felt like the fingers of a long-dead corpse. He knew magic took heat from the air and objects around it, but it appeared she'd also used all the heat from her body. He feared she had killed herself trying to siphon that curse.

Red looked down at the bite on his arm. There was still a gash, though the prickling sensation had disappeared. The gash had already closed, as if it had started to heal but was interrupted. *Had Aly finished?*

Shaking Aly as hard as he could, Red shouted at her over and over again. "Phoenix! Phoenix! What did you mean?"

He could not lose her. Not here. Not now.

Healed or not, he would not lose her.

Because, for the first time, he needed her—and not only for her magic.

"Aly!"

He was the crown.

"Can you hear me?"

She was the scepter.

"Wake up!"

He could not rule without her.

"You can't have her!" he shouted at the darkness.

He didn't *want* to rule without her.

The Canyon seemed to close in around them. Walls looming; river raging, grabbing, reaching. It wanted them.

He kicked his weakened legs as he tried to push them away from the water's hungry edge. Aly's shoulders slipped from his grasp, her head clunking unmercifully against the stone. He hissed and pulled her head into his lap.

The curse. It must have entered her. She'd taken it into herself and not fully released it into the river.

The death curse.

Has it taken her so quickly?

Shaking her shoulder over and over, he shouted at the darkness. He revealed thoughts he'd never spoken aloud to anyone, truths he hadn't even admitted to himself; it all spilled from his mouth.

There could have been more.

There should have been more.

She was supposed to reign with him.

With him.

That first day in her rooms, he'd wanted to fire her; now he couldn't face the rest of his reign without her. It wasn't her magic. It was *her*.

"Come back," he whispered, voice hoarse from shouting. "Come back to me."

Even if she had the curse inside her, he would not leave her here. She'd taken it from him; they would find a way to take it out of her.

Aly's father.

There were only two viable options to rid a person of a death curse: pour it back into the river or back into the one who'd cast it. Whatever it took, he'd bring her to her father. She might not want to face him, but now they had no choice.

A scratching sound behind him seized his attention. A foxblood's claws clicked against stone as it trotted toward him, its unusually long snout boasting large fangs.

The cloak! He'd left it where Yin had fallen. Consumed by the Canyon's lies, he'd thrown it down in a moment of weakness, a moment when he hadn't trusted Aly.

What a fool.

He didn't have time to worry about the cloak. The foxblood trotted closer.

He gently positioned Aly on the stone away from the reach of the river, before turning to face the animal now merely a lunge away. Red didn't even have his dagger. He'd dropped that, too.

The animal eyed the still body on the rocks.

"You'll have to kill me first."

Red unhooked his belt and snapped it out, whipping it toward the foxblood. The animal paused his advance, dancing to the side. Several more whips toward the foxblood and it sat down, just out of reach.

"We can do this all night."

The animal cocked its head.

The beast suddenly hopped forward. Red stepped backward, his foot plunging into ice cold water. He slipped. Lurching forward, his head cracked against the unforgiving rocks.

As his mind dissolved into blackness, the last thing he saw in the fog was the foxblood walking over to sniff Aly's limp body.

ALY

Aly's head rolled and her nose crunched against a hard surface as her body was flipped over. Her limbs were limp, useless, but her mind began to sharpen.

Her legs, arms, and chest peeled off the ground, her head hanging limp. Something snarled.

Finally, she came to. The fabric attached to her arms and legs was rippling in the breeze, lifting her upward. It was night.

She was still in the Canyon. A foxblood's claws clicked on the stone as it scampered away from the rising form. Beneath her, she saw a man in a waistcoat, his arms flat out by his sides, his pale face blank as paper. Red's eyes were open, staring at nothing.

"Red!"

He didn't move. Her cloak was fully unfurled now and she had only seconds. She reached out and grabbed at his clothes with both hands. She couldn't hold him! Flashing back to a recent dream, Aly Pulled on his Truthwell to strengthen her hands and pry his body from the earth.

Her hands didn't strengthen. Nothing happened, except that her body floated farther away from his.

"No...please." She closed her eyes and mentally tiptoed

toward his Truthwell, afraid of what she would find. If he'd stepped in the river, all her effort might have been undone.

Her magic sensed nothing. No light, no rhythm, no familiar pattern of the king's Truthwell. No Truthwell at all.

With all her physical strength, she hauled him off the ground as the magic in her cloak lifted them both.

A quick adjustment made it easier to hold him. She wrapped both arms around his chest, embarrassed at his closeness. His body was cold. His clothes were wet.

What have I done?

"Red!" She squeezed him, her hair whipping against both their faces. His heartbeat bumped against her stomach. He was alive. She tried to hitch him up, hold him better.

As if bumping into an invisible energy source, her magic found power, and she Pulled, finally able to grip Red with ease.

Something about the magic she was using felt wrong, like the spell itself was a greased spoon, easy to drop. Her arms loosened around Red. A blistering headache splintered into her brain. She nearly dropped the king.

Like shuffling cards, she thought back through what she could remember from the Canyon. Foxbloods. Woodwolves. A lyth. Red's abandoned cloak. Yin—he'd been hurt, right? The river. Elise's phantom likeness. Phoenix.

She gasped, swallowing a mouthful of freezing Canyon fog. When she'd begun siphoning the curse into the river, she'd felt all its evil, all its pain, as it moved through her, back into the water. Halfway in, she'd known that the effort would take everything she had. More importantly, it would take all of Red's energy.

To fully siphon out that curse, she would have had to Truth-strip him.

So, even as she siphoned, she built in a spell that would cut off her magic if she reached a point where she wasn't capable of stopping the spell work. The word *phoenix*. It was also a way of telling him the phrase that would activate her cloak. She'd known he could hold her and rise with her, even if she didn't wake.

"You said the right words," she whispered to the top of his head. He was slipping from her grip, despite the fact that she was employing magic to hold on. "You saved us both. I'm sorry I couldn't do it. I'm sorry I failed. Again."

But you stepped in the river. Why are you alive? Again she reached for his Truthwell. Nothing. There was no darkness in him, like those whose Wells had been corrupted. Frantic, she pushed her magic outward, searching for the light that should be coming from the distant Canyon walls. Until they lifted clear of the walls, there would be no other Truthwells nearby.

Her magic stretched and stretched, until she was fairly certain she should have found the walls, Caridan, maybe even the Forgotten Cities. No light at all registered in her mind.

The river had taken her ability to see Truthwells.

She was blind.

～

Aly's knuckles slammed into the paved stones of Isardra's palace courtyard. The force cracked the pavement all the way to where a man stood, champagne glass in hand and a look of shock on his face. Red's body slumped onto the stone beside her, far less gracefully than she'd intended.

The man, she realized, was Lord Weston Grey. "The king! Help the king!" he yelled, turning toward the person beside him. Sebastian Thorin. One look from Aly stilled Grey's approach.

"Grey?"

If Grey is here, that means we came to… Isardra. Why did we come here? Her enchanted cloak hadn't brought them here—it had merely lifted them from the depths. The only reason they would be here was if *she'd* chosen to fly this way. Magic only obeyed her thoughts.

Did I choose to come here? As she thought about it, her mind grew dull and she slumped forward on her hands. Nothing made sense.

She was exhausted, not physically but magically. Her mental strength had been sapped from the effort of holding onto Red all the way from the Canyon. Pulling from him while she couldn't sense his Truthwell was like trying to catch lightning bugs that never lit up.

Red lay still beside her. She lifted her hand to press it to his chest, ready to heal whatever bones she may have just broken, but as she moved, another figure caught her attention in the corner of the courtyard.

Her father stepped out of a shadow at the edge of the courtyard as if he had been waiting for her arrival.

Though she'd never once laid eyes on the man, she knew him immediately. This man in the white owl mask was Kassia's Royal Sorcerer. Her father.

She jumped to her feet, stumbled in her weakness, and attempted to Pull on Red's Truthwell. She missed. She reached out again, frantic, grabbing at the air with her magic, hoping to find that his energy was somehow hidden from her. Her father took deliberate steps, his owl mask as unsettling as the stories claimed.

Her magic latched on to a fringe of Red's Truthwell. She yanked, but the magic slipped away like oil slipping off her fingers.

What has happened to me?

Only one answer made sense.

She had the magic of the Deep within her, the curse that had been residing within Red for the past few weeks, the curse that she'd been certain would turn her wicked the moment it infected her.

Dimitri Patrenko stopped a few feet away, watching his daughter with a tilted head. He wore a crisp white suit, no cloak.

"Welcome, Alyana."

"How do you know my name?" she snarled, tensing for a fight she knew she'd lose. If she couldn't Pull magic, there was no fight to be had. She still didn't know if Red was healed, if their plan had even worked. Yet here they were, more vulnerable than they'd ever hoped to be when facing Dimitri.

There was one other way to eliminate a death curse. She balled her hands into fists.

"I have been waiting for this moment," he said. The courtyard grew silent around them.

"Have you?" she asked, uncertain. "Did you bring us here?"

He shook his head and walked closer. "No, but I imagined that once you attempted your little stunt, you would come to see reason and return here."

When she took a step back, she distanced herself from Red. "Return? I've never been here."

"You were born here, Alyana." His voice was smooth, deep, full of power.

"You killed Renna. You killed her."

Suddenly, she wondered why no one in the courtyard had moved to help Red. All the faces stared at them. They were not invisible.

The men and women standing in the courtyard were dressed as if they had been attending a fine dinner. Perhaps Kassia had been celebrating. *Did she know why we were in the Canyon? Did she know we would end up here?*

There was so much Aly didn't understand. She reached for Red's Truthwell, knowing it was her sole hope of surviving the man who stood before her. This was the moment that she had feared ever since the night when Grey had brought her the news of Renna's death, the night she'd found out about her father's vendetta against her.

Dimitri chuckled. "Yes, but you'll be happy to know the woman revealed nothing that proved useful in finding you."

Mama. Aly's heart ached. She'd missed her mother every day of the past six years. She'd wanted her smile, her hugs, her voice. Her chastisement. Her orders. Anything. *Everything.* He'd taken all that from her.

Red moaned. Aly's attention flashed to him. Her chest imploded in pain and guilt. *And I took Gevar from you. Can you ever forgive me?*

Then she looked up at her father. "No," she said aloud. "*He* took Gevar from us." She balled her fists.

"Do you really think you can fight me?" he asked, amused.

Aly knew she couldn't. She was blind to Truthwells, only able to Pull from one if she happened to knock directly into it. This man had the queen as his source and, Aly knew, the Black River. She knew he Pulled from it, despite how far away it was, because *she'd* Pulled from a river once as a novice, though the water had been far away as well.

Her magic that day in Kitrel, years ago, had been what launched her to this very moment.

Of course she could Pull from a faraway river. She could do it because he could do it. That had been the moment Grey had noticed her, the moment that had drawn her toward the palace, toward King Gevar, toward the position of Royal Sorcerer, and now, inevitably, back toward her father.

The look on his face suggested that he knew all of this.

"Why? At least tell me why?" she demanded, sputtering out the one question that she had wanted answered her whole life.

As her father walked a few more steps toward her, she tried to sense the evil inside of her and push it back. There had to be truth somewhere in the recesses of her memory that would push away the curse and heal her. There *had* to be, or she would die and so would Red.

Inside of her was a death curse, even if only a fragment of it, and she wasn't certain what it would do to her. She stepped between Red's motionless body and her father. That was when Seb broke from the crowd and ran toward the king.

Movement resumed in the courtyard as people started shuffling about, unsure how to use their gloved hands and long tail coats to serve a king who appeared to be dead. Someone snapped their fingers at a pair of attendants, who ran off into the palace.

Aly wished she could help Red. *I'm sorry*, she said into his head, but her words weren't reaching his mind. Somehow, she knew it. She stared at her father.

"What will you do now?" She knew the answer. He had wanted her dead since the day she was born. *What prevents him from killing me now?*

"I see you have a lot of questions. I will not answer them; instead, come with me."

"No." She would not leave Red here.

"Oh, but you will."

At that moment others burst into the courtyard: a pair of Bulvarnan guards clad in navy blue with silver wolf heads snarling on their chest. The queen stepped into view behind them. She wore a midnight blue ballgown and had white makeup caked to her exposed skin. Diamonds sparkled in her hair, on her neck.

"Ah, Dimitri. You brought them to me. Thank you, my darling."

He took her outstretched hand and pressed his lips to a ring the size of a robin's egg. The gesture startled Aly, but the rest of the people in the courtyard seemed unfazed by it. Here Kassia was, cavorting with her sorcerer like it was nothing. The look she gave him was one of pure adoration. Of love.

Is she in love with my father?

Kassia reached out a shoe to nudge Red's shoulder. His face lolled sideways and flopped onto the stone.

Wake up, Aly begged him, knowing he couldn't hear. Without her ability to see his Truthwell, she couldn't tell if the Black River had given him another curse. She had no way of knowing if he would wake up again.

She wanted to reach down and pull him up, but her limbs were frozen. Each time she tried to bend down, she made it no more than an inch. Everything about her was melting away into something that made no sense at all. The curse. It was already twisting her away from Red.

Then Kassia moved her shoe and nudged Red's face, kicking slightly.

Aly leaped toward her, enraged. Her movements slowed. The curse—or was it her father's magic?—kept her from attacking the queen.

Kassia smiled. "Careful, girl."

The crowd in the courtyard did not seem to be able to hear them. The people chattered amongst themselves, pointing at Red. Perhaps her father's shroud was changing the sound of their words, changing what the people could hear. She tried to push against his shroud, but her efforts failed, her magic weak as damp leaves.

"Your next actions will decide his fate," Kassia concluded.

"The curse hasn't taken her fully," her father said. "We must wait."

The words rang in Aly's head. She would lose her mind to the point where she would actually harm Red. *Could that be possible?* She had no idea, but the fear of his words rattled her very bones.

"I have a better idea," said the queen. "It is what you suggested. Oh, this is perfect!"

What had they discussed? What am I missing?

Right then, her father reached a hand into the air and, before Aly processed what was happening, he slammed her to the ground in a burst of wind. Her elbow then her head smashed into the stones.

Dazed, she rolled over and felt for a Truthwell, any Truthwell she could Pull from. Her magic hit something and she yanked, throwing the cobblestones up from the courtyard, one by one and slamming them into her father. They dissolved before they ever touched him.

She leaped to her feet, calling on all of her knowledge of magic as she dove into whatever Truthwell she had hold of. It was resisting her, but she Pulled harder.

One of the stones managed to knock her father square in the jaw. He stumbled backward. Kassia gasped.

"Do it now," she hissed.

Aly's father picked up the stone that had hit him in the face and hurled it toward Red. Like a cannon shot, Aly pushed her magic toward that flying stone, knowing that if it met Red's body, it would kill him. She sent all of her power, all of her energy into stopping that stone.

The stone's trajectory faltered and smashed to the ground beside Red's face.

"Do not hinder me again," said Dimitri.

"Hurt me, not him," she blurted. "You're here for me. You've always wanted to kill me."

"No. In fact, I haven't," he said. In that one statement, he shattered everything she believed to be true. "What you think you know to be true is not always true." His magic lifted another stone in the air. "You will serve Kassia now." Dimitri stepped to Red's body, rock hovering beside him.

She looked at her father's hands. One of his fingers barely flickered. He was invoking magic. It took no physical movements to keep a shroud going, but a direct spell toward a person took hand movements, the concentration to direct a spell. He was bewitching Red in some way.

"If you refuse, I will kill him; this time you will not stop me."

She wilted to the ground beside Red, knowing she was defeated. "Don't hurt him."

"The choice is yours. You will serve Kassia alongside me, or he will die."

"I will serve," Aly said, scrambling up. "I will serve Kassia," she said again, making sure each word was audible and steady. She wanted everyone in the courtyard to hear, even though she knew there was a shroud around them.

"Say it again," her father whispered.

"I will serve Kassia," Aly breathed, her gusto from a moment ago already fleeing. A few people shouted in response, some happy, some angry. *He removed his shroud so they could hear.* One of the men watching her was Weston Grey. The look on his face was one of betrayal. She had betrayed him; she had betrayed Red; she had betrayed Tandera.

She marched away from Red's body, her elbow clasped by her father's hand. All eyes followed her. Seb's mouth hung open. Elise, who Aly now noticed stood beside Seb, had one gloved hand pressed to her lips. When Aly made eye contact with Elise, the princess's hand fell away, her expression hardening like fired clay.

Of course they hated her. They believed what she'd said.

Only Aly knew something no one else did, that she had just spoken a lie, and with that lie, had broken whatever magic she had left.

27

RED

Red woke up to the smell of peppermint wafting under his nose. The sharp but pleasing scent pierced the fog in his brain. Blinking, he glanced at the drapes above his head, wondering why they were deep blue instead of gold.

His attempt to sit up brought a fit of gagging as he clutched at his sore ribs. His right arm pulsed with dull heat.

"Moving isn't the best option right now, Chief."

Red peeled open one eye and stared at Seb. Elise sat beside him, stoppering a bottle of peppermint oil and smiling beneath wet eyes. He softened his expression and smiled back at her.

Behind them, Bernard hopped up out of a chair, a look of relief surging across his exhausted face.

"I will inform the others you are awake," Bernard announced. He sputtered out a laugh that sounded suspiciously like it was concealing tears and bowed before rushing from the room.

"How are you feeling?" asked Elise.

Memories flooded his mind. The Canyon. He'd been in the Canyon. After a loud groan, he drew a few shallow breaths and asked, "What happened?" *Am I healed?*

Elise glanced at Seb. "We were hoping you could tell us."

"Yeah, we all thought you were asleep, then you landed in the courtyard, and Kassia's guards carried you off on a stretcher. You looked dead."

Another failed attempt to sit up dropped him back against his pillow. "Kassia? Where are we?"

"Isardra, Brother. You brought us here, remember?" Seb shrugged at Elise.

Elise dabbed at one eye. "You did not respond to anything. For hours."

"Hours?" Red tapped at the side of his ribcage, recalling the impact of stone but not what had happened in those hours since. He didn't understand why Kassia would grant him medical treatment if his memories were correct.

Gingerly, Red sat up. He stared at Seb, Elise, the lavish room. He remembered now. "Where is Aly?" Then he cringed, remembering that they didn't know who Aly was.

Narrowing her eyes, Elise said, "You mean Alyana Barron? What about her?"

"Is she all right?" he asked, wondering how they knew her name.

Seb and Elise exchanged another glance. They weren't telling him something.

"The Tanderan sorcerer has pledged her allegiance to Bulvarna," said Elise.

"What?"

Scratching his chin, Seb said, "I was up, having drinks with Grey in the courtyard when you, uh, fell from the sky. You were tangled up with a *woman*. Kassia was there by then, and, well, so was her sorcerer." He ran a hand over his short hair. "Things got a little tense—your sorcerer and Kassia's sorcerer seemed to know each other—and then your sorcerer fell to her knees and said she wanted to serve Bulvarna."

Red shook his head. *No.* That couldn't be right.

Not Aly.

"Frederick, there is something I need to tell—"

"Yin? What about Yin?" he blurted, silencing his sister, who looked away.

"He'll be all right." Seb nodded as he spoke. "The bites were nasty, but magic can work wonders. Even the magic of an enemy."

"*Dimitri* healed him?"

Seb shook his head. "No, Aly did."

"You said enemy?"

"She's Bulvarna's now."

No, she isn't. Red had to find her. He mustered the strength to stand, flinching in anticipation of a wave of pain.

Elise laid her hand on Red's. "I really do need to—"

Suddenly, it occurred to him, "My headache is gone!"

Seb half-chuckled. "Now that's a relief. You fall from the sky and hit your head and then don't wake up for hours, and our once-faithful sorcerer has just pledged her power to another country—and you're happy that your headache is gone. Excellent." With an elbow jab, he added, "You could have *told* me she was pretty."

A loud breath hissed from Red's nose. Slowly, he rotated his legs off the bed, thinking through what could have happened to cause Aly to pledge fealty to Bulvarna. Maybe her father had forced her. Red had fallen in the Canyon. *Did I step in the river?* The memories were like dandelion seeds puffing away from him. "Where is she now?"

Seb shrugged. "Everyone's still preparing for the ball tonight."

"Ball?" He cupped his hands to his ribs, regretting the outburst.

"The masquerade ball? You know, the one scheduled to celebrate the peace talks?" Seb looked a little concerned, as if Red's mental state resembled Bulvarnan bread pudding.

It was only then that Red noticed that Seb wore tails and his sister wore a pale blue evening gown.

Red stared at the wrinkled covers for a moment, images haunting his mind. The Canyon beasts. Aly, passed out on the rocks. Yin's bleeding body. *Did I dream all of that?* "When does the ball start?" He had to find Aly first.

"In about twenty minutes," Seb said with a shrug.

Tossing the covers off his legs, Red grimaced through the pain as he stood.

"Whoa, Brother. You should at least drink this." Seb handed Red a cup of cold tea. When Red frowned at it, his friend added, "Has bimara in it. It'll help."

Red downed the cup. Bimara was a rare, expensive herb used when magic was not available for healing. He glanced at the suit laid out for him.

"Tell me," he asked, "what on earth are we celebrating?"

Elise reached out and squeezed Seb's knee, a gesture of care that Red previously never would have thought her capable of. He expected Seb to tease her or gloat or say something inappropriate, but Seb merely deflated and looked at Elise to clarify.

Alarmed, she said, "The peace agreement you all signed."

The navy and crimson tails Red wore seemed a little too bold, a little too anticipatory of a victory. They were the sole clothes he'd brought. How childish of him.

At least the soreness in his ribs and arm had evaporated with that pinch of bimara in his tea.

Elise and Seb had, with the help of Bernard, dressed, styled, and prepared their king in record time, ignoring the strangeness of the situation with nothing but kind smiles every time he winced in pain. By the time the suit was on and his hair was to

Elise's liking, his pain had dulled and he could walk down the stairs on his own.

He held Elise's arm, grateful he wouldn't enter the ballroom alone, not knowing what lay on the other side of the doors. He didn't know if he could bear to see Aly standing beside Kassia and her father. Whatever had coerced her to do it, Red would expose the truth.

Lies can affect our ability to see the truth. Aly's words. She'd also said the Canyon could twist reality. His memories were foggy, but he recalled the way the walls of the Canyon had seemed to move, the way the river's edge had leaped and darted, as if in a game. He wasn't really sure how he'd escaped, though according to Elise, a cloak was left behind in the courtyard. Aly's cloak, then, had been what brought them out. *Had she woken and said her secret phrase to lift us out?*

"Ready?" Elise asked. In her hand was a small item. A mask. "You do know this is a masquerade?" She raised her mask to her eyes and turned so Red could tie it. A simple twisting wire mask with jewels mounted around the eyes.

Elise projected elegance in her pale blue dress. Briefly, Red wondered if she'd chosen this color to draw Lucien's attention, by way of reminder that she could have been his daughter-in-law, or if she simply chose it because it looked lovely beneath her red hair.

"I do not wish to hide tonight." He finished securing her mask and lifted his elbow toward her. In his mind, the black mask he'd given Aly lay abandoned on the floor.

They set off down the hall behind two Bulvarnan palace guards. To Red's amazement, Veeter Yin limped behind them, dressed in a formal Okwan nitku, the stiff fabric jutting out at his shoulders. The man's strength bordered on mythical. Despite his recent brush with death, he likely had blades stashed all over his body to defend his king. The King of Tandera had his armed guards, and that would have to be enough for tonight.

Red burned with a single question: *The curse, is it gone?*

In the Canyon, he'd felt the curse leaving him. It had been an odd sensation, but it had been real. Then Aly had passed out. She'd used every drop of her energy to heal him.

She doesn't trust her father. Something about this is wrong.

Approaching the ballroom, Red muttered to Elise, "We went into the Canyon to rid me of my death curse."

"You *what?*"

"I'm not sure if it worked."

Elise blinked at him. "Brother, I must tell you something. I made a mistake."

"I may have too. Perhaps I can ask Lucien to have his sorcerer check me for curses." He glanced at his arm. "Though I do think the bite has fully healed."

Head down, Elise said, "That was Grey. He sent up his sorcerer to heal you."

His body stiffened. It hadn't been Aly, then. "Well, at least it wasn't Dimitri. *He's* the one who cursed me to begin with. I couldn't trust—"

"It wasn't him."

Red uttered a few more words before he realized what she'd said. "Pardon me? What do you mean, it wasn't him?"

"It was my handkerchief," she whispered. "The one that cursed you."

Over the general buzzing in the foyer as guests congregated before the ballroom doors, Red wasn't sure he'd heard her correctly.

"Pardon?"

"The handkerchief." She pressed her lips together, appalled at her own confession. "It was *mine*. But I had no idea when I gave it to Josephine that it had bad magic in it."

"Josephine?"

"When Lordan...when I no longer had a reason to keep the gift he had given me, I threw it away. Josephine asked to keep it. I let her." Elise dabbed at one eye with a gloved finger.

"How does this relate to the one in my pocket that day?"

Elise huffed. "When you were unconscious, Josephine told me she'd been asked to put that handkerchief in your pocket that day. The one *Lordan* had given me. Which means it was cursed by someone in our palace."

The floor threatened to fall out from under him. "The magic in that cloth could only have harmed me, no one else. It was intended to awaken when it touched the sorcerer's magic." He glanced up at Elise's watery eyes. "It could have been cursed when Lordan gave it to you. Elise, he may have intended all along for that cloth to end up in my pocket."

"Did you say you need a handkerchief, my lady?" asked a passing Bulvarnan man, reaching a hand into his pocket and withdrawing a white cloth.

Elise shook her head, tears spilling down her cheeks. The man backed away.

Red could barely contain the shock on his face. "Who asked Josephine to do it?"

Of all the people he'd suspected to have participated in activating the death curse, his sister and her attendant were not on the list. Elise's role, however, was one of innocence. Josephine, however, he couldn't trust. For a moment, he could only stare at her. The double doors to the ballroom opened and the crowd began to move, leaving them as river rocks among a current.

"She didn't know his name." Elise made a hissing sound in her throat. "Do you know that when Lordan saw me at the funeral, he told me he still loved me?" She used both index fingers to dab at tears.

"Loved you?" Anger surged through the king's veins. "If he loved you, he would have married you! That liar." *Lies make us do terrible things.*

Elise nodded. "It took me a while to realize that."

"Because you wanted him to be telling the truth."

She nodded, eyes down. "I am sorry. If you die from this curse, I will never forgive myself."

If I die…

"You didn't know it was cursed. It's not your fault." Red exhaled loudly. "How did *Lordan* know I was even going to give Mother a handkerchief? And why in the blazing Black River did *he* give me a death curse?"

Crying silently, Elise did not answer.

"You realize that Lordan's father is in that room? If Refere, for some unfathomable reason, wants me dead, *and* Kassia wants me dead, and if Aly really did pledge to serve Bulvarna, I have little chance of surviving our time here, regardless of whether or not my curse was healed." He grabbed her shoulders. "*You* have little chance of surviving, as you are my successor. I can't believe I brought you here. Take the guards and flee."

He spun around, ignoring her whimpering cries, and tried to think. His mind was reshaping with this new information. Refere was his strongest ally—or had been.

He adjusted the circlet on his head. "It was Riode Liere who suggested we come here." Spinning back around, he hissed, "It *was* Refere. I only wanted to go to the Canyon. To visit the soldiers. Liere suggested we meet with Kassia."

Red and Elise now stood in the small foyer alone, save for two of Kassia's footmen posted at the double doors. Violins hummed in the ballroom and the guests were taking their seats at banquet tables piled with flowers.

He glanced through the doors, knowing that the ball itself was a snare, waiting for him to trigger it. All his enemies waited in that room: Kassia, Dimitri, Lucien, maybe even Aly, if her pledge to her father was genuine. He still didn't believe it could be. As a king, he was bound to have enemies. He couldn't figure out *why* he had so many, and why they were all here.

Elise's hand on his upper arm drew his mind away from the

glittering ballroom. "It was Aly, wasn't it? The person I pledged to discover by the time we reached the Canyon?"

He grunted.

"I am truly sorry. I know what it feels like, almost like you would kill to have that person really love you back."

Love. He shrugged the word off, incapable of processing it amid everything falling to pieces around him. "It isn't that. I simply can't believe Aly would agree to serve her father. We're missing something or someone's lying."

Elise narrowed her eyes, as if she didn't buy his words about love. "You believe she is still on our side?"

His last memory of Aly was her limp body, nearly frozen from her effort to save his life. "Fully," he said.

"Then don't let her go." Elise tilted her head toward the ballroom. "Don't let Kassia win. Don't let Lucien and Lordan win."

A man in a striped suit poked his head into the foyer. "King Frederick? We are waiting for you."

Elise looped her arm under her brother's and nodded. "I am not leaving. Truth will rise, right?"

Red clicked his heels to attention. With a deep breath, he thought of Carolyn. His mother. All of Mardon. Seb's family. His *people.* Whether he left this ballroom or not, he would not resign his people to the whims of a wicked queen without a fight.

Stepping forward, Red felt the rising fury of a hunted fox.

28

ALY

When Red stepped into the ballroom, Aly's gasp was diluted by the violins. Magic clogged her throat. She couldn't speak. Her father was bewitching her tongue as well as her movements. When she tried to talk directly into Red's mind, even her mental voice was silent. Her magic was too weak—a risk she'd chosen.

Red was on his own.

Waning light diffused the room from the vast windows that reached toward the ceiling. On a dais at the end of the room sat Queen Kassia, to Aly's right. Kassia's throne stood between Aly's chair and the one for her father. Aly's father lounged in his seat, his white suit glinting with a silver sheen. Aly wore no sorcerer's cloak but instead wore a black ballgown she'd made in the hours since her father brought her, captive, inside Isardra's palace. She'd demanded fabric, supplies. The dress took very little magic, considering she'd made her clothes before she ever moved to the palace in Mardon. Magic merely made the garment come together faster. She'd had enough strength in her magic to build this dress from a pile of black bolts.

Above the dress, resting on her nose, sat the black feather mask Red had bought her.

If he is not blind too, he will see. He will know. Her heart tripped with glee simply to see him walking.

He paused when he saw her. Elise stood at his side, elegant in her slim mask. Tonight, all were masked, all were a half-truth, except for two people. Red's face was unmasked, as well as Ondorian's. The High Priest never hid. To him, even a mask was a lie.

Aly's father still wore his white owl mask.

Several sorcerers wove around the room, their masks as elaborate as their cloaks were plain. Grey's sorcerer wore a green bird mask while hovering near the table reserved for Tandera's councilmen. A large, cloaked figure in a horned gazelle mask sat at the table with the Referen king.

As Red and Elise followed a man to the dais, Red kept his eyes on Aly, his shoulders stiff, his jaw iron-wrought. She sat up straight, her frame rigid, unmoving. *See me. See the truth*, she begged.

Again, she tried to sense his Truthwell. Her magic flooded the room, yet she couldn't sense a single spot of energy.

The orchestra dropped to a low hum as Red and Elise bowed before the dais, their names called out by a crier standing to the left. A gentle round of applause followed their introduction.

Red finally met Kassia's eyes as he lifted out of his bow. His eyes betrayed the hatred there, the contempt, the betrayal. Aly scooted forward on her throne. The anger on his face meant he knew Kassia was up to something.

Yes! See the truth, Red.

Aly's trip to the Forgotten Cities had shown her that the Canyon could blot out all ability to see the truth. Red had stepped in the river, which meant he might be as blind as Alef or Burdi. But Aly sensed he was not. Or maybe it was just a mad hope.

I'll take mad hope, she said to herself, reciting what he'd told her before they'd left Mardon.

This night would not conclude without answers, without the truth.

Ondorian's face popped into Aly's mind. She glanced around for the priest. The priest had proposed to see the library in Isardra while on this visit. Aly wondered if he'd been allowed entrance. She might not have the ability to speak to Red's mind, but she could still speak aloud. For now. As soon as the meal concluded, she would find Ondorian. Then Red.

Red and Elise took their seats at the table for the guests of honor, set with more than a dozen utensils for each person and a cityscape of crystal. Lucien lifted his glass as they sat. Red did not return the gesture, an odd choice.

Red wouldn't snub an ally. Maybe the curse has corrupted his mind! Aly played with her Master's ring, sending the smoke and ash looping around and around all ten fingers.

When everyone else was seated, Kassia rose and descended to the lone chair at the head table. The tables for the honored guests peeled down from the queen's table like drying lily petals. As customary, no sorcerer sat *with* her. However, contrary to all customs Aly had ever known, not one but two sorcerers sat *behind* her, one at each shoulder.

Aly's stomach growled as the room filled with the scent of grilled meat. She hadn't eaten since before leaving Caridan. Her father, it seemed, wished to weaken her in every way. Why he'd asked her to serve alongside him, she had no idea. He'd wanted to kill her for so long, she couldn't imagine why the sudden change of heart.

Every few minutes Red glanced up at Aly. His expression was uncharacteristically unreadable. His eyes were piercing, as if trying to rend the darkness around him. If the Canyon had polluted his mind, he might not even see the black mask on her face. She'd hoped it would be enough to show him whose side she was on. Tapping her toes in rapid succession, Aly waited to rise. She didn't think her father would allow her to speak to Red, but she would find a way.

Truth will rise, she mused.

The official call to the dancefloor was given, and Kassia excused herself from the table, taking Dimitri's hand for the first dance. A bold move. It said she was in complete control here, dancing with magic like she dared anyone to question her.

As couples began to move toward the dancefloor, Aly waited for Kassia and her father to turn away, then Aly darted from her chair. Red stood and wove around a table toward the same place Aly was headed: the High Priest's table. Aly glanced at Dimitri. He was twirling Kassia around the dancefloor.

Red was intercepted by a Bulvarnan palace servant.

"My lady would like the next dance," said the man. Behind him stood Mira Mirkova in a stunning red gown.

Aly's mind flashed to the single time she'd worn red. She'd felt as beautiful that night as Mira now looked. Heads turned to stare at the queen's niece. Automatically, Aly found Grey in the crowd, who was talking to Lord Alexander. The smile that crossed Aly's face was one of fondness. Perhaps after all this, if she could extract herself from this mess, she'd thank Grey for finding her, for training her, for bringing her to the palace.

Without Grey, Aly would never have met the king.

Her cheeks burned as Red, a bit dumbfounded, accepted Mira's invitation and led her onto the dancefloor. Mira's dress seemed to bleed life into the room. Her blond hair piled around her head and tumbled down one shoulder. A thin band of diamonds rested among her curls.

Kassia was up to something, first by forcing Aly to stand by her side and now with Mira dancing with Red.

Elise moved to a table where Lady Alexander and Leeta sat sipping wine. Leeta's gaze stayed pinned on Red. Perhaps she, too, felt a sting of jealousy. Aly moved through the crowd to Ondorian's table, wishing she could be invisible.

The violins churned up a Tanderan waltz, and Red led Mira around the floor with ease. He was a much better dancer, of course, than Grey had been.

Bulvarnans enjoyed two things: vodka and dancing. Paired with the lingering heat of early summer and the density of the crowd, the dancefloor soon became a twirling, sweaty mass. Hired Comforters stood along the walls, cooling the room, but their efforts did little to combat the nerves and political maneuvering on the dancefloor.

Aly smiled, staring at Red as she took a seat by the High Priest.

"Ah, my dear," he said. "You are glowing."

She blushed scarlet. *Does he mean my attire or the way I am looking at the king?*

"I can't see Truthwells anymore," she said. If her father spotted her, he might lock up her tongue again. She didn't have long. Fortunately, it appeared dancing with his queen was occupying all of his thoughts for now.

The priest stilled, his goblet halfway to his mouth. "That is most alarming. Tell me what happened."

Aly began to tell Ondorian of their trip to the Black River. Applause scattered around the room as the couples parted. Aly didn't notice, absorbed as she was recounting the hour they'd spent in the Canyon.

Ondorian's goblet sat abandoned after Aly spoke. "You believe you are cursed?"

"I don't feel different, but then again, wouldn't a curse meant to make me believe lies be hard to detect?"

"It would indeed. You have no way of knowing if the king is healed?"

Aly shook her head. "I was hoping you could Reckon the truth for me. I almost had it out of him when I lost consciousness. I was going to kill him if I Pulled anymore from him."

"No, you would not have."

"Sir? I could feel the edges of his Truthwell, there was nothing left."

"Aly, how many times do I have to tell you, Truthwells are infinite. They are not used up. To Truthstrip someone is to use up all that can be attained. Theod's mark is like him, unending."

Aly's fingers drummed on the tablecloth. "But I found the bottom of his Truthwell before we went into the Canyon."

"No. You found all he had given you."

Her eyes snapped to Red, who spoke to his sister. He'd stopped dancing. Mira was nowhere in sight. Neither were Kassia and Dimitri. Aly stiffened.

"Well, now I'll never know if there was more."

"You know there is more, Aly. Lies alter our perception of the world around us. Think about a lie you may have believed. I am not speaking of a lie you may have heard recently. I mean perhaps one you may have lived for years."

Her breathing became shallow. "How would I know it, if I've believed it my whole life?" Images of Alef and his scarred face flashed in her mind. A shudder of fear, of repulsion shook her frame. *Could I be like them, lost in a lie?*

Ondorian placed his hand on hers. "Truth. It is our only weapon against the lies."

"Can you Reckon it and tell if Red is healed?"

He sighed. "I will when I speak to him."

"Thank you."

"Of course. It will serve us all to know if our king is fully healed of his death curse. Now, we have much to do."

"Sir, I can no longer sense Truthwells to perform magic. I have to Pull at random. I can barely do anything."

His brown eyes softened. "Ah, but not everything that matters takes magic." He winked at her. "Now, I suggest you step away because Frederick is headed this way, and if your father catches you speaking to our king, I imagine Dimitri's reaction will go poorly for you."

Ondorian rose to greet his king. Aly slipped away, darting between two groups of courtiers.

Not everything that matters takes magic.

One thought occurred to Aly at that moment. She brushed through the crowd and faced Red just as he was reaching Ondorian's table.

"Before you speak, I have one thing to say. When I pledged my fealty to Bulvarna, I lied."

2 9

RED

Red stared in shock at Aly, who backed her way to the queen's dais with stiff, jerking motions, almost as if going unwillingly. Her green eyes pleaded with him from beneath her mask. The mask he'd given her. He hadn't even known she'd kept it, much less brought it with her.

Even with her face half-covered, she was beautiful.

If Aly had lied, then she still retained loyalty to him. But if she'd lied, then it wouldn't matter anymore.

Lying broke her magic.

After all she'd taught him about magic and its purpose and purity, if she'd lied now, even to keep from pledging allegiance to Kassia, she'd ruined any chance she had of defeating her father.

He closed his eyes, trying to push away the happiness he felt at her words. She walked away before he could ask if he'd been fully healed.

She was faithful to the point of giving up her magic to protect him. Hope surged through him, followed immediately by the sting of despair.

As if someone ripped each column out of place, the room seemed to crumble around Red as his mind sank into a deep darkness. Fear, cold as the Canyon bottom, crawled over his hot skin, chilling him into marble. She may have remained loyal to him, but when her father found out, he would kill her, leaving Red alone anyway. If the curse was still in him, even just a sliver, he would die too.

"What's wrong?" Elise whispered from beside him.

Ondorian cleared his throat, cutting off Red's response. "I believe it would be of interest to you both that the document we are celebrating tonight was drafted and signed before the negotiations even began. I only just discovered this truth earlier today. I tested the document's age and authenticity."

"Doesn't that require magic?" asked Red.

"No. Much simpler. I inquired about the palace, found the man who drafts all the queen's official documents and asked him about his work, mostly under the presumption that I admired his penmanship and wanted to know how he treated his paper to preserve it. He did not mention the treaty directly, but I was able to glean that he had not written an official document for the queen in several weeks' time."

"Not lying now, are we, priest?"

"Of course not, Your Majesty. A man of the book does not lie. I *am* interested in the preservation of documents, as much of my day is spent in copying ancient texts. Simply because my intentions were two-fold does not mean I was lying." The man never joked, but Red, to his surprise, saw in his dark eyes a strange flash of what might have been humor.

Red removed his coronet and raked a hand through his hair. "Before the negotiations began? That's pretty confident, even for Kassia. And you said I *signed* it?"

"A forgery or, perhaps, a deception of even greater power." At Red's lifted brows, he added, "Kassia had your father cursed. Then you. She was determined to weaken the strength of Tandera's crown and her sorcerer. This, I believe, is because Kassia knows something that terrifies her. Something about Aly."

"About Aly?"

The priest nodded. "Why else the endless attempts to ruin her magic? Even now they have weakened her by forcing her to lie. They *knew* she would choose your life. They wanted her as weak as possible. *Think* about why."

Red's gaze moved across the room, finding Aly's masked face as she sat in the chair behind Kassia's.

Aly had said her father hadn't wanted them coming north, perhaps because he didn't want them to attempt to heal Red in the Canyon, thus restoring Aly to her full strength. Everything Kassia and Dimitri had done was to weaken Aly. Red was simply a pawn in the process.

What do they know about her that I do not?

It hit him like a punch in the nose. Aly had been keeping something back from him; he'd felt certain of it several times. There was that night in the garden, when her magic had accomplished something *new*. What if Aly was stronger than she'd let on?

But why would she hide that? Or had she?

He recalled her words when speaking of his Truthwell, *Didn't I tell you how bright you are?*

She'd told him over and over again that he burned with more light than any she'd seen. He was her source of power.

Kassia had dimmed his light and cut Aly off from him.

It was Aly, yes, that frightened Kassia, but it was Aly *and* him. There was something to his Truthwell and to how it powered Aly's magic, something even Aly didn't understand. But Kassia did, and she'd spent *decades* trying to stop it.

Steadying himself, Red placed two hands on the back of the nearest chair as his mind spun.

Kassia may have drafted the treaty recently, but she'd been planning this for *years*, before they'd even arrived in Bulvarna, he was certain of it. Before the Bulvarnan ambassador arrived at his father's funeral, even before the handkerchief had released its curse.

The queen dealt in empires and death, and her strategy was such that all the winning cards did not enter her hand until the end of the game. Dimitri. Gevar. Lucien. Lordan. Elise. Now Aly and Red. All these people were players in her hands.

Kassia had won. Her plan had worked. He'd played right into her hands.

Red squared his shoulders toward Aly. *I'm sorry I doubted you.*

He'd brought this entire mess on them both. Gevar had been smart to simply let the curse take him. Now Red had given Kassia everything she'd wanted.

Trumpets blared, drawing all eyes to the back of the room.

Two footmen marched up to the dais carrying a scroll between them. White gloves kept their fingers off the document, and perfectly timed steps kept the fragile paper from twisting or turning as they moved toward the queen.

The ballgowns and suit tails ceased twirling, and everyone stopped sipping wine or vodka to watch the unfurling of the treaty. The reason for the celebration.

The lie.

Red balled his fists as he stood next to Elise and watched the fat men bow before their queen—their wicked, lying, conniving queen.

It took all of Red's practiced composure to keep his gaze steady, his breaths even, as Kassia stood to celebrate the success of the week's deliberations. Now was his chance to expose her deception.

"…Have agreed to end our war against the Canyon, accepting it as the gift it is," the announcer finished reading. Red's temples burned.

When the announcer reached the part where he read the signatures, Red tensed. At the mention of his name, he would call out Kassia's lie.

Right before his name was called, Red felt a binding sensation around his throat. Immediately, he began to gag, air not reaching past his clogged throat. When he moved to clutch at his neck, his hands remained by his sides, immovable. Some invisible force was immobilizing him.

Elise noticed his curt gasp and saw the color fleeing his cheeks and neck. "Frederick!"

Her shout drew eyes and ears, including Aly's. Then Elise's mouth pressed together, her eyes as round as dinner plates in pained surprise as she moaned against the tightness of her own lips. Then her moaning fell silent and she tossed her head back and forth a few times before the magic held her still.

One glance at Aly told Red it wasn't her. Her hand cupped her mouth, as if she knew exactly what was happening to them.

The others who'd been watching Elise and Red turned back to the queen and listened with ready smiles as she read off the names of the kings of Refere and Tandera. Red lashed against the magic pinning him, but his entire body was held captive by invisible bonds.

Helpless. Useless. Weak.

The old triad. His head seared with pain.

He hated that no matter what, magic always won. Even as king, he'd not had any real power.

He should have spoken up sooner. He should have blurted out the truth when he had the chance—before Kassia's sorcerer suspected his intent and prevented it.

He knew Elise suffered too, but he could do nothing to stop it.

Aly. His eyes found her again. She'd worn the mask to tell him to trust her. When she couldn't speak, she'd shown where her loyalty lay.

As the man finished his reading and bowed to Kassia, Red's jaw clenched as he waited for the magic to let him go. Aly's words from weeks ago rattled in his head, *I'd kill you as soon as it was out of your body, and you wouldn't have a chance at stopping me.*

No, Red thought. *She can't be cursed.* Aly had saved him. She hadn't killed him, and she hadn't left him to be the feast of a hungry foxblood. She'd broken her magic to save his life.

Inside him, hope surged. Aly was his only hope, weakened magic or not.

She was his mad hope.

In that moment, he knew she'd cured him of the curse. He was clean, and there was no doubt in his mind. To rid him of the curse, she'd poured it through her own body.

Now that they'd both survived and Aly had saved him again, Red would not sit by and watch as Aly's father's magic ripped them away from each other.

Tandera's power was like that of a phoenix, always rising when it appeared defeated. In the Canyon, she'd used the word *phoenix*, but he hadn't understood. Until now.

She was the flame. He was the bird.

Together, they were Tandera.

Truth will rise.

Like scales falling from his eyes, clarity dawned and he smiled. Kassia's powdery face looked like dried, cracking clay. She did not wear a mask, but still she hid beneath a false face. She was *ancient*. Red startled at the realization.

Then it hit him, he could *move*.

He stumbled forward, his bonds failing. At the same moment, Aly gasped and shouted, "It's a lie!"

All eyes focused on Aly. Even Kassia, craning around in her throne, seemed shocked at Aly's outburst, too stunned to say anything.

The hold on Red's limbs broke like a sheet of ice over a rushing river, and he stormed toward the thrones and the useless treaty still held up by the two large men.

"This is a false document!" With eyes pinned on Aly, he moved directly in front of the dais, barely more than an arm's length from Kassia's gown, which spilled down the steps before him. "My signature is a forgery!"

Pursed lips preceded a slight turn of her head as Kassia glanced back at her sorcerer, whom she'd been counting on to keep Red silent.

"This entire summit has been a sham." He pointed up at Kassia, not caring that his breach of decorum technically slapped on him the penalty of offending the queen, which in Bulvarna warranted prison. A few horrified gasps followed his words. "And she is using her toy back there," he indicated Aly's father, "to try to keep me from telling you all the truth." He spun toward the room full of people, Bulvarnans and foreign guests. The hairs on the back of his neck lifted in fear, but he couldn't worry about that now. "This document must be destroyed."

Someone dropped a wine glass and the shattering sound barely registered above the shrill scream of a half dozen women at once.

Bodies collided and a channel cut through the crowd, revealing a wolf as white as Kassia's powdered skin. Beside it sauntered a leopard, white and silver tail draped out behind it like the queen's train—no, not a leopard, a garland cat, the twisted, maned version of the snow leopard that, previously, had only existed in stories.

A flicker of panic rose in Red's stomach.

No one fled. No one even moved, other than to clutch at the nearest person. Perhaps they were all under a spell.

Drawing his dagger, he jumped up on the dais and sliced the treaty in half. The two men holding it, a little shaken at the appearance of the white beasts, stumbled apart, sputtering, each holding one riven half.

Kassia shrieked in anger. Instinct told Red to lift his blade.

Metal rang out as one of Kassia's guards attacked him. Kassia shrank behind her sorcerer. As Red shoved the guard away, he nearly lost his balance when he caught sight of Aly.

She shouted and a shard of wood burst into dust just before it could stab into her neck. Her father lifted his hands, but Red didn't have time to wait to see what his next move would be. Kassia's guard lunged.

Scraping and shattering and screaming filled the air. Magic thunder-clapped.

"Aly!"

Clang! The guard stumbled off the dais as Red shoved him. Then, in one of the stupidest actions he'd ever performed, he turned and knocked fully into Aly's father, barely moving the man's shoulder. Red spun away.

People ran from the animals, no spell holding them hostage now. Part of the ceiling crumbled and swarmed around a dark-skinned man with a ponytail and a large, white cloak. Around his neck hung an antelope mask. Refere's sorcerer. Red had no time to watch which side this man was on. Red's aim was simple: stay alive and save Aly.

Dimitri whirled, a look of pure hatred on his brow. On the other end of the dais, Aly fell to her knees and sucked ragged breaths of air. Red's dagger flew from his hand as a pulse of magic drew it easily from his fist.

Hands lifted, Dimitri slammed Red to the floor with such force that his lungs nearly popped.

Seconds passed before Red could breathe. His whole body ached and his dagger now hung in Kassia's powdered hand.

He scanned the room, looking for his sorcerer, his limbs pinned by magic.

A Bulvarnan soldier battled Veeter Yin, who fought as if uninjured. Steel weaving like ribbon, the two fighters matched each other's strikes, as if trained by the same master.

Mira appeared to be weaponless, though a blade glistened on the floor near her. An odd, wavering, red light near an alcove spoke of magic, but Red didn't have time to ponder it. Kassia approached him slowly, a trusting smile on her face that told him she knew he was immobilized.

He managed to struggle to a kneeling position, his breathing still shallow. His heart stopped at what he saw next.

Elise stood by the dais, cornered by the silver garland cat. The white wolf lay sprawled out on the floor, his mouth open and eyes vacant. Aly was nowhere to be seen.

Red wanted to snap his fingers and vanish too. It'd be much harder for Kassia to fight him if he were invisible.

As if Aly read his thoughts, the room fell silent, save for one person's noticeably heavy breathing. Aly materialized in front of him, panic in her eyes.

Freed instantly from his magical cage but too stunned to say anything, Red leapt to his feet and glanced back at Kassia, who snarled at his sudden disappearance.

"Red," Aly croaked, voice hoarse. "For a while there I couldn't see your Well. But then, when you broke out of my father's spell, your light—all the light—came back. *You* healed me." She smiled. "And I was worried you were corrupted after stepping in the river!"

"I stepped in the river?"

"You were soaking wet when I lifted you out of the Canyon. But it was all a lie—the curse is gone, *fully* gone! Maybe what we thought we knew about the Black River isn't all true."

A loud bang drew her attention. "Lucien's sorcerer is holding off the other Bulvarnans." She nodded toward the faint red glow. "But I can't *do* this anymore. I can't protect you. When I lied, I broke my magic!" Her body trembled.

He grabbed her shoulders and pulled her against his chest. For one second, he wanted to feel her alive, to feel her breathing and close and safe. "Aly, listen to me. Thank you. For saving my life."

A sudden movement nearby caused him to instinctively place

two hands on Aly's shoulders and move her farther away. Elise had slipped out of sight.

Red looked back at Aly, whose eyes were huge and desperate, her breathing ragged. "Wait." He lifted the mask and tossed it aside. It snagged on her hair and pulled a curl loose. "There. Now I can see you."

The silence cracked. A ripple coursed through the invisible shroud around them.

"It's breaking. He'll get through." Aly stared up at him. "He'll win." Her face held a sadness that chilled Red's heated blood.

He squeezed her shoulders. "No, he won't. You told me that your magic comes from the truth. Either the truth is still strong, or you lied a long time ago." He ducked down to eye level with her. "Fight the lies with truth, right? The curse didn't turn you against me, Aly—that was a *lie*. I'm healed, and you are still powerful. I'm not sure how, but I know it's true. As far as I see it, your father hasn't won until we give up."

Around them, the battle raged. It felt unfair to stand here in strange silence while the world fell.

She reached one hand up to his cheek—a gesture that stole his breath from him in ways magic never could.

"I can't beat him now," she said, voice hoarse. "But I can try to get us out of here." She moved her hand and slid her fingers up and through his hair, his coronet gone, tumbled somewhere near the dais. Her palm lit a trail of fire where it went. She pressed against his forehead, and blazing heat flared in his body. Was it magic or just her touch? "Thank you," she muttered, "for trusting me."

Lightning coursed down his body.

And the sounds of the room crashed in around him.

The shroud disappeared. Aly surged up from the dais, her black dress billowing around her, swirling in the current of her magic. The look on her face rose the hairs on Red's arms.

Power seeped from her lips as the words began to rise.

Swords clashed all around. A few pistols fired. The walls were coming down as the magic of the sorcerers ripped the room apart. The garland cat closed in, inches from Elise, who had reappeared holding a dagger.

A descending blade diverted Red's mind away from his sister. Kassia lunged, his own dagger still in her hand. He leaped aside.

A few people scrambled for the exits. The temperature plummeted as magic drew the heat from the air. As Red rolled out of the way, a glimpse of Seb's golden suit jacket whirled by as he battled someone in Bulvarnan white. Light flashed as if a storm had woken in the rafters.

Fire exploded in an alcove to his left. A flash of orange. A shattering of marble.

Kassia dove at Red, a wildness in her eyes that screamed for blood. Red scrambled to his feet, and someone jammed a sword hilt into his hand.

Lucien shouted, "Take it!" Red grabbed the blade. "I am with you, Brother." He nodded to a column of smoke rising from the uplifted hands of the Referen sorcerer. Red swung the sword toward Kassia. Her white-rimmed eyes danced between him and Lucien.

Refere was a true ally. He'd been wrong to question Lucien.

"You think you can win this?" hissed Kassia. "You think you can resist the magic of the Deep?"

Talking meant distraction. Red tried to feel the room around him, to sense the dangers.

Aly had crashed to the floor, but her father appeared tangled in a knot of twisting ropes as he cried out curse after curse at his daughter. Her mouth moved as she whispered her weapons.

"The magic of the Canyon is a lie!" he bellowed above the din. He could try to distract her too. Maybe convince—

Thunk!

With a flick of her wrist, Kassia had tossed Red's stolen dagger right into Lucien's chest.

"No!"

The awful sound of limp muscles and hard bone hitting the floor was louder than the clashing of blades. It was the sound of a friend falling.

In that moment, Elise caught Red's eye, backed against one of the thrones. The cat primed its haunches to leap at its prey.

"Elise!"

He had one shot. Turning from Kassia, from Lucien's twitching body, Red dove for the cat right as it sprang toward his sister.

Glass shattered. A thousand daggers fell through the air as the windows on the south wall of the room collapsed at a sorcerer's command. In a great rush of wind, the shards turned to sand as they fell, saving everyone below from cutting glass.

Grit stung Red's eyes, blinding him. He slapped at his face. Elise screamed from under the cat's body. He was too late.

Lunging again toward the spotted beast, he willed his sword to save his sister as he collided with fur.

Snarl and grunt. Claw and tooth. The cat snapped at Red's shoulder. Then a loud blast and it whimpered and slumped off onto the floor.

Weston Grey stood a few feet away, pistol in hand.

Screams and a whooshing, crushing sound of items moved by magic filled the room. Everywhere he looked, his eyes saw ruin. Blood splattered the floor, the columns, the swinging blades. Pistol shots echoed.

He'd come for peace; he'd brought a war.

A warm breeze blew across his face before he noticed the outer wall had cracked. Summer air wafted in as mortar clouded the air like blown dust. Then the south wall burst apart, stone by stone, as a sorcerer called out the command. A moment of awe held Red rooted, then a brick crashed down onto his shoulder, taking him with it.

30

ALY

"Red!" Aly screamed above the chaos as he fell.

At the edge of the ballroom, his Truthwell burned like the noon sun. It was pure and bright and free from all traces of the death curse. He was right; she'd healed him. Her magic surged as she Pulled and prepared a spell.

The king tried to rise. Aly blasted a wall of wind at her father. He waved it away.

Red's borrowed sword spun across the parquet floor away from him, bumping into rubble. Steps away, Seb locked blades with his attacker. A Bulvarnan soldier bore down on Red.

With a shout, Aly pushed the sword back toward Red's hand and raised both arms to deflect a bullet aimed at her. It exploded against a column.

Sound and instinct and fresh air lured her out the back of the ballroom, through the now gaping hole, and into the warmer garden. Pale gray mortar dust frosted the plants, pathways, and Aly's lungs as she tried to lead her father away from Red and the others. The air smelled of grass, rubble, and flowers—better than the metal scent of blood in the ballroom.

Dimitri blasted fallen stones out of his way as he pursued her. No one else followed; she was on her own.

With a glance at her ring, she tightened her jaw. This was what she'd been preparing for since she had become a Master.

She slapped away a large brick as it hurtled toward her. Then gravel, like a hundred bullets, pelted at her from the ground. Twisting into the air, she burst all the pebbles into powder with a word.

Stone dust shot into her eyes; she fell to the ground, her concentration broken as she dug at her eyes with her knuckles. Backing up, she tripped and fell down hard on her wrists.

With a silent thought, she erected a dome above her to stop whatever was heading her way. It was a strong spell and it required all her attention. A lightning bolt sizzled against the outside of her dome. The dome cracked and disappeared.

He's Pulling lightning from the air. There was no storm nearby. Even when she reached outward, searching for the electric energy in the clouds, she found none. This was strange magic.

Halfway across the garden, she managed to strike her father with a rose thorn. He would never think to fight with something so small.

His hand cupped his neck, then withdrew with a bit of blood on it.

"You hit me," he said, amused. "Smart girl."

Footsteps crunched in the gravel as someone else brought their fight outdoors.

Aly had to keep her eyes on her father.

With lifted hands, her father intoned a line of words that made her skin prickle. Beneath her feet, the ground began to swell. Leaping up, Aly suspended herself above the garden, seeing now the pair who fought near the fallen outer wall of the palace.

Red battled a navy-clad guard. The man catapulted over a

bush to boot Red right in the thigh. Red's fingers raked the gravel as he faceplanted. Aly wobbled in the air, her magic faltering.

Aly's father rose to meet her. No, he lifted the *ground* beneath him.

"Why do you want him dead? Your fight is with me," she shouted at him.

A rosebush struggled to remain in the earth as it was lifted. The sight brought a spell to mind. At Aly's command, the rosebush unfurled, wrapping its limbs around her father's ankles. He shouted, kicking at the thorny branches. With a blast of fire from his hands—*how did he draw fire from nowhere?*—he obliterated the bush.

"Your king has come," her father said with a wicked grin. The earth sank back down. Dimitri turned to Red, who for some unfathomable reason now stood within striking distance. "Ah, you will make this easier."

"Stop! Red!" she screamed, slamming to the ground. The look in his eyes gave her pause. He was bleeding on one side of his head. "Oh!" She cupped her hands to her mouth for only a moment, as if startled, then shoved her palms down toward the earth.

At her command, the earth unfurled. Roots wormed their way into the air, grabbing at Dimitri. For a moment, he was occupied blasting them to smithereens.

When Aly next saw Red, her heart catapulted against her ribs. His face was now a sheet of blood. He screamed and touched his cheeks, then yelled again when he saw his hands.

"No!" Aly ran to him as snare after snare of roots looped around her father's hands and feet.

Blood began to drip off Red's chin. He fell to his knees, red spots appearing on the gravel. His skin was sloughing off like a snake's. Her father was torturing him.

Aly directed the roots around her father, who just as quickly sliced the roots with thorns the size of sabers. Red reached up to her and gripped her wrist, leaving a bloody handprint.

She muttered an undoing spell—more difficult than a healing spell. It required she know exactly what spell her father had used to melt away the king's skin. Her first three attempts did nothing. His face was deteriorating.

Think! Her pulse was too high. She was about to pass out from the sight of—*Oh!* She uttered one more version of the spell, and his skin reappeared, fresh, soft, and freckled. She reached out two hands, pressed them against his warm face and wept one single note of joy.

He toppled toward her in thankful tears, but she shoved him aside and stood.

"Leave!" Her back pressed against him, her arms twisting around her head. Light grew between her palms. When she flung the light at her father, it smashed inches from his face, not even touching him.

"I want to help!"

"Red, please!" Aly sent another blast of pure white light at her father's feet, barely singeing him as he hopped out of the way.

"Aly, you can—"

She wasn't listening. Feeling for weapons, she sensed fire burning nearby. Within seconds, it crackled in the air before her in a half dozen fiery orbs. One at a time, she shot them at her father.

Something grabbed Red's ankles and yanked him down, face first in the garden path. His chin smashed gravel, his chest dragging along the ground as if he'd been tied to a whipped horse. Dimitri's magic moved Red's body like a doll—toying with him.

Aly's eyes bulged as she stared at his retreating form. Her hands trembled as they reached for him. "Let him go!" She lunged after him.

Red's chin frayed until bone carved a path through the pebbles. His eyes sagged, then closed.

Aly caught up to him, sliding to the ground beside him as she conjured a blue dome of light above their heads.

Her hands cupped his head, then lifted his butchered chin. Aly set his head across her lap, cradling his temples. Soft healing words poured from her mouth.

"Truthstrip me," he grunted, eyes opening as his skin again reformed.

Aly sniffed. "I can't." Her thumb rubbed against the freckles beneath his eye.

"The garden," he muttered. "Like in the garden."

Her thumb stopped. "What do you mean?"

But she knew what he meant. Suddenly, it made sense. That night in the garden, he'd somehow given her more of his Truth-well. Ondorian had said a sorcerer could only Pull from the part she could see, the part she had access to.

Like a gale force wind, another realization hit her. "I could have healed you a long time ago, if only I'd been able to see. I've been blind long before tonight." His trust gave her more of his light. She had never realized it worked this way until now. *Why didn't you trust me sooner?*

He squeezed her arm. "Take it, Aly."

Because I didn't give you reason to. I'm sorry.

She removed the hand not pinned under his head and used it to tilt his face toward her. "Better now?"

He smiled, the blue light of her magic shield reflected in his eyes. "Much. Now, as your king, I command you to use the truth in me. Defeat him. You're stronger than he'll ever be."

The light above them shimmered. Something jostled it. Her father would break it soon.

Aly smeared a tear off her cheek and shook her head. "But—I might kill you." More tears dripped.

Red lifted a hand, traced the edge of her jaw. "I won't die. I'll be right here."

"Shh." She cupped her hand around his, pressing it to her skin.

"Listen to me. I want to live past tonight, to see you again. But right now, I can actually help. I can finally do something. I want to save my country. And you. Take it all, Aly, every bit of light inside me. I'm giving it to you." He wrapped one hand around her wrist. "I trust you."

Her eyes closed and she nodded. A tear hit Red on his forehead.

Without a word, she carefully slipped out from beneath him and stood. Beside her, he rolled and stood too, an eagerness in his eyes. A fierce hope.

With one hand toward Red and one hand toward her father, she called on Red's light. It ran to her. Like a thousand horses stampeding, his light barreled into her. She swelled with power.

Eyes open, she stared at her father through the cracking blue dome. Her Master's ring caught her eye, like a black snake swirling around her middle finger. With a twitch of her lip, she sent all her magic, all the energy from Red's Well, into that ring.

Aly's hands started to glow. An amber-gold light emanated from her skin, mottled and moving like reflections on water. The light spread up her arms, and as it neared her chest, she inhaled, as if gasping after almost drowning.

Wonder filled her. She lifted her hands, ready with a spell for the moment the blue shield broke.

The dome dissolved and, with one sweep of her hand, a dagger made of fire and ash appeared in her grip. Her ring was gone.

With the blade she stabbed the darkness around her father. A splintering sound accompanied the rupture of his own magic shield. Aly reeled backward from the explosion of her father's spell.

Red was there to catch her.

Before Aly could regain her balance, before her mouth even

finished uttering her next spell, Dimitri's hands lifted, a growled word peeling from his lips. Red jerked the magical dagger from Aly's hand and hurled it at her father. It sailed straight through Dimitri's conjured green shield and sank into his chest.

Dimitri gaped at the glowing, unnatural blade, at Red, at his daughter. A howl of anger sprang from his mouth. "So, it is true. You are the Beholder."

Panting, she raced forward and yanked the blade free, ensuring that the man could not take the blade and use it against them.

Her father stared down at his chest, his body already falling. At the sight of the blood and the sound of his words, Aly began to cry. He moved a hand across his wound but nothing happened. Blood continued to spill.

"It was all a lie, wasn't it?" she said, words stumbling out over her sobs. He'd done all this—curse after curse—to keep her from Red. From the Beacon.

She'd doubted it for so long, but her father had known.

Her father fell to his knees. "She will never let you live now."

She. Was Kassia after the Beacon and Beholder too? Aly glanced around, but Kassia was nowhere in sight. Likely still fighting indoors.

Aly's sobs intensified. Red stood beside her, eyes wide with shock. Her father flopped sideways onto a bush, crashing through it with limbs splayed. *He's gone.* His words echoed in her mind, but she shoved them away.

Fingers shaking, Aly turned and dropped the magical blade like it was poisoned. On the ground, it emitted a faint orange glow. Red grabbed her hands, then pulled her into a hug, squeezing so tight she could barely breathe.

She squeezed back just as hard.

Red's smile vanished as he pushed back. He studied her face. "I told you I'd be all right."

She pressed her eyes closed, releasing two tears. "He's dead…"

"And now we're safe. You can explain that blade to me later," he said. Their closeness felt strong and warm and right. He leaned his forehead against hers, the entire world in the pressure of his skin on hers, his lips hovering so close.

He tensed to pull away from her.

Then she whispered, "Stay."

31

RED

King Lucien did not recover. Neither did a pair of Bulvarnan guards nor one noblewoman who'd not escaped the ballroom before the pistols began firing.

Aly stood from where she'd knelt beside another injured soldier inside one of the palace's dining halls, which had been converted to a ward for the wounded. The man she'd just saved was a Bulvarnan. Her mercy to those in blue only increased Red's admiration for her. She'd been hunted by Bulvarnans her entire life, and now she stooped to heal their wounds. She and the other sorcerers soon managed to heal the remaining wounded.

Kassia had fled with a flurry of white-clad palace guards. Plenty of Bulvarnans would remain loyal to the Lady Wolf, ready to do her bidding at a moment's notice. But she was no threat now that her source of power lay lifeless on a bed in the queen's guest quarters.

But Dimitri's last words echoed in Red's mind. *She will not let you live.* Kassia's disappearance refuted any fears he had that the Bulvarnan queen would pose them danger in the near future. When and if she resurfaced, Red would wait to see if she retaliated for what they'd done here. To kill her Royal Sorcerer, no matter what she'd done to initiate the attack, could be seen as an act of war.

As he walked out of the dining hall, ready to speak to Aly and Seb and Elise and forge a path forward, he scoffed. Poisoning the sovereign of another country was a deed deserving of the strictest retribution, and Red had given her the utmost mercy by allowing her the opportunity to redeem herself by securing peace. She'd ruined that option. At least Red was alive, healed, and the man who'd crafted his death curse was gone.

Red swallowed and led the way to a drawing room in the guest quarters where he'd told Seb and Elise to meet. Aly walked silently behind him.

He had not mentioned Dimitri in front of Aly, and she had not protested when she saw his body being lifted and carted away on a stretcher to be prepared for burial. He may have been wicked, but he was not to be eaten by crows on the palace grounds.

And Red had not asked about her last words to her father. She'd explain them in time, if she wanted to. Instead, he'd let her cry against his shoulder until she'd steeled herself and gotten to work healing the injured. She needed to mourn the man they'd killed. She may have feared him, but there was something else going on with her that Red couldn't fully understand. Her sadness was more than he'd expected, but it seemed like whatever he expected in regard to Aly was always wrong. He simply stood beside her.

"Can you do anything about Kassia?" Seb asked, staring out a tall window with a poor view of little other than the white stones of Isardra's palace.

The summer sunlight, slicing in as the sun crested the palace walls, illuminated dust floating in the angled light, mimicking the muddled zoo of Red's thoughts.

Aly sat in a stiff chair by the empty hearth, which was topped with a painted wooden mantle and a mirror. Facing her, Elise sat with hands in her lap. Seb leaned against the blue windowsill with his arms crossed. His brows caterpillared above worried eyes, the way he looked when a girl had cold-shouldered him or when he'd lost a bet.

Red wished it were so trivial. "No. She'll search for another sorcerer—we can be sure of that." He swatted at a mosquito and perched on the edge of a wide, polished desk, his surcoat unbuttoned.

"I was talking to *her*," Seb said, nodding at Aly.

Aly, who'd been tapping the flat edge of her magical blade against her thigh, pinned Seb with iron eyes. She'd officially given the ash-like dagger to Red after the fight, but she had asked to hold it, as if trying to discern its secrets. When she'd first made the blade, it had dripped flames from its tip, but now it glowed like the coals from an overnight fire. Every now and then the blade would flicker as if a fresh wave of air had touched its embers.

She no longer wore her original Master's ring. Where there had once been a ring of smoke and ash, there was now a dancing whirl of pure white light.

Seb lifted a hand toward Aly, still not accustomed to being in a room with the Royal Sorcerer and also not exactly sure how lethal or offendable she was. "So that knife, uh, doesn't burn you?"

Aly flipped the dagger in the air, then caught the blade end with her outstretched palm. "No."

"Right. It's magic," said Seb.

"Like your Master's ring," Elise said.

Aly nodded. "Yes. And no. The ring is held together by magic, but it's natural." She held up her hand. "This one is made of tiny little bits of light. My first ring was of smoke and ash. Like what a phoenix is born from. Then my ring became this." She held out the blade. "It's hard to explain, but I was able to make the ring become the knife."

"Can you make one of those and stick it in Kassia too? That'd be pretty handy."

Aly frowned at Seb and spun the knife so that she held it properly again, tip toward Seb.

"At least we know Refere was on our side," said Elise, ever the optimist, trying to diffuse the tension. Elise had avoided asking about the Canyon, thought Red could sense in her a mild hesitation, a wariness around her brother, as if his trip into the Canyon had brought back something contagious, something wicked.

"*Lucien* was, at least," Red said, eyeing his sister. "Lordan, we still can't trust."

Elise emitted a barely audible huff. "The real threat is gone. Your curse is healed and," Elise looked at Aly with a sadness that suggested she hated to have to say her next words, "your father is really dead, then?"

"Yes." Aly's eyes found Red. "But the threat is not gone." She stepped toward him, feet soundless on the thick rug. Even without a shroud, she moved so quietly. She'd spent her life traveling as a ghost, unseen and unheard.

He blinked slowly and listened for the sound of her dress swishing, to give him the simple pleasure of opening his eyes and finding her right before him, visible to all, an step closer than anyone else would have stood. It fanned the embers in Red's already-burning cheeks. He wanted to wrap his arms around her and tell her they would be okay, that the world would be righted.

But the world wasn't right. No matter how much he wanted to return home, laugh with her as she turned water into steamships or daisies into dahlias, he could not do that. She was right that the threat was not gone. Kassia was still out there. To make things worse, once Red's council had learned of his descent into the Canyon, they'd recoiled with fear, shadows of distrust growing in their eyes. It would take time and a decent amount of explaining to convince them it had been the right course of action.

"My father was merely Kassia's tool," she said. "It was always her." She pinched her eyes shut, then peered up at Red with an apologetic frown. "All along, we feared the wrong person." She handed him the dagger. It fit perfectly into a sheath Aly had also conjured out of what had once been a handful of rubble from the ballroom. A magical sheath to hold a magical blade. Only a faint orange glow peeked out around the handle.

"Well, I'd say you were close enough. He was the power behind her evil." Seb made a face. "What about Kassia?"

"Would you let her finish?" said Elise.

"My father's last words revealed something I'd never considered." She nodded at Red. "*He* had considered it, but I'd missed it. Last night, I realized that my father had believed a lie for a long time. Ondorian asked me to search my past for any lie I might have believed for years. But what if the lie I believed was a lie my father had believed as well? When he saw the blade, something changed in him. It was as if he was seeing reality for the first time. I *felt* his Truthwell surge, as if trying to rid itself of the shadows that darkened it. He tried to heal himself, but he couldn't. I think it's because he was realizing the lie he'd believed."

"What lie?" asked Elise.

"I'm not entirely certain. But he…called me something I've doubted for some time. Something I didn't think anyone else could know." She glanced at Red. "He sounded like he'd been proven wrong, like his entire vendetta against me had been proven baseless."

"What did he call you?" Seb asked.

Aly half-smiled beneath hooded eyes. "If I am right, Kassia, not my father, feared me from the day I was born. I think she conceived lies that I would believe my entire life. Lies about my father. Lies about my magic. Lies about my birthmother. I'm not sure now if my birth really did kill my birthmother. I'm not sure of anything that could have been filtered through Kassia's schemes."

Red ran a hand through his hair, exhaling. "She fabricated an entire reality just to make you *weaker*." Kassia's plan had stretched back farther than even he'd surmised.

Seb shook his head, pointing one finger in the air. "Nah. There's more to this. *Toss me* if Kassia wasn't up to something more. Only to make one sorcerer weaker? That's way too elaborate."

The room quieted. Red watched Aly for a response, but she stared at her hands.

Red stared at Aly. This was the secret she'd been keeping.

"Seb is right," she finally said.

Seb's arms lifted by his sides in a victorious gesture.

Turning to Red, Aly's green eyes burned with a strange intensity that prickled his skin. "There's something I never told you. I didn't believe it myself until recently. Remember how I said your Truthwell is the brightest one I've ever seen? Well, before he died, your father's former sorcerer told me that at rare times in history a person called a Beacon is born." She nodded at Seb, as if to say she hadn't forgotten his question. "That person's Truthwell acts like a blinding light to a particular sorcerer, known as the Beholder."

Her father used that word last night.

She grabbed his hand, sliding her palm under his. "He said that when a Beacon exists, the world is about to undergo something significant, and the sorcerer who sees that light is the one who can use it to change the world."

Seb walked up and slapped a hand on Red's back. "Brother, I knew you'd make a good king, but going for world changer is, well, the most arrogant thing I think you've ever done. Way to go."

Elise sank back into her chair, face in bewildered shock. Red squeezed Aly's hand as his heart, encouraged by her touch and by her mysterious words, thundered behind his ribs.

This was the part she'd kept back from him, the secret she'd brought with her. The hidden hope that he could be some strange and mysterious agent of change.

Whatever a Beacon was, it was secondary to the way she returned the pressure on his hand. It was as if she had measured Seb's and Elise's reactions, rejected them, and reached for him anyway.

"The strangest part," Aly continued, "is that Kassia must have somehow suspected I could be a Beholder, which is why she instructed my father to inspect every new sorcerer in her kingdom, and it's why she made him pursue me, to kill me. Kassia didn't want me to find the Beacon, and I think my father had bought into some lie Kassia forged about Beacon and Beholder, some reason why we needed to be eliminated." Aly shrugged. "But I think, in the end, he saw her lie for what it was."

Seb strolled back to the window. "She might be wicked, but blazing Black River, she is smart."

Elise shot him a narrow look. Aly dropped Red's hand, her brow furrowed with dread and possibly a bit of regret. If Kassia was the mastermind, then Aly had been right: Dimitri was no more than a pawn, a tool in the queen's hands.

Red drew Aly into a hug and said over her shoulder, "He was still evil." If what Aly had said was true, and it seemed to be, then her father wasn't the one they should have killed. But her father *had* been the power behind Kassia's wishes, the one weaving death curses and enchanting Canyon beasts to execute the queen's bidding. He, too, had embraced the magic of the Deep, even if it was initially Kassia's design.

Red had not killed an innocent man; he'd eliminated the man who'd murdered his father, who'd killed Aly's own mother years ago, and who'd nearly ended his and Aly's lives as well.

When she pulled away, Aly's eyes were turning red. "My father was wicked because she pushed him into it. She twisted his mind with lies and drove him to the Deep." She inhaled to calm her now frenzied voice. "We may have won against my father, but Kassia is still out there."

Elise and Seb exchanged a frightened glance. Red had not called his council members to him today; he'd wanted only his sister and best friend with them for now.

Seb rubbed the back of his neck. "So we're not safe?" He, like Red and Aly, had suffered personally from the evil of the Canyon. His fear was well-founded.

Aly shook her head. "As long as Kassia is at large, we can't anticipate what she will do. I imagine she hasn't simply given up her life-long goal of removing Beacon and Beholder from the world. And as long as the Canyon is open to spill its evil into the world, we will never be free from its lies or those who believe them."

Elise exhaled. "Then we will never be safe."

Walking over to her, Aly placed one hand on Elise's upper arm. "I will keep you safe." She glanced at Red. "*We* will keep you safe. All of you."

"How?" asked Seb.

Red's memory flashed to his first official council meeting as king. He'd faced a room full of worried men. He hadn't solved the problems they'd discussed that day. The creatures of the Deep would still threaten his countrymen, as well as all the Sarovian Continent, if they were not contained, and Kassia had not agreed to defend her border from these wandering beasts. He hadn't really done anything other than heal himself and remove the man who'd wanted Aly dead for years. Tandera was still at risk. Everyone was still in danger.

Change the world, he said to himself, mulling over her words about a Beacon and Beholder. Aly fixed her eyes on his, and the longer her gaze held, the stronger he felt, the more certain of the truth in her strange revelation, despite the doubt whirling in his mind like an unsteady top.

Perhaps, if he really was a Beacon, they would change the world.

Aly finally broke her gaze. "We fight the lies with truth," she said.

"And we defend against the Canyon," Red added.

Seb clicked his tongue. "Sorry, guys. You were going for inspirational, but that was…anything but. That's what we've *been* doing. Look where that got us. I want to know what you two"— he pointed his finger at Red and Aly—"are going to do to *change the world.*"

Red bristled a little, but Seb was right. They needed a concrete plan. "I will return Lucien's body to Refere, and I will personally ask Lordan for more aid at the Canyon. If he was knowingly involved in my curse, he'll reveal his true allegiances and refuse, or he'll be appalled that he was part of such a plan and come to our aid."

Seb shrugged, unimpressed.

Red was glad he'd chosen Seb as a councilman. Few had the nerve to call out Red's plans as mediocre. "Fine. As king of Tandera, I will do all I can to secure our border and ensure we can withstand whatever retaliation Kassia sends our way."

Aly pursed her lips at Seb, then to Red added, "If we've been given some greater power than most, we will use it to defeat the evil of the Canyon in whatever way we can. I don't really understand how the whole Beacon thing works, but we'll figure it out."

Red smiled. "Together."

Red settled onto the velvet seat of the carriage, ready for the breeze of movement that would push out the hot, caged air. The white walls of Kassia's palace glinted down at him, the scaffolding of her renovations a strange reminder that her work was not finished. Not here. Not in Bulvarna.

Red's work was not finished either—it had only just begun. He needed to be ready when Kassia reemerged, as he was certain she would. And more than that, he wanted to ensure his people were safe from the beasts of the Deep.

He slipped the ash blade out of its sheath and twirled it absently, mesmerized by its pulsing glow. It did not burn him; however, if he set the blade down anywhere other than in the sheath Aly made, it would leave scorch marks. A strange thing. A beautiful thing. Perhaps it had to do with him being a Beacon. He and Aly had a list of questions for Ondorian, and a list of topics to study once back at home.

But they had a more pressing agenda—one that involved a dead king and his soon-to-be crowned, and possibly traitorous, son.

If Lordan was allied with Kassia, Red needed to know. Until he had all the facts, he held out hope that Lordan, like so many others, was simply under Kassia's wicked influence, or possibly even unaware of his own hand in the near death of Tandera's monarch. To sever their longstanding peace would be foolish.

Elise climbed into the carriage from the other side. "It is good to be leaving this place."

The king nodded.

Then from the open door, another figure climbed in and sat facing Red.

"Hello, Aly."

"Hello, Red."

Elise pressed her hands against a copy of the *Verad* and smiled.

"Glad you could join us," he said.

Her face remained steady, but her eyes sparked. "Glad you asked."

At the train station in Excheter, they were a safe distance—if there was one—from the Canyon, where Red could leave his sister and the rest of his royal council behind to travel by train to Refere with Lucien's body. Escorting Refere's deceased king back to his homeland was the suitable course of action.

At the other end of the train platform, Seb heaved trunks onto the third car. Men and women shuffled about, some bringing fresh supplies to the train, others huddled up along the platform to catch a glimpse of the king and princess.

They'd survived the trip back across the Canyon without incident, and now the royal council would return to Mardon while Red traveled on with Lucien's body to Refere's capital, where Red would remain until they crowned Lordan. Red planned to question Lordan about the handkerchief, and then recruit him to join them in the fight against the Canyon. Maybe it was because Lordan had nearly married his sister—or because he *hadn't*—Red fully believed Lordan would join their side. Whatever lies Kassia had poured into Lordan's head, Red was determined to strip them out. He had to. Refere was too great an ally to lose. He needed Refere if they hoped to hold back the throne of evil.

After facing Dimitri and Kassia, both of whom had wanted him dead, traveling to Refere to face a young king—one too cowardly to threaten Red directly—didn't feel nearly as dangerous.

Elise pressed gloved hands together at her waist and peered up at her brother in the back of the royal train car, which had been brought up from Mardon. "You look like the boy I used to watch riding off into the wood with Father. I was always jealous of that, you know. I had to sit inside the palace with Mother and Carolyn."

"I know. You've told me many times."

"I thought it needed saying again, I suppose." She knotted her fingers and wrung them like a cloth. "I would not be a burden."

Red chuckled. "We discussed this. It's not that you would be a burden. It's that I need you back at home." He couldn't bring himself to say the real reason he thought she should stay behind. If Lordan had affected her once with his lies, then he could do it again. Red trusted and loved his sister, but he also knew that her heart hadn't fully healed from Lordan's rebuff.

Her chin dropped as if she too thought of the heartache she'd face in Refere.

A few feet away, Weston Grey hefted himself onto the train. The council wanted to send a member along with the king—a more experienced member than Seb—and Grey volunteered. Despite his unease about Grey and Aly, Red couldn't very well forbid the man from accompanying them without arousing suspicion. Steam hissed from the engine several cars down.

Elise stiffened. "I am nervous."

"We'll be fine."

"I never said otherwise." She lifted her shoulders high, her chin higher. Passengers dressed in dark wools or pale sun hats drifted across the platform, curtseying or bowing as they caught the king's gaze.

"Right. We'll be three weeks. Four at most. We will, of course, be obliged to stay for Lordan's coronation."

Elise blinked. "Of course." She loosened her hands. "And when you return, we will be one nation stronger against the Canyon."

"Let's hope."

He watched as a long white box emerged onto the platform, carried by four Referens, who lifted it onto the train with gentle, synchronous movements. These men, dressed in their finest, had come to escort their king's body back to his home. One of them was the Referen sorcerer, in a brand-new lion mask. He seemed to have no qualms about remaining visible while the country was between sovereigns. Until he could be present with Lordan, the man couldn't Bind with the crown prince, and he'd promised to travel with the late king's body.

With a sigh, Red glanced back down at his sister. "Refere's loyalty to Tandera is not as strong as we might like to think. Lucien was a rare king. He treated us like we were of the same blood, but no blood unites us."

Elise blinked darkly up at him. "Not yet, anyway."

"What do you mean?"

In her quiet eyes was a dogged determination. "Lordan will be king."

A sinking sensation weighed on Red's stomach. "We still don't know his involvement. Why would he have known about the handkerchief? Why would he have wanted to harm me?" Red had argued *against* these ideas just yesterday, as Elise tried to talk him out of a meeting with the young Referen prince. Now he used Elise's own reasoning against her—because he knew where she was headed, and he didn't like it.

"He could be a threat." She'd spent the past few days insisting on it, after all. "But for some reason I do not really think so."

Theod, help us. She still loves him. Elise could not come with him. She was still susceptible to Lordan's lies. A broken heart was too risky to bring along with him, when he needed to give Lordan every reason to agree to help Tandera.

Elise curled one side of her lips. "He is still unwed, you know."

"Elise!" He lowered his voice. "You can't mean it!"

Two hands rose to her hips. "And why not? You said yourself that this alliance means everything."

"Not *everything*. It is important, but if they say no, we will manage, figure something out. It is not worth *that*." He felt a flip of anger in his stomach. "Lordan left you." A bullish snort punctuated his words. "If I see him, I will slap him for you."

I'd do more, but we need his allegiance.

Elise turned her head aside with a flustered sigh. "You will not."

"I will too. He deserves it." Red shook his head. "More than that, really, but I might not be helping our treaty if I punched their new king."

Elise snapped back at him. "No, I mean, *you* will not slap him. He does deserve it, but I will be the one to do it."

"What?"

Seb walked up.

"Did you get them?" Elise asked.

"Yes, my Lady." Seb took her hand and pressed a small, conspiratorial kiss to it.

"My thanks." She withdrew her hand quickly, then placed it on the railing beside the car door. Her other hand refused Seb's offered support. "I am coming with you." She bounced onto the train beside Red.

Forced to make room for her, he let out a nervous laugh. "Elise, why?"

"Because if he sees me, he will have to agree to help you." One hand pushed away loose hairs from her face. "He will either feel so ashamed—and rightfully so—that he will swear his allegiance to make up for it, or he will fall at my feet and ask me to marry him, making us allies anyway."

For a moment, Red stared at his sister. He'd never suspected she was the politicking type. Maybe a broken heart was a good weapon to bring with him.

"And which do you hope he does?"

She darted narrow eyes at him. Then, her face relaxed. "Honestly, I have no idea. Come on, Aly."

Before Red could say a word, Aly materialized in the narrow space between him and the back railing of the train car. Her traveling attire of pants and tucked-in blouse had been replaced by a dress of pale green silk, simple enough but also stunning. No mask. No cloak. He recognized the dress as one of Elise's, but it had been hemmed to fit Aly perfectly.

Elise, head turned to greet Aly, caught her brother's stare and said, "She could not very well travel in her old clothes, now could she? We had to make arrangements." With pursed lips, she shuffled off into the train's car, skirts swishing through the narrow door.

Aly stepped after Elise, her body brushing against Red's chest in the small space. He reached out, letting the back of his hand just touch hers. She paused, eyes wide, looking over her shoulder. She offered the smallest of smiles and pressed her knuckles against his.

"Does this mean you don't wish to stay hidden anymore?" he whispered, his own smile playing at the edge of his mouth.

Her fingers lined up against his, hidden by the folds of her dress. "I've always wanted this. More than anything else. To not sit in the shadows."

Such a simple wish. What did he want more than anything?

He wanted to twist his palm, latch onto hers, and pull her toward him.

But before he could, she lifted her hand to the doorframe, her eyes pinched with worry. "She's out there. When she finds another sorcerer, she'll come for you. I know she will."

Red exhaled. He wanted to reassure Aly that he'd be fine, but she was right. If the Bulvarnan queen had been hunting Beacon and Beholder for over twenty years, she wasn't about to stop now. They'd survived Kassia's attempts thus far, and that gave him hope.

He leaned forward ever so slightly. "But I have you."

Aly's shoulders tensed, but she remained silent.

After a moment, he changed the subject. "Who are you supposed to be?"

"For now, I'm a friend of your sister's. No one on this train needs to know I'm your sorcerer."

"You know that people will wonder who the beautiful woman is who's traveling with the king. People don't ignore that sort of news. Besides, most of Elise's friends are distantly royal, and they all know each other."

She blushed and looked down. "I *want* to be seen, but I'm nervous."

Red stepped closer, his shins brushing against the folds of her dress. His hand braced against the thin doorway, right above Aly's. He could feel the heat from her arm and wanted so badly for her to turn to him. "You'll be just fine. I'm right beside you."

"But what if no one even looks at me?"

"I assure you, they will."

Her chin down, she whispered, "And will you?"

She was giving him permission. Even though it broke the rules of logic, Red didn't care. In that moment, he was on fire.

His hand dropped over Aly's, so that his fingers slid between hers. "I already am."

To read the backstory on Lord Weston Grey and get a glimpse of his spy life, sign up below!

vip.cfeblack.com/join

ALSO BY C. F. E. BLACK

Scepter and Crown series:

Shield of Shadow

Crown of Dust

Scepter of Fire

Other titles:

The Veritas Project

If you enjoyed this book, please consider leaving a review on Amazon.
They help more than you know!

ACKNOWLEDGMENTS

This book is the result of the help, support, and encouragement of so many people and the gracious will of the Lord, who has allowed me to pursue my dreams in ways that I hope honor Him. I will do my best to include everyone who helped this book find its way into the world.

First, to my husband. You've put up with a lot as I've chased my dream. Thank you. Also, thank you for never telling me it was a silly dream.

To my dad, this book really wouldn't exist without your brilliant insight and hours and hours of plot help. You could have been an editor in another life (though I suppose you've always been telling stories and teaching others how to as well). To Mom, your unwavering enthusiasm means more than you'll ever know. Everyone needs a cheerleader like you.

To my beta readers, Peter Last, Rhia G. Adley, and Levi C., you guys were pivotal in the development of this book. You helped me see the glaring problems, inconsistencies, and cliches that I was blind to. Peter, your wisdom shaped the story. Rhia, you woke me up out of fairly land and spoke some needed truth (I'm a better writer because of you). Levi, you encouraged me more than you know. Special thanks to Hudson O. for your words of wisdom.

To the amazing authors who've held my hand and answered my questions with kindness and sincerity: D. L. Wood (my author-angel), Kortney Keisel, Rachel L. Schade, Victoria McCombs, and Alisha Klapheke. There are many others, and I'm sorry I didn't include everyone.

To my street team and ARC readers, you guys made this book happen. Like really. You all are awesome.

To my readers, you are this girl's dream come true. Never forget that I write to bring light into your life. I hope I have.

To my son, you may be too small now to know it, but I do this thing called writing books while you're asleep. I appreciate all the long naps you took while this book came to be, but I love our playtime even more.

A special thank you to Marian A. Jacobs, Selah R., and Mindy B. for keeping me on the straight and narrow. I'm thankful to God for each of you for speaking truth to me and ensuring I did not stray into the dark with this book.

To my editors, Monica and Claire, you two are gems and I consider you both a blessing. Thank you for your work to make this book the best it could be. To Claire Evans, thank you for putting in the elbow grease necessary to straighten out this story.

Every book is a team effort. Thank you to my team.

ABOUT THE AUTHOR

C. F. E. Black loves to get swept away in books, both reading and writing them. Fantasy and science fiction have been her bread and butter since childhood, and she can't imagine life without her beloved fictional worlds. She lives in beautiful north Alabama with her superhero husband, sons, and fur-family. Connect with her and find free stories at www.cfeblack.com.

CROWN OF DUST

The enemy is dead. The battle has only just begun.

Red and Aly thought they had eliminated the greatest threat to their lives, but as they return from their trip north, a new enemy rises from within their own ranks, threatening to rip Red and Aly apart.

Lord Benedict Alexander has a distant claim to the throne, and he will do everything in his power to usurp Red's rule before the official coronation at summer's end. Convinced Red was corrupted by his trip into the Canyon, Lord Alexander fights to destroy Red's kingship, and with it, Red's Binding to Aly.

Now Red must regain the trust of his countrymen, not only to retain his throne and continue his fight against Kassia and the Canyon, but to keep Aly as well, for Aly is bound to serve the crown, no matter who wears it.

Fight for the crown. Fight for love. Or lose them both.